THE LIFE AND TIMES

OF

JODI WORREN

Michael S. Bromberg

THE HAMPTON STREET PRESS

SAG HARBOR, NEW YORK

Copyright© 2002, 2020 Michael S. Bromberg

All rights are reserved. No part of this work may be distributed, reproduced, or transmitted by any means in any form or uploaded or stored without the prior written consent of the author.

This is a work of fiction. The characters and events are fictitious. Any similarity or resemblance to any person living or dead or to events is not intended.

At a Critical Point in Time

Great problems—the kind you think you'll never walk away from feeling whole—ritually caused Timothy Kelly, the head of the conglomerate's company security, to rock slowly in his high back chair, his eyes closed, trusting that solutions would appear to him.

This time was different. As he pondered how to contain the vast turmoil "the accident" was going to cause the array of interlocking companies, his thoughts were interrupted by her call.

"I know this is an imposition, but I need you to find these three people." She told him what she remembered about them, but did not add that only one of the three knew how Judy became Jodi.

The troubled tone of her voice told him this search had to be his top priority. His response to her concerns could only be, "I'll handle this right away, Miss Worren."

As he hung up, he wondered if her request was an imposition at all. Instead of just sitting and rocking, maybe doing the familiar tasks that he had learned, as a special agent for the FBI, would act as a better warm-up for facing the aftermath of the accident.

Pleased that his assurance of immediate action seemed to comfort her, he said to himself, "Before anything else," as he placed the short list of names she gave him in the middle of his well-organized desktop.

Years earlier —

ONE

"**G**od! Who the hell would pay to have sex with this!" grumbled Clarence Gibbons, Madison High School's round faced, roly-poly guidance counselor.

Harry Daweson, looking out the ground floor office window to decide if the weather would force him to keep his first period gym class inside, shook his head as he heard the crass remark about the new student. He turned to Clarence just as he was tossing the folder onto Harry's desk. Opening the file to see what provoked the comment about paid sex, he again tried to imagine careers Clarence would be less suited for than guidance counselor, but as always, he came up empty. Clarence just didn't care about kids.

Harry, with his short dark brown hair and brown eyes was just six feet tall with a sturdy trim build. He had been a good enough play-making guard to lead his Rawlings College team to their best record ever, but he knew that any future in basketball would be in coaching and playing in pick-up games to stay fit. Three years ago, after graduation, he had taken this first job at Madison High School as physical education teacher and the assistant coach of the basketball team. The job came with the promise he'd be head coach when Jake Wilson retired. That retirement now looked like it was only one season away. Meanwhile, since there was no room in the locker area, and he didn't have a Home Room assignment, he was still stuck with a desk in a corner of the guidance office.

He looked at the two Polaroid pictures Clarence had just taken for the student's file. They showed a scrawny young girl with stringy blonde hair. She looked familiar. He looked for the name. Judy Jarrolson.

"I know this girl. C'mon Clarence, you remember that kid John Jarrolson who moved here from New York City his junior year? This is his kid sister. He sat the bench two years for the varsity. He was a senior when I got here. We helped pull him together to graduate and enlist in the Marines."

Clarence had no clue.

"C'mon Clarence, you gotta remember her brother. He died in a chopper crash on a training exercise in Korea about five months after their mom died. They put up a plaque on the front lawn about two years ago. You were standing there next to me."

"Oh, yeah," Clarence said. But he still had no clue what Harry was talking about.

When Harry started at Madison, John Jarrolson, Jr. was a student in his senior boy's gym class. Harry immediately called him "3J." He knew the boy had been on the basketball team the year before, and wanted to play on the team again, but the boy was distracted all the time. John would stand apart from the team as they huddled together. After class one day, Harry pulled the boy aside to see if he could find out what was happening. Letting the boy talk it out, he heard that when John was eight, his sister was born, and his father abandoned the family. The father, an alcoholic, died shortly after he left the family. Now, John's mother was dying of liver disease. Harry wondered about her abuse of alcohol, but since John didn't mention it, he didn't either. The boy's only goal was to graduate and join the Marines so he could send money back to the family—because he was "the man of the house." John was already behind in school.

Harry's own parents had died in a car crash when he was only ten. He knew what it was like growing up without parents. He thought about advising John not to come out for the team—to concentrate on graduating. From what he saw of John's play in the gym and what he heard about him from the coach, it didn't look like he was going to be playing much anyway. But he realized that basketball, or at least belonging to the team, helped John cope.

Harry made some calls to Madison Town Social Services Department and found there was help available. The little amount of home-health-care assistance the Town could provide was enough to take some of the pressure off. It helped free John from always being the father to his dying mother and his sister.

As basketball season started, Harry kept an eye on John, to make sure the extra work of being on the team didn't pull him under. When things got bad, 18-year-old John would come to 24-year-old Harry and talk about anything from help with school and basketball to dying or dead parents.

One day, because they talked so long after practice, he gave John a ride home. John insisted he come in and meet his mother, Jennifer. Harry was reluctant, unsure of what he would find, or how he would react. He was surprised at how young and pretty Jennifer looked. Except for noticing how thin and pale her hand was when they shook hands, he never would have thought she was dying. Harry then met John's young sister. When he heard her name was Judy— he dubbed her "JJ."

When the children were out of the room, Jennifer whispered, "Please, can you help me? Getting the Town help for me was wonderful—thank you—along with my kids that's the only help I get. But I don't want my children to have to spend all their time here with me." He nodded that he understood. After that visit, he would come by, sometimes on weekends, and take the kids to a park or shopping, or to the only movie house in town.

Now, when Clarence said the girl was outside with her grandmother, Harry remembered when he first met the Jarrolson grandparents. They were both born in Madison, both close to six feet tall, rail thin with long stringy, gray hair and deep blue eyes. If they could afford a pitchfork to pose for a picture, their image would be complete. Jennifer had told Harry that her in-laws blamed her for their son's death, even though she felt they had raised him badly and she had found him with all his fatal alcoholic faults fully formed. She was sure that when she became ill, they only suggested she move to Madison to see the local faith healer, not because it was the proper thing to do, but because they wanted to be nearer the grandson named after his failed attempt of a father. She felt that if they just had "their John Jr." without her and her daughter that would have suited them just fine.

He remembered helping to bring Jennifer to John's graduation. Right after graduation, John got his wish and enlisted. When he finished boot camp, he was granted emergency leave to come home. His mom was failing. John called and asked him to come to the house. When he arrived, John was in his dress uniform. Jennifer could hardly lift her head, but she insisted on sitting up. Her raspy voice said, "Coach, I am very proud of my son. Thank you for making these last months so much easier for me." He couldn't speak. He noted she said "last months," not "past months." Standing at her bedside with

"3J" and "JJ" alongside, they both folded him into a hug. Everyone had tears in their eyes.

Jennifer did not wake up the next morning.

After the funeral, with John going to be stationed in Korea, the grandparents made no effort to keep Judy. As soon as John left, they packed her off to a little town outside of Philadelphia to live with her only other living relative, her mother's much older sister.

The aunt, knowing early in life that she could never care for a child had decided—after her last abortion, at twenty-six years old—to have her tubes tied so she would never have a child of her own.

All Harry heard was that Judy had gone to live with her aunt. That reminded him of his own past. He hoped things would work out for her.

Judy had trouble adjusting to the new place and new rules. From the moment she arrived, her aunt treated her like a maid and told anyone who would listen about the great burden she was assuming by taking in her "dead sister's kid."

Judy was starting to accept her loveless position when word came that John was killed in a helicopter crash while on a training exercise. She felt even more alone, but she made the best of her bad situation for the next two years. Then, three days after the aunt's much younger boyfriend moved in, Judy ran away.

From the police report in the student file, Harry learned that Judy, then a frightened fourteen-year-old, had arrived in New York City by bus. The vice squad covered the bus station—aware that young runaway girls were being preyed upon by what the police called "chicken hawks." These pimps would attempt to snare young girls, who had little or no resources, and try to turn them out as prostitutes.

The police report stated that as Judy got off the bus, she was marked by what the report called a "flashily attired gentleman." They were both spotted by a female police sergeant. As the "gentleman" moved in the girl's direction, he had "an unfortunate mishap." He "happened to trip" over the sergeant's foot and went sprawling on the gray plastic seats next to Judy's backpack. While the sergeant's female partner "helped the gentleman to his feet and slowly ran her hands over every part of his body—to make sure he had not suffered any injury," the sergeant grabbed the girl and her backpack and led her to an unmarked car.

The report continued that since the obviously-ill-suited family placement with the aunt had failed, the sergeant informed the grandparents that if "this child" didn't come to live with them they would be responsible to reimburse any child care agency where she could be placed.

Judy was on the next bus to Madison and her less-than-welcoming, aged grandparents.

Now, Judy and her grandmother were sitting on a bench outside the guidance office waiting for Clarence to finish the registration process.

Handing the file back, Harry went out to see Judy and her grandmother. He could see that Judy recognized him, but then she turned her head to keep looking at the floor. He was surprised at how tall, thin, and withdrawn she looked. Knowing her history, any feeling of reassurance he had in seeing her back in Madison was tempered by knowing that, even though she would be living under her grandparents' roof, she would be living all alone.

Standing next to the end of the bench near the young girl, he told the grandmother that he had known John and his family during Jennifer's last months, and reminded the grandmother that he had met her and her husband when John's memorial plaque was placed.

He looked to Judy, "And how is JJ?"

"Fine," she said, but still didn't look up.

Harry assumed she was downcast about running away only to be returning to this situation. Looking at the 5'10" blond teenager, he tried to sound upbeat,

"I've got one word for you."

She looked up, "What's that?"

"Basketball! In addition to the boys, they want me to work with the girls' team until their regular coach gets back from maternity leave."

He looked at the grandmother.

She nodded it was OK.

"Oh, I don't know," Judy moaned, looking back at the floor.

"That's OK. I do know. This one's easy. You're an entering freshman, right?"

"Yes"

"And you are a girl, right?"

"Yes"

"OK, it's settled. You're on the girls' basketball team!"

He smiled at the grandmother.

To Judy he said, "I've gotta go to a gym class. I'll see you later."

TWO

It took more discussion between Harry and the grandfather, who was mainly concerned that Judy have enough time for her household chores, but Judy was allowed to join the girls' basketball team. Before the start of the boys' first practice, Coach Wilson announced he would be retiring at the end of the season.

With only one gym at the school, the boys had the use of the basketball court until 5:00. Harry had the girls do stretches and sprints on the track above the gym until they could get on the court. He secretly thought the girls were better conditioned than the boys. He enjoyed teaching the girls. Many of them, like Judy, had never played before. No bad habits. She learned quickly.

The girls' season was only eight games. Not many schools of similar size had girls' teams. His aim was to make sure everybody played. The team as a whole didn't embarrass itself. Toward the end of the season, when it looked like they could have a winning record, the girls lobbied to have the better players play the whole game. He went along with their request —while still playing everyone—by cutting back on the playing time of some of the less skilled players. Judy wasn't one of the better players.

The boys made the playoffs but were eliminated in the first game. Coach Wilson, of course, would have liked a better ending to his career, but both men knew they had done the best they could with the players they had. Harry used to tell both boys and girls, "We can give you the ball and we can teach you, but we can't play the game for you. This is your time. Coach and I had our days on the court. These days are yours. Make the most of them. Do not regret later that you could have tried harder, now."

He talked about life-living-lessons. One of the lessons was about the importance of balance both in sports and in life. He urged each player to strive for balance both in the physical sense and in the way they lived their lives.

He explained, "On the court, if you are leaning on someone and they move, you could fall. In life, if you reach out for something that isn't within your control to get, when you don't get it, you'll be unhappy."

The next year with Coach Wilson gone, Harry was made head coach on a probationary basis. He was pleased to have the job, but not pleased with his team. It wasn't just the fact they had lost three starters to graduation—those who remained and those who came out for the team seemed to have a poor work ethic and a poor attitude in general. These kids were cocky beyond their skills. He didn't like how they blamed each other rather than taking responsibility for a mistake. With the door open in his new office off the locker room, he heard racist comments and boorish talk about some of the girls in school and women in general. He wondered, If my office was down here instead of up with Clarence, would I have been aware of these problems sooner?

Preparing for the season, he was curious how long it would take this group to learn his new system and how long it would take the returning players to understand he was not merely substituting for Coach Wilson but he was really the head coach. Even so, he decided for at least this year, in honor of the former coach, his team would continue using "Wilson's Wildcats Conduct Contract." He knew this group of kids was going to continue to be called "Wilson's Wildcats" until he could start molding the team to his own style so he didn't mind keeping the name on the conduct form. The decision was made easier by the fact that at the start of his last season, Coach Wilson had so many forms printed—with the small number of players at this small school—the supply of forms could last for another decade.

The signing of the contract signified the player had made the team. The school was too small for a football team, so basketball was its major sport. At the pep rally before the start of the season each player stepped to center court in uniform and signed the contract which included the prohibitions about smoking, drinking, and sex and added the "does not lie, cheat or steal" clause stolen from West Point's Honor Code.

Harry thought about all the variables that went into the makeup of this team. He could give life-living-lessons or talk about civility and racial justice but he knew what they lacked at home, he couldn't give them in the gym. As he wondered if he would be able to help these boys learn to be decent men, he reminded himself about the danger of getting the job you wish for.

Judy sprained her ankle in the third game of the new season and was on crutches. She lived a few blocks too close to the school to be eligible to ride the school bus. Since her grandparents no longer drove because they couldn't afford insurance, and his drive to work passed by her house, Harry gave her rides to school. It was a simple transportation solution. After school she went to practices and games with her team and afterwards her coach or a teammate, would drop her home.

On their morning rides Harry and Judy talked about her school work. She was an average student who wasn't motivated enough to put in more work to get better grades and too shy to want to stand out. Most of all, she talked about how difficult it was living with her grandparents. When he talked about whether she wanted to go to college, her main focus was getting freed from the restrictions and boredom of her grandparents' home. When the conversation drifted to her mom and brother, she spoke about her feelings of loneliness. Harry shared what his life was like growing up without his parents.

When the weather turned cold, he was concerned she didn't have a warm jacket. He thought of saying something to her or her grandparents but then thought better of it because he could see they were barely making ends meet and he sensed they were too proud to accept charity. He realized there was only one way he could help. He picked up a jacket he had seen at a thrift store. The next day after his team's practice, while the girls were at an away game, he stopped by her grandparents' house. He was not invited in—he thought the grandfather had been drinking—but through the partially-opened door he told the grandparents that he had found the jacket in the Lost and Found in the locker room and it had not been claimed in over a year. He couldn't tell if the grandparents knew he was lying, but they accepted the jacket.

The next day, wearing the jacket, Judy thanked him when he picked her up.

As soon as she was able to walk to school, the rides stopped. Harry made sure she knew he would make himself available if she wanted to talk. But Judy also knew that while she could talk to him about her problems, there was no way he could fix her living situation. So, if they ran into each other in the halls or at the gym, and he asked how things were going, he would usually get a grimace or a grunt. He was pleased to see that she had healed enough to be able to play a few minutes in the final game.

THREE

Harry never considered himself a creature of habit, but as an athlete in college—and a serious student—he came to admire the economy of effort that a schedule provides. So, as he settled in after being hired at Madison High School, his laundry time would be Tuesday evenings and Wednesday evenings were for shopping.

On the first Tuesday as he was arriving at the Laundromat, he saw a large cylinder-shaped pop-up mesh hamper approaching the door from the other side. Instinctively he held the door open; it was only after the burdened person passed him that he saw the person, whose upper half was obscured by the clothing, was a pregnant woman. She politely refused his offer of further help.

The next Tuesday his laundry was in the washing machine when he heard a voice say, "Either I'm late or you're early." Looking up, he recognized her as the woman from the doorway. She was a light-skinned black woman with long black hair and brown eyes. She looked about 20 years old.

She started her laundry and sat down on the hard bench opposite his and, after finding as comfortable a position as her condition would allow, simply said, "Jacqui."

Thinking the one-word introduction meant she wasn't interested in small talk, he nodded, "Harry." He wanted to return to reading a book of essays without seeming rude when she asked about his book. That started a conversation from which he learned Jacqui had come to Madison to live with her older sister Naomi. But, arriving at her sister's basement apartment, she found out her sister had been in a serious car accident the day before she was to leave Oakland to return home.

She had broken her leg, her hip and both wrists. With better medical and rehab facilities in Oakland, her return home to Madison would be delayed. Naomi did not know about Jacqui's pregnancy.

Hearing that Harry was at the high school, she asked him to check into her getting a General Education Diploma. He told her he would check in the morning and asked if he could stop by her apartment on his way home from work the next day.

He saw her hesitation about him coming to her apartment, so he quickly added if it could wait for a week, he could give her the forms the following Tuesday. Just the fact that he took her feelings into consideration assured her that his stopping by would be OK.

The next day when he brought the GED paperwork, as he knocked on her door, he reminded himself of her initial hesitation and wasn't surprised when she opened the door part way to receive the forms but didn't invite him in. That was fine with him. He didn't want her to think that he had any expectation of anything else—because he didn't.

As their Laundromat meetings continued, they became friendlier. He learned she had run away from her home down South and wound up in Chicago. Four months after they met, Jacqui Fykes had her baby. She named the light-skinned little girl Patricia.

At first, she was unsure if she could raise this child on her own, and unsure if she wanted to. But Harry, prevailing upon the school nurse, was able to put Jacqui in touch with agencies which could help them.

Her apartment was not far from his. Sometimes he would stop in on his way home just to chat, see how they were doing, and help out however he could. Sometimes they would push the stroller down the aisle of a grocery store and Harry would pay for what things she needed. He liked having someone to talk to who was not part of his work, and he could see she needed his help.

One night, with Patricia sleeping, now fully comfortable with the idea that Harry was a friend she could talk to, Jacqui told him about her past. He listened with feelings of shock turning into sadness, then rage, as she told him how she had been held captive and forced to do things in order to survive. He now understood when she confided that her feelings about Patricia were darkened by the fact that she got pregnant as a result of one of the many times she was sold and raped.

Going home from that discussion two thoughts rotated though his mind. He realized that no matter how much rage he felt toward the faceless sadists who controlled her in Chicago he could not turn back the clock to give her a better past. The other thought was more about himself.

He remembered conversations—he was not meant to hear—between his probation-officer aunt and the black police detective from across the street, about their work with the domestic violence center. He wondered how these conversations had sensitized him at an early age to one of the topics athletes at his college heard lectures about at the start of each practice season. He wondered why he had instinctively known not to show any physical closeness—no matter how comfortable Jacqui appeared talking with him—as the time they spent together had grown. He fell asleep pondering that. How, as soon as they met, he just knew she would not want to be touched?

Ten months after Patricia's birth, Naomi had still not returned and Jacqui was still struggling with taking care of the baby on her own and providing for their needs. One night when Harry was in a small local grocery store, the grocer complained that his refrigerator had conked out and that he was going to have to throw away a lot of milk and other good food. Harry bought the items he came for, but the thought of good food being thrown away, and the grocer's loss, made him sad. He remembered giving part of his lunch to hungry kids at school or PAL teammates. Still, there was nothing in the refrigerator he wanted or thought he would use.

Then he thought of Jacqui.

He looked at his watch to make sure it wasn't too late. He hadn't seen Jacqui for a couple of weeks but he decided to take her some of the food.

As he pulled up, he was pleased when he saw the flickering light of a TV in Jacqui's apartment. His arms loaded with the bags of food, he managed to knock on the door and waited. Jacqui shuffled to the door trying to keep paper-thin slippers on her feet. Seeing it was him, she opened the door.

She looked terrible. Her thin robe was open and the T-shirt she wore under it was torn and stained. Her hair was a matted mess. He smelled marijuana as she opened her door. She looked like she had been sleeping but he noticed the marijuana cigarette in her hand was almost finished.

Deciding to ignore the marijuana, he told her, "I was in the grocery store and the grocer said his refrigerator went out and we should take what we wanted before he had to throw it away. I thought you and Patricia might be able to use some supplies."

Without a word, she gestured for him to put the bags on the kitchen counter behind the door. Taking hold of his sweatshirt, she guided him to a spot that allowed her to close the door. Still without a word, looking up at him, she started to kneel down in front of him while her hands pulled to open his belt and take down his pants.

For a second, he was outside of himself watching what she was doing. Then the blank look on her face assured him she was not making some kind of joke. Pulling her hands from his belt—he grabbed her by the arms near her elbows and pulled her to her feet in front of him. She was surprised by his stopping her.

Still holding her arms, he backed her down into a kitchen chair next to the table. She slumped in her chair and pulled her robe closed. He took a deep breath and let it out slowly.

Not knowing if she would think to do it, he found room for the groceries in her refrigerator, then walked to the door.

"How has it come to this Jacqui? Have you so little respect for yourself—is that what you think of me?"

She started to cry.

He didn't want to leave her like that, but he wasn't sure what to do, so he started to sit down at the table opposite her. But, starting to sit, he bounced back up almost in one motion as he thought to go check on Patricia.

She was sleeping peacefully.

Sitting back down, he slid the ashtray across to Jacqui. After using her sleeve to dry her eyes, she took the ashtray and crushed out what was left of the joint.

"My last one of those," she said, but she wasn't talking to him. Getting up, she shuffled to the sink. There was an empty liquor bottle on the drain board along with a couple of white pills. He wondered if she was going for the pills. But she tossed the bottle into the trash, looked at him, turned on the water and dropped what was left of the cigarette and then the pills into the sink.

"My last of that, too," she resolved as she let the water run and watched the cigarette follow the pills down the drain.

"Naomi called. Getting back here is going to take even longer than she thought. I just kinda lost it. So, I decided to invite myself to my own party. Old habit."

She sighed, and shook her head, "And I'd been doing so good!" She turned off the water. "I'd seen the bottle the first time I looked in her cabinets. The grass and the pills were in the bottom of the old knapsack I used when I ran away and hitched here after I found out I was pregnant. I was pleased that all this time—even after the baby was born—I could know that stuff was there but never. . ."

She sat back down at the table, "But now that stuff's gone."

She sighed, "All gone.

She yawned as she pulled the belt of her robe tighter,

"I'll be OK now. If you don't mind, I need to go to sleep."

As he got up and opened the door, she said, "Thank you for the milk and things, as always; it's very thoughtful of you. And I'm ..." Her voice trailed off.

Looking at her, he said, "OK, you know you can't undo your past. Tonight, you slipped. But Jacqui, you must know you don't have to slide all the way back. It was a slip. Now you turn the hourglass over and start from a new day one."

He looked at her and nodded, "Have a good rest of your night."

After a few days, Jacqui called. She had enrolled in the course to get her GED. Her teacher was going to help her get a part-time job in the mayor's office as a receptionist and get childcare and counseling.

Jacqui and Harry never spoke about that night.

FOUR

It was dark as Harry drove home from the last session of a mandated CPR course for high school head coaches. Needing the CPR card to continue coaching, he was pleased he passed. But, like most of the students, he wondered if he'd be able perform in a crisis. He hoped he'd never find out.

Where his road merged with the one used as a detour off the interstate, his headlights picked up someone walking alongside the road. At first, all he saw was a lot of bare leg. Getting closer, he could make out a girl in a short skirt carrying a backpack and walking slowly backwards trying to hitch a ride.

Getting closer, he recognized the jacket. It was Judy.

A big tanker-truck was coming up behind him. It was pulling to the side of the road to pick her up. Harry stopped alongside her. She looked at him and then at the truck stopping behind him.

Opening his window, he heard himself say, "Don't even think of it. Get in here. Now!"

Her shoulders dropped. She put the backpack down, looked at the trucker, and then put her backpack on the back seat of his car. She got in and sat in silence.

All he said was, "Seat belt." Hearing it click, checking behind him, he pulled back onto the road. He drove in silence to the end of the block, then pulled into an empty parking lot.

"OK. You wanna tell me about it?"

She hesitated, then burst into the story: "I decided to go to the mall after school instead of going straight home. Even though I had no money to buy anything—I never have any money to buy anything—I just wanted to go look in the windows. It got later than I realized and I missed the bus. I had to walk to where I could get a different bus. I got home much later than usual. My grandmother was upset that I was late getting home and hadn't cleaned up their room and my room. She yelled at me that I should have called and told them I missed the bus. She was so upset. I couldn't make her hear that I only had enough money for the bus. If I made a call, I couldn't take the bus. They never understand anything. After they went to sleep, I threw some of my stuff into my bag and went out my window."

He thought about it. "I think I have a friend I'd like you to meet." He drove to Jacqui's apartment.

She had turned her life around in the two years since that night he brought the groceries. After starting that receptionist job in the mayor's office, she learned quickly and was now working at the town's day care program. It was 9:45, but Harry took the chance she'd be awake and was pleased she was.

Introducing them, he asked if Judy could stay for a short while so he could go and talk to her grandparents. Jacqui sized up the situation and quickly agreed.

When he left, she asked, "You were running away?"

Judy didn't answer.

Jacqui said, "I used to do that. This your first time?"

Judy shook her head, "No."

"How far did you get the first time?"

"I got to New York but didn't get out of the bus station before the cops picked me up and sent me here."

"Well, girl, you were lucky. I'd never been with no-body 'till I made it all the way out of my bus station. You wanna know what's outside the bus station? A lot of painful times where they force you to do shit, and a big dude who likes beating on you and sticking his dick up your ass to make sure you know he's the boss."

Judy cringed. Just then, Patricia woke up and came into the living room in pajamas, rubbing her eyes. Jacqui, scooped the child up in her arms, "This is my souvenir of outside the bus station." She looked to see if Judy was listening. Then she put Patricia back in bed.

Coming back, she saw Judy sitting on the floor next to the couch hugging her knees. Sitting down on the couch next to her, "The people you were running from—"

"My grandparents"

"They beat you?"

"No."

"Try to touch you?"

"No. The first time, when I ran from my aunt's, I didn't get touched yet, but I saw it coming."

"How do you know Harry?"

"He was my brother's basketball coach. Mine too for a while. And he —he found me on the road trying to hitch a ride."

When Jacqui heard Judy was hitching, she winced.

"Well, maybe you can't appreciate it now—'cause bought is always better than told—but what you were runnin' toward is a thousand times worse than what you're runnin' from."

Judy let that sink in.

She found Jacqui easy to talk to. She told Jacqui about her mom's death and how she came to live with her grandparents. And they talked about Harry.

Jacqui said, "When I had Patricia and the money was real tight, Harry invented what I called "the shopping date."

Hearing the word "date," Judy wondered aloud, "You and Coach dated?"

Jacqui laughed, "No, no, we're just friends. But he had a job and I had nothing." Then, thinking back on that time—"I mean nothing!

"So, instead of sitting in a restaurant and eating and talking for an hour or so, we would talk as we walked through a supermarket and he bought food that would last me and her a week instead of paying for just two dinners. When I really needed a friend—there was Harry. It took me by surprise that he didn't seem to want anything from me. All the other men in my life—well, you know. But he's different, and he don't even brag. Did you know he played on the same team as Julius Anderson?"

Without waiting for an answer, "I saw JayA in an interview the other day, when he won MVP again. He said, 'You can't get here alone. Like on my college team, we had this point guard that kinda glided around the court like he was wearing slippers. No wasted motion. It was like having another coach on the court. I tell you what, that man knew where I was going before I realized I had to go there—and when I got there, the ball was in my hands in catch-and-shoot position!'

"He said, 'Talking to him about why he passed the ball to me when he did, taught me a whole lot about my game.'"

Jacqui laughed, "It was Harry! I checked. He was talking about Harry! It was Harry. And Harry never said a word!"

She smiled and shook her head, "And Harry's deep! Real deep. I wasn't sure if I should keep my baby."

Looking at Judy she explained, "I didn't know which of those bastards who forced sex from me was the father."

She tried to imitate Harry, "He just said, 'Events are neither good nor bad. It's your perception of the event that makes it good or bad. You can choose to look at this child as a burden or a blessing. You can hate this child because of her father or love her because she's yours.'

"And after we talked, I chose to love her because she's mine. And, like Harry said, 'Why should she have to take a chance with strangers? She didn't do anything wrong.'"

They were still talking when Harry came back and told Judy it was time to go home. Before they parted, Jacqui and Judy decided they could continue their talks.

In the car, he asked, "JJ, what do you think of Jacqui?"

Not sure why he asked, she hedged. "She's nice, I guess. She asked me if I would like to come back to talk or babysit for her sometime."

"Do you think you'll do that?"

"Sure. I think I know why you brought me to see her instead of taking me straight home—another life-living-lesson?" Harry smiled and stopped the car in front of her house.

"There is an old black proverb that says, 'I wept because I had no shoes and then I saw a man who had no feet.'

"Jacqui is doing OK now, but she knows she fell into a deep deep hole. She managed to pull herself out. I'm sure she would like you not to fall in— so you won't have to pull yourself out."

"Well, she says you helped pull her out."

"No JJ. No one can really help pull someone out of that kind of a hole. The best anyone can do is to be supportive and try to point out the opportunities for the climber to help themselves."

He smiled as he saw her pondering and said, "Goodnight."

FIVE

A few weeks after stopping Judy from running away, Harry was in his office at the back of the locker room thinking about the next game when he heard a girl's voice saying "No! Leave me alone!"

Going to check what was happening, he saw his senior starting guard, Richie Archer, with his hands on the wall on both sides of Judy. He was keeping her from moving, and leaning in to kiss her, saying, "You did it with Brian Thomas and told him you want me."

As he leaned again to try kissing her, Harry grabbed his shoulder and spun him around. "What the hell do you think you're doing?"

"Er—Nothing, Coach! I wasn't doing nothing. We were just playing around."

"It didn't look like 'nothing' to me and I really don't think she was playing. Get to my office. Wait for me. Now!"

When Richie left, Harry asked, "JJ, are you OK?"

"I don't know what he was talking about. I never went out with Brian. I was on my way to the girls' locker room," motioning toward the door, "and Richie just came up and said he wanted to—"

"Did he touch you?"

"No, you got here pretty much as it started." She looked at him and emphasized, "I never went out with Brian."

"I believe you, JJ, and in this situation, it wouldn't make a bit of difference if you did."

Harry took Judy to the principal's office to report the incident, left her there, and sent word for Brian Thomas to meet him in his office.

When Harry got to his office, Richie started, "Coach, Brian told me he had—well he had sex with her, and she had said she really wanted to have sex with me."

Harry thought about that for a moment.

"You're a starting senior, we've got a big game to-morrow—if we win, we go to the playoffs—and you pin a young girl against the wall because one of your buddies said—"

Harry just shook his head. "Did you ever stop to think of what she wanted? Did it appear to you she wasn't in-terested? Did it appear to you she wanted you to leave her alone? Which—by the way—is what she said."

Sitting down at his desk, he put his face in his hands, then looked up and continued, "Let's suppose Brian comes in here and says he had sex with this girl. Does that make what you just did right?"

"I didn't —"

"You didn't what? Are you telling me I didn't just see what I just saw? You had a girl up against the wall and tried to kiss her while she was telling you to leave her alone."

Harry paused, "Didn't you sign a Conduct Contract in front of most of the school?"

"Well—"

"Remember the part that says, "Wildcats won't lie, cheat or steal?""

"But Coach she's just a little—this isn't—"

"You lied to me out there when you told me you weren't doing anything."

Just then Brian came to the door. "You wanted to see me, Coach?" Then he saw Richie sitting behind the door. "What's up, man?" But, the look on Richie's face told Brian there was trouble. Harry motioned for Richie, the team's shooting guard, to stand next to Brian the senior, power forward.

Looking from one to the other, Harry said, "Judy Jarrolson."

Brian thought for a second—trying to figure a way out. He knew if he said he had sex with her, as he told Richie, he would be admitting a violation of the Conduct Contract. If he denied the sex and said he lied to Richie, he would also be admitting a violation of the Conduct Contract.

"Hey Coach—it was just a joke!"

"Well, she didn't think it was very funny when Richie had her pinned against the wall out there."

Brian turned to Richie, "Oh man! You didn't!"

Then to Harry, "Nobody told him to do—"

"What did you think he was going to do? Did either of you gentlemen stop to think about her? Did you guys think she was fair game because she doesn't seem to fit in? Did you think she was going to be easy because she's alone and doesn't have any friends? Did you think you were throwing her some kind of honor—some kind of big-jock life line to the in-crowd? Did you think she'd be grateful for your attention?"

He paused, "You've got a big game to prepare for—and above all you have a Conduct Contract. I can't think of anything you two have done here that brings honor to our team. How many other guys does she need to look out for now?"

"It was just a joke, Coach. We heard she—"

"You heard what? And from whom? Did you hear how her parents died when she was really young? And did you hear about her brother—who played on this team, died in the Marines—there's a plaque for him outside. Did you hear about that? And what does whatever you heard about her have to do with you?"

Brian started again, "It was just a joke, Coach. There's no need to get upset."

Harry thought about that remark for a moment. "Gentlemen let me assure you —if you think I am upset, it just shows you haven't seen me when I am upset. Let's get up to the principal's office and you can both explain your actions to him and probably the police."

Harry was surprised that by the time they got to the principal's office, a detective was already there. Judy was sitting in a chair next to the principal's secretary outside the office. Harry sat the boys on a bench on the other side of the waiting area away from her, told them not to speak to her, and knocked on the door.

When the door opened, the principal and Clarence Gibbons were inside with the detective who had Judy's student file in his hands. Harry was sure Clarence had made the detective aware of how she had come to be in school here.

"Those are the boys?" The detective asked, looking at Brian and Richie. He asked Harry to step into the principal's office while he went outside and talked to the boys.

Harry stepped in as the door was being closed behind him.

Clarence said, "Harry, what are you thinking of here? What outcome are you looking for?"

Harry thought for a moment. "They should probably be suspended."

"For what? The girl wasn't hurt?"

Just then the detective knocked on the door and let himself back into the room.

Harry thought, That was one really long interview he just did with these kids.

The principal told the detective, "Harry was just saying he thought the boys should be suspended."

"I don't know. That's a school matter. I don't see anything criminal here. The girl wasn't hurt—"

"Physically hurt? No," Harry interrupted. "Maybe if I was a little slower in getting there—but what about emotionally?"

"She seems OK to me." The detective continued, "I understand you drive this girl to school?"

"What?" Harry said in disbelief.

Then he caught himself. "When she was on crutches, I gave her a lift to school because her house is on my way. That stopped long ago—what does that have to do with—?"

The detective sat down in the principal's chair, made a big show of lighting a cigar, and continued—"and she hangs out with that black woman with an illegitimate child?"

Seeing where this was going, Harry nodded, "As I understand it, she occasionally babysits for the assistant director of the town's child care program. But as far as I'm concerned, I would feel the same if these boys acted the same toward any girl."

"Thank you, detective," the principal said.

"Harry," the principal continued, "I think what we have here is a misunderstanding and I don't see any reason to suspend either boy from school."

Clarence added, "And, since they can't be suspended from school, Harry, I see no grounds for them being suspended from the team."

Harry knew they were concerned about the next day's game, and letting him know they were in charge. He also knew he couldn't change the way they thought. It was a battle he couldn't win if he chose to fight it.

Deciding he had to stay with what was in his control, he said, "OK, if that's the way you both see it. Will you tell the boys? I'll tell Judy and then I have to get back to work—we've got a big game coming up." He knew they didn't need reminding.

Harry didn't want her to feel she had any responsibility for what had just happened. He took Judy aside and told her about the discussion, leaving out the part about her file, the lifts he had given her and Jacqui.

She thanked him for looking out for her and assured him she was OK.

When he told Jacqui about the incident that evening, she supplied some information he had not known. "From my work in the mayor's office I get a better view about who's who in this zoo. For example, I know the police detective has an approved second job. He works for Brian Thomas' father. You want more?"

Harry just shook his head.

In his apartment that night, he wondered about what he was going to do. But he also wanted to come to terms with his motivation. He said he would have reacted the same way if it was any girl and not Judy. Was that true? How could he ignore the history they had together? What did the detective say that was not right? He had given her rides to school and Jacqui was a black unmarried woman who had a child. He ruled out the idea of any attraction he had to either of them. But that was the easy part.

He had to acknowledge what it might look like to others even if their perceptions were incorrect. Could it be that he overreacted because the girl was Judy? He knew he was disappointed with the team he was coaching—because of the sexist and racist comments he overheard coming through his locker-room-office door and from the seats behind him on the bus for away games. Maybe the boys sensed more anger while he did not. He pondered the Conduct Contract prohibition against lying.

It should prevent him from lying to himself.

With the principal and Clarence, he knew he had given up his end of the rope to avoid a tug-of-war he couldn't win. But he also knew that the decision as to what happened next was truly his. He wanted to make sure he was not going to make a bad decision just to show that it was his decision to make. Above all, he wanted to make sure that he wasn't seeking revenge on these two boys because he couldn't change their attitudes or because they chose Judy as their target. He thought long and hard about what should happen and whether he really was in a position to be a fair judge.

His decision was informed by the example of his college coach. Just before a crucial game in Harry's junior year, Julius Anderson—who was a senior and the leading scorer and rebounder on the team—missed a team meeting for the second time.

The first time he was held out for the first half of the next game. He came storming back in the second half and they won going away. But then, even with the big game on the line, the second offense had to be punished more severely. The whole team knew that violations of the team rules had to have consequences. Julius was benched for the game.

Harry smiled when he remembered that game. It was the best he ever played. Not having to feed Julius, he took more shots. As happened for him at times, the rim looked as big as a hula-hoop, and almost every shot he put up went in. They won.

The lesson of discipline was learned, and Harry was proud to play for the coach who put teaching character and discipline over winning.

The next day, he continued to review what was fair for the two players involved and the team as a whole.

As the tip-off for the game approached, he became more convinced of what he had to do. He would not evade his obligation to help the team learn how to be responsible men.

Madison didn't make the playoffs.

During pre-game warm-up, he saw players watching him for any indication of what he was thinking. He gave none. The team went through the drills as they always did, but neither Brian nor Richie made it off the bench during the game.

The game was close. But they lost.

Harry was aware he was only on probation as the head coach. Pondering whether he could be effective as a mentor if he was allowed to stay, he concluded this was not the place he wanted to spend his life teaching or coaching.

As the game was ending the season, Harry was resigned to making some inquiries about other jobs.

If asked about it after the game, he was prepared to deal with the fallout. He was prepared to say, "The boys that played tonight put up a good fight. Tonight, the better team won. But life is more than a game. The school has its rules and the Wildcats have a Conduct Contract. The school can tell the coach who is eligible to play, but my responsibility to the boys as their coach means I have to decide who represents this school and who sits."

He was prepared, but nobody asked. He thought that was because those who knew what had happened, knew what he would have to do.

His first call the next day was to his alma mater, Rawlings College, to see if his old coach—with his vast array of coaching contacts—might know of an opening somewhere.

As luck would have it, he fell into a job he would have left Madison for anyhow. His coach, Gus Barron, told him that at the end of the season it was going to be announced that he was being promoted to athletic director. His assistant, Buddy Tabor, a teammate of Harry's, was taking over as head coach.

Within minutes of his hanging up, Harry's phone rang.

Buddy said, "Man, this is great. I'd love to have you come and take this job. You know our system and now I don't have to do a big search for my replacement. What a break for me. There'll be a lot of travel because we still play a national schedule, and you'll be out recruiting."

As the old teammates talked, Buddy told him of the interview he saw when Julius Anderson won MVP. Harry laughed when he heard the line about the slippers.

The next day Harry gave his notice. He told people his dream job had just opened up and he felt he had to take it.

In the final weeks of school, he and Judy spoke often. Aware she already had too many losses in her short life, he was concerned she might consider his leaving another loss. He knew his leaving was nowhere near the magnitude of the death of her parents and her brother but still, he wanted to be sensitive to her feelings. He made it a point to say goodbye while Judy was visiting with Jacqui. He wanted to make sure they understood how much he valued them as friends. He would miss them, but had to move on. As Judy went into the bedroom to pick up Patricia, he quietly asked Jacqui to keep an eye out for Judy.

Jacqui winked, and whispered, "We'll keep an eye out for each other."

Leaving town, after a goodbye hug with Patricia sandwiched in the middle, Harry didn't know if he would ever see them again. But he did know he felt like he was going home.

rriving in the town of Rawlings, following a tip from Buddy, Harry found a small, furnished apartment within walking distance to the campus. Then he checked into a nearby motel for a few days until he could move in. He brought in his bags and threw himself on the bed.

After staring at the ceiling for about half a minute, he jumped into the shower, got dressed, and headed to the gym on the other side of the campus. After Madison, he thought the Rawlings campus, with its building and grounds and 35,000 students—seven times the population of the whole town of Madison—seemed huge.

It was late afternoon. Rawlings's main gym building was unlocked. Harry walked past the trophy cases and the banners to the gym floor, and was surprised to find no one around. But that was OK.

In fact, it was perfect.

He went onto the court and looked up at the empty seats, remembering them full of spectators. Looking up he shot an imaginary ball at the hoop and whispered, "Swish."

Before leaving the building, he found a campus phone and left a message telling Buddy he'd arrived.

Looking to see what changed, Harry took himself on a tour of the campus.

What he noticed was a lot of young women. Even in summer session, women of all shapes and sizes were walking, jogging, and riding bikes. Some were on roller skates and a few on scooters. Seeing all these young women while he was walking to a deli for food, he realized how little social life he had in Madison. As he carried the food to his room, the fatigue of the long drive started to catch up with him. He fell asleep before he finished his meal.

Buddy called the next morning to invite him to breakfast and tell him it was time to go to work. Buddy, at 6'10" and about 275 pounds, had played center. In Buddy's senior year, Harry, as a sophomore, started at guard.

He had encouraged Buddy to think about coaching if the pros didn't work out. After a few NBA tryouts and a season in Italy, Buddy came back as assistant coach in Harry's senior year. With this step up to head coach, Buddy was the first black head coach in the history of Rawlings College.

The two men ate breakfast, talked about old times, and Buddy told Harry his vision for the team.

After breakfast, Buddy aimed him in the direction of the personnel office to fill out the new employee paperwork. Harry said, "I want to stop off and see the Coach first." As soon as the word "Coach" had cleared his lips he grimaced, realizing that title now belonged to Buddy.

Buddy grinned, "That's OK, he'll always be 'The Coach' to those of us who played for the man. I've got the job now, but I have to earn the title."

They parted ways, planning to meet later that morning to look over reports on prospective players.

At the athletic department, Harry introduced himself to the young woman working there. Her name was Corey. She was about 5'8", with red hair and green eyes set off by creamy white skin. She was wearing slacks and a loose-fitting school sweatshirt.

She smiled, "Coach Barron is on his way to the office."

While he waited, they made small talk. Harry was taken by her warm smile and easy manner. She told him she was a Business Administration major. She had heard of his being hired.

"I'm just filling in at the Athletic Office part time until, the secretary, Mrs. Olson, gets back from sick leave." Harry was impressed enough to note she wasn't wearing a ring.

When Coach Barron—a bear of a man—arrived, he threw an arm around Harry's shoulders and he swept him into his office.

An hour later, when Harry emerged, he was disappointed to see Corey was gone.

The next few weeks were filled with moving in, learning the new job and getting ready for the fall term. After the first scouting trip with Buddy, Harry made four trips on his own to see prospective players.

Harry thought about Corey. A few times he made it a point to walk by and peek in the Athletic Office. No Corey.

His walk-bys stopped when he saw an older woman sitting at the desk looking like she had been there forever.

He thought, I guess Mrs. Olson is back.

Wondering how he could manage to "run into" Corey again, finally, he asked Buddy if he knew anything about her. Buddy pointed to his wedding ring saying "Don't know—you could ask Coach though, he probably has the lowdown."

Seeing Harry's face react to that suggestion, he chuckled, "Yeah, I know that's kind of like having the big sex talk with your father," not remembering Harry lost his dad when he was ten. "OK. Plan B. She was filling in for Mrs. Olson who had minor surgery. She is due back next week. Maybe —"

"I think she's back already." Harry frowned.

"Hey! Wait a minute" Buddy laughed. "Why am I trying to help here? When do you think you're going to have time for women?"

Harry shook his head, knowing Buddy was serious about recruiting players in the month ahead.

Two days later, Buddy called. Buddy was one of those people who never introduce themselves on the phone—he just starts talking. Harry recognized the voice, "Remember Coach always yelling, 'You've got to shoot to score?' Well, I asked around for you. Here's the scouting report. Her name is Corey Winsloh. She doesn't work for us. She was just on loan to Coach to cover for Mrs. Olson. She works part-time for Liam Doyles, the assistant dean of Admissions, who's the liaison for athletics. She also babysits for Liam and his wife sometimes. His wife doesn't think she's seeing anybody, but she's not all that sure. You want me to give you her number, or do you want me to call her and ask her out for you, too?"

Harry laughed. "Thanks for the info. Good lookin' out. Just give me the number. If I run into trouble, I'll let you know."

"Sure. Just don't let it keep you from your job."
He knew Buddy wasn't kidding.

Making the call he was relieved Corey just said, "Oh, hi," when he told her who he was. He didn't have to explain how he got her number. They had a few awkward silences, but he thought the call went well. They made a plan to meet for lunch later in the week.

He had to cancel the first meeting because Buddy needed him to go look at a kid who was just added to the roster in an all-star game. Corey said she understood. He realized how interested he was when he noticed he was trying hard to hear through the phone if she sounded disappointed. They rescheduled.

On the way to meet Corey, he was getting nervous. Walking across the campus to the Rawhouse restaurant, which he remembered as his team's favorite eating place, he tried to notice other girls to assure himself God had made so many of them.

It didn't work. He was still nervous when he got there.

He wasn't helped by the fact she was ten minutes late. He was sure she had forgotten. When he saw her coming, he was not only glad to see her but also to notice she was hurrying to get there.

He was surprised he hadn't remembered how pretty she was.

"I'm sorry I was late. Just as I was leaving, my mom called to tell me the results of some tests from the hospital. She was telling me she was fine and how relieved she was. I realized I was going to be a little late and hoped you wouldn't mind too much."

"No. It's fine. Everything is OK." He chose not to tell her he was hoping he hadn't been stood up.

They took a table in the back corner of the restaurant and she took the seat with her back to a brick wall.

As they talked, he was surprised to learn that, even though she was a going to be a senior, she was a year older than he was.

"I grew up in a little place named Smalsville—"

"Wait a minute, isn't that the name of the place Superman grew up?"

She smiled, "The two names sound alike, that place supposedly had 45,001 people in it, but it doesn't exist. Mine hardly exists, it has only about 750 people in it. That place has two L's in the name. Our local joke is our village was so small they couldn't get four L's on the sign.

"I stayed there and I worked for six years after high school to earn money for college and to figure out what I wanted to study. I had to be kind of goal directed. I don't have the financial resources to keep changing majors."

He was impressed that once she decided she wanted to attend Rawlings, she moved from Smalsville, and took a job in town near the campus so she could work while at school and also establish residency. That way, when she started school, she had the much lower, in-state, tuition payments and some savings to pay them.

He commented, "That was mature planning."

She smiled and kidded him, "I looked for ways to save money because I knew I wasn't going to get a basketball scholarship." With a twinkle in her eye, she asked, "Since scholarship has so little to do with a basketball scholarship—why don't they just call it a 'sportship or a basketballship?'"

He chuckled, "I'll bring it up at the next athletic committee meeting." Then added, "But, seriously, Coach always stressed the student part of the term 'student-athlete' and Buddy and I feel the same way. Our school has one of the highest graduation rates in the nation in terms of its basketball team and our other sports are up there too. We want our players to prepare for a life after sports, no matter how far their athletic skills take them."

During lunch, he talked more about coaching and trying to relate what happens on the court to real life. And they talked more about Coach Barron and the recruiting part of Harry's new job.

She asked, "What's going to be the difference between this new job and the high school job you just left?"

"In high school it's more about fundamentals: shooting technique, passing and defense. At least, on the small-school level I was on, there was no recruiting. You got whoever was in the school district and tried to get their skills up."

"And here?"

"On this level, it's much more complicated. For example, we might practice a zone defense but, if we are winning big and don't need it, we won't use it in the game. We don't want a team scouting us for a future game to know we have it. It's that kind of strategy stuff. But one thing the two levels do have in common: I think a good coach always wants to turn out good citizens."

As they talked, he liked the way she leaned back in her seat with her shoulders against the wall as though she was fully at ease and had nothing better to do than sit and listen to him. She seemed sincerely interested in him and what he had to say.

They talked so long they became aware the staff was starting to set the tables for the dinner crowd. They continued the conversation as they walked toward her dorm.

Realizing they were getting close to the dorm, he asked, "Can I see you this Saturday night? I can try to find a concert or a movie on campus or near here and then we can get something to eat afterwards."

She smiled, "I'd like that."

As he opened the dorm door for her, she said, "I'm looking forward to Saturday," spun toward him, gave him a quick kiss and a big smile. He was caught by surprise. By the time he reacted, she had disappeared into her nearby room.

He stood there, holding the door, cocked his head to the side, and thought about what had just happened. He smiled as he started walking to his apartment, thinking about the way she had leaned against the wall in the restaurant as they talked, seeing her on Saturday, and the kiss at the door.

Harry was very pleased.

SEVEN

Harry called before Saturday night, to check that the plans he made would be OK with her. Their talk lasted over an hour. On Saturday, they went to a local music store which had a small stage and seating for about forty people. They listened to a bluegrass band made up of students from Rawlings.

On the way to the restaurant, he put his arm around her shoulders. She fit right under his arm. He liked when her arm tightened around his waist. After a few steps they stopped, turned, and kissed.

He smiled, "I'm glad I was ready for this one."

"I'm glad you were ready too."

They took a shortcut across campus. She said, "Sometimes I look at these old buildings and can't believe that I'm really here. Neither of my parents went to college. My older sister, Deborah, went to a secretarial school. She got a job at NASA in Florida and married an aerospace engineer."

She laughed, "We know he went to college. We try not to mention anything about 'rocket science' because that's what he really does."

He smiled.

At the restaurant she said, "I kinda liked the bluegrass but it really wasn't something I was familiar with. My folks usually had Big Band stuff playing when I was a kid. What about yours?"

The look on his face told her the mood had changed.

Harry shook his head, took a deep breath and let it out slowly. He said softly, "OK Corey, so this is the hard part and it's going to be a bit awkward—please let me just get it out, OK?"

Puzzled, she just nodded.

"Corey, my folks were killed in a crash with a drunk truck driver when I was ten."

He saw her reaction, "Like I said, it's the hard part. I never know how or when to get that into a conversation."

He paused, "My little sister was killed with them."

"Oh, how awful," she said softly, reaching for his hand.

"I was away for the first time at camp and they were coming up to get me to bring me home. They never made it.

"I remember being at the camp and waiting while all the other kids got picked up. Finally, my mom's sister, Jean, showed up. She was the emergency contact person, so when nobody came to get me, they called her. Nobody at the camp knew why my folks weren't there. And it took my aunt six hours to get there from where she lived."

He continued as she listened quietly. "I later learned my sister was killed instantly. Because the small hospital closer to the accident couldn't handle two trauma cases, and my mom looked worse off, they took her there with my sister's body. But my dad was taken to another hospital further away. By the time my aunt came to get me, she'd already found out what had happened and where my family was. They all died. Mom in the hospital, and then my dad an hour later.

"I remember, my aunt cried, 'It was like she and your sister came and got him and they all went off together.'"

Corey wiped a tear from her eye and squeezed his hand. They were both choked up. As he leaned forward he whispered, "So, I don't really know about the kind of music they liked. But I do remember my father had a good singing voice. That's not much to remember," he shook his head, "But, that's what I remember."

He brightened just a little, "And I also remember he used to make my mom laugh a lot. She had a nice laugh."

Corey just looked at him. He knew there was nothing she could say.

He sighed and sat back, "As I said, I never know how or when to get that into a conversation when I want someone to know me, but I don't want them to feel terrible about having asked.

"It happened. It's a fact of my life."

He looked to see she understood.

"I think the last time I spoke about this was with a kid I coached in high school. This poor kid was taking care of his mom while she was dying and he was taking care of a little sister too."

He paused as he remembered the rest, he shook his head. "And now he's dead too."

Seeing the questioning look on her face, he added, "All this kid ever dreamed of was being in the Marines. He made it. And then he was killed in a helicopter accident. But before his death, he had to deal with his mother's. I honestly never figured out, if I had the choice, what type of death I would want my loved ones to have.

"Is a sudden they-aren't-coming-to-get-you death better than a long-slow, burden-on-the-family death?"

Corey just shook her head. She couldn't know the unknowable either.

He nodded, "But, truth told, my parents' dying is how I got interested in basketball."

She leaned back and listened.

"My aunt took me to live with her. She had no children of her own and worked as a probation officer. There was a friend of hers who lived across the street, Ralph Chase. He played in high school and college ball. He was a detective and he coached Police Athletic League teams. He also ran a small construction business and made some extra money as a referee for high school and college games. Having two grown daughters, he just kind of adopted me as his white son.

"When I came to live with my aunt, I was a pudgy kid. He got me into playing on the PAL team. He took me with him when he refed games. In the car going, we talked about the tendencies of each of the teams, and on the way home we talked about the games and each team's weaknesses and strengths. We talked strategy. He really knew the whole game. We were always talking basketball. He took me with him when he jogged around the local reservoir—we talked basketball. And he ran me and the rest of the team ragged with running and dribbling drills on the court. We put a basketball hoop up in the back of Aunt Jean's garage and with all the running—and when I wasn't running, I was out back shooting hoops—I really lost some weight and got into good shape.

"By the time I got to high school, I realized I might be good enough to get a basketball scholarship for college. The side jobs I did for 'Uncle Ralph's Construction' were not going to pay my way through school. But a basketball scholarship and a Phys. Ed major might be the way to go. And the rest as they say, is history."

She sighed and shook her head, "So much, so young."

He looked across the table at her, smiled, and kissed her hand, "Yeah, but, so far so good."

After kissing goodnight at her door, Corey called her sister to tell her that she had found the man she wanted to marry.

EIGHT

The first time Corey was at Harry's apartment, while snuggling on the couch, she remarked on the number of books.

He smiled, "My real interest in school was Greek Philosophy. But I didn't have any money. I needed that basketball scholarship. I knew early on that after I graduated, I was going to need to get a job. Getting a job as a physical education teacher was something I could do without an advanced degree. So, I majored in Phys. Ed but I had a minor in Greek Philosophy.

"You know the saying, 'A sound mind in a sound body.' Both basketball and Greek Philosophy have a beauty about them."

He laughed, "There are also some surprising overlaps. On the same day that I was reading Epictetus's teaching that 'things are not so well with your servant that he can give you peace of mind,' I heard Buddy telling one of our teammates not to let the critics 'rent space in your head.'"

Corey nodded and smiled.

He continued, "But also in both basketball and philosophy, you can study and come to understand the principle and still have a hard time putting the idea into action. In basketball you can understand the mechanics of making a shot and still miss the shot.

"In philosophy you can understand the concept of why you should keep your composure when someone dies and still not be able to keep yourself together after the loss. I learned that lesson when my Aunt Jean died at the end of my junior year."

Corey snuggled closer.

After that night, as the time they spent together grew, they became so comfortable with each other it seemed less like dating and more as if they were an established couple.

After a few weeks, Corey started spending the weekends at his apartment. One night, after they had gotten back from dinner, she remarked on a couple they had seen at the restaurant.

"It looked like he was really hot for her and didn't pick up that she didn't like to be touched or at least not in public."

He added, "Or at least not in public by him."

They drifted into a conversation about when chemistry was just not right. Either the person or the place or the timing was wrong. He thought for a moment and then decided to tell her about the night he brought groceries to Jacqui Fykes.

"…and in the grocery, when the man said the food would be going to waste, all I thought of was Jacqui and Patricia needing it. So, when she looked like she was going to pull my pants down with that sleepy, drugged look on her face I wasn't sure what was happening—it was so out of nowhere—I wasn't sure if it was some kind of a joke. I was frozen for a moment when she started to pull them down."

Corey studied his face as he talked. "Would you have let her do it if you were ready for it?"

Slowly, trying to make sure he was telling the truth, "It was just so out of place. I realized if I let her do it, it would change things between us, and it wasn't going to make me smarter, stronger, younger, or faster. It would have been just— And then I remembered what she had told me about being kept drugged and locked in a room, and guys would pay to be let into the room."

Corey said, "She was like a prisoner."

"She was a prisoner," he replied softly. "And there was something else. There was a full-length mirror on the bathroom door and I could see myself standing there with her starting to get on her knees—and that look on her face. I just couldn't— It was almost like I had just paid to be let into her locked room."

"Why do you think she treated you like that?"

"I don't know. She was drunk or stoned. Maybe she saw all men like that. When she'd told me about all that stuff that happened to her, I thought she felt that I was a friend."

"Maybe she thought you wanted more than just friendship."

"I don't know, I never thought I wanted more than friendship. She was attractive when she wanted to be, but I just didn't think about her as a 'girlfriend,' in the lover sense of the word. She had a lot of emotional issues, but I will tell you, that night must have been a bottom for her. She flushed the pills and marijuana and the next day she went for counseling and help to get her GED. Before I left there, she had completely turned her life around."

"Did you two ever talk about that night?"

"No, Corey. I've never talked about that night with anybody, and probably never will."

She looked at him intently. She put her hands on his cheeks and kissed him softly on the lips. She looked into his eyes. Then she slowly started to unbutton his shirt.

After their first two months, Corey was spending more than just weekends at his apartment. More time at his place than she was in her dorm room. One night after they made love—as she was resting with her head on his chest—a small voice within him said he should ask her to marry him.

He fell asleep, thinking about being married to Corey.

With the start of her senior year just weeks away, they decided Corey should give up her dorm room and move in with him. She told him she had a babysitting job for Liam Doyles the first Saturday night after the semester started. Liam and his wife were going to a wedding. She had accepted the job before she met Harry and asked if he wanted to come with her while she watched the children.

When they arrived at the house, Liam and his wife Nancy greeted them, and reminded Corey about the kids' bedtime routine.

Harry was truly in awe of the way Corey could handle the three young children. She seemed to have unlimited patience; she listened to them, treated them with respect, and was able to respond to them in a way that made everything, including baths and putting them to bed, go so smoothly.

He heard the voice inside himself softly say, She will make a great mother for your children. He knew it was true.

With the last child asleep, she came out of the bedroom and sat close to him on the couch. He took both her hands in his hands.

"I think we should get married."

Leaning forward, she kissed him and snuggled her head on his chest, "I agree."

When Liam and Nancy returned home, Nancy asked if everything went alright. Corey reported, "The children were fine."

Harry chimed in, "Yeah, the kids did so well we decided to get married and have our own."

Liam thought he was kidding, but Nancy, looking at Corey, knew right away. She nearly flew over to Corey and hugged her. When Liam saw Corey accepting Nancy's congratulations, he realized it was no joke. He laughed and shook Harry's hand, "Is this for publication?" Harry smiled and nodded it was.

Walking home, they stopped for a hug and a kiss on every street corner. When they got home, they realized it was too late to call Corey's parents. He had no one on his side to call.

The next morning Corey called Smalsville, introducing Harry to her parents on the phone. They made plans to see her folks in person at the Thanksgiving break in the school and team schedule. They also thought that might be a good time for the wedding.

Buddy laughed when Harry asked for the break time off. He thought about Harry meeting her parents and getting married at the same time. But nobody could see any reason not to.

It was set. After the team's sixth game of the season, which was a home game on the Monday before the holiday, they drove the two days to Smalsville to get married.

NINE

It was dark when Harry and Corey arrived. He had spoken to her parents on the phone several times since she had told them about their wedding plans. He had seen pictures of them but was looking forward to their face-to-face meeting.

He liked Bill and Barbara immediately.

He was surprised at how old Bill looked and decided it must be the white hair parted in the middle, the wire rimmed glasses and the stooped stature. He also noted Bill wore both a belt and suspenders. His pants were so high he looked like he had no torso, just a waist and shoulders. Bill shuffled when he walked.

Harry thought Barbara was a preview of what Corey would look like when she aged. Her red hair was slightly faded, but her green eyes were still bright and her skin showed very little sign of aging.

He liked what he had to look forward to.

Barbara and Bill were very comfortable with him.

Heading off to bed, they promised him a tour of the area in the morning. Like Corey, they warned him there was not much to see in the village, nor the surrounding area.

Main Street in Smalsville was just a few blocks long. Bill's hardware and supply store was on Main Street toward the south end of the village. On Sundays, the store was only opened half a day and Corey and her mom took Harry for a tour around closing time.

Bill had been a plumber and electrician until he opened the store twenty years ago.

He said, "I realized it was easier to sell the pipes and wires than to pull and push them into place myself."

Harry told them, "Every summer, from the time I was fourteen until the summer of my junior year in college, I worked as the 'gofer' on a construction crew. I was told 'go for this or go for that.' I spent lots of time in stores like this and lumber yards fetching supplies and tools."

Having shown Harry around the store, Bill closed up and they all took a drive. The village was not much more than the few blocks of Main Street. There was a bank, two churches, a few other stores, and a restaurant. There was a post office and the Village Hall, but not much else. The volunteer fire department was up on the end of Main Street furthest from the store. Bill had been a member for forty-five years and was an ex-chief.

Most of the buildings between the store and the fire department were old and none of them was higher than three stories except for the steeples of the churches. There was a movie theater that had long since closed.

Barbara said, "Each year there's a new rumor as to what's going to become of the theater building. But, so far. . ."

Bill added, "Ten years ago at a department meeting, we were told it wouldn't be safe to go above the first floor if there's a fire in the movie house."

On the way out of the business part of the village there was an old brick schoolhouse. Half a mile away there was a lake, and the surrounding woods had trails where kids still rode their bikes.

One mile further up that road from the lake was the Winsloh house. It was a big, old two-story brick house with stone fireplaces, sitting on thirty acres of land with a small pond and a view of the lake beyond the pond. With a sense of nostalgia, after the last of their chickens were gone, the house had been dubbed "The Coop." Corey had grown up in this house and was pleased to think of getting married there. The house had very new-looking plumbing and electrical fixtures that Harry thought were an upgrade befitting a man who owned a hardware store.

Corey and her mom planned the wedding. A small wedding in a small village. They realized with so few people to invite they could do the food preparation themselves. Corey's older sister, Deborah, came from Florida to be the Matron of Honor and insisted on baking the cake. Her husband Jack agreed to be Best Man.

Harry laughed, "My part is easy. I wear a decent suit, make sure there's a ring and remember to say 'I do.'"

He remembered what Corey had told him about Jack's work with NASA and decided not to add, "It's not rocket science," although getting to know Jack, he would have expected Jack to reply, "No, it's a slam dunk."

The wedding was on the lawn overlooking the pond and the lake in the distance. The mayor, who had been fire chief before Bill, performed the ceremony. Corey wore her grandmother's wedding dress just as her mom and Deborah had done before her. The party went into the night, but bride and groom had to get to bed before the others left because they had to get up early to get on the road. The wedding had been planned for their last day in Smalsville, so when they drove back home it would be as husband and wife.

As they drove back to Rawlings, Corey talked about the basketball schedule and kidded, "When you start recruiting for next year, I guess you are going to be spending a lot of time looking for another Julius Anderson."

He shook his head, "If I am hoping to find another Julius I might as well not get started. Here's the deal with Julius most people don't get. When Julius was a sophomore in high school, he was 5'8". He was very fast and very agile, I mean, he really had moves. And he was constantly working on his game. But when Julius was a sophomore with us, all of a sudden, he's 6'10" and he's still very fast and still has all the agility. And he still has the same work ethic. Now, he's a monster. There's no one else with his quickness and agility for his size. So, he's too quick for the tall guys and too tall for the quick guys. And, to make it even worse for the defenders, he shoots just as well with either hand. All I had to do was figure out where he wanted the ball. For some reason he liked lower passes on the right side of the basket and higher passes on the left side. I don't know why—even he might not know why—but all I had to do was notice it and make the passes where I knew he wanted the ball.

"Don't get me wrong, I'd love to find another one like him, but I doubt that guy exists on Earth."

On a whim they decided to extend the trip rather than drive four more hours back to their apartment. They stopped at a hotel they had seen advertised on roadside billboards to see if a room was available.

When they got to the front desk the clerk said, "There's a rock concert in town this weekend and the hotel is pretty much booked. But if you can pretend it's your second honeymoon, you can have the bridal suite—it's the only room available."

Harry laughed, "It's our first honeymoon and we'll take it."

The clerk laughed too.

In the room, he jumped into the shower while Corey looked at the TV schedule. When he came out, he was barefoot and bare-chested wearing just a pair of basketball shorts.

She told him there was a movie on she might want to see but first she was going to shower. He sat down on the end of the heart-shaped bed and was reading the blurbs about the movies in the guide when she stepped out of the bathroom.

She was barefoot and topless—wearing a cutoff pair of his basketball shorts slung playfully low on her hips.

She asked, "Are you tired from all the driving?"

He stared at her, smiled, and shook his head.

They never got to watch the movie.

TEN

Judy and Harry had written to each other for a while after he left Madison. He encouraged her to try making friends at school, and urged her not to be too hard on her grandparents. After all, they had no experience with raising a girl and they were most likely doing the best they could.

He wrote it, not sure he believed all of it. He reminded her to look for balance and not to let other people's opinions of her count more than her own.

Reading his letters, she could remember his voice, his life-living-lessons. Judy liked getting Harry's letters. They comforted her, but she wished she had better news to share with him.

Because of a big increase in rent, Judy and her grandparents had been evicted. She came home from school one day to find them sitting on the curb and what little she owned on the street.

They were homeless until a church group found an affordable place further from the school. Judy no longer wanted to bother being on the basketball team where she rarely saw playing time. Feeling Harry would be disappointed, she put off writing to him. Finally, not having returned his letter for a while, she decided she would rather not write than disappoint him.

When Harry did not receive a response from Judy—and his follow-up letter was returned to him as undeliverable—all he could do was hope for the best for her.

Naomi returned home to pack up Jacqui and Patricia and move them to Oakland, where they could be together while she continued treatment. A friend of Naomi's, named Francine, came to visit and help Naomi and Jacqui pack.

Meeting Judy, Francine said if Judy came to New York, she could stay with her until she found a place of her own in the city. Francine said she would also put in a word for Judy at a couple of stores near her work that always needed help.

Judy was not sure what she would find in New York. But she knew she needed to leave where she was. She started counting the months until she would finish high school, leave Madison and—with Jacqui's warnings in mind, and Francine's promise—try to make her own way.

Judy Jarrolson was graduated from high school. The next week she had her 18th birthday. Packing her few belongings in a backpack and a small cheap suitcase that was left over from Jackie's move, she said "goodbye" to her grandparents and headed for New York City.

She arrived to the news that Francine was going to be moving in with her boyfriend in North Carolina. She was quitting her job at the drugstore, and recommended Judy as her replacement. The apartment was hers if she got a job and could pay for it. It would be her first taste of living on her own and a regular income.

It was a small apartment on the fourth floor of an old building, the only apartment on that floor. The flights of stairs creaked and the old wrought iron banisters wobbled. The rugs in the bedroom needed to be thrown out and the whole place needed to be painted. Judy thought it would do until she could get something better set up.

The drugstore was on the ground floor of an old building on a side street on the west side of lower Manhattan and was a short bus ride or a long walk from the apartment. It carried the usual products for that type of store but also had an emphasis on theatrical makeup since the Theater District was not far from there.

The pharmacy was run by Tom and Joe Leonard.

Their father had been a pharmacist and owned two stores. When Tom finished pharmacy school, his father gave him this store. When Joe finished three years later, his father retired and gave him his other store in Queens. Unfortunately for the brothers, the Queens store was driven out of business when a big chain drug store moved in up the block.

Now, they both depended on the Manhattan store for their living. Tom, the older brother who still thought of this as his store, was a control freak. Joe was much nicer and could see the big picture; he knew there was life outside the store. Not surprisingly, Tom was incensed that Francine was leaving on such short notice. But Joe was happy that Francine had brought Judy in, and would stay on for at least two weeks to help train her.

Once the brothers agreed to hire Judy, Francine took her around past the office to a storage area where a corner of the space had a small bench and a couple of beat up, salvaged, school lockers standing along the back wall as well as hooks for "the girls" to hang their coats and bags.

There Francine introduced Judy to Connie Depanici, a young Italian woman from the neighborhood, who was the other "girl" who worked at the store. Connie stood about 5'3", with a dark complexion, long black hair, brown eyes and was on the heavy side.

While Connie went to attend to the first customer of the day, Francine showed Judy the two cash registers that sat about six feet apart on the waist-high glass counter near the wall, which led up to the glass-enclosed, raised pharmacy area. When Connie was using one cash register at the end of her sale, Francine was explaining what Connie was doing to complete and record the transaction.

Connie smiled at the narration. Both she and Francine cautioned Judy that no matter what she learned about the various products they sold, she should never put herself in the position of giving advice to the customers when they asked what they should buy for different problems. Connie did make an exception to that rule with regard to advising people who asked her about the makeup and other beauty products.

For the two weeks before Francine left, Judy slept in the apartment on a mat on the floor. At work, those weeks also saw Judy looking at the displays that lined the walls of the store from the front glass door to the raised pharmacy area. She was intent on learning where everything was.

Toward the end of Francine's "tutoring time," Judy was happy that when Francine let her attend to customers on her own, she was able to walk out from behind the counter and show them where to find the items they were looking for.

After Francine left for North Carolina, alone in her own apartment, Judy reflected on the simple interactions with appreciative customers. It assured her that she had found a place for herself in the "Big City." She was also assured by having made a friend, Connie.

She learned that Connie had a three-year-old son named Paolo. Connie's sister, who had two daughters in elementary school, lived in the building next door to her and watched Paulo while Connie was at work. Connie had married right out of high school, and had not worked outside the house before. But, when her husband, Carmine, went to prison, she needed to find a job.

Judy enjoyed their conversations and Connie's insights. It was clear to Connie, if not to Judy, that Tom Leonard was starting to fancy Judy. He seemed nicer when he was around her, even though that still wasn't nice enough.

Judy learned that when Connie married Carmine, she also wound up making dinner for "the boys," he had befriended: the twins, Frankie and Johnnie Zingaro, and their cousin whose given name was Cosmo Puglesi—but, everyone called him Gort. The whole neighborhood helped to raise these three boys. But they had mostly hung out with Carmine before he was sent upstate to prison. Connie had grown up as the oldest of eight children so cooking and cleaning for these boys seemed natural to her.

The Zingaros, identical twins in their twenties, never dressed alike. They were both 5'11", with dark eyes, black hair, and Roman noses that stood out from their skinny, pockmarked faces. While Frankie experimented with different styles of beard, Johnnie wore a mustache. They were slim, bordering on skinny, with rope-like veins on their arms; the effect of the hard construction work they did whenever they had to.

It was Gort who stood out in any crowd. He was 6' 4" with a head like a big round pumpkin covered by light brown hair that he wore in a flattop crew cut. He always wore a pork pie hat. But as big as his head looked, it was not out of proportion with the rest of his oversized body.

He had almost no neck, was broad shouldered, and a had barrel chest on top of legs that looked like they would support a small elephant. His arms, the size of most men's thighs, ended in thick, powerful fingers.

It was said he could lift the front end of a car and split tennis balls by squeezing them. He got the nickname Gort after the fearsome robot in the old movie, The Day the Earth Stood Still, because of the "train thing."

Like the robot, Gort was thought to be indestructible. This notion was promoted by his most distinguishing feature—a long raw-looking one-inch-wide scar—and the story of how he came by it. The scar ran from the top of his head, just over his left eye, down the right side of his face and chest to the middle of his right thigh. The scar made him look like a picture that had been torn down the middle and not quite put back together.

He got the scar ten years before, when he was twelve and was jumped by four teenage boys on a subway platform. Even at twelve he was holding his own in the fight, until one of the boys hit him from behind with a baseball bat and together the four bigger boys managed to throw him on the tracks in front of an oncoming D train.

Word of the attack went around the neighborhood and made the evening news. The police never caught the other boys, but as word spread of Gort surviving the collision with the train, rumors began to circulate that maybe the police were just going to let him and the neighborhood deal with his attackers. Thirteen months after "the train thing," when Gort was released from the physical rehabilitation center, it was obvious that physically he had more than gotten back to where he had been. The joke on the street was, "Now the train won't stand a chance."

The injury made him quieter. He had grown up while spending all that time in pain alone in the hospital and then in the rehabilitation center. The neighborhood was surprised that he showed no interest in finding the boys who had almost killed him.

When Connie told Judy about Gort she said, "So, since the 'train thing,' no one has ever seen Gort get angry except for with guys that hit women. Other than that, I don't know if it's possible to get him angry because I don't know anybody crazy enough to try."

She looked around to make sure they weren't overheard. "So now, you gotta know that Gort's mother was a drunk who died when he was seven and his older sister, Justina, had to raise him. I mean the neighborhood tried to help but they really had no one else. She had to quit school to take care of him. She worked when she could—cleaning other people's apartments, or whatever work she could find. She was pretty, a cute little thing, which you wouldn't imagine from looking at him.

"Sometimes when the money ran out, she would turn a trick to pay the rent or buy food. The only way we found out about that was seeing how this poor girl seemed to be a magnet for scumbags who'd rather hit her than pay her. Even when Gort got older, and he could earn, so she didn't have to turn tricks, she would still wind up with guys who used their hands on her.

"So, Gort goes ballistic with guys who put their hands on women."

Checking to see they could still talk, Connie continued, "So, one night some guy beats his sister really bad. Gort gets home and finds her with blood all over the place. So, he goes like on a mission to find this guy. He's like an avenging demon. I mean he's ready to tear buildings down in his search. So, he finally finds out where the guy stays in the Bronx. Gort goes up there. The guy is looking out this window and sees Gort charging up the stoop. So, this guy probably figures he can't get past Gort by going down, so he runs up to hide on the roof. So, he goes up there and Gort finally figures that's where this guy's gotta be.

"So, now, as it happens, there's a couple of cops on the roof of a building across the street. They're dealing with a complaint of kids dropping water balloons on people from that roof. So, they're talking to these kids up there and they see this guy rush outta the door onto the roof across the street. The cops watch this guy run over to the front of the roof like in a panic and he looks down at the street. Then, they see Gort burst outta the door onto the roof. So, they watch as the guy takes one look at Gort and jumps off the roof."

She paused, "I mean what are the odds that there's two cops on a roof across the street and they watch this guy decide he'd rather take his chances with the six story drop than deal with Gort?"

Judy watched as Connie stopped and crossed herself then said, "The guy didn't make it. So, Gort skates on that one because he's got two cops who see he never touched the guy.

"So, Gort's like an equal opportunity avenger. He gets pissed at any guys who hit girls even when he don't know the girls.

"So, like about a year ago, Gort is out with the twins at a diner uptown where they don't know anybody. While they're eating, some guy across the room reaches out and slaps his date.

"So, Gort sees that and before the twins can react, quick as a cat, Gort is outta his seat and across the room. He yells, 'So, you like to hit women, huh,' and just shatters the guy's jaw. Boom! Like that. Just one punch. Boom!" She acted out the punch.

"OK so the twins manage to grab Gort and drag him away from this guy. They hustle him outta there before he throws another punch and totally destroys the guy.

"But, Gort ain't all that hard to find. And the idiot that hit the girl has a brother who works as an investigator for the DA in Brooklyn. So. . ."

She looked at Judy, "But, you gotta laugh.

"I come home one day and find two detectives just pulling up to my place and they tell me they're looking for Gort. I tell them if it's dinner time he's probably up- stairs waiting for me to cook. They go up with me and Gort is there and they tell him they have to take him in.

"So, the young cop goes to put his handcuffs on Gort, but the cuffs won't fit around his wrists. So, the young cop says he is gonna go back to the station house and get some leg-irons that he can use as cuffs. The older cop looks at him, shakes his head and says, 'You're gonna do what?'

"The young cop takes the older cop aside, but I heard him whisper, 'Look, this guy's a nightmare in a hat. I wouldn't want to run into him even in a well-lit alley. Let's follow procedure and transport him in cuffs.'

"So, the older cop's shaking his head, he can't believe it. He says, 'Look Gort, I don't have any problem with you and you don't have any beef with us, right? Let's all just act like the fine gentlemen we are. Now, we'll all just go downstairs, and you and I are gonna get in the back of our fuckin car.'"

Connie looked around to make sure they are still alone in the front of the store, "So, because of the Brooklyn DA thing, even though this scumbag shouldn't be hitting his date, they're talking about prison time for Gort. So, Carmine's uncle, Leno Giambroni, has to get involved."

Connie saw Judy's quizzical look and explained, "Leno kinda takes care of people in the neighborhood. So, he gets involved and talks to a few people. Gort winds up with a sentence of 30 days at Rikers Island," she paused, "with the understanding that if it's only 30 days, he's gonna only do 20 with credit for good time, and then Leno can guarantee that when Gort gets out, he doesn't go looking for this guy to finish the job."

Connie laughs, "So, welcome to the big city, kid. You just gotta love New York."

ELEVEN

After Judy had been working at the store for a couple of months, one of Connie's favorite customers came in. Sol Magenwise was a short, older, white-haired gentleman, a widower who got prescriptions filled there. His coming to the store predated Connie's working there, but when she started, she recognized him as a man who knew both her uncles.

At first, he came in to pick up medication for his aged mother, who still lived in the neighborhood. Then, after his mother was gone, he came in for himself and his wife. Now, and for the last four years, he came only to get his own prescriptions filled.

He had a voice softened by the cigars his doctor made him give up years ago and he always made time to chat with Connie. This was his first time in the store since Judy started working there. She greeted him like any other customer when he walked in, but Connie said she would take care of him. Judy went to the customer who walked in after him.

He commented to Connie, "I have not seen this new girl before.

"I really see something in this young lady. Some potential about the way she looks. But her clothes do not fit well, and she is not being helped by the way she wears her hair and no makeup."

Connie nodded and moved her hands to say he should go on.

"You know I still do a little work for models. Nobody very famous now, since your friend left, but I think I have a bit of an eye for this sort of thing. You and I have talked about your interest in cosmetology. Why don't you take your friend aside and, if she's willing, you can help her out? I think she would really look beautiful with her hair shorter and off her face so her eyes would be presented better. A soft blue or purple eyeshadow would be a good shade for her to compliment and bring out her unique eye color."

Connie nodded. She had noticed Judy's clothes but never said anything. She hadn't looked for nor seen the potential. Looking at Judy—as though for the first time—she could see he was right.

Holding up a finger to pause the conversation, he slowly walked up to the magazine rack and studied it. Finding the issue, he was looking for, he opened it to a page he had seen while looking through his copy at his office.

He handed the magazine to Connie opened to the picture saying, "She might do better with a hairstyle something like this but with her makeup more understated than this."

He reached into his pocket and handed Connie his card. "Please give this to your friend if she is interested in talking about modeling. I know it's not for everybody, but if she wants to talk. . ."

When he and the other customer left, Connie gave Judy, "my sweet old gentleman's" card and told her about his suggestions.

She nodded to Judy. "Forget the name on the card. Everybody just calls him 'Pops.' He's really good people."

"How do you mean?"

Connie said, "So, this girl Agneta Colisimo was from around here. I was in high school with her older sister. So, I hear she's interested in becoming a model. I mention her to Leno's brother, Luigi. He mentions Agneta to Pops and his wife Bea, and they helped her to become a model.

"But as soon as she starts to make good money, she changes her name to Anna Cole. Now she ain't got nothing to do with the old neighborhood. All of a sudden, it's like she's too good for us. So, with Pops and Bea she's making all this money, but she was impatient to make more money faster. So, despite Pops and Bea trying to advise her to take care of herself, she starts to go out with a fast crowd and soon she's drinking heavy and into drugs.

"So, now she gets convinced that she needs to leave Pops and Bea and go to a more glamorous agency. I think one of the guys at this big agency was getting her the drugs.

"So, her drinking and drugging gets worse and worse. Now she's got this big party-girl life and it's starting to mess up her work. She's missing things she's supposed to be at and stuff like that. Soon she ain't modeling anymore because she's just too out of control. So, she's strung out on drugs and broke.

"I mean she starts getting into some crazy wild shit like this Central Park West thing."

"What does that mean?"

Connie looked around to make sure the brothers couldn't hear her, "One day our big shot druggist brothers have to do a favor for a big wig friend of theirs. They fill a scrip on a rush basis that he calls in just at closing time. So, the deal is they give me money to take a cab uptown to deliver the meds in person and pick up the scrip they filled in advance. So, I deliver and pick up and on the way back downtown in the cab, we're stopped at a light on Central Park West and I hear the cabbie yell, 'Wow, wouldya look at that!'

"I turn around and I see Agneta with these three guys. They all look wasted outta their minds. They're staggering outta the door of an apartment building. Her makeup is smeared all over her face and she's barefoot with one high heel still strapped to her ankle. Her skirt is pulled up so high I can see that she doesn't have panties on and her blouse is unbuttoned down to her waist.

"She's laughing. She's got a cocktail glass in one hand and the other hand is down the front of one guy's pants."

Connie shook her head as she recalled the scene, "Two of the guys are kind of supporting her and dragging her staggering ass toward a limo. So, one of these guys has got her purse and her other shoe and a bottle of booze. All these guys are in suits and ties and she's half naked. I couldn't believe it—this is Central Park West—and she's half-naked on the street. She's lucky she didn't get her dumb ass arrested. In another half a block there's a museum full of kids. The doorman is runnin' to get the back door to the limo opened and looks like he can't wait till they get the hell out from in front of his building.

"So, Pops used to come in and ask if I seen her or how she was doin' after she left them. After a while he kinda heard that she was going downhill and he was concerned about her. He asks me if I can find her. He says, 'If she's in trouble, maybe I can help.' But after I saw her in the street like that, I knew there's no way I'm gonna tell him about her. I mean his wife was sick and his mother was dying and I knew, even after what she done to him, that he would still try to help Agneta deal with her demons.

"I knew he would not hold it against her. See, he was in here once to get a scrip filled and I was waiting on a girl who was obviously buying supplies for a few girls that musta been working in a cathouse somewhere around here. I mean like she used to come in every couple of weeks and buy like 30 boxes of condoms with 54 in each box, and several tubes of spermicidal gel and lots of lube—then she just stopped coming in. So, I figured the place got shut down—but anyway, Pops is here one time, when she was still coming in. I finish with her order and when she walks out I look at him and I shrug, What do you think about that? And that sweet old man says, 'Constanza, I never want to be the judge of what some people have to do to get through their lives. You know some people do not have an easy life. I think most people think these women sell themselves to buy drugs, but I suspect that they need the drugs to medicate themselves, to help them deal with the fact that they have to sell themselves to survive.'

"So, then he says that he and his wife had just seen a gospel concert in Harlem and this choir sang, 'When I look back over my life, and I think things over, I can truly say that I've been blessed.' He says, 'Have you and I not been truly blessed? Who knows what hole in their soul some people are trying to fill?'

"So, I realized you know he's right—Gort's sister, Justina, was a nice kid but, like I told you, she sometimes had to sell herself to put food on their table. So, I don't think she was really into drugs, but I realized that most of the time I saw her dressed all slutted-up she was usually drunk, so maybe that was her thing for getting by with it. So, from then on, I call no woman a whore. And, the more I thought of it, I realized that what I couldn't forgive

Agneta for was the fact that she turned her back on the neighborhood and the way she turned on Pops and his wife. That's what I couldn't forgive.

"Like I said, before I saw her with those guys, when Pops would ask about her, all I told him was I hadn't seen her. So, after I saw her on the street like that, I knew. He's too good a person. No way I want to see him get involved."

Judy asked, "What about her now?"

Connie crossed herself and said, "She's gone. AIDS—about two years ago now. So, like I said, that Pops is real good people. I think we should listen to him. If he thinks he sees something in your looks and things that can help you, we should really pay attention.

"Don't you think you'd be interested in modeling? Didn't you dream about that stuff when you were a kid?"

"I didn't dream about modeling. I honestly never thought about it at all. I don't want to bore you with details, but with the way things were before I got to New York, I never thought much about makeup and those kinds of things."

Connie said, "My girlfriends and I, all we talked about was makeup, and boys and that stuff. Didn't yours?"

"I didn't have any girlfriends. And we couldn't afford makeup."

Connie was taken aback by the answer but only said, "Well you're here in the Big City now. So, maybe it's time to think more about what colors are better for you and wear your hair and some makeup to set off your face and those eyes. He knows I wanted to go to cosmetology school, but Carmine always wanted me to be home. Even before the baby, he refused to let me work.

"So, now, with him away—well, at least we sell some cosmetics here and I can give girls some suggestions."

Connie was pleased that Judy seemed interested.

After that, they started talking about makeup and hairstyles. Soon Judy accepted an invitation to Connie's to allow her to cut her hair and "put her together," as Connie called it. They chose a night when Paolo was scheduled to have a sleepover with her sister and his girl cousins.

Arriving at the apartment, Judy finally met the Zingaros and Gort, who were waiting for dinner. She thought them cold and standoffish. She couldn't understand why, but Connie just shrugged and told her they'd get used to her.

While the boys watched TV in the other room, Connie was assembling the things she would need to cut Judy's hair when Gort announced, "I'm starving. Could you do that stuff after you make dinner?" With Judy's help, Connie started the meal preparation.

After dinner, Connie cut and styled Judy's hair to look like the picture Pops had pointed out in the magazine. It was the first time her hair had not reached past her shoulders and Connie cut it and brushed it so it swept back away from Judy's face. Connie liked Pops' suggestion that she use the makeup sparingly to enhance, rather than hide Judy's natural beauty. She especially wanted to draw attention to her eyes. Connie was impressed with the transformation. Once Judy saw herself in the mirror, she liked it too. She was sure she should wear her makeup the way Connie had applied it and her hair the way it was styled.

When the boys came in for dessert, they said "Wow! Who is that?"

"So, where did she come from?"

"Hey. What happened to the other girl that was here before?"

The next day at work Connie took pride in her handy work— everybody noticed the "new Judy."

Just before closing time, in walked Peter Warrin.

TWELVE

Peter, about 5'5" wearing black boots with heels, to make him look taller, had a stature complex as big as he was small. He wore tight pants with a shirt open in front to show off several thick gold-looking chains. With dark brown hair that fell down to his shirt collar, Connie thought if he had on a big hat and fur coat, he would look like a neighborhood pimp. He strutted past the girls and interrupted Tom's phone call at the pharmacy counter to ask for some film. Shrugging him off, Tom told him to talk to Connie. He asked for three rolls of fast black and white.

Seeing Judy come out of the back with a package, he walked up to Judy, and put his face in both hands, and leaned on the glass counter with his elbows. The chains popping out of his open shirt clanking against the counter.

He asked, "Who might you be?"

Judy was taken aback by the attention. She had never seen anybody like him. Connie was instantly suspicious of him with his flashy clothes and forward attitude. Coming up to the counter opposite him she said, "Her name is Judy and here's your film."

He repeated the name "Judy! Judy! Judy!" It seemed like he was trying to do an impersonation of Cary Grant. Each time he said Judy, it sounded like he was saying Jody.

"I'm Peter Warrin," but sounded like he said Worren.

Connie asked, "Where are you from?"

"Australia! I'm a photographer and a promoter. First, I moved to Montreal and now I've come to these gold-lined streets to seek my fortune, and I think I just found it."

Connie looked at him. "If you're really a photographer why are you buying film in a drugstore? By the way, that's $19.79 with tax."

"How 'bout dinner with me some night, Luv? I can really make you a star." Connie could see Judy was flustered by the attention.

"That's $19.79, friend," she said, protectively stepping in front of Judy. Lifting his elbows from the counter, Peter made a big show reaching into the pocket of his tight fitting slacks and pulling out a roll of bills to pay for the film.

"I'll be back tomorrow for my answer," he told Judy. He walked slowly out of the store making it a point to look back at her as he left.

"What do you think?" Judy asked Connie.

Connie put her hand on Judy's shoulder. "Any girl older than twelve knows what he wants. What do you want?"

Judy thought about it for a while.

Finally, she told Connie, "I guess, I really don't know."

"So, I suggest you go real slow until you figure it out."

When he came in the next day, he brought a large, expensive looking bunch of flowers. Connie was the first to see him opening the door.

Judy turned to see the grand entrance only when she heard Connie mockingly say, "Oh! Be still my heart!"

He pretended he didn't hear the remark and presented the flowers to Judy with a slight bow and asked for her phone number. She was surprised. Judy looked away and looked to see if the bosses where watching. She was uncomfortable with the approach and refused to take the flowers or give him her number.

The next day he showed up again with an even bigger bouquet of flowers and a big white stuffed dog. Connie just shook her head when she saw him. Judy giggled, "They're lovely."

"Judy, make this quick." Connie whispered nodding toward the office where Tom was working.

Realizing what Connie meant, Judy whispered, "Thank you, they really are lovely. But could you give them to me when I get off this afternoon?"

She told Peter she could meet him at a café down the block from the store.

Just after he left, Tom came out from the office. Judy and Connie looked at each other and went back to dusting the bottles on the display shelves.

After work, Judy told Connie she was going to meet Peter.

Connie just said, "If you have to, you have to. But if you see his lips moving you know he's lying to you."

When Judy arrived at the café Peter seemed to take no notice of her. She saw the flowers on the table and the big stuffed dog on the seat next to him. She was sure he had seen her come in. Finally, he looked up as she hesitantly sat down across from him.

Peter quietly told her how beautiful she looked. But added, "The hair is OK luv, but you need a bit more makeup. I can fix it for you. I know what a man likes in a woman."

Pointing just above her breasts, "I think you should wear tighter sweaters instead of shirts unless you keep the shirt buttoned down to here. Not when you're at work, of course. I don't want other men coming on to you—but when I say it's OK— when you dress just for me."

She was uneasy that he came on so strong. But she thought that meant he cared.

He told her he was a student of mixed martial arts in Canada and proudly said he had earned a black belt when he was 15, and had won several tournaments. He had also managed the career of a heavyweight martial artist but, "This guy never appreciated all the work I'd done so I dumped him and decided to come to the States. I've been here two months and I've got lots of irons in the fire. And then I saw you. You come along with me and I can make you a big star. I've got a meeting next week to talk to a guy about a whole new way of promoting martial arts fights. We're gonna do it in rounds and you can start out being the girl that carries the cards between rounds."

She was fascinated by his talk, his excitement about his and her futures, and she was flattered he was interested in her.

She listened.

When they left the café, she was carrying the flowers and the big dog. She agreed to have dinner with Peter the next night and decided not to mention anything about this to Connie.

The next day she was surprised that Connie did not ask about Peter—she was sure Connie would want to know—but then Judy realized that Connie was brought up knowing not to ask too many questions. Judy was relieved when Connie didn't ask.

A week later, on their third date, Peter bought her an expensive meal at a nice restaurant. Arriving at her home, after some kissing at the door she let him come up to her apartment. It was clear Peter wanted to go to bed with her.

She let his advances progress like something she thought she was expected to want rather than something she actually desired. Never having had sex before, it happened for her more out of curiosity and to please him. When he assured her he had a condom she thought she would go along with letting him do what he wanted.

He finished quickly and was pleased with his performance. When he rolled off her, all she felt was surprise that this first time hadn't been as painful as Jacqui said it would be.

In the weeks that followed, his demands for sex were more frequent but the meals and restaurants less nice. She'd never been to his apartment. For one reason or another they always wound up at her place. She found the sex more comfortable even if not more satisfying. Her only pleasure was pleasing him.

They never went out socially with anyone else. All he talked about was his latest money-making schemes. He said he was getting ready to launch her career. He was going to take pictures and send them to some magazines. He bragged about all the things he could do for her "when the time was right."

He told her he was going to take her for a trip to Coney Island. He would buy her a bathing suit for the occasion and take his camera. This self-declared photographer never showed her any pictures. She had rarely seen his camera. She never saw a darkroom.

Soon his flatteries—that she could be everything with him—started to alternate with his forewarnings—that she would be nothing without him.

Judy just listened—unsure if she deserved any better.

Now, on the rare occasion that he took her to dinner before wanting sex, he was more agitated, when paying the check. His roll of bills was getting smaller and easier to slip into the pocket of his tight-fitting pants.

THIRTEEN

At work it was "the girls' job" to open and close the store since the Leonards only kept the pharmacy part of the store open from 9:30 to 5:30 but the store was open from 9:00 to 6:15. The actual unlocking and locking up took a few minutes, so even though "the girls" supposedly got off at 6:15, it was really later. They took turns checking out the store and locking it up at night.

The Leonards knew of "the girls' arrangement" and had never said anything about it.

One morning, on Judy's arrival she could tell something was wrong. It was ten minutes to nine, and both bosses' cars were there, and a police car was parked outside. Connie was near tears. The door to the office was closed and the blinds were down. Judy heard Tom's very loud voice. But she could not make out what he was saying.

She whispered to Connie "What's wrong?"

Connie whispered back. "Oh Judy! I'm gonna get fired!

"I screwed up and the store was unlocked all last night! The cops called the bosses and they're talking about it now and I could hear Tom screaming and I heard him yell 'she's got to go.' I got Paolo, I need this job, I can't—"

Judy put her finger to her lips saying, "Shush. Have they asked you anything? Have you told them it was your turn?"

"No, they were already in there when I got here. But—"

Judy put up her hand to cut her off, "I think it's going to be OK."

Connie asked "How?"

Judy turned and went to knock on the office door. Tom opened the door and Judy said she needed to talk to them right away. She went into the room. Tom failed to close the door all the way. Connie could hear Judy tell them she was so sorry she screwed up. She thought she turned the lock on the door but apparently not all the way, and she now knows she left the store unlocked.

Tom started to stammer. "We —we thought—"

She continued "—was anything taken?"

The police officer, amused watching this new scenario unfold, smiled and nodded slowly realizing that while Tom was ranting and raving about "she's got to go" when it looked like it was Connie's fault, he seemed less in a hurry to fire Judy.

The officer smiled at her and said, "Nah, the place was undisturbed. I only noticed it on a door check this morning."

"That's good, I'm so relieved. I'm really very sorry and I'll be much more careful."

Connie, was now near tears for a different reason. When Judy walked out of the office, Connie hugged her friend and whispered, "Thank you so very, very much!"

She returned the hug and whispered, "Shush! No problem. You have Paolo to provide for; I could probably find another job if I had to. I just fell into this one and I've got enough saved so I could probably make it for a month or so until something turned up. Maybe losing this job would even push me to try something different—maybe even modeling."

Coming out of the office, the cop looked at them and, pointing with his chin toward Tom, whispered, "Boy, he sure is a piece of work. If my dad built up a business like this and gave it to me, I think I might manage a smile now and then."

They just nodded to him.

The cop said, "I was just making up my mind whether I should try telling the brothers that if they fired Connie, they would probably get a visit from her uncle Leno. Then this one came in and turned the whole deal around. I was wondering if I should I try to explain to these two clueless bastards, that with Leno's niece working at the store, they had nothing to worry about. They could probably leave the damn door unlocked all the time and the money laying on the counter and no one would dare touch it unless they had Leno's say-so."

When he walked out, Judy asked what the cop was talking about. Connie was agitated, "Just because we're Italian the cops think we're all mobbed up. There is no Mafia! I got this job by applying for the job. But, while Carmine's away, Leno hasta take some care to look out for me and Paolo. So, the money I make here doesn't hafta come out of Leno's pocket.

"So yeah, maybe he woulda tried to talk to the brothers to—"

She paused to think of the right word "— suggest to them to keep me, but you stepping up the way you did headed off what could have been a—situation."

Judy nodded.

Connie went on, "So, ya see, Leno is known in the neighborhood and he's kinda used to people taking his suggestions. The bosses don't know Leno, and Tom is pretty arrogant. So, there could've been a situation that could've gotten outta hand if Tom disrespected Leno. Since the cops already have a fixed idea about Leno, they would think he was trying to strong-arm the brothers if they went in with any complaint.

"In the neighborhood no one would talk to the cops, but the bosses aren't from around here."

Judy just listened.

"So, you ever notice that in the movies all the biker chicks are dressed real sexy, but when you see any of them from the clubhouse around the corner from here they don't dress like that at all?"

Without waiting for a reply, she continued, "That's 'cause in real life these girls know that if they get all slutted-up and some idiot does something stupid around them, then things can get real violent real soon. So, in real life they dress to avoid those—situations."

Connie pulled Judy to her for a hug and then held her at arm's length, "So, you stepping in saved me and took a whole lot of possible crap outta the picture. So, you prevented a situation."

That night was Judy's turn to close but Connie said she would do it. "You closed up last night, remember?" She gave her another big hug.

As Judy approached the door, Gort loomed on the other side. He took off his hat when he saw her. With his hat over his heart, he held the door open for her and his deep voice growled, "You did a good thing."

She heard Connie yell to her "Don't worry. I'm gonna have Gort check to make sure the damn lock is locked."

When she saw Peter that night, she told him about the door and what she did. He said she was a chump for risking her job for someone else.

She said, "I figured this job was something I fell into and I have no reason not to try other things. I don't have a kid to feed like Connie does and since I think Tom might have a thing for me. . ."

She saw him getting angry, but wasn't sure why.

That night he took her to see a movie about a stripper who also worked as a call girl for an escort service. As they walked home he said, "If you want to try other things, you can make a ton more money dancing like that and I can—"

She stopped walking.

She told him she wouldn't even consider anything like he was starting to suggest. He retreated to the only hole he could find by saying he was only kidding. He didn't want other men looking that way at her and in fact was annoyed that she had to work for Tom if he was hot for her.

They walked the rest of the way back to her place in silence; Peter scheming another way to exploit her, and Judy thinking about girls being sold for sex.

Her thoughts turned to Jacqui Fykes.

FOURTEEN

After their "honeymoon in the bridal suite," getting back to Rawlings, Corey resumed her senior year and Harry rejoined the team. The day before New Year's Eve, Corey found out she was pregnant. They were both very happy, and also pleased Corey would be able to graduate before the baby was due. She quipped, "Luckily those graduation gowns are pretty big."

That next summer, Dayna was born.

Shortly after Dayna's birth, they took her to Smalsville to meet her grandparents. Because of Harry's schedule, the plan was for him to stay two weeks but Corey and the baby not having a schedule, could stay an extra two or three weeks.

As it turned out, the duration decision was made for them when one week into the visit, Corey's mother, Barbara, fell and broke her hip. Harry went back to work as planned but Corey would stay as long as was needed to take care of her mom.

Harry and Corey spoke on the phone each night. He was looking for any break in his schedule to get to see his family.

One morning, after Corey had been there a month, as she and Bill were helping Barbara into a chair so Corey could freshen Barbara's bed. Bill started having pains in his chest.

They put Barbara back down in the bed and he sat down in the chair. Both women were worried.

After a couple of minutes, the pain subsided.

Corey tried not to show how worried she was, but she was very worried. She suggested her dad make an appointment to see his doctor. He resisted, but Barbara insisted that if he didn't agree she was going to crawl out of bed and call the ambulance right then.

He made the appointment.

When Corey spoke to Harry, he could tell she was worried. He realized with Dayna and Barbara, Corey had her hands full, and if Bill's condition got worse. . .

Buddy was aware of Harry's situation, and told Harry he should grab a week to get to "Smalltown," as he called it, before the season started in November.

Harry left for Smalsville after practice the next day.

When he arrived, he found Bill napping in the living room. He had a follow-up appointment with his doctor the next day. When the appointment was discussed at the dinner table that night, Harry, with a silent cue from Corey, asked if he could ride along with him to the doctor's office.

Bill came home after having closed the store an hour early, and asked Harry if he would drive. As they were departing, Corey gave Harry a glance to make sure he understood things must be pretty bad if her dad was not insisting on driving himself to the doctor's office.

The doctor did another EKG, took blood samples and scheduled Bill for more tests. The doctor told Bill even without the test results, he thought he should consider slowing down.

Harry, Corey and Dayna had rooms upstairs and Barbara and Bill had the big bedroom downstairs. That night, lying in bed and talking about ways to handle the situation, she said, "If my dad can no longer work at the store as much, they're going to have to hire someone to run it, and I don't know where the money is going to come from for that. They couldn't afford help for the past several years. They may have to close the store. If I'm going to have to take care of my parents, I'll need to be in Smalsville, unless we can figure out how they can come and live with us. They can't afford anything else."

They were thinking about their options when Dayna woke up. He got up to get her and change her and then brought her in to Corey. The three of them shared a bed together for the first time in a long time.

As they lay there together, he realized there was only one option. "My job with the team involves too much travel for us to be together and to take care of Dayna and your mom and dad. To do that we both have to be in Smalsville and keep the store open."

She was surprised by the matter-of-fact tone in his voice. Her eyes started to tear as she listened to him say, "If you can hang on until the end of the season, I'll quit basketball and learn how to run a hardware store. Hopefully, your dad will be well enough to show me the business. I'm not going to root against the team, but if we don't make any post season tournaments, I could be back as early as March."

"You would do that for us? Give up basketball?"

"Being 'us' is all that matters."

They wouldn't say anything to her parents for now, but he would talk to Buddy as soon as he got back to Rawlings.

When he got back after calling Corey to tell her he had arrived, he had his talk with Buddy. He was relieved that Buddy was quite gracious when he explained to him what was going on.

Buddy said, "You know that the team you helped to put together—particularly with those two guards you brought in and taught—is going to be very strong. We're gonna to be up there in the national spotlight—maybe even playing for the championship.

"I'm sure you know what you have to do, but it would be great if you were around to see our seedlings bear fruit."

"I'm just sorry I'm leaving you in the lurch."

"Well, you put me in a position to lurch my way to the championship. If you gotta run a hardware store, you gotta run a hardware store. I'm just sorry I didn't check out Corey's family medical history before I gave you her phone number."

They agreed they wouldn't say anything to the team about Harry's plans.

As it turned out, the Rawlings Raiders had a better season than anyone expected and they did get into a post season tournament, only to be eliminated in the second round.

Anyone could see—with everyone coming back next season—if they stayed healthy, this team had a chance to go all the way.

After the last game, Buddy announced that Coach Daweson was leaving. Harry was surprised how emotional Buddy got.

Harry explained to the team that he had to leave for family reasons. Then spontaneously, the players lined up and each of them told him they were sorry he was going and thanked him for all he had done for them.

He called Corey with a full report on the game and the announcement afterward.

He realized he was soon to be with Corey and Dayna, but there was still a twinge of sadness in the departure. However, the rightness of the decision left no room for regret. Even though he had spent very little time is Smalsville, since that was where they were, he felt like he was going home.

FIFTEEN

S hortly after Harry arrived, he started going to the store with Bill while Corey stayed home with her mom and Dayna. At dinner, after his first full week at the store, Corey laughed, "The boys go off to work and the girls stay home and someday soon both mom and Dayna are going to be walking."

They bought Dayna some toys called Weebles because they liked their motto: "Weebles wobble, but they don't fall down."

Barbara said she wished she were a Weeble.

As it turned out, Dayna started walking before Barbara. When Barbara got back on her feet, she had to use a walker. She was encouraged to try to use it less and less, but she relied on it more and more. She was less confident somehow.

Harry learned the hardware business very quickly, and soon there were days when Bill would just let him go in by himself.

Things settled down to a quiet routine. Barbara and Bill started talking about moving to the warmer climate of Florida. Corey's sister, Deborah, and her husband said they could renovate their garage and create an apartment for them.

Bill talked to Harry about joining the Smalsville Volunteer Fire Department. He wanted to propose Harry for membership before he and Barbara moved. Harry went with Bill to the next fire department meeting and his application was approved.

But Bill's move to Florida with Barbara was not to happen.

One night a severe chest pain awakened Bill. He called out, and Harry and Corey rushed to his room. Harry called for an ambulance as Corey tried to comfort her mother.

Harry knew Bill didn't look good. He drove to the hospital right after the ambulance had left the house.

On the way to the hospital Bill died.

He could not be revived in the emergency room.

When Harry arrived, he could tell from the faces of the ambulance crew, that Bill was dead. Harry let the news sink in and thanked them. He listened as they talked about what happened on the trip to the hospital.

He thought, What must it be like to see someone die in front of you and you can't stop the process. He went home to deliver the news of Bill's death in person.

Corey and Barbara knew as soon as he walked in the door.

As dawn was breaking, they sat around the kitchen table and Corey and Barbara told him stories about Bill. Taking their cue from Barbara, the decision was made; Harry would go and open the store. People in the area depended on the store and even though Bill would be remembered and missed, no one would think ill of them for keeping the store open so the local people could pick up their orders. In fact, many would know it was the right thing to do.

After he went off to work, Corey reminded Barbara about Harry losing his family when he was so young. She said she felt so lucky to have had her father in her life as long as she had. With tears coming down each of their faces—even though neither of them thought of themselves as particularly religious—they agreed that it was a blessing Bill had lived to see his grandchild.

The burial of a Chief follows Fire Department tradition. The casket was carried to the cemetery on one of the department's trucks as the firefighters in their dress uniforms—their polished axes on their shoulders—marched slowly behind it.

Deborah drove up from Florida for the funeral. She decided she could stay for the rest of the week. She hadn't been back since the wedding. Even though she had seen pictures of Dayna and sent her presents, this was the first time Deborah saw her in person and she could not take her hands off her.

Watching Deborah play and make faces with Dayna made Harry reflect on the procession of life—from a baby in arms, to a body in casket being carried on what he now knew was a hose truck.

Deborah helped with the preparations for the gathering at the house. After the funeral and the reception at the house, Corey talked with Deborah and Barbara, and it was decided that Barbara would go to Florida when Deborah returned home.

At the end of Deborah's one-week stay, as planned, she and Barbara left for Florida.

That night, with Dayna asleep upstairs, Corey and Harry sitting in front of the fireplace remarked how the empty the house felt. They spoke of the twists and turns that brought them to where they were. On the couch she snuggled up to him.

This night felt like it was the first quiet time they had spent together in a long, long time.

SIXTEEN

In Smalsville, things went along in quiet routine. Harry worked in the store, and sometimes he closed up and came home for lunch. Trying to make friends in the fire department, he was aware he would always be the outsider—the one who wasn't born and raised in Smalsville.

He made acquaintances rather than friends. He would always be the one who hadn't grown up and gone through school with the other firemen.

Soon after joining, he became aware that no matter who had the title of Chief, the leaders of the department were the brothers, Mark and Tony Torey. They were born a year apart, were both about 6'2" with dark hair and strong builds. Like their father Tom and his brother Matt, who had each served one term as Chief, they joined the fire department right after high school.

After the older generation passed on, the brothers took over Torey Motors, in a nearby town, selling and servicing new and used cars, trucks, and farm equipment. "TM" employed several of the fire department members. Those who worked for the brothers marveled at how easily they could agree on everything concerning the business, and yet agree on absolutely nothing concerning the fire department.

After a while, a steady customer at the hardware store named Jack Bargers—a big ruddy-faced redheaded building contractor—invited Harry to the luncheonette across the street from the store on a Wednesday afternoon.

Willy Cooper, the local real estate and insurance sales-man joined them each week. Then, Frank Peterson, the local banker joined the group. Since none of these men were in the fire department, Harry joked to Corey that Wednesday lunch was with his non-firefighter friends.

Soon Dayna started talking and climbing on every-thing. Harry arrived home from the store one day to the news they were going to have another baby. That evening at dinner they told Dayna she was going to be a big sister. She was excited and they hoped she would continue to see the new addition as a good thing happening for all of them.

With the Rawlings Raiders having a great season that year, making it to the final four, and playing on nation-al television, Corey worried that Harry would regret not being with the team. She thought, If they get better and better and he has to watch on TV as they win it all—I hope he won't feel that he had cheated himself out of his dream.

When they were alone, she asked him whether he saw himself as a candidate for what she called "5th Beatle syndrome.

"You know the guy who leaves the band just before they make it really big?"

He smiled, "I'm happy with the life we have right now. That's all that matters. I'm sure, if I wanted to, I could find something in the future to worry about. And I could probably find lots of things in the past to regret. Why would I?

"What would I be doing if I was still with the team? I would be running around, traveling and working with the team, and all the time trying to squeeze in enough time to do what I really want do—which is be with you and Dayna.

"Sweet girl, I wake up with you by my side, I come home to you each night, and I am with Dayna. I'm happy.

"Now that I'm finished with fire school and I'm no longer on department probation, I don't have to go to every meeting and drill. I'm feeling fewer outside demands on my time. Why should I regret any of this? OK, so there are no bands to welcome me when I walk through the door. But a hundred years from now, no one will remember who was the assistant coach for the Rawlings Raiders. In fact, if I hadn't told Buddy who I thought would be a good replacement, I don't know if I'd remember who the assistant coach was.

"No, sweet girl, I don't regret that I'm with you more. I don't think the fantasy grass is any greener. In fact, I'm pretty damn sure it's not."

He laughed, "Do you remember JoBob Trask, the legendary baseball coach at Rawlings? I know he was a bit before your time but I'm sure you saw his picture on the Wall of Fame outside the athletic office."

"That good looking blond guy with those blue eyes and great smile?"

"Oh, yeah. This guy cut a huge path through the women on campus. He was a real playboy. Women couldn't get enough of him. He was married maybe three or four times. Heck, I think he ended one marriage and started another in my freshman year.

"Anyway, when I came to school it was pretty obvious I was going to have to work harder than the other guards to see any playing time on the team that we had. So, this one night we have a big all-teams party and, after the party, I go back to the gym by myself to work out in the weight room.

"I'm working with the weights and I'm almost done with my routines. It's after midnight, and in walks JoBob. He's a little drunk. Well, maybe more than a little.

"He says he promised his doctor the next time he takes a drink he's going to ride the exercise bike for 20 minutes. Makes no sense to me at all, but there he is in his sweats, and he's starting to ride the bike. I was about to leave when he came in, but I figure this guy's such a jock legend maybe I can learn something from him. I get on the bike next to his, and we're just riding. And then he starts like he is trying to beat me to some imaginary finish line. I pedal faster and we keep it up until his timer rings.

"He looks like he's about to die. Then he turns to me and says, 'Ya know kid. This is the exact opposite of extramarital sex!'

"He can see I've no idea what he's talking about so he explains, 'I always dread doing this—but I always feel great afterwards!'"

She just shook her head as he laughed at the memory.

He continued, "Corey, I don't think anybody has it any better than me. Do you think you would have wanted to be a Beatle's wife?"

Sure of the sincerity, she grimaced, "And have to deal with groupies and Beatle mania? Not in this lifetime! Dayna and I are so lucky to have you as our man."

"I think we all got lucky, sweet girl. I think we're all very lucky to have each other."

SEVENTEEN

Walking home from work one day, Judy saw life-size photos of models in evening wear in the window of a store and thought, If I was so willing to risk being fired for leaving the store unlocked, maybe I could risk finding out about modeling. That night she showed Peter the card Connie had given her of Sol Magenwise, and said maybe she should go see him.

Tossing the card on the table he said, "I think this guy, Sol, is nothing. We should look into one of those big modeling agencies; that's where the money's going to be. I think the real money is posing nude. You should let me take some pictures like that and send them to magazines."

"I don't think I want to do that kind of stuff. Besides, Connie thinks he's OK, after all he's the one who made the suggestions about my hair and makeup, so I should at least hear what he has to say."

"OK. Since you have the card, you can call to set it up, but we're going together. We can use him as a starting point and go from there."

When Judy called, she mentioned Connie had given her his card. He was very gracious and she felt at ease. He had not been in the store since Connie followed his hair and makeup suggestions, so she told him about that, but she didn't think to mention Peter.

The office was a small single room in an older building. They walked up a flight of stairs. Before she knocked, noticing the name "Sol" on the door, just as it was on the card, she told Peter that Connie said everyone called him Pops.

The one-room office was full of pictures and wall-to-wall books. It had a large but not overly ornate mahogany desk with a small maple wood inlay of the scales of justice. The desk looked out of place and took up almost half the room.

Even though she hadn't said anything about bringing Peter, Pops greeted them both graciously. He was pleased with the way his suggestions for her look turned out. But he was surprised when Peter introduced himself as Judy's manager. It was the first time Peter had granted himself that title within her hearing but she said nothing. Peter dominated the conversation. It was quickly obvious to Pops that Peter was an opportunist who had no knowledge of the business. But, in an attempt to be helpful to her, Pops tolerated him.

At the end of their discussion, Pops gave her a make-up kit and the address of a reputable photographer, Gary Blake, to get a small set of photos taken.

Pops said, "I'll make the call to set it up. From there, who knows. We will wait and see what the camera thinks of you."

Because of his strong feeling about helping her, Pops made the gesture in spite of Peter's involvement. He knew that doing anything that would involve Peter was going to be problematic, but he hoped there would be time enough for a fatherly talk about him and his smothering possessiveness if it was still needed down the road.

After leaving the office, Peter declared the place looked like a loser's office, and grumbled that the old man wouldn't be able to do anything for her. But, as long as he gave her the kit and was willing to pay for the pictures, he'd go along with it.

When they arrived after Judy got off work the next day to take the photographs, Peter noticed how impressed Gary and Jimmy, who did makeup and hair, seemed to be with Judy. She was handed a form to fill in her name and address and a release so they could send the pictures to Pops. Peter insisted she pick the name he felt she should use for her "career." She told him when he said "Judy" it sounded to her like he was saying "Jody," and she liked the way that sounded. He said, "Jodi" with an "I" was less common, and it would help set her apart. He insisted his last name was a better name for her than Jarrolson and she should use it so when they were married, she wouldn't have to change.

The mention of marriage surprised her, but since she had no expectation this would amount to anything, she reluctantly decided not to fight about it. She hadn't seen his name spelled out anywhere. Just as Peter pronounced Judy and it sounded like Jody, she thought Warrin sounded like it was spelled W-O-R-R E-N.

While Peter went off to look at the lighting, that's how she spelled it on the forms.

The photo session was almost called off. Peter, saying he was also a photographer, insisted on checking the lighting, the focus, the lenses, and the camera angles. He also didn't like the way Gary sometimes touched Judy as he moved her into a position.

Peter was so overbearing, that while she was in the other room with Jimmy combing her hair and repairing her makeup from the hot lights, Jimmy whispered, "Girlfriend, did this guy pull you out of a burning building or something?

"Do you owe this guy your life? —'cause he's the kind of bad news that nobody wants to deal with."

Coming around to look her in the eye, "Girlfriend, it's like a burglar, see? The burglar's going to pick the house that doesn't have the big angry dog, and break into that one. You have to ask yourself why you really need this kind of a handicap. You sure have the look—but lots of girls look good. People are going to lean toward the girl who's not with this chump."

Peter continued to pester Gary as he took the pictures.

When they went back to see Pops, Peter was insufferable. Even before the pictures were sent to Pops, Peter wanted to know how much business Pops could get for "Jodi" and what percentage Pops wanted. And, he wanted Pops to be sure to bring any offers to him.

He was particularly incensed about Gary and Jimmy.

"What kind of guys did you send us to?

"The makeup guy is as queer as a three-dollar bill and the photo guy kept coming on to her."

Pops said softly, "I think you might have been mistaken about Gary."

He came up to Pops, and poked him in the chest with his finger, "Look, I know what I saw and you weren't even there!"

Pops, stepping back, said quietly, "Not that it is any of your business, but my two friends are in a committed relationship together. I have seen Gary work with dozens of beautiful, sexy women, some of whom were quite famous. Many were attracted to him. Some made advances, not knowing of his relationship with Jimmy.

"Gary has been nothing but professional at all times."

Pops shook his head, "Any business that I may have with this young lady cannot include you. I think you should leave."

Peter ordered Judy to leave and made a big show of slamming the door on the way out.

EIGHTEEN

Two weeks after the disastrous meeting in his office, Pops was in the drugstore having his prescription filled. When he saw Judy, he told her he liked the pictures but he was surprised by the name "Jodi Worren." Telling him how it came about, she said Peter had discovered the spelling mistake of the last name when he saw it on her copy of the release as he was putting it in the file he was keeping.

He said she would have to change it.

Pops thought the talk of marriage to this man, and Peter's keeping a file didn't sound good for her. Having seen the way Peter acted toward her, knowing he knew nothing of the business, and hearing about what happened at the photo session, he thought Peter was abusive and would only jeopardize any possible career.

"Do you have a formal management contract with this man and I am sorry for prying—do you really think you could marry such a man?"

Connie, nearby, chimed in, "So, this I gotta hear!"

Judy sighed, "I'm not really sure about anything. I don't know if I want to go through with the modeling idea."

Pops said, "I can understand that. It is not for everyone and everything would be different. Even your name—Jodi Worren, it is different. I like it. But—"

Connie interrupted, "So, if you take the chance and try modeling and if you lose your mind and really marry this guy, you can deal with the name then, but for now the name Jodi Worren has nice flow to it. It has my vote."

They both looked to Judy, letting her know it was all up to her.

"My vote, too," she said, "If I decide to try this, I'll stay Jodi Worren."

"Well, Miss Jodi Worren, the pictures are quite good and I think you can do well, if you decide to do this—if anything changes from the time you came to see me—or if you just want to talk—please give me a call."

As Pops was walking out, Peter saw him from down the block. Coming into the store he started in on Judy. "Wasn't that that Sol, or whatever-his-name-is guy in here? Are you trying to go behind my back to make a deal with him?"

Before Judy could open her mouth, Connie, jumping in, and said "So, the man came in for a prescription. He does that." She lied and said, "I waited on him. Judy was in the back and didn't even see him in here."

When he finally left, Connie said, "So, I can't stand this anymore, Judy. Just where do you think you're going with this guy? Is he all of a sudden your manager? You're not really in love with him, are you?"

"Well, I don't think I am in love with him. But, I'm not sure I know what love is. I don't think I've ever seen it. I'm certainly not used to being sought after. He cares for me. He says what we have is special. He says he wants to do things for me. I need someone to care for me. I don't think my grandparents or my aunt ever cared for me. It feels good to have someone love me. I like that I make him happy. I never made anyone happy. Or at least not that anyone ever said. But it does feel like I'm always on edge with him."

Connie asked, "Why did you agree to use his last name?" She laughed, "Even when you couldn't spell it?" Then, thinking about what Judy had just told her, it dawned on her.

Connie sighed, "Wait a minute. Is this guy the first guy you've been with?"

Judy nodded, he was. "I never had a boyfriend. I didn't even have girlfriends. A woman my coach brought me to see one night had a child after she was raped. I watched her child sometimes. Then one night she gave me the whole sex-talk. My grandmother was really old and drunk a lot of the time—she wasn't going to tell me about that stuff—and my aunt never had time for me."

Connie looked her in the eye.

She wanted her to understand.

"OK. So, be really really careful here. Just because you've done things with this guy doesn't mean you have to rush into anything long term with him. And for damn sure it doesn't mean you gotta marry him. I'm sorry, but I don't think he's right for you. Hell, I don't think he's right for anybody. You deserve better than him. I think he's just a wannabe-controlling-scumbag snake with a hard-on."

They both laughed.

Knowing how Connie felt, Judy knew she couldn't tell her that Peter had been living in her apartment for the past week. He'd told her his landlady was having his apartment painted and he needed to stay with her until the job was done.

Peter was there when she got home. He had spent the time waiting for her getting angrier and angrier, convinced she was going to start a modeling career without him. He imagined his best way to keep control was to marry her. But even if they married he'd need something to hold over her.

As soon as she walked in, he started to pressure her to set a date for a wedding. At first, he started to talk about all the good things he could do for her.

Then he said, "I know that you love me. You know what we have is special. But you don't show that you love me. You need to prove it. I want to photograph you nude."

She shook her head.

He demanded, "If you love me you'll do it. You don't have to worry—the pictures are going to be just for me."

"I don't want to pose for those kinds of pictures."

When the soft words were not getting her to say "Yes," he started to get angry and told her she was nothing—he loved her, but he was the only one who would ever want her. He had told her many times before about her being nothing without him.

This level of anger and verbal abuse was different. More often, his comments about her being nothing alternated with his professions of love—and that mixture was interrupted by periods of a silent treatment in which he would just ignore her. She could see his face redden with anger as he walked over to get his camera.

When she insisted she would not pose nude for him, he backhanded her across the face.

Stunned—she fell backwards on the bed.

He complained, "Look what you made me do."

Raising his hand he ordered, "Don't make me do that again." He pushed her on her back and used his free hand to start ripping off her blouse.

He made her strip off the rest of her clothes. He forced her to pose on the bed while he took his pictures. Then, he dragged her to her knees in front of the bed and ordered her to perform oral sex. He demanded, "Look up at me," while taking close-ups of her tear-streaked face as she performed the act he knew only his violence made possible.

"Don't move." He left her still on her knees, went into the kitchen, and returned with an empty beer bottle. Throwing her back onto the bed, he demanded she open her legs so he could insert the bottle into her and take what he called "hotter, more edgy shots."

She refused, and he hit her again.

She curled up naked on the bed and wept uncontrollably.

He got into the bed. Holding her to quiet her, he told how much he loved her. He repeated no one else would ever want her. Then he told her that to prove how much he loved her—instead of keeping them for himself—he would give her all the photos as a wedding present, then she would know that no one else would ever see them.

He lied. He had no intention of ever giving up the control he felt the pictures provided.

After he had sex with her, he went to get another beer and watched television while she cried herself to sleep.

The next morning, he was sitting at the table in his shorts, drinking his coffee and looking at a magazine as though nothing had happened. She waited in the bedroom doorway, studying him, not sure of what his reaction would be. He didn't look up. He didn't acknowledge her as she made her way to the bathroom to take a shower. He didn't look up when she went back to get dressed. He was still silent and acting like she didn't exist when she left for work.

Judy decided to walk to work. She didn't want contact with the bodies of strangers on the crowded bus. She had tried to cover a black-eye with makeup she had at home but it was still visible. As she walked, she felt ashamed.

Knowing that she had let him into her apartment, she was fearful about what might happen when she got home after work. She thought, How could I have been so stupid? How could I have believed he ever loved me? What will he do if I said I was leaving him? How could I leave? It's my apartment. But how would I get my things? Where would I go?

Connie was alone in the store when Judy got there. The black-eye and a bruise on the left corner of Judy's lower lip were still visible.

One look, and Connie started seething.

But she knew she had to calm down. Putting her arm around Judy, she led her into the back room, sat her down, and hung up her coat.

"I'm sorry I wasn't honest with you. I should've told you when I let him move in—"

"—This was not your fault!"

Judy's words started pouring out amid tears. She told Connie everything that happened. Connie gasped and bit the index finger of her fist when she heard about the forced sex and pictures.

She had to take a deep breath to calm herself. She took another deep breath and then got Judy a cup of water.

Judy sat there while Connie got some theatrical make-up to better cover the black-eye. Taking a tissue, Connie made sure to slow down and be gentle as she slowly dried Judy's eyes and applied the makeup.

Returning to rage, Connie stormed over to the phone on the back wall, ripped the receiver off the hook and made a call. Judy could hear only part of what she was saying. But she heard Connie telling someone her friend was beaten by a guy in her apartment and he took some pictures.

Then she heard, "Yeah, that's right, my friend from the store, the one who stepped up and took the weight for the unlocked door thing."

Hanging up, Connie told her that she needed her keys. Without asking why, Judy handed them to her.

"So, I just suggested to Leno that maybe this scumbag would be happier if he was back in Canada. Maybe Leno should get the film and then just take this scumbag, asshole to the train station and make sure his skinny, scumbag ass gets on the fuckin' express."

By the time the bosses arrived at 9:30, Connie and Judy were restocking the shelves and putting items that thoughtless customer had left in the wrong places back where they belonged. Working behind the pharmacy counter in the back of the store, the bosses did not see a car pull up and Connie slip out the front door.

She leaned over to the dapperly dressed Leno in the front passenger seat, handed him Judy's keys, and told him her address. Frankie Zingaro was driving with Johnnie and Gort in the back seat.

As the car was pulling away, Judy looked out the store's glass door and caught a glimpse of Gort, sitting behind Leno. Gort was staring at her. From the way his eyes narrowed and his jaw tightened, she was sure he could see the bruises through the makeup. She started to worry.

Connie, seeing her expression said, "I know what you're thinking—but Leno can control Gort. Leno will be a calming influence. He won't let things get out of hand. So, he's just gonna suggest to this bum that he destroy whatever pictures he took, get on a train, and never bother you again."

Judy went back to restocking, wondering if it could be that simple.

The four men arrived at the apartment. Peter, in his shorts, was coming out of the bathroom with an empty cup from his coffee when he heard the key in the lock.

Wondering why Judy had come home early, he was stunned when the apartment door opened and Gort was standing there, his massive frame blocking the light that would normally flood in from the naked bulb in the hall-way.

Peter yelled, "What the fuck is this, now?" As Gort stepped through the doorway. No one said a word. Peter threw the coffee cup down and took a karate stance. Bouncing on his toes, he looked at Gort to see if he got the message that he was tough.

Gort just stared at him while he bounced. Then he took another step forward to let the others fully enter behind him. Peter, making a spinning move, kicked Gort in the face and still bouncing, admiring his kick, looked to see what damage it had done.

Gort straightening his hat, stared at him, and just smiled.

Leno, looking at Peter, shook his head, and said quietly, "I think that was a mistake. We came here to talk to y—"

Peter spun and kicked again.

Gort, blocking that kick with his elbow, grabbed Peter's crotch with one hand while his other hand grabbed him by the throat. Lifting him off the floor, Gort held him at arm's length—squeezing the crotch and tightening his grip on the throat.

As the hands tightened, Peter struggled, but the grip on his windpipe stifled his screams. Watching as the pain registered on Peter's face, Gort lifted him higher—banging his head on the ceiling—before cartwheeling him upside-down and slamming him into the floor.

"Ooh!" Winced Johnnie, as Peter thudded onto the floor face-first.

It took Peter a second to recover. In pain and in panic he tried to crawl away.

Gort went after him.

"Gort! No!" Leno yelled, "We need him to be able to travel."

Gort frowned and put his foot in the middle of Peter's back—pinning him to the floor.

Leno leaned over him and asked, "Where are the pictures you took last night?"

"Who the fuck are you? Did that bitch send you? I'll kick—"

He never got out the rest of the words.

"Wrong answer," Leno exhaled sharply, shaking his head in exasperation. He motioned for the Zingaros to search for the film. "Look hard, but don't make a mess. This is her place not his."

Gort grabbed Peter by his hair and shorts, and threw him head first into the bathroom, Peter's face smashed against the partially opened bathroom door as he flew into the tiled room. He groaned as his upper body doubled over the rim of the claw-foot tub like a life-size rag doll.

Gort quickly grabbed Peter's head from the tub and rammed it into the toilet bowl.

Leno, standing outside the doorway, said calmly, "At this point, you've got a choice. If you give us the film, me and these nice gentlemen will take you to the train and export you back to Montreal. Anything else—and you're gonna die right here."

Before Peter could answer, Gort flushed the toilet.

When Gort pulled Peter's head out of the bowl, he sputtered that the film was in the camera. Still cowering, he took them to the bedroom and pointed.

Frankie grabbed the camera, ripped out the film and flushed it down the toilet.

As they let Peter get dressed, Johnnie took a new roll of film he found alongside the camera and clumsily loaded it.

Before leaving the apartment, they told Peter to gather the rest of his clothes, but made sure he took nothing but his clothing, his passport, and what was left of his roll of bills.

Johnnie made a show of taking pictures of Peter with his packed bags and holding his open passport up next to his face. Looking admiringly at the camera, then to Leno, Johnnie hugged it to his chest—indicating he wanted to keep it. Leno shrugged and waved that he didn't care.

Cowering, Peter was squeezed in the back seat of the car between Gort and Johnnie, and they headed for the train station. They stopped at a nearby construction site, where Leno was—in name only—a union representative. The concrete foundation was being poured.

Pointing to the concrete flowing down the chute, Leno, in a matter-of-fact tone, told him, "We're putting you on a train to Canada."

He lied and said, "We'll have someone on the train watching you and they'll know if you try to get off before it gets to Montreal. If you ever try to get back into this country, we will have our friends in immigration and the

CIA tell us. And then you'll become part of a concrete foundation at some building job just like this one."

Leno added sternly, "If you ever contact this girl, or if you ever say a word about this girl, about your pictures, or any of this, we're gonna know. Wherever you are in the world, we're gonna know and you're gonna be dead and in concrete in 24 hours. Capisce? Do—you—understand?"

Peter mumbled, "I understand."

Leno turned away as the car pulled from the curb. But Peter leaned forward and poked him on the shoulder with his index finger several times to get his attention, insisting, "Hey listen, you don't understand. You have to understand. You can't blame me. This bitch loves me and she knows she's nothing without me. I don't want to be in trouble when she finds me and starts calling me."

As Gort pulled Peter's hand down—and pushed him back in the seat—Leno spun around and glared.

"Oh, I have to understand? So, I'm the one who needs to understand here?"

Then he paused—he took a breath and exhaled slowly through pursed lips, he nodded pensively—knowing, now, what he had to do. He tapped Frankie on the shoulder, and gestured for him to pull over.

Leno stared at Peter and spoke slowly, "OK. So, let me tell you what I understand. First, I'm gonna tell you what I don't understand. So, what I don't understand is why I let myself step into the middle of this put-him-on-a-train idea in the first place. That's what I don't understand. I don't understand why I even considered that this train idea would put an end to this friend's problem."

Getting out at the curb, Leno looked at Peter through the open passenger door, "Now, let me tell you what I do understand. So, what I understand is you're absolutely right. You shouldn't have to go on living your life worrying about being in trouble from us because of this girl—this girl who you think you own—keeps calling you."

He nodded slowly, "For a man like you, what's needed here—is a more permanent solution. So there's no more worries about trouble and no more misunderstandings." Without taking his eyes off Peter, Leno said, "Frankie, I'm gonna walk the few blocks back to the drugstore. I'm gonna give Constanza's friend her keys and pick up a few things for my wife."

Closing the car door, Leno made a gesture like he was washing his hands. As he finished—when the palms of his hands were faced toward the ground—he turned to walk away and pronounced, "Gort! He's yours."

Connie was surprised when she saw Leno coming up the block to the store on foot. Stepping inside, he stayed near the door, out of earshot of the Leonard brothers in the back. He handed Judy back her keys, "Don't worry. The pictures are no more—and we made sure you won't find any trace of this guy in your apartment."

Judy, her mind racing—trying to comprehend the meaning of what she had just heard—took the keys.

She managed to quietly say, "Thank you."

Connie asked, "Did he agree to go back to Canada? Did you put him on the train?"

Surprised that she would ask him any questions, especially in front of Judy, Leno, masking his annoyance, closed his eyes for a second—as if searching for the right answer—nodded and answered slowly, "Close enough."

He paused, "After he gave up the film, we told him we were gonna put him on a train back to Canada and he shouldn't get off 'till it gets there. So, we were heading for the station. He said he understood our plan but said he was worried—that he had some concerns.

"I was just thinking that we needed to lay his concerns to rest, you know, so he wouldn't have to worry, when all of a sudden, I remembered my wife asked me to pick up some things for her on my way home. So, I told Gort to finish off with our end of the agreement."

Looking at Connie, he reached into the inside pocket of his neatly tailored suit jacket and took out his wallet.

"Constanza, get me a bottle of that shampoo and a bottle of that other hair stuff that your aunt uses."

Walking his fingers through a bunch of big bills, he handed Connie his rarely-used credit card.

She smiled, "So, why don't you just let me treat you to that?"

"Constanza, basta. Just do as I say. Put it on my card and put my receipt in the bag. Capisce?"

Looking at Judy, "Before we headed for the station, we took the roll of film outta the camera and flushed the film down the toilet. The only things he had with him when he left was his clothes and his money."

He smiled as though he just remembered, "Oh, and we made sure he had his passport. We told him he should never try to contact you again."

Then he added, "He said he understood, but if you ever hear from this guy again," he winked, "you just let us know."

Judy whispered, "OK. Thank you again," and went to the back room and put her keys back in her bag. Then, sitting down, quietly, she picked up her feet and put them on the bench with her arms wrapped around her legs, and rested her head on her knees. She thought about what had happened to her, retracing the events—from entering her apartment last night, him hitting her, and forcing her and taking the pictures, to now, Leno giving back her keys and telling her not to worry.

It was hard to get it all to sink in. Peter was gone? And the pictures he wanted so badly, they were gone?

Finally, when Connie was finished with Leno, she came back to check on Judy. Connie sat down and put her arm around her shoulders.

Looking at Connie—more to reassure herself—she said, "Events are neither good nor bad. It's your perception of the event that makes it good or bad."

"That sounds smart. What does that mean?"

"It was one of the life-living-lessons—something my basketball coach used to say."

She started slowly, holding Connie's hand, "I thought what happened last night was terrible—it was terrible—but it could've been just the beginning of something much worse. And now what happened means I've found out the truth about him, and, thanks to you, it sounds like he's gone from my life."

Connie, thinking about the life-living-lesson phrase, stood up and straightened her skirt to go back to the counter. She put her hand on Judy's shoulder. When she looked up at her, Connie smiled, shaking her head, "Events may not be good or bad—but arguing with Gort can only be bad. Nobody—fucks—with—Gort!"

NINETEEN

That night, having refused Connie's offer to spend the night at her apartment, Judy arrived home, hoping that Leno's words were true.

After cautiously opening the door, she found that, except for a small puddle of water in bathroom, her place looked as it had before she let Peter move in. She set about soaking up the water with the towels from the rack. She stuffed the wet towels into the pillowcase, along with the sheets, the other bedding, and the clothing she had worn the night before. She was taking it all immediately to the Laundromat. She saw the empty coffee cup on the floor in the corner of the room and trashed it as well as anything else she thought would remind her of Peter.

Thankfully, the cleanup didn't take long— allowing her time to take her second shower of the day.

After a month with no word from Peter, Judy stopped dreading that he would show up any minute. She started to stretch back into her life—believing she was free of him. Walking to work one morning, she thought that all she had was her apartment, her job, and Connie. It was as if she was starting over just like when she first arrived in New York. But then she realized it was different. She looked different and she felt different. She had to be more careful.

Then she thought, Connie told me Peter was wrong for me, and she was right. Connie's old friend, Pops, thinks I could have a career in modeling—maybe he's right too. Before putting her purse in the back room, she found Pop's card. Running her finger over the lettering, she thought of Harry's yelling from the sidelines, "You have to shoot to score!"

Her call was very brief. Pops was gracious, "I'm delighted to hear from you." Hoping her call meant she was free of Peter, all Pops asked was, "And how have things been going with you since—?"

"Since I saw you at the store? He's not around anymore."

"Wonderful! I hope you are OK."

"I'm fine."

"Good. When might you want to come to see me? If you want, I can wait for you in my office this afternoon after your work."

"I'd like that."

Connie was pleased hearing about her plan to meet Pops after work. "I'm happy for you even though I know it means," pretending her hand was a rocket taking off, "that you'll be outta this place soon."

After work, she took the subway the few stops to Pops' office. She again noticed the desk looked out of place. It looked too big, too expensive and just too grand for the rest of the office.

Trying to put her at ease, he asked if she wanted something—a bottle of water or a soft drink, but she declined. Noticing her reaction to the desk, as he escorted her to a chair, he sat in a chair near hers, instead of sitting behind his desk.

He patted the desk, "You are wondering, 'What is a nice desk like you doing in a place like this?'"

He chuckled. "While I was still in law school, I met a young woman who became a model. Her name was Beatrice Gold." He pointed to the highest row of pictures on the wall. "From the day we met I started falling in love. Silly as it might seem, she fell in love with me. After we got married, I gave her a break on tax work;" he chuckled and looked to make sure she understood he was joking.

She did. She smiled.

"After she made a big name for herself in the business, she started looking after some younger models—helping them."

He said softly, "We could not have children so she looked out for other people's children. There are some people who are not very nice to young girls. My Bea was on top and wanted to help others get there too. So, we started working as agents for some of the girls—I also looked after their money. One thing you have to know, not everybody makes a lot of money. If you make any money, you have to be smart with it. There are too many people who were big and now they're broke. Not any of our girls that I know of, thank God.

"We called it Gold Shield Agency. Gold for her and Magen means shield in Hebrew so, for the agency name, I dropped the 'wise' and just went with the shield. Then, after forty-six beautiful years, my Bea got cancer and God took her."

He paused and sighed. Going to a little refrigerator behind the desk, he took out a bottle of water for himself, offering one to her. This time she accepted. He sat down and continued. "I didn't know what to do with myself after. . . I kept my license and kept the agency open. I moved into this place when I semiretired but I couldn't part with the desk she gave me so. . .

"OK. Now we talk about you."

As she talked, he listened intently. She was surprised to find herself talking so freely about her past and her feelings to this kindly, old man in the slightly rumpled suit. She told him about her childhood. She told him what it was like going through her mother's illness and death, and the death of her brother. She mentioned that the only other man she had spoken to about those feelings was her basketball coach, Harry Daweson. She repeated some of his "life-living-lessons."

Pops nodded, "A truly wise man. Do you still speak to him?"

When she told him she had not stayed in touch he said, "Such a pity."

He looked at her, "In some ways you are very much like my Bea. Growing up with no mother and few girl-friends, she never gave much thought to makeup or clothes either. When we met, she was shlepping equipment for her uncle who did lighting for photographers. I was making some money, helping a cousin who sham-pooed carpets. I was in law school, but in those days, if it was legal, we did whatever we could to make a little money to help out.

"One night, my cousin and I were cleaning one part of a department store, after it closed for the night, and a pho-tographer was shooting in another part of the store. Bea and I met that night and spent a little time talking together and walking around the empty store. Later, we went to a coffee shop. We really hit it off. It turned out she was the younger sister of a friend of mine.

"That first night, I thought she was the woman I want-ed to marry. After we were married, she admitted that on our first meeting she knew too. Anyway, on that first night we knew we would both be back at the store the next night, and we made a date to go out again after work. They were doing an appliance layout.

"When I finished, I went over to the appliance department to wait for her, but they had hardly gotten started. They were waiting for the model they had booked and they were just shooting anything they could think of that they did not need her for. Finally, when she did not show up, they put Bea in the chair, did her hair and makeup, put her in the other clothes, and threw her in front of the camera, smiling and opening an oven. After that they moved on to refrigerators. Then they redid her look, put a lot of volume in her hair and put her in a shot with a washing machine. I watched as they transformed her.

"When she finished and we went back to that same coffee shop, the difference in the way people reacted to her—with her hair and a little makeup—was stunning. We could tell they were watching us—like they were trying to figure out who she was. It took us by surprise. We talked about it. She was a bit uncomfortable with all the stares. Talking about how she felt about being put in front of the camera she said she never thought of herself as beautiful—like a model—but she did not dislike it. And, it was a lot easier than dragging heavy, hot lights around. She did not know it then, because she had not asked, but it paid a lot better too."

He looked to see if Judy was as interested in his story as he was in telling it.

"When the photographer and the store people liked her look in the photos, he started asking her to do more ads. Her brother was already out of law school and was working in the legal department of a big agency. He knew people in the business and was able to open a few doors. Soon many photographers and agencies wanted to work with her. While I was finishing law school, and we were planning our wedding, she started to become quite well known."

He paused, "My Bea had to get used to her new situation. You see, some girls in the business are beautiful as children and they grow up knowing the world sees them that way. They have a sense of entitlement. Their image of themselves is of a beautiful person and they expect to be treated like one. They expect to have people behave around them in a way that is consistent with their self-image. You and my Bea did not grow up that way. I certainly did not grow up beautiful and I never changed.

"But you and Bea did change. People treating you like a beautiful girl or a celebrity may feel a bit strange to you."

He got up from the chair to get the pictures Gary had sent and sat down.

"You need to know that this business is not for everyone. Some girls cannot handle the rejection, and some girls cannot handle the success. There can be a loss of privacy. You might not like what comes with this business. Believe it or not, you are a little old to be starting out—some of the girls have contracts while they are still in high school. But your pictures are very good. Actually, they are far better than very good."

He showed them to her.

She didn't recognize herself. Pops smiled at her reaction. "I know, if you are not used to seeing what the camera sees—and then there is the lighting and the makeup and all. But the camera sees—and what it sees with you, it likes; I think it will sell. I think I can get you work."

He could see the idea made her nervous. He understood.

He said, "It is sad that sometimes people get so used to things being the way they are that, even if they could do better for themselves, they never try, either because of fear that they will not succeed or they are just afraid of change."

He told her about a lawyer who used to say, "I'm not opposed to change as long as it doesn't happen now!"

She laughed and was more relaxed. He told her when Bea was nervous about all the changes and all the attention she was starting to get, he'd relate a story about his visit to the circus and he repeated the story to Judy.

She smiled that she understood. "I think I'm ready to do this."

"Good! First, I know we talked about the name—Jodi Worren— I like it but if —"

"—No, no." She said, "It's really fine. I like it too."

He tapped her bottle of water with his as though making a toast. "OK. To Jodi Worren. We can start slow and small. Well, realistically," he said motioning to the one-room office, "if you are starting with me, you are starting small—but I know a lot of people in the business. At first, I will try to work around your schedule at the store, but that may not be so easy. The important thing is to start to get work. In this business, the first question is, 'What has she done?' In order to get work, you have to have already done work. I will look for jobs where they are asking for a group of girls. While you are learning something of the business, and what is expected, you can also learn more about fashion and about what colors and styles work better for you. You will also be building your portfolio. Then, God willing, that phone will keep ringing for Jodi Worren. I have seen it happen more than a few times and it can be quite a ride."

She agreed, "I'm willing to take the chance."

"Wonderful, we can talk about fees later when you start to make some money."

"Do you need me to sign anything?"

"No. A handshake is fine for me. I do not need anything else. I have not done anything yet. We should get a more extensive set of photos from Gary. I will make the arrangements."

He leaned toward her and said softly, "And that man—should I even ask?"

She thought about the question for a second, and said softly, "Not yet."

He sat back in his chair and sighed, "OK. Fair enough, but I do have to ask—he said he was your manager—was there ever any kind of contract?"

"No."

"Good."

As they were leaving his office, he stopped at one of the book shelves that filled all four walls, and took down a book.

He handed it to her saying, "If you look at the part called, "The Manual," you might find some of your coach's life-living-lessons in here."

Going downstairs together, he told her he was going to hail a cab.

"I can get home on the subway like I got here."

"It is dark. And, if I am right about you—you better start thinking about raising your sights a bit."

He hailed a cab.

He opened the door for her and handed her eighteen dollars for the fare.

"Thank you, Pops."

As she was getting into the cab, he said, "One more thing. Since you are in the business—now you are Jodi Worren."

To make it official he told the cab driver, "Take good care of her. This is Jodi Worren!"

The cab driver grumbled, "Yeah. Whatever you say, Pops."

Jodi and Pops looked at each other and laughed.

When she called him the next day, she asked about the eighteen dollars. He explained: "In Hebrew the letters have numbers, and in the word 'Chai' which means 'Life' the letters add up to the number 18. I gave you the eighteen dollars for luck."

He added, "I set up getting the new photos with Gary so you will not have to miss work."

When she arrived at the studio, Gary was pleased that she came alone. He yelled, "Hey, Jimmy, you can come out now. I told you Pops said that jerk wasn't going to be around anymore."

Jimmy was glad he was out of her life. "When you were here before, it wasn't until you left that Gary told me that you were with Pops. Way to go! Nice lookin' out for yourself. He's such a sweetheart. His wife was a little before my time but I've heard stories—everybody says she was really a very classy lady. She always looked out for other people. She and Pops helped a lot of people get a foot in the door. They talked about everybody deserving to be happy. They made it happen for a lot of people. They helped Gary get started before he and I hooked up."

He nodded toward Gary setting up the lighting. Lowering his voice, he whispered conspiratorially, "Girlfriend, I've always liked older men."

Then he added, "By the way, he and I have a shoot coming up for an ad agency next week. They're doing a soft drink shoot with a group of people. We liked your first pictures so much we asked Pops if we could show them to the agency people, and he said it was OK.

"They called Pops right away. He asked me to tell you he can book you for it. He wants you to give him a call for the details."

She got nervous.

He saw the frightened look on her face. "Oh, Girlfriend, is it your first?"

She nodded, "Yes."

He shook his head and laughed, "Well, you better get ready. Be prepared. Get your bags packed. The camera really loves you! You better just give notice at your day job and hold on tight."

Then he added hesitantly, "Pops deputized me to check, 'that she has what to wear'—that is, if you have the right clothes to wear to this booking. First impressions really count. When you were here the first, time I saw that you didn't wear heels and I knew you couldn't with that short chump, but now—"

"I've never owned a pair of high heels."

"Well, Girlfriend, Pops will pick up the tab and you and I are going shopping. I want to be able to report back to him that you have 'what to wear.' Don't fret; high heels are easy. I can show you."

Jodi wasn't prepared to give notice at the drugstore. She called Pops and he confirmed he wanted to book her for the job next Friday. He hoped getting the day off wouldn't be a problem. "I know we talked about starting slowly, but when these people called and wanted you. . ."

The next day Jodi told Connie about the job, what Jimmy said, and about the shopping.

Connie smiled, "I hate to say, 'I told you so'—but I did!"

To Jodi's surprise, when she told Tom Leonard she needed to take off next Friday, he said she couldn't have it. She thought of reminding him that in the almost two years she had worked there she had never taken a sick day and never asked for time off before. Instead, she explained to him why she needed the day. But he still refused. Even though she hadn't planned to quit, she wasn't going to sacrifice the opportunities this first modeling job might lead to. Thinking of the story Pops had told Bea, she told Tom she was sorry, she would work the rest of this week but Thursday of next week would be her last day. He grumbled it wouldn't give him much time to find someone else. She decided not to remind him she hadn't planned to quit, but he was leaving her no choice.

She was shaken by the confrontation.

Connie could see from her face it hadn't gone well.

Jodi reported what had just happened, and then added, "I feel like I just took a plunge off a diving board and I'm not sure there's water in the pool."

She paused, "But when Pops and I were talking about how things change, he told me a story that he told his wife about when he was a kid and he went to the circus.

"He said that he saw these huge elephants being tied with these really flimsy thin ropes. He asked the trainer if the elephants couldn't just break those ropes any time they wanted to. The trainer said they were sure strong enough to do it, now, but the trainers had used the same thin ropes on them when they were young and small, and the elephants learned that they couldn't break the rope then, so now they don't even try.

"Pops said the elephant—not understanding its strength had changed—accepts the situation and doesn't test it. I'll never forget when Pops said, 'The elephant is forever bound because it fails to try.'"

"Wow. So, now you tried. I told you Pops was good people. You'll be fine. Worse comes to worst, you can sleep on my couch. Besides, what does this thing next Friday pay?"

"I forgot to ask."

Connie shook her, "What am I gonna do with you?'

Then paused, "OK. So, if it pays what you make here in a day, you're even. And if it pays what you make in a week, you only need one of those a week while you're looking for more. And—you don't have to deal with Mr. Wonderful back there. Hell, if I didn't have Paolo, I'd quit with you!"

"You better lower your voice or you won't have to quit."

"No. No. Not now, baby. So, I'm the only girl they got. Do you think Tom is gonna get his ass out from behind that big pharmacy counter? Hey, you ever seen either of them dust bottles? No way! They need me now."

When Jodi called Pops to tell him about quitting, she was surprised when he said, "Good!"

He went on, "Gary and Jimmy have been talking to people. Since we spoke last, I had calls for a couple of shoots the week after. Now, we do not have to worry about your work schedule at the store. Three weeks from now, they need girls for the boat show at the Coliseum— that should be a solid couple of weeks. Your new pictures look really good. I am sending them around to the people booking for the boat show and some other ad agencies. The automobile show is coming in soon after the boat show. All these things build up your book and pay the rent."

"I'm glad to hear that—the couch at Connie's place didn't look all that comfortable. Although once when my grandparents and I were evicted because the landlord raised the rent—my grandfather reacted to the news of the increase by going on a binge and drank up most of the rent money. We spent some nights on the street and then had to live on inflatable mattresses in a church basement for three weeks until the pastor found us a place they could afford. So, I guess Connie's couch would really be a step up if I needed it."

She couldn't see the sadness that came over him as he heard this story. But she heard it in his voice when he said softly, "God willing you will never face that kind of want, again." After a pause they set up a meeting so he could show her the new photos.

This time she was more relaxed and Pops smiled when he saw she was wearing high heels and a smart looking dress. She said she didn't think the photos looked any more like her than the first set.

"I did not think they would. This is the fantasy image business. There is a story of an older woman hearing some young girls saying that they wished they looked like the girls in Playboy. The older woman told them that the girls in Playboy wished they could look like the girls in Playboy."

She smiled.

"Jodi, most people cannot live their lives from the outside—they do not usually see themselves as other people see them.

"I had a cousin who was the only woman scientist working on a project. Back then, there were very few women doing that, some more now, but still not many women scientists.

"She was very overweight. But then she lost a lot of weight. Looking more like what this culture wants to think is the norm, she was surprised when the men she worked with treated her like she was so much smarter than they had before. We both agreed it was sad, how much looks matter in the world, but my cousin said, 'I just didn't see that change coming. As a scientist it was interesting to see such a big change in the men's attitudes based only on that one variable.'

"Jodi, you might not like the fact that looks are so important to the way people treat other people. We should not like it, but you need to understand it. You also need to make your peace with the fact that this is the business we have chosen. To some extent our 'selling-of-fantasy-image' business perpetuates the 'looksist' problem.

"It is important to understand the basis for certain re-actions. I told you about the circus elephant and you said you thought about it and it allowed you to take the risk to quit your job. Well, you can also, unless you are an ele-phant, change your perception of yourself. When I say we cannot see ourselves from the outside, I mean not even in a mirror. When a person looks in a mirror, all they see is their own reflection. But from other people we can get feedback."

She cocked her head to the side and he saw the questioning look on her face.

"The idea of feedback is like the signal an orbiting satellite sends to gauge its relationship to the earth. That signal says, 'I think I am five miles above the North Pole.'

"If the signal comes back, and the satellite can judge it is accurate, it can behave accordingly. If the satellite is lower or higher it can change its orbit.

"But it has to be receptive to the feedback; it has to have its antenna out ready to receive the feedback to make its adjustment.

"Most often, people will only accept feedback as long as it fits with what they already assumed. Usually, if a person thinks they are good looking and you were to tell them they are ugly, they would reject your opinion—your feedback—and they would feel insulted."

He laughed, "They may even question your parentage. But, if a person thinks they are ugly and you tell them they are good looking, they may question your eyesight."

She smiled.

He nodded, "But if you really care about a person and trust that they care about you, you can work with their feedback and adjust how you see yourself."

He checked to see if she was following. "Jodi, when you look in a mirror all you see is your reflection. I look at you and I see a beautiful woman. If you trust what I tell you of my vision of you—my feedback as being real and genuine—slowly you can start getting used to it and maybe learn to see yourself that way too. The mental image you have of yourself can evolve. You might slowly come to realize you are not a caterpillar anymore. You are a beautiful butterfly."

She smiled and thanked him.

As it turned out, Jimmy was right.

As her pictures started to appear in ads in magazines and newspapers, Pops' phone kept ringing.

She started working steadily.

Before the end of the year, she had appeared on the cover of several major magazines and had been to Europe twice.

Once, after being in Paris and Milan for five weeks, she brought home some things from Italy for Connie and Paolo. Calling the phone number she had, she found the number was disconnected. She mailed Connie a note, but it came back, "Moved. Left no Forwarding Address." Finally, she stopped at the store.

Joe was glad to see her. He told her that he had seen her picture on the cover of some of the magazines in the rack but hardly recognized her. Connie had to tell him who it was. But Connie had just failed to show up for work one day months ago.

They were holding some pay for her and didn't know where to send it. Jodi agreed to let him know if she found out anything.

When she left the store, she saw the cop who had been involved in the door incident when the store wasn't locked up, walking by.

Saying "Hello," she told him, "I came to the store to look for Connie."

"Good luck with that! Word in the neighborhood was, with Carmine getting out early, people are wondering if he was talking. The old code of silence isn't what it used to be."

"Connie said there's no such thing as the Mafia."

"Yeah, that's what they say. Look, I ain't no old time Irish-mick cop. My folks were born in Naples. I know this neighborhood. You might not have known it, but you saving the other one from getting fired probably saved the owners from getting a beating. And then the shit would really fly—cause if you get in a beef with a 'citizen' sometimes you can't be protected if they go to the cops. That's why Carmine was locked up to begin with. He gave a beatin' to some guy who owed a ton of money on gambling debts, but the guy Carmine beat on had a mother-in-law who worked for a judge.

"Anyway, if I happen to run into the other one, I'll tell her you were looking for her. Best I can do."

She was sorry to lose track of Connie, but she would always be grateful that Connie had aimed her toward Pops.

When she told Pops what the cop had said, all Pops could say was, "We can only hope she is well and happy."

TWENTY

Jodi's career grew rapidly. She crossed easily between print and fashion work. As the top photographers and designers saw her photos, heard how easy she was to work with—how easily she could use her eyes and face to show a range of emotions, and how giving and comfortable she was with their needs for her to create the moods and looks they needed to capture—they all clamored to work with her.

Before long, she had walked hundreds of shows—all the top tiered shows—and appeared on the cover of all the major magazines, some more than twice. She was one of the top earning models in the world.

Through her discussions with Pops, Jimmy, and other acquaintances she made in "the business," she quickly developed her own sense of what looked good on her and her own sense of lighting and timing. Even though models were often in competition for the same jobs, they saw each other as kind of friendly rivals. They hung out together on locations. If, as was sometimes the case, a group was sent to a remote location for a shoot, the only people to socialize with were the other models and the crew. She fit in easily.

Reflecting on her new life—with her new name, Jodi often thought of the life-living-lessons of Harry Daweson. The book Pops had given her that first day contained excerpts from Greek philosophers and included "The Manual of Epictetus." She recognized most of the ideas behind the lessons as coming from that work.

Pops suggested a wide variety of things for her to read and she enjoyed the lengthy discussions about the books and anything else on her mind in their at least twice-daily phone calls.

She took comfort knowing she could rely on Pops and his wisdom. He handled her bookings, collected the fees for her, and invested her money. She liked not being involved with the day-to-day issues of getting the work or dealing with the finances.

He tried to show her where every penny came from and where it went. She was truly startled to learn what she was earning and to see that he grew what she had earned into more than she would ever need. But she was just not really interested in the details of how he did it. Though he saw her lack of interest in details as a sign of trust, he was concerned for her future and wanted to make sure that she was at least aware where her money was invested.

One night, almost five years from the day of their handshake agreement, she realized that while they were always in touch by phone, her travels meant she hadn't seen Pops in a long time. Knowing she was heading home, she called from London to invite him to dinner for their "anniversary."

Pleased by the thought, he picked his favorite French restaurant.

It was a beautiful summer night in the city. Arriving a few minutes early, she decided to wait outside on the corner. While waiting, she happened to look at a newsstand and noticed her picture on the cover of two magazines. Thinking how much she owed to him, she looked up as he was walking toward her.

She was surprised at how stooped over he looked and to see him using a cane. As he got closer, he was pointing with the cane to something behind her. Turning, she saw, covering the side of a passing city bus, an ad she had done for an herbal shampoo. In the picture she was lying on a luxurious white rug wearing a slinky, low cut white satin gown with her hair full and flowing.

He came alongside her, "Has it been five years already?"

Smiling, she leaned down and gave him a kiss on the cheek.

Pointing to the magazine covers, she said, "I was thinking, he did all this for me in just five years?"

"Next month, I think you are going to be on four. Come inside, I have something to talk to you about."

Walking to their table, she was curious, while waiting for him to start.

"Well, how do you feel about what has been happening for you so far?"

"Pops, I think it's great. You've done wonderful things for me."

Putting up his had to stop her, "Jodi, I was not asking for you to throw flowers at me—although it is very nice. And thank you for thinking of this anniversary," he said kissing her hand.

"What I am trying to find out is if you are really OK with all this. You have been working almost nonstop for all these years. I do not hear anything from you about a boyfriend or even any friends outside the business. Jodi that is what I mean when I ask how you feel about the way you are living your life.

"Thank God, you have more than enough money if you wanted to take some time off. Actually, with what little you spend, I think you have enough if you never want to work again."

"No, Pops I'm fine."

"Jodi, are you sure? Over the years you have talked about this life-lesson coach of yours and his talking about balance—to work all the time is not balanced."

"No, Pops," she said, taking his hand and looking into his eyes, "I'm fine. I really am. I don't need a boyfriend in my life. I grew up without many friends. And as long as I have you— And, now, thanks to you and your reading suggestions, I always have a great book to wander around in.

"Getting lost in a book is like my time off and like having friends."

She cocked her head, "But, what about you? Do you need some time off?" Imitating his inflection, she asked, "What is with the cane?"

"My doctor said I should have it. I just use it to get sympathy. Thank you, but no. I do not need any time off. I do like having only one client, though. But, believe me, at my age, there is an eternity of time off just around the corner. If it is all the same to you, I will try to keep active while I wait."

"Is slowing down what you wanted to talk to me about?"

"No. Actually a few other things are coming up. Since you have been on those TV talk shows, people realize you can talk and hold up your end of a conversation as well as look beautiful.

"I am dealing with three more offers for you to be a spokesperson, two for major cosmetic companies and one for another car company. And I have two offers for movies."

Sitting back in her chair, she thought out loud, "Movies?"

"Well, yes. A lot of the girls move on to films trying to build on the name they made for themselves as models. There are not many great roles for older actresses, but they still find more work than older models.

"Not all of the girls are successful, of course, but some are. Anyway, what is happening for you is now that they know you can talk, the movie people are wondering if you can act."

She smiled, "You know the answer to that, Pops."

"Of course, that is what I tell them— 'You see the swimsuit ad? It was 35 degrees out there and she is in a two-piece suit smiling like she is on a warm sunny beach.' They know that stuff. They get it. Anyway, one of the movies is a low budget indie that might be good to start with."

"And the other?"

"Well, the other is what I wanted to talk to you about. It could be something special. Sharin Mersor, the 'Grand Dame of Hollywood,' has taken a shine to you. She thinks you look just like she did when she was starting out.

"Frankly, I think she wishes she looked like you any day of her life—"

Jodi blushed.

He went on, "—but anyway, she is looking to do the story of her life and insists you are the only one she wants for the part of her as a young woman. In addition to being pestered by her people, she has already called me about it herself three times. How does that sound to you—being a young Sharin Mersor in the movie they are calling 'The Life and Times of Sharin Mersor'?"

"Really? How serious is all this?"

"Well, with the spokesperson things, I am ironing out any conflicts with other endorsements and making sure you have the freedom to do what you have been doing—and the movies too, if you want them. I am talking to both teams with the movies to see what they are expecting if you went with them."

"Like what?"

"Like so far you have not been seen wearing less than a bikini. We never discussed your doing any nudity. I know many young actresses say that they will do it as long as it is in keeping with the character, and sad to say, the starving girls will do it if there is a meal in it for them.

"As long as it does not hurt anybody, I do not think it is up to us to judge how some people try to get the happiness I think everybody deserves. But not everybody has an ad campaign paying them a huge number of dollars, for a company that might not want the person most identified with their brand getting into a bathtub in front of the whole world."

She smiled, "I'm glad I've got you looking out for me. Who knows, maybe, just maybe I could become a serious actress. I could take an acting class. Maybe I could learn acting as a craft—not just the smiling-on-the-freezing beach trick."

"—or that print ad where you are looking longingly at the guy with the new sports car," he interrupted.

She laughed, "Maybe people didn't think it was acting. Maybe they thought I was really longing for the car or the guy who you and I know Jimmy dumped to move in with Gary. Who knows?" Then pensively, "But, this Sharin Mersor thing is interesting."

"I was sure it would be. They are talking about only playing her as a young woman. They have someone else in mind to play Sharin in her older years."

She nodded.

He continued, "From what she says about her plans for this film and its high production values, using a top director, a top cinematographer and a top screenwriter to work with her, it looks like it will be some time before they actually put all the working pieces together. I think she may also run into some budget issues with wanting these high-price professionals to shoot at the actual locations like Anzio where she was a nurse.

"But one thing she is sure of is that she wants you. As things are looking, now, if we wanted to take all the offers on the table, you could probably wrap up your current commitments, maybe even fit in an acting class, do the low budget indie and still be done in plenty of time to do the Mersor film."

Moving his wrinkled hands above the table like he was massaging a crystal ball he intoned, "Who knows, three or four years from now, if God is willing and we stay healthy, we could be sitting here again with an Oscar on the table."

She just laughed.

During their meal, while they were talking and getting a few stares from the other patrons, she noticed a young girl approaching the table with a pen, a piece of notebook paper, and an aghast mother hurriedly getting up from her seat to try and rein in her child. Putting her hand up to signal the mother that it was OK, Jodi reached for the paper and talked to the child as she signed the autograph.

Pops was pleased watching her take the time to talk with the girl, listening to what she had to say, and making her feel special during the brief time they spent before the mother and father apologetically took the child back to their table.

"That's the first time someone asked for an autograph when I was out socially—not working. I didn't think of models as people who are sought after like that."

"Some of the top models are. You should try to get used to it, especially after the talk show work. You sort of turned a corner.

"I loved the way you treated that young girl like you were the only two people in the room. You gave her a lot more than just your name on a piece of paper. You are very much like my Bea in that way. I am proud of you."

"Thank you for that, Pops. It means so much to me."

"You know, before you were getting used to your wings as a beautiful butterfly, now you need to see that you are a more recognizable butterfly. We have talked about this coach of yours talking about self-esteem."

She nodded.

"Well, what we are talking about is esteeming or valuing your self-image—the idea of who you are as a person in this world and that, of course, is more than just how you look. In order to do this, you need to have a sense of yourself, a kind of emotional balance, a sense of not only who you are in the world, but where you have been, and where you are in relation to others in your world."

She listened, aware that what he was saying would be helpful.

"When Archimedes discovered the principle behind the lever he supposedly said, 'Give me a place to stand, and I will move the Earth.' Jodi, you do not need to move the Earth, or even to try to, but you still need a place to stand—a place to secure your footing. You need to know who you are, and trust yourself, before you can trust others. Once you know who you are, then you can try to verify the position of others in relationship to you."

"I think I am starting to understand. The idea of a solid, centered place to stand reminds me of my coach's talks about balance. Just like Epictetus talked about knowing what is in your control and what is not. I think the idea of being solid or centered means not wanting or being needy; not trying to grasp things not within your reach; not leaning for things or leaning on others."

He liked that she was learning.

She sighed, "The autograph request surprised me in this setting, but I am getting more comfortable with people coming up to me or just staring at me. I think I'm getting the 'Jodi' bearings, growing into the wings, as you say. I'm getting more comfortable being 'Jodi Worren.'"

She smiled, "But, Pops, I don't think these people are staring at me as much as they are staring at us."

He looked around, put down his napkin and smiled.

"When my Bea and I were younger, when we went out, I was aware of the glances in her direction. But after my Bea was gone, I did not go out much. I have forgotten what sitting in public across the table from a beautiful woman feels like."

He patted her hand, "And thank you again for inviting me out."

He noticed her absentmindedly run her finger over an embroidered butterfly design on her napkin.

He asked, "Where did you just go?"

She cocked her head and, clearing the lump in her throat, she said, "Speaking of butterflies. When I was living with my grandparents as a kid one winter it was freezing cold. We couldn't afford any warm clothes for me.

"This coach bought me a warm jacket from a thrift store. He lied to my grandparents—"

Seeing his puzzled reaction to the word "lied," she made it right. "He told them that he found it in the Lost and Found at school. And he said it must have been abandoned, it was there so long. See, I'm sure he told them that so they wouldn't think it was a handout. They would never take a handout.

"He never said anything to me about the jacket, and I never told him I knew where the jacket came from. But I'd seen it in the window of the thrift store. I recognized it because of the embroidered design, like a butterfly, that was used to patch a tear in the sleeve. I cherished that jacket. I still have it in my closet. Before you gave me this life, that jacket—and the thought behind it were the nicest things anyone had ever done for me."

"Thank you, Jodi, but no one gives someone a life. I just showed you the right door. You went through the door on your own and now you are living on the other side. We talked, but all the decisions about your work were yours."

She nodded.

"Now, this coach with the jacket is the coach you said you lost track of, no?"

"Yes."

He sighed, "Losing track of a mensch like that is such a pity. He tried to give you lessons to live by and he cared enough to step in and even lie to make sure you had what you needed."

Choking up, "What he did—and how he did it— sounds so much like something my Bea would do. Giving without any expectation of recognition or reward other than the quiet pleasure of knowing you did for someone what needed to be done."

After finishing their meal, walking slowly out of the restaurant, he accepted her silent offer of her arm.

"Thank you. And thank you for getting all dressed up for the occasion. I like that you felt you could wear high heels."

Then added, "The first time, when you came in with that guy, I noticed you wore flats. I guessed he was too insecure for you to be taller than he was."

Cautiously he added, "You know that time, when you first came in without him you were not ready to tell me. I never asked again but—whatever happened to that guy, do we know? He did not seem like the type to give up a good thing too easily."

Standing on the street corner, she took a deep breath, remembering how concerned he was that day. She wasn't ready then.

Now, there was nothing she couldn't tell him. Looking around to make sure they couldn't be overheard, she took his hand and told him about Peter hitting her and the pictures he took. Pops winced when she told him about getting hit and then got angry as she told him everything that happened to her that night.

As he listened, he felt he had let her down. He questioned himself as to whether he had missed something. If, when he first saw them together, he could have tried to warn her. If, when she came to see him and told him she was free of Peter, he had let his feeling of satisfaction blind him to some sign that she needed something more from him in the way of help. She had said she didn't want to talk about it and he had just left it at that.

Now, he asked, "Did you get any counseling about this? Maybe it could have helped? Maybe it might help even now?"

She smiled and patted him on the shoulder and assured him that, for now, she felt OK. Then she told him of the next day and Connie calling her uncle Leno to get the film and put Peter on a train.

Pops said slowly, "Leno Giambroni. Oh, what a small world! I know Leno. Actually, I knew his older brother, Luigi, much better. This restaurant used to be an Italian restaurant, Luigi's place before he passed. I did his tax work for him. My Bea and I came here for Italian food all the time. Connie is married to their sister Angela's son, no?"

"Carmine."

"Yes, right, Carmine. Leno took care of this thing for you?"

He paused, looking around and lowering his voice, he said cautiously, "OK, now you must wonder if they might have killed that guy, right?"

She nodded. That thought had occurred to her.

He took a deep breath and let it out slowly, "You should not worry. Let me tell you. Unless they have to lay their hands on somebody to collect money, usually when these people get involved with civilians it is a measured response—a 'beating-for-a-beating' type response."

He went on. "The train idea sounds a bit far-fetched, but if that is what Leno said—Leno is old school—he is a man of respect, he would not order his people to do murder because of a beating—even what happened to you. A man of his generation would not think such an order was honorable. He would not think it was fair. He would want to know that he had taken care of you, but he would stay within his unwritten code."

Shaking his head, "But, on the other hand, if that guy mouthed off to these people in the same pushy way as he did with me and Gary—if he acted with disrespect, or talked out of turn, then to use their term, 'He'd get what-ever his hand called for.'

"In that case I could speculate that Leno, by want-ing to pay with a credit card and getting a time-and-date-stamped receipt, was looking to establish an alibi. But as I said that is only my speculation."

Checking again to see there was no one around to hear them, he said slowly, "Anyway, you should not have to worry yourself about it. You did not do anything wrong."

He looked up at her, "Whatever happened to that guy—it would have been something he brought on him-self. Besides, Leno told you they flushed the film and made sure he had his passport. And he told you if you ever heard from that guy again to let him know? Right?

"Well, that could have been some attempt at misdirec-tion—again, we should not speculate because we just do not know. But I think if Leno had killed him, or ordered it done, he would have let you know that you would not to have to worry ever again.

"Without any bragging or any specifics, he would want you to know that he handled your problem for you. Just as he told you the film was destroyed, he would have let you know you will never hear from this man again. But he did not say that. If Leno had just seen that guy laid in a grave, he would not have talked about wanting to know if you ever heard from him.

"From what little I know, these people are not believ-ers in reincarnation or in getting messages from the spirit world.

"Anyway, it has been five years without word from him, no? Then I guess whatever Leno said or did to him, it must have worked."

She brightened, "I'm glad we talked about this, Pops. She bent down and gave him a kiss on the cheek.

She sighed, "As always, I'm so glad we talked."

She hailed a cab for him. Smiling, she handed him eighteen dollars cab fare.

He was touched. He was pleased she remembered.

Getting into the cab, his eyes got teary. "My Bea would have loved you so much!"

Watching his cab drive away, Jodi got teary too. She felt her life was so full and she owed so much to this stooped-over, little, gentle man.

She thought, And Coach Daweson would have liked you so much, Pops.

TWENTY-ONE

On a sunny afternoon, one month after Corey told him they were going to have a second child, Harry was in the store finishing a sale when the phone rang.

Corey was sobbing. "Harry, come home!"

"I'll be right there. What's wrong?"

"I'll tell you when you get here. Please hurry."

Locking up quickly, he was home in minutes. He found Corey upstairs in their bathroom on the toilet.

Blood was pooled on the bedroom floor and was smeared on the bathroom wall.

"I think I lost the baby. No, I'm sure," she cried.

He sat on the rim of the tub so he could be next to her. She turned and put her arms around his neck and continued sobbing. He smoothed her hair as her head pressed next to his.

"Did you call the doctor— an ambulance?"

"No. I don't need the ambulance. I've stopped bleeding."

"Are you sure you don't want me to —"

"No, I'm sure. Just stay with me for a while. Then, I'll need you to help me clean up before Ruth drops Dayna off."

"Look, I'll stay with you as long as you need and I'll clean up. But I need you to go to the doctor."

"No, Harry—but I will go lie down."

"Let me at least call the doctor and see what he suggests."

He fought back tears, "I don't want to lose you too."

She thought about that and finally agreed.

Helping her clean herself and then to bed, he got her a fresh nightgown and a glass of water before he called the doctor's office.

He was told that the doctor was on his way to the office from the hospital and would return his call soon.

After cleaning the bathroom, and the bedroom floor, he lay on the bed, over the covers, next to her waiting for the doctor to return his call. He held her when she started crying again, as they waited for Dayna.

As she regained control, she told him she had started feeling stomach cramps around 1:30 and went up to lie down, thinking maybe it was from something she had for lunch. She tried to close her eyes for a nap but couldn't sleep. She wasn't sure how long she was lying down when she started to feel her underpants were getting wet. She got up to go to the bathroom and saw she was bloody. There were some large clots in it and she was sure she had lost the baby.

Corey's head lay on Harry's chest until they heard Ruth's "Hello" at the front door. Dayna came running into the house. Corey and Harry looked at each other, quickly deciding they wouldn't say anything to anyone just yet.

Going down and thanking Ruth, he prompted Dayna to thank Ruth for allowing her to play at her house. He told both of them Corey was upstairs resting. Ruth lifted her son Robin to her hip and said she understood Corey's need for rest.

Helping Dayna get her coat off, he wondered how you tell a child she is not going to be a big sister after all. He sighed and realized whatever the way, Corey would surely find it and take the lead in making it as meaningful to Dayna as anyone could.

Sorting out Dayna's stuff, he heard the phone ring and then realized Corey had answered it upstairs. Taking Dayna to her room, they looked in on Corey.

She was just hanging up the phone.

She nodded in answer to his unspoken question—it was the doctor who called.

Just as Corey took her eyes off Harry, Dayna jumped up on the bed before he could stop her. Corey, nodding to him that it was okay, reached out her arms for Dayna, hugging her and in her typical animated way, asked her about her day.

Harry stood there and choked back a tear. Except for the fact that Corey was in bed in her robe, nothing between mother and child looked abnormal.

The next day, the doctor confirmed what they already feared.

He alerted Harry to be particularly watchful for any hormonal mood swings Corey might have over the next several weeks.

They assured the doctor they would be OK.

For the next few months, they socialized less and spent more and more time together. They decided he could cut the store hours by one half hour a day and he would come home for lunch more.

One dark night while they were alone cuddled together in front of the fireplace, she observed, if it wasn't for Dayna sleeping upstairs, it would feel like they were on their honeymoon.

Jarringly the fire whistle sounded and his pager alerted him to a fire just outside of town.

He sprang up.

"I wasn't in the fire department on our honeymoon."

The car fire was quickly extinguished and he returned home in less than half an hour. Coming in, he curled himself around Corey and asked, "Where were we?"

She yawned, "Right here, but where we need to be is in bed."

After checking that Dayna was asleep, they got ready for bed.

As they lay the in the darkness, she kissed him and asked, "Are you tired?"

Harry grinned. He knew, that when Corey asked him that question, it meant she wanted to make love.

TWENTY-TWO

Slowly, Harry, Corey and Dayna settled back into their old routines. Harry added the half hour of open-time back at the store, and Corey was looking forward to Dayna starting kindergarten. Money was a bit tight and Corey was hoping to get some part time work.

There was a medical building opening up not too far away and she hoped to put her business skills to use in one of the doctors' offices. But soon she learned the building was not going to be opening as quickly as planned and the doctors could not expand into their new offices as they were anticipating.

When Dayna started kindergarten, Corey's search for employment was still ongoing. Then she got pregnant again. She and Harry were cautiously optimistic. But they decided not to tell anyone about the pregnancy until it was further along.

After three months and a prenatal test with good results, they felt comfortable making the announcement. Soon Corey got busy with her friends and so she and Harry decided Wednesdays would be a good day for both of them to schedule lunchtime activities with others.

Shortly after Dayna started first grade, Henry William Daweson was born. He was named after both his grandfathers—Henry, the one only Harry had known, and Bill, the one that Dayna only slightly remembered.

Dayna was proud to be a big sister. She could not believe how small Henry was when she was allowed to hold him on the day he came home from the hospital. She drew lots of pictures of Henry. They hung in various places throughout the house. A few made it to the back of the cash register at the store along with some photographs.

Corey was pleased at how helpful Harry was in dealing with the baby and spending more time with Dayna to allow Corey to either take care of Henry or rest.

Harry as always, was pleased to watch the way Corey interacted with the children. Remembering the inner voice prompting him to propose, he remained in awe of her patience and stamina.

Henry seemed like an active baby until he was about two-and-a-half years old. Then Corey started noticing he seemed to bruise easily. At first, she thought maybe he just bumped into things more than she remembered Dayna doing. But then she saw bruises which had no cause that she could recall. He was quite pale and she noticed he was becoming less active.

One day, when he fell and cut himself, she thought he bled more than she expected from such a minor wound. Talking with Harry, they decided they should talk to the children's pediatrician. Since Dayna had an appointment coming up, they decided to both go and talk to the doctor about Henry as well.

The frown on the doctor's face told them he didn't like what they reported and what he saw when he looked at Henry.

"I need to do some tests. I'm sorry Harry, you've got the unpleasant job of holding Henry still, while I draw some blood."

Having drawn the blood, he tried to hide his disappointment at how long it took for even the small stick he made to stop bleeding.

"I'll send the blood out to the lab right away and I don't want to talk about any of the possibilities until the test results get back in a few days."

When he called, Corey was home alone with Henry. Telling her he needed to do one more test, he suggested it would be best if they could have someone watch Dayna when they brought Henry in.

The next day, Harry closed the store early. Henry was asleep as they took him from his car seat and stayed asleep in Corey's arms in the doctor's private office.

"I need to do a bone marrow test."

Looking at them he sighed, "It's to see if maybe Henry has leukemia."

Then he sat back in his chair, to give the worried parents a chance to take in what he had just said.

It took a moment.

Corey leaned down and gave Henry a worried kiss on his head while a tear escaped from her eye.

Harry putting one hand on her back and the other lightly on Henry's shoulder asked haltingly, "How sure are you from the tests you've already done?"

"I'm sorry. We're quite sure. But we can't be positive without the bone marrow test."

"And if that confirms it?" Corey asked.

"Well, if it is leukemia, there are treatments—depending on the type of blood cells involved. But there is a chance that he will—"

"Die?" Corey whispered.

After a pause the answer came softly "Well, the treatments are getting better and we'll have to discuss treatment soon but—yes, Corey, there is that chance."

She looked down on Henry, asleep in her arms. He was starting to wake up. He stretched and rubbed his eyes.

Harry slid out of his chair and kneeling down next to her, hugged her, and then looked up.

"This is going to be tough on Dayna too."

Henry, awake now, was standing on Corey's lap. His little shirt was pulled up around his chest and before she could pull it back down, Harry, crying softly, kissed Henry's exposed back.

Standing up, the doctor said, "Let me give you a couple of minutes," leaving them alone in his office.

The break was as much for him as for them. He was overcome by the weight of what his science had found out about Henry's condition. He knew he couldn't promise the child wouldn't die.

His emotion was in large part due to the fact that he had a son who was three months older than Henry. He said a silent prayer that his son was healthy and home in his mother's arms free of the misfortune that had befallen Henry.

Regaining his composure, he returned to his private office, outlining the plan for the bone marrow extraction and the initiation of treatment if that test confirmed their fears. They agreed with his timetable.

Thanking the doctor, they took little Henry home.

That night, with the children asleep, Harry and Corey clung to each other and between the tears tried to figure out the best way to tell Dayna, knowing she would take her cues from how they acted when they told her.

They also wanted to try to anticipate how to minimize the impact Henry's illness would have on her life. This was a major crisis for the whole family, but they wanted to spare Dayna as much of the upheaval as possible.

They were aware it would not be easy.

Soon the family was living lives that revolved around Henry's visits to doctors and hospitals for tests, checkups or treatment. On one visit, while Corey was in the hospital's treatment room with Henry, Harry sat in the waiting room with Dayna. She was supposed to be doing the little fourth grade homework she brought with her, but instead she was fascinated by the pictures in a magazine. It was a clothing ad with four women wearing different outfits at a scenic point overlooking a waterfall.

Taking the magazine over to him, Dayna said, "Look how pretty this girl is. She's wearing a sweater like the color of the one that grandma sent me. Isn't she the one who talks about the shampoo on television?"

He put down his paper and looked as she pointed to the picture.

"Yes, she is quite pretty."

He started to resume reading, when she said, "I wonder who she is." He put down his paper to see if he could help. Sitting Dayna on his lap, they looked at the captions, with the names of the models and the designers of the outfit each wore.

"Here it is," he pointed, "Her name is Jodi Worren."

Dayna asked if she could keep the magazine. He sent her over to ask the receptionist.

Seeing the picture, the receptionist said "Sure, you can Dayna. It's an old copy."

Getting up from her desk, she picked up another magazine saying, "If you're interested in Jodi Worren, this magazine has her on the cover and a little story about her inside. It's last month's issue, so if it's OK with your dad, you can have this one too."

Harry, agreeing it was OK, was pleased Dayna thanked her. He watched as she sat down with the magazine on her lap looking to find the pictures that went with the cover story. His eyes started to fill with tears he didn't want her to see. He was both so terribly sad she had to go through the ordeal they were going through, and yet he was touched she found something to distract her. He watched as she intently pored over the pictures.

When Corey came out of the room with Henry, and they were all getting ready to leave, Dayna wanted to show her mom what she had found. Henry was fussy. Corey tried but couldn't devote much attention to Dayna. Dayna knew and didn't demand much. As Dayna thanked the receptionist again, the receptionist was embarrassed being thanked twice for something she saw as such a poor attempt to bring just a little happiness to a child in Dayna's situation.

The drain on the whole family was visible. As word of Henry's treatment spread through the small community, people came by and brought lunch or dinner. Friends offered to do the cleaning or take Dayna for a day or even a sleep over. The fire department started a fund to raise money to help pay some of the medical bills. Corey and Harry were deeply touched by the response of their neighbors.

As they had feared, over time, Henry's illness became even more of the driving force in their lives. Yet they fought hard to find ways to keep Dayna from becoming swallowed up by Henry's problems.

After he failed to achieve a remission as hoped, they decided to accept his doctor's suggestion that they all get some counseling.

Margaret Solomon was the therapist they chose. She was a gray-haired, kindly, grandmotherly woman in a nearby town.

She wanted to meet with them before she talked to their daughter. Then, after seeing Dayna, she mentioned some concern about Dayna being overweight. She wondered if the turmoil was keeping Dayna from getting enough exercise and if the pressure she was under was making food her only source of comfort. When she asked them what interests Dayna had outside of school, the only one they could tell her about was that, for some reason they could not explain, she had become a fan of Jodi Worren. She looked for the woman's pictures and read anything they could find published about her.

Over the next two years, Henry got sicker rather than better. Whatever the doctors tried did not achieve the result they hoped for.

One dark and freezing, windy winter afternoon—at closing time—Harry set out to join Corey and Dayna at the hospital visiting Henry. Driving along, a small boy ran in front of the car. Harry barely avoided hitting him. It was Jerry Pawl. Getting out, Harry heard Jerry screaming, "My brother Billy fell through the ice on the pond." Looking where the boy was pointing, Harry grabbed his flashlight and took off through the woods.

He saw a glove stuck on a branch overhanging a hole in the ice. Quickly surveying the scene for something solid, he found a six-foot section of a wrought iron fence lying partly covered by dead leaves. He dragged it to where it could support him as he plunged his arm into the icy hole. He could hardly feel his fingers. He reached around under the ice until he felt something he could grab onto and pull.

He pulled.

It was Billy Pawl's jacket.

Dragging the child on top of him, he rolled both of them off the section of fence onto solid ground.

Billy was not breathing. Not knowing how long Billy had been in the water, Harry remembered from his Coach's CPR class "cold kids" could be revived even if submerged for a long time.

No phone—no ambulance. He did what he remembered from his class. He thought ABC—Airway, Breathing, Circulation.

It worked.

Billy started to sputter and cough. Knowing the nearest phone was at the hospital, he got out of his fire department winter coat, wrapped it around Billy and took off for the car. He could barely get his cold hands to work as he clicked the seat belt around Billy, and yelled to Jerry to buckle up in the back seat.

They barged into the emergency room. Harry carried Billy in the coat with Jerry hanging onto a dangling sleeve.

Staff came and whisked Billy away. The doctor asked Harry how long Billy had been in the water. He quickly told him all he knew and what he had done.

Harry sat with Jerry for a while until someone saw them and started paying attention. First, they took Jerry to be warmed and looked after. Then, someone came and brought a shivering Harry a blanket and helped him out of his wet shoes and clothing.

Putting on the dry scrubs, Harry asked, "Please, someone go up to the pediatric ward and tell my family I'm here."

As he wrapped himself in the warm blanket, looking at the emergency room door brought to mind arriving and being told that Corey's dad had died.

Upstairs, the volunteer aide found Corey sitting next to Henry's bed as he slept. The aide whispered, "Your husband's downstairs in the emergency room."

Seeing her face, he quickly added, "Oh. He's OK, but really cold. Damn if he didn't just save Billy Pawl's life!"

Corey looked at Henry and then told the nurse she and Dayna were going down. Finding Harry wrapped in the blanket, still shivering, Dayna asked him what the man meant about saving Billy Pawl's life. It was then he remembered Billy and Dayna were classmates. Harry asked how Henry was before he told them about nearly hitting Jerry on the road and somehow finding Billy under the ice.

The doctor came over with another warm blanket and sat next to him.

"How long ago did you take a CPR class?"

Harry thought for a moment, "It must be more than fifteen years now," he said trying to narrow it down in his mind.

Getting up, the doctor patted Harry on the leg, "Well, I'm here to tell you this kid is alive because of you and that class. Once he stopped breathing and his heart stopped beating, this kid was clinically dead. He's gonna be fine now, but if it wasn't for you this kid would have stayed very dead."

Just then, Bill Sr. and his wife Donna rushed into the emergency area. Harry didn't know the boys' parents other than by sight. Walking swiftly past him, they were led to Billy and Jerry. Harry and Corey looked at each other.

They could fully appreciate the concerns the parents were having about their son.

Three days later, four-year-old Henry William Daweson lost his battle for life.

In the village of Smalsville the fact that Harry had brought a child back to life followed by the loss of his own child was viewed with awe and sadness. Those who wanted to glad-hand Harry—slap him on the back for his heroism—wanted to respect the family's grief and found it awkward to approach him.

The day after Henry's death, the Smalsville Fire Department had its regular monthly meeting. Harry stayed home.

One of the members asked about admitting Henry as an Honorary Member. Never having honorary members before, some voiced concerns about setting a bad precedent. The discussion ended when Mark Torey stood up and said, "It's a good idea. I move that we admit him. I think it's proper for our department to honor the struggle for life made by the grandson of our three-term Chief and son of our absent member who's a Smalsville hero."

From across the room Tony stood up. "I agree and second that motion."

For the following week the Smalsville Firehouse was draped in purple and black bunting to honor the passing of its newest member.

In their grief, Harry and Corey dealt with the funeral arrangements, and were united in their concern for Dayna. During Henry's short life, they tried to make sure Dayna knew that the attention paid to him didn't diminish their love for her.

But despite their best efforts, Henry's illness had in fact colored and encroached upon her young life. While she had only a limited memory of her grandfather and slight understanding of the miscarriage, she was old enough to know she would never see her brother again, and yet young enough to believe he was in a better place.

As the parent's hoped, Margaret Solomon was able to help them all in their grief. They were grateful Dayna was comforted by Margaret's analogy to the life of a dragonfly.

They were all sitting together as she told her, "There are many differing views on what happens after death. I think of it like the life of the dragonfly."

She paused then explained, "Dragonflies start life underwater. There comes a time when they grow wings and leave the water to live in the open air. Once they leave the water they cannot go back. They enjoy a wonderful life flitting around in the sunlight. The young, still underwater, wonder what happened to them. But, those with wings cannot return to tell the young what their life will be like on the other side.

"That is very much like our life and death. We cannot know what it's like on the other side because no one can come back to tell us. The death side of life is a world the living cannot know.

"We can hope there is light and peace—and we can hope there is no pain."

The service was simple. Of the many villagers and townspeople who attended, the two people who Harry and Corey knew the least, Bill and Donna Pawl, seemed the most upset.

No doubt they were haunted by knowing, if Harry hadn't been on his way to see his dying son, it could be their son being buried.

Harry, in tears, carried Henry's small coffin down the steps of the church to the grave. Corey and Dayna walked tearfully alongside. Harry kneeled and placed Henry's coffin on the straps suspended between the brass poles at the corners of the grave.

After the mourners left, Henry was lowered into his grave next to his grandfather Bill.

Later, a small plaque was placed on the grave:

Henry William Daweson
Age Four
Please Step Softly
Here Sleeps Our Dream

TWENTY-THREE

Sharin Mersor came to her legendary career as an actress on a unique path. She was the only child of Winston and Marleta Mersor. Her father, a former governor and vice-presidential candidate, had been the United States Ambassador to Spain.

After having served as ambassador for several years, he married a cousin of the Spanish king. Sharin grew up with the beauty and bearing of a princess, but she was not opposed to shelving that image and getting her hands dirty.

Wanting to be more than a débutante, as war approached, she trained as a nurse. When war was declared, she joined up and went overseas. She got bloody.

Most of the blood belonged to the men she was helping. But she shed some of her own when a piece of shrapnel ripped through the field hospital tent she was working in and the uniform she was wearing. It tore through her side and killed the man she was treating.

After the war, she turned to acting. As her fame as an actress and philanthropist grew, this aging icon continued to garner awards, and she became the "Grand Dame" of Hollywood. She was an elegant hostess who was a prized member of the gala-and-benefits committees of nearly every major charity in Los Angeles and New York.

Sharin had seen Jodi on the covers of several magazines, in commercials on television, and then on a couple of late-night talk shows. She would hold one of the magazine covers up next to a tastefully framed picture of herself in uniform as she lobbied to have Jodi, who she had never met, play the part of "young nurse Sharin" in the autobiographical film she was trying to get green-lighted at one of the major studios.

Knowing Jodi had a small part in a low budget film, Sharin had her agent get her a private screening of the film. She was surprised and disappointed to see Jodi had been totally cut out of the final version. She asked the producer to show her the outtakes, and when he obliged, she thought they showed that Jodi was very promising.

Jodi, as was typical of her, was nervous coming to meet Sharin for lunch at a restaurant in Los Angeles. She arrived a few minutes early and was shown to the reserved booth. By this time, she had read about Sharin having two Oscars, one Emmy, and four Tony awards, including a Lifetime Achievement Award on her mantle. On the opposite wall of her Hollywood Hills castle-like home, she had a Master's Degree from Yale's School of Drama, surrounded by an abundance of Certificates of Nomination for various awards.

People who were with Sharin knew they were in the presence of greatness. Even though the 79-year-old actress had not starred in a movie or play in several years, most of the patrons stood up and applauded Sharin as the maître d' escorted her to the booth. When Jodi realized what was happening, she stood up too, but before she could decide whether she should join in the applause, Sharin grabbed her hand to shake it and, with her left hand on Jodi's shoulder, gently eased her back down to her seat.

Sharin tried to make Jodi feel at ease and to make a connection with her by mentioning that years ago she had met Pops and Bea at a charity auction. Also, she and Bea had once spent a couple of days together in Vienna, where they'd met by chance when they were stranded by an airline strike.

Jodi noted in her what Pops would describe as a "sense of entitlement" that came—not only from her vast success—but from her beauty and her background. She admitted that she had taken on acting as a form of rebellion against a mother who would prefer that her daughter be a débutante rather than a creature of the stage or screen.

Sharin saw in Jodi a young woman who was strikingly more beautiful in person than any photographs or the movie out-takes she had seen. She was aware that Jodi had a meteoric career as a model and, from what Sharin knew about Pops, was sure she must be financially secure. She wouldn't need acting to earn a living.

In their conversation Sharin learned that while Jodi was curious about acting, the movie she had been in heightened her concern about her lack of training and acting experience. She still wasn't sure she wanted to challenge herself by taking on a new career.

It was clear to both of them that Sharin was the one who wanted something. She was courting Jodi with the talk about Pops and Bea and, at the same time, trying to intrigue her with a description of the freedom, often rapture, of inhabiting the life of others, becoming anyone you want to become.

She explained that the movie was going to be biographical and contain scenes from movies and plays in which she had starred and won acclaim. There would be a remake of the scene from the movie *The Epic Journey* and also the demanding scene from *A Teacher's Tale* for which she won her second Oscar for playing an abused teacher.

"If you say 'Yes', which I hope you will, I'll be there to help you with anything you need. And you don't have to worry about the more challenging scene in Teacher's, because I want the shooting to be in sequence and that scene's going to be played by Dame Gwyneth Spensor, the British stage actress who will be playing me in my—shall we say—less-young years."

As the two of them were talking, the waiter interrupted to present them with a very rare and expensive bottle of wine. The waiter motioned to a gentleman at another table who had sent it for them. They smiled at their would-be beverage benefactor, looked at each other, and politely refused the gesture. They both knew from experience the expensive gift was an opening gambit from a man who would follow up with an attempt to join them at their table. Neither felt like they wanted to entertain anyone but each other at the moment. As the waiter was consolingly explaining to the gentleman that his gift had been refused, Sharin continued to outline her project.

Jodi was intrigued. By the time lunch was over, anybody would have thought they were, if not mother and daughter, at least the closest of friends.

After their lunch, Sharin's campaign to get the movie green-lighted and to have Jodi cast in the part intensified and met very little resistance.

Over the next three years, Sharin worked on getting the script polished up to her liking and waited for the director she wanted to finish one project so he could start this one. All the while Jodi worked steadily as Sharin's plans progressed.

Sharin continued to insist that the movie be shot in sequence. This was not typical, and was more costly, but once she had raised the money and lined up the people, it was a battle the studio, the producers, and director finally agreed to let her win. Jodi's part as the young Sharin covered her time as a débutante—turned nursing student who was flirting with acting—and then the rather unglamorous war years. Her part of the shooting would end with her playing Sharin as the Oscar winning young actress, in a re-enactment of the famous "watch scene" from Journey, Sharin's first movie.

After production of the movie finally started, there were delays related to weather at some of the locations but Jodi handled all these situations with such poise that Sharin was sure her selection of Jodi was a triumph. She made no secret of her growing admiration for Jodi's performance.

As Jodi's part of the project was coming to an end, Gwyneth Spensor, cast to play the "older years," made the miscalculation of deciding—at the last minute—to hold out for some script changes, and a bigger part.

Sharin thought the belated demands might be evidence of a newly-found reluctance to do the part because of a possible comparison with Jodi whose reputation as a rising new star was spreading as the filming progressed.

Sharin wondered if Spensor was also having second thoughts about the inevitable comparison with Sharin's own performance in Teacher's. After all, she thought, Dame Spensor has a reputation to protect and she's seasoned enough to be afraid of the Teacher's role.

Jodi could play her scenes which no such worries.

Faced with this new development, Sharin insisted, in her force-of-nature way, that Jodi was able to handle the older-years part as well.

Jodi was not as sure.

"Sharin, I really have no grasp of what I was doing in the scenes we've already done. People are telling me it's going well. I hear that, but to me it seems like I am just going through the motions. I'm saying the words and looking like I am happy or sad or scared depending on what I'm told you were feeling at the time, but I don't really feel any of it."

"Jodi, all you can do as an actress is to give every part all you've got."

"But Sharin, I don't know what I've got to give. This is more than me just sitting on a beach and pretending it isn't freezing. I'm supposed to be a different person who's motivated to do things for a reason."

"Jodi, I don't know what to say. You played the scene, caring for the soldier who gave you the watch as he's dying, and you appeared stricken with grief.

"Sitting behind the director, I was so moved, I cried with you—watching as you closed his eyes. If you're telling me that you just go inside yourself and can bring that out without any effort or actual emotion or understanding, all I can tell you is—that's a wonderful gift. It works. Just keep doing it. The crew are all seasoned professionals, some have been with me for years. When they cry with you and applaud you—it's for real. Believe me. It's for real."

"But I cried because when you played that scene you cried. For me, I was thinking of my brother who was a Marine and died when I was young. I thought of what it would've been like if his eyes were being closed. I remembered how I cried when my aunt told me we couldn't afford to travel to his funeral."

"Jodi, I am sorry you had that loss. But using the memory of that—that's acting."

"But it feels like I was cheating. I wish I could feel it as the character is supposed to feel. It doesn't feel like it can be any good unless I can do that. And playing you older—I just don't know."

"Jodi, I always had to do a lot of research to inhabit the character. It took a lot of work for me to become that person—for me to feel like I was getting what I needed to meet the challenge of getting it right. If it comes that naturally for you—to tap into those feelings, you should just go with it. It's called sense memory and it's exactly what they teach you to do in acting school. It's great. You'll be fine."

Jodi sighed "It doesn't feel fine. But I can trust your judgment. I trust that you think I can do this. I made a commitment to you and I don't want to disappoint you or Pops."

Sharin asked, "Will you let me do a test?"

When Jodi agreed, Sharin scheduled the three hours that were needed to have her made up to look like the old Navajo woman she wanted her to play in one of the later scenes. All she told the studio was that she made a screen test of someone she might want to cast for the part.

She showed the director and the studio executives the scene.

One of them commented, "Wow! She's really good. Who is it? You've given up on your idea of using Jodi?"

Sharin, smiled her victory smile, "I never give up. That is Jodi! Like all the great ones—you see the character, not the player."

After the screen test, what little skepticism the studio had was gone. Jodi was Sharin Mersor.

As production progressed, the word spreading—that a new star was beginning to shine in Hollywood—was likened to the phenomena that took place while James Dean was making his first movie, *East of Eden.*

Some others thought Sharin was behind every rumor.

Sharin was very generous with her praise and it was obvious to some she thought Jodi winning an Oscar would be the same as her winning her third. When asked about the movie she said things like: "I'm embarrassed to see how well she played the parts I won my Oscars for because she was so much better."

And, she admitted to a talk show host, "I wanted Jodi at first because I thought she looked like I did when I was her age. When we met, I realized there's no comparison. Even without makeup she looks like a more beautiful, fuller bodied version of Grace Kelly with Elizabeth Taylor's deep-purplish-blue eyes."

One of the actors who had early scenes with Jodi was Richard Princeton, Jr. His father had been an actor who was teamed with Sharin in several movies. The son had been an All-American soccer player. His rugged good looks and growing up in the business had gotten him into acting. Early on, because of tagging along with his father—who at that time was playing the part of Richard II—someone started calling the son Prince Richard.

The nickname stuck. Recently, he had done poorly in a series of bad movies and it was thought this movie was his last chance to continue working in anything meaningful. Sharin thought he was a pain-in-the-ass as a child when his father brought him on the set, and she was unsure of him as an actor. But, because of his remarkable resemblance to his deceased father, and her hope to help resurrect the career of the son of the man she respected, he was her natural choice to play the parts his father had played.

Around Hollywood, rumors spread of marital difficulties between Prince Richard and his opera-singer wife. Neither Sharin nor Jodi was close enough to him to know if the rumors were true. He took no one into his confidence. Still, there were times he arrived late and obviously upset.

During shooting, Sharin introduced Jodi to Edgar Wingate. He was 6'1" tall, tan and distinguished looking, with graying hair and light gray eyes. He owned a privately-held conglomerate, Wingate International. That holding company either wholly owned, or had controlling interests or large—but undisclosed—percentages in more than two hundred and sixty large companies. The companies were in such diverse areas as electronics, electric power plants, oil drilling and refining, major construction of buildings, and shopping centers. He also owned the Winamart mega markets. The Winamarts were spread out across the country selling everything from the company's brand of electronic equipment to food, hardware, snacks, tires, and toilet paper.

He was also one of the people Sharin turned to for financial help with the movie. Wingate had been a major contributor to some of her favorite charities, and she was encouraging him to spend more time, and more of his money, on philanthropic work.

When he came to the film set, it was obvious that he wanted to meet Jodi. Sharin was more than happy to oblige.

Jodi was cautious about men. She knew she had made a bad mistake in choosing Peter, or, as she later realized, responding to him when he chose her. Moving past the time with Peter, she kept pretty much to herself. And as her modeling career accelerated, she threw herself into her work so much that she had neither the time nor the energy for much of a social life. She associated more with other models and the hair dressers or makeup artists who were more than likely gay. As time went on, when she did accept an invitation to go out, the men, unlike Peter, were usually at least ten years older than her and it usually was only once or twice. But Sharin had been too generous to her for Jodi to refuse when she asked her to meet Wingate.

He was obviously very taken with Jodi.

After the introduction, Wingate stayed around the set for a while, but then some business matters called him away.

After his reluctant departure, it took less than a minute before Sharin asked, "Well, what do you think?"

"What do I think of Mr. Winamart?" Jodi mused, then put her hand to her lips, embarrassed for having let the secret name she created for him slip out.

Sharin just chuckled, "Yes silly, Mr. Winamart? But you don't want to call him that to his face. Why do you think he showed up on the set? He tried not to let me see it, but he wasn't here to check on his investment or to see me. I had told him I wanted him to get more involved in social things. I think you could be good for each other."

And without waiting for a response continued, "OK, here's the scoop. He's 59, divorced for ten or so years, and has a 17-year-old son who lives somewhere up north with the ex. He has a gorgeous big house on the ocean in Malibu, but his main office is in New York. I hear he just bought a huge place overlooking Central Park. I lose track, he's either the fourth or sixth richest man in the country. But I only know him from charity boards and committees where people are always on their best behavior because they're all there to look good."

While Sharin listed some of his financial assets, Jodi drifted off for a second, wondering about his interest in her. She was suddenly brought back to the conversation by Sharin saying: "And, if you're not busy Saturday night, I'd like to have the two of you come for dinner."

They both knew the answer could not be "No."

Sharin saw this as a win-win situation. She liked Jodi and she liked what little she knew of Edgar, so she didn't feel like she was pimping Jodi to him for his contributions. She felt Jodi could do a lot worse in terms of future security and connection—no matter how much she already had.

Before the week was over, Edgar called while Jodi was doing some exercises before going to bed. "Can I pick you up on the way to the dinner at Sharin's? When I mentioned it to her, she gave me your number."

She felt at ease with him calling and they spoke for several minutes. He tried to impress her by showing her how thoughtful he was when he said, "I know enough about the business to know that you have to get up early to go to makeup so I don't want to keep you on the phone."

When she finished her exercises and was in the shower, she started to think of him. He seemed pleasant enough. She had noted that he was tall enough for her to wear high heels.

Before bed, she spoke to Pops and reported, "I'm going to a dinner at Sharin's, which she arranged for me and Mr. Winamart. He just called and asked if he could give me a lift. He said Sharin gave him my number. By the way, Sharin again mentioned that she spent some time with Bea in Vienna."

"Yes, she reminded me about it when she first called about this movie. Bea thought she was nice—but between you and me—Bea thought the man Sharin was with was an overbearing bore. That was a long while ago though. Wait a minute, you called the other guest 'Mr. Winamart.' Is this gentleman really Edgar Wingate, the man who owns Winamart?"

She laughed, "Yes, do you know him?"

"No, but I know of the family. His father was a self-made billionaire. He really came up from nothing. He was a bit of a bully from what I heard. But I do not know what kind of a father he was, except I heard that the son once said he moved to Malibu to be as far away from his father in Manhattan as he could get.

"When he died, his son took control of a vast array of the major companies and had really big shoes to try to fill. I imagine it can be difficult for a man who is just handed vast wealth to be seen as making his way through the world on his own achievements."

Even though it was out of his way, Edgar was prompt when he came to pick her up. She was pleased the dinner was very casual. She felt relaxed with Sharin and Edgar.

As the evening wore on, it became more apparent that he was smitten with Jodi. When he excused himself and left the room to make a call, Sharin pointed out the obvious, "I think he's really taken with you."

Jodi just shrugged and said "We'll see."

In the back of her mind she thought, I wonder where I'd find Gort if I needed him.

Sharin—noticing the sly smile crossing Jodi's face as she told herself her secret joke—asked, "What?" But just then Edgar walked back in.

He apologized, "It looks like I have to fly to Paris tomorrow and I'm sorry but I'm going to have to cut this evening short."

Jodi said, "I'd like to stay with Sharin a little longer. I'll get a cab and take myself home."

He was clearly disappointed.

Sharin was impressed.

When he left, she asked, "Was that what I think it was? You not wanting to have to deal with the 'good-night-kiss-at-the-front-door scene'?"

Jodi shrugged, "I'm honestly not sure I want a man in my life that way right now. Like that bumper sticker I saw on the freeway yesterday, 'A woman needs a man like a fish needs a bicycle.'"

They both laughed.

Sharin shook her head, "I could see if a woman my age said that, but when I came back from the war, I felt like I always needed a man and was a little wild about the way I got some of them.

"A man in your life can be a great cure for loneliness. Even if you're not looking for sex or don't have the time or energy to work on a serious relationship. Even now, when love and sex are more like a fond memory, I don't like being alone."

They moved from the dining table to the living room couch as Sharin continued.

"During the war there were all these guys. Many were away from wives or girlfriends for the first time and there weren't many women. Some girls took advantage of the situation and made a fortune. Some just went out with the guys for their own pleasure and to take care of the men's needs. No matter, if they were caught violating the no-fraternizing policy they got shipped home. It was sad because some of them were great workers and we really needed the help."

Jodi listened and thought of the chaos of Sharin's war.

"As a nurse I couldn't see socializing with the men. They all seemed to look alike—to have the same young face. And each time a guy made an approach to me, for some reason, all I saw was the mangled corpse I feared he'd become. I felt my gut tighten like a big hand was inside me squeezing my heart. So, I built this wall around myself. I hid behind it. I just didn't see them as men."

Still thinking back there in time, she slowly brightened, "After I got home, everything just flipped."

Jodi waited for what followed.

"I was 33 when I got back home and all I could see was men. After all the blood and gore, I couldn't go back to nursing. I was burned out. I would have gone mad if one more person depended on me to care for them. I dedicated myself to the pursuit of men.

"I started tearing down my wall—one guy at a time. If I needed a little extra courage, I found that a gin-and-tonic or two made the perfect fuel for my rapid wall-removal projects.

"When I decided I could escape into acting—I'd just dabbled in it before the war—I was accepted at Yale's School of Drama. Finishing up there, I got cast as Janeen, the nurse, in Journey. The rest of the story you know.

"What you don't know—" she looked Jodi in the eye, "—all the while, I thought all this double standard—this 'good girl' or 'bad girl'"—stuff was a load of bullshit. My definition of a nymphomaniac?"

She paused, and smiled at Jodi as she answered her own question. "That's what society calls a girl who likes sex as much as a man."

Jodi nodded.

Sharin laughed, "Luckily for me, in my runnin'-around days, I had the studio public relations people to keep my sex drive out of the papers. But now I think a lot of that is changing. Last year I went back to Yale for a reunion. Some of the students were our hostess-guides.

"Sitting down for lunch I overheard our two guides talking about 'friends with benefits.' I asked, 'Is that what I think it is?' One of them smiled, 'Why should you have to be in love, or pretend to be in love? Who has time for all that? It's just sex.' The other one laughed, 'Hester Prynne got pregnant by the Reverend Dimmesdale and they gave her a scarlet letter A. Today she'd only get a C plus.'"

Sharin chuckled, "They're right! It is just sex. They say that for any man the sanest time in his whole life is when he is lying with a woman after he's had an orgasm. In my younger days I found that if I had a lot of tension—like from having to make big decisions—I always felt I could put it on hold and go out and seek that same kind of sexual release.

"For me, I always found cuddling in a man's arms after good sex was a time of calm and confidence. It provided a kind of quiet clarity. I still don't fully understand why it worked that way for me, but why shouldn't we be allowed to have it?"

She looked at Jodi, who was weighing the question, and continued, "Still, no matter how things have changed, in our fishbowl world—with all these paparazzi—it would be hard to keep anything like my past adventures out of the papers these days."

Jodi nodded, "I have Pops. I'd never want to do anything that would make him feel disappointed or be ashamed of me. Besides, I've never found the type of completion and serenity you have. Maybe I haven't found the right man."

Cautiously Sharin asked, "Do you think you'd find it with another woman?"

Jodi, sensing the unease with which the question was asked, was not offended as Sharin feared.

She knew Sharin was honestly trying to be helpful and was pleased she cared enough to risk asking.

"No. It's not that. It's just that after spending time with lots of models and gay men, hearing them brag about their sexploits, conquests, and raging desires, I realized I must not have much of a sex drive. I think with me it's more like I have a sex 'coast,'—like I'm in 'neutral."

She continued the analogy, "I mean—I am not in 'park'— I'm not afraid of sex, I can enjoy that I please a man. I just don't feel all that motivated to seek sex if it's not fulfilling."

Sharin was concerned that her friend mainly saw gratification in terms of pleasing the man, but thought there might be a time for them to talk about female fulfillment.

For now, she decided it would be enough to ask, "What about having children?"

Jodi sighed, "I don't know. I was a child. It wasn't all that great."

Getting up from the couch, Sharin nodded, "Well, with Edgar, I think you two would be good for each other. One thing's for certain, whatever else he may be interested in, you can be sure that he's not after you for your money. But I think I've done my matchmaker part—at least for the night."

As the movie progressed, despite her fear of failure, Jodi started to feel more comfortable with her work on the film. Her concerns about her ability and her fears never disappearing completely, but she didn't let them keep her from using her feelings and intuition to act and react in the scenes in ways everyone who saw the work said was first rate.

Everyone, that is, except Prince Richard.

Even though he said almost nothing to her while they were working together, it seemed clear that he saw her as an outsider in his world. Because of the shooting schedule, their scenes together were over by the time she heard a rumor. When asked about the word going around Hollywood that a new star was emerging, it was reported that he thought her work was "beginners' luck." And added, "It's too bad our Academy doesn't give an award for rookie of the year. She might have a shot at that."

She wouldn't bring herself to try to find him to ask if he had really made those remarks.

Pops called the night after the shooting of the Teacher's scene. She had spoken to him the night before the scene and now he was checking back.

"Jodi, you told me when you played the scene from Epic Journey, you brought up the memory of your brother."

He paused, "Did the abused teacher scene dredge up bad memories for you—are you OK?

The Do you want to talk about it?"

She sighed, "No, Pops, getting ready for the scene I went back in my head and thought about what that night with Peter felt like. But I got though the scene. The crew stood and applauded when the director yelled 'cut.'

"I was not going to talk to anybody about my personal experience. But, playing this scene did help. Before, I had thought that I was over it, but now, I know that I really am over it. Now I can think about that night and not feel like I'm reliving it."

She whispered into the phone, "Pops, I love that you asked. I truly love that you're always there for me."

"Being there for you, as you call it, is my pleasure, my sweet Jodi. Lord willing it might be for a little while longer."

He paused, "Jodi, people know that principal photography on the movie will end in a week or so. They are talking to me about your acting talent and they want to talk about more movie business."

"Pops, I don't know if the talk of my talent is based on what I am actually doing or Sharin's bullying people to say that. I can't tell if any of that feedback is real or if it's just the Sharin effect."

"Well, I am also hearing Prince Richard had done his best work on this movie. I have been approached about a possible deal to cast you and him in a remake of *The Epic Journey.*

"You would again play Sharin's Oscar part, and he would still play the part his father had been nominated for opposite her.

"Of course, I will find out more about it, but we might be inclined to say 'Yes.'

"What do you think?"

From the long pause, he could sense there was reluctance—that something about the idea made her uncomfortable.

"OK, I hear it—what is going on?"

"Sharin mentioned that project to me. But, whenever I was around him, he seemed to have this attitude that he was raised in the movie business and I was this outsider who got in on a pass.

"I could see he really was upset with me when I missed my mark in a scene—they were shooting me from over his shoulder— it was a long scene and we had to do it again. Then I heard he's made some comments about beginners' luck. I'm fearful enough I may be discovered to be a fraud at any minute, without going into another project. I don't want to worry that if I think I got something right, it'll still never be good enough because I am just the newcomer who gets all this hype from Sharin."

"From what I am hearing about your performance—from a lot of people—you are doing great work. Sharin is not the only one telling me you have a great future in the business. I wonder if what you were sensing from him was his feeling of discomfort about how good you are. Envy is a very potent poison. The fact you seem to have a natural talent has got to be threatening to someone with a legacy who has been hacking his way through the business for as long as he has."

He paused, then added, "But, I am also hearing rumors about some marital problems he has been having, so whatever was going on with him may not have anything to do with you at all. But if you are not comfortable —"

She sighed, "I know. You're right. It's Epictetus and the old life-living-lessons again. It's not up to someone else to give me peace of mind.

"Thanks for the refresher course," she laughed, "I'll try to remember it. Let's just wait for a while and we can get back to it after this one is actually finished."

"Good girl! There is no decision you have to make right now. We can take it slow and see how you feel about it when the time comes. By the way, I am getting calls. Should I start to book some modeling work for you? Or would you want to take some time off?"

"No. After almost a year with this movie, it'll be good to get back to something where I feel I know what I am doing. The studio wants me to do appearances to promote the movie, so we'll need to coordinate with them, but there's been so many delays and so much sitting around waiting for the weather to clear that I feel I've already had my time off. Book the work."

TWENTY-FOUR

At the end of that last day of shooting, they had the wrap party at the producer's house. There was a smaller after-party at Sharin's home. Edgar got himself invited to the smaller party but he didn't see Jodi there.

He had pulled into Sharin's driveway just after Jodi left.

She hadn't stayed long.

As soon as Jodi arrived, Sharin took her into the den where they could be alone. Jodi could see from the time Sharin had left the producer's party, to get ready for her own, something had happened to upset her. She sat Jodi down on the sofa—sat facing her—and took both of her hands.

Jodi, getting nervous, could see Sharin trying to find the right words.

"Jodi, I'm so sorry to have to tell you. Pops Magenwise died."

Jodi sat there for a moment and then silently folded into Sharin's arms.

Both women quietly held each other and cried.

Jodi sobbed for a man she truly cared for, a man who had taken a chance on her, preparing her for the life she now had.

Sharin cried because she truly cared about her protégé and knew how deeply wounded she was by the news. The two women could hear the party going on outside the door. But it was not a party they could join.

Sharin finally said, "Jodi, please stay here with me tonight. I don't want to think of you spending the night in your hotel alone."

"No. Thank you Sharin, but I really want to be alone. Pops' Jewish religion will require him to be buried the next day and I want to make plans for getting back to New York for the funeral."

"Can I help or have my people make your travel arrangements?"

Jodi stood up and hugged her,

"No. Thank you, this is something I want to do for myself."

Jodi had a limo take her back to her hotel.

When she arrived, there was a message to call Sharin. She called.

"Edgar arrived right after you left. When I told him why you left, he insisted he be allowed to take us both to New York tomorrow in his corporate jet. He's stopping in New York on his way to a meeting in Madrid."

"I don't want any man in my life who insists on anything about me."

"Oh, Jodi, I'm so sorry. Let me back up here a second. I know this is a terrible time for you, and maybe my use of the word 'insisted' was too heavy a way of saying the man really does want to be helpful to you.

"I wish you would reconsider. With the three-hour time difference a private jet does make the most sense."

Jodi thought about the offer.

"Did I hear you say 'take us both to New York?'"

"Yes. If you don't mind, I'd like to attend Pops' funeral with you."

Jodi sighed, "Perhaps that would be best after all."

Jodi couldn't get much sleep that night. Her visions of Pops played over and over. She started to relive the funeral of her mother. She wondered how this one would be different. Now she was weeping for her mother and brother too. Her sleepless mind drifted to a passage from Epictetus. She remembered his words about knowing the nature of things—and, it being in the nature of man to die, not being disturbed when death strikes.

It didn't help.

The next morning, Jodi thanked Sharin and Edgar for their thoughtful generosity as they picked her up and headed for the airport. Boarding his plane, she fought back tears as she took a seat next to Sharin.

After seeing them seated, Edgar excused himself and went into the cockpit. Jodi was surprised to hear that he would be flying the plane. Before the copilot closed the cockpit door, Edgar explained, "This is my greatest passion. Concentrating on things like keeping the wings level allows me to free my mind from the many distractions my businesses create. It's a time I feel I can think clearly. There's something majestic about being in control of a powerful machine that makes the Earth glide beneath its wings."

At the funeral, Jodi was comforted by the large turnout. She knew Pops had been in the business a long time and was well thought of, but the sight of all the people who took the time to come to the service was heartwarming.

Many people just nodded to Sharin as a way of saying they knew who she was but weren't going to encroach during such an occasion. Most of the people there were aware of Jodi's closeness with Pops and they also wanted to give her all the space she needed to deal with her sadness.

There was a big murmur in the crowd as people turned to look when a huge vintage Bentley limo pulled up and a chauffeur and two muscular aides got out. They set up a walker and helped multimillionaire Becher Gold, the owner of the Worldwide Perception Agency, steady himself in his walker.

WPA was, by far, the biggest and most prestigious creative talent and modeling agency in the world. His entire world knew Becher had not been well. Those present were surprised he could make the effort to attend this funeral, especially since, by the way he looked, it seemed it would be close to his own.

Becher was the older brother of Bea, and was Pops' lifelong friend as well as his brother-in-law. Pops, an only child, usually just referred to him as "my brother, Goldy." As he made this reference, he was always aware of the levity that could be inspired by their total lack of any resemblance and was prepared with a good-natured explanation if anyone asked if one of them was adopted.

As tall and beautiful as Bea was, Becher was a bit taller and very handsome. But unlike Bea, whose beauty was discovered relatively late, Becher grew up knowing he was good looking and always had a sense of self-assuredness.

Now, appearing as infirm as he did and feeling as poorly as he felt, this usually carefully-dressed man would normally not let himself be seen in public. Today he had to make an exception.

With great difficulty, and the help of the two large, athletic-looking aides, he made his way toward the graveside. The president of the congregation hurried to greet him, "It's good to see you. I am surprised and pleased that you had the energy to come."

Becher nodded slowly, "I would come here to honor my Pops Magenwise if I had to crawl."

Jodi, overheard that remark, and turned to watch Becher slowly making his way to her. Pops often talked about Becher, but she only met him once.

She remembered their one meeting fondly.

Early in her career, she and Pops had just come out of a business meeting and were starting to walk the ten blocks back to his office when they were struck by a sudden downpour. They were taking cover in a doorway when this same vintage Bentley, happening by, pulled up and Becher yelled, "Pops, come on, get in."

They made a dash for the car and once inside Pops introduced them. "Jodi Worren, this is Becher Gold, call him Goldy. He is my Bea's older brother.

"When I met her, I had already known him for most of my life. He and I attended the same grade school, high school, college and law school, all the while he was three grades ahead of me. But since I had not been to his house in quite some time and she was so much younger than him, it was not until she told me her last name and we played some Jewish geography, that I realized she was his sister."

Goldy laughed his high-pitched laugh, "We used to say I had to be the guinea pig and check out a school to make sure it was OK for my Pops to go there."

"It was Goldy who gave me the nickname, Pops."

Goldy laughed, "I was always full of all kinds of ideas and Pops made a great partner and sounding board. When we were in high school, I would have these ideas about promoting this or that, and he would tell me, from a very sound and sober adviser point of view, how to do it better.

"And I would always say, 'Well one of us has to think and act like a grownup, and I guess it must be you Pops.'"

Pops said, "The nickname just stuck. After I met my Bea, and we realized the connections, then even my Bea starting calling me Pops."

Jodi remembered the warmth and mirth of her ride in that big car with these two physically dissimilar lifelong and loving friends. It was a kind of friendship she wished she'd had growing up.

At the cemetery, when Goldy inched his walker next to her, he put an arm on her shoulder, mainly to comfort her, but also to steady himself.

"Miss Worren, I am so very sorry for your loss. Everybody knows how much you and Pops meant to each other. I had just spoken to him earlier in the week and he told me how very pleased he was you had just finished shooting your last scenes.

"He knew you had done very well, and the whole movie would wrap in a few days. Now, it looks like he waited, until he knew your part was finished, before he could die peacefully in his sleep. That was so much like him. Pops and my beloved sister not only believed in Tikkun Olam—which is the Jewish concept of healing the world—they acted on it. I think everybody, in their own way, tries to live a caring and helping life."

He sighed and choked up, "Pops and Bea—may they both rest in peace—they were just so much better at it."

She could only manage a whispered, "Thank you. I know how much you will miss him too. He talked so often and fondly about the three of you."

As Goldy turned to accept condolences from others, Gary and Jimmy came up to her with hugs. Gary was fighting back tears.

He told her, "Jimmy and I had an appointment to meet Pops at his apartment in the morning. When he didn't buzz us up, we got worried and called but. . .

"So, we had the super let us in and we found him in his bed."

Jimmy was crying. "There was nothing to be done for him.

"He looked just like he was asleep."

He shook his head. "No one will ever replace Pops, for any of us."

Gary paused to gather himself, "We're going to look after his apartment and the office to try to sort out what needs to go where. We'll keep you up to date on who is calling for bookings for you until you tell us who to forward that stuff to."

She closed her eyes and sighed, "I think Goldy would be the obvious choice for an agent except for his health—I don't know if I could go through —"

"Just take whatever time you need, Girlfriend, take whatever time you need."

"You guys are truly great. I know of some of the things coming up Pops booked and I will do those. And, then we'll see."

Gary said, "I think one in the Bahamas in a few months is one we are on too. We'll keep in touch, my girl. We will keep in touch."

Jodi wondered how many others who came to the funeral were living the life they wanted because Pops and Bea took the time and helped them get started or helped them along the way. Her mind recalled the pictures of Bea and she thought about Pops, the man who had meant so much to both of them.

During the service she was moved by the message from the woman rabbi when she said, "We know that a person who lives righteously never really dies. They live on in the lives they have touched. All of you know Sol, who—even when he was much too young for the name— everybody called Pops, was a real mensch. A man who truly had a good, kind, old soul. He used to quote the aphorism in which the philosopher Hillel asks us: 'If I am not for myself, who will be for me? But if I am only for myself, who am I? If not now, when?'

"He was for himself but he was always for others. And 'When' was now, and all the time. Pops used to talk about the happiness that everybody deserves. Today, those of us he helped to obtain that happiness know he will have his well-deserved eternal peace."

As Pops was being lowered slowly into the earth, seeing the words "Beloved Wife and Sister," on Bea's headstone next to the newly dug grave, brought some comfort to Jodi, as she thought of Pops and Bea finally resting together side by side.

Pops was dead. She already missed him, but he and Bea would be together for eternity.

Once the unadorned pine casket reached the end of its downward journey, the rabbi picked up the shovel—embedded with its handle up—midway to the top of a pile of earth. Turning the shovel face down, the rabbi used the back of the shovel to drop earth on top of the lowered casket.

She explained, "The task of burying the dead is a different use from the other uses of the shovel. The shovel being inverted for the first shovelful symbolizes that the task is to be done with difficulty, because it needs to be done, but it is not done out of any sense of joy for accomplishing a task."

Then she put the shovel back in the mound.

She explained, "You put the shovel back in the earth, rather than handing it to the next person, so you won't be passing your grief along to the next person as we perform the last act of kindness we can perform for Pops—burying him.

"This is a task of the highest order, it is the ultimate act of loving kindness, because we know he can never say thank you—it is as though we are tucking in a beloved, sleeping child."

Whatever solace Jodi took in thinking of Pops and Bea peacefully resting side by side did not survive.

As the first shovelfuls of earth thudded on the lid of the coffin, the mental image of Pops lying face up in this box vanquished all consolation and brought uncontrollable tears to her eyes.

When a weeping Jimmy placed the shovel back in the mound close to her, a deeply distraught Jodi, with tears pouring down her cheeks, had to summon all her resolve to enable her to pick up the shovel so she could take part in the ritual of helping to bury Pops.

As she put the shovel back for the next person, she envisioned her mother and her brother lying in their graves far from where she stood. She mourned that she had not helped to bury them as she had just done for Pops. She agonized over not even seeing her brother buried. She resolved she would go back and put some earth on their graves, now, and offer them each a silent apology for making them wait so long for her to take care of them.

Soon the earth no longer resounded on the top of the coffin.

Now the earth merely fell on the earth that had fallen before. As others took their turn, the grave was filled—and Pops was tucked in forever.

Then the rabbi led those who could join in the recitation of Kaddish, the traditional prayer for the memory of the dead.

Jodi, sobbing next to Becher, heard the tears in his halting voice as he recited the mourner's prayer in honor of Pops' memory.

Then they all turned to walk slowly away from the grave.

Jodi was crushed. She felt lost. She felt the center of her world had just been ripped away and nothing would ever make it full again. When it looked like Jodi's legs would not support her, Sharin enlisted Gary and Jimmy to help her get grief-stricken Jodi back to the car.

The next day, Sharin, even though she hated leaving Jodi, had to go back to the coast to start working with the editing and other post production issues on the movie. They needed to get the movie released by the next November to get favorable consideration for the Academy Awards. As it was, the post production process of dealing with the music and the special effects of the battle scene would be stretched out for nine months.

Jodi decided she would stay in New York. She needed to be back in her own apartment. She needed to feel she could return to Pops' unmarked grave whenever she wanted. She had learned that a headstone could be placed within the year but not during the first thirty days. She vowed to herself to take part in the placing of the headstone. She knew Pops lit a candle to honor the anniversary of his Bea's death. She vowed she would do the same for him.

Thinking of all her conversations with Pops, she regretted not changing the subject often enough, from the business of her life, to tell him how much he had meant to her. But, she sighed, knowing he would never hear of it.

She knew she had lost the only father she ever had. A father who took for granted that he owed everything he could ever do for his child. He neither expected nor wanted anything in return.

With Pops gone, Jodi tearfully decided she would honor just the bookings and the studio publicity obligation they had committed her to, and then she would take some time off after all.

TWENTY-FIVE

Returning from Spain, Edgar moved into his 20-room triplex overlooking Central Park. As the weeks went on, his calls became more frequent, but Jodi was not ready to go out and socialize. She talked with him about it and he would back off—for a while.

Knowing what the loss of Pops meant to Jodi, Sharin would call her in the evening to make sure she was OK. The timing of the calls reminded Jodi of her routine with Pops.

After a while, she began to make peace with the fact that the calls would never be from Pops again. She would never hear his voice except in her fond thoughts.

Jodi felt Sharin, in the guise of keeping her up to date on the post-production process, was trying to fill the void in her life left by Pops' death. But more and more Sharin expressed an almost motherly concern about how being with Edgar could provide security for Jodi's future, and at one point asked if she wanted Edgar to fly her to one of her modeling commitments.

Jodi thanked her and politely refused the offer.

"I can get myself to wherever I need to go. Thanks to Pops' taking care of my money, I don't think I need to worry about my financial future. I'm a bit more fond of Edgar than I was, but I don't know if I want it to be any more than that. At least not now."

Sharin knew that Jodi intended to honor the commitments Pops had booked. Jodi agreed that Mattie, one of

Sharin's assistants, could field and screen business calls for Jodi. It was not like every day was booked. It was a series of choice assignments that stretched out for several months. Usually, if she had wanted, Pops would fill the spaces in between this framework and the studio's promotional work. But she was satisfied that the modeling work that was locked in place was limited.

She confided to Sharin, "I have no question of whether I could do the work. Besides Pops used to say, 'Anybody can do what they like and do it well—the mark of a mature person is to do what they don't like and do it well.' I thought by going back to the familiar work it would ease me back and help me move on, but it hasn't.

"As I'm doing these jobs, the work and the people I'm working with, only remind me more of how much I miss him. I can't report back to him after finishing my assignments, and we can't talk about books or laugh about the long flights, or getting stuck in airports, or three weeks of rain in Anzio and what happened on the set. I'm reminded that he will forever not be there.

"At least when I was worried about my acting, I couldn't get too bogged down in being stressed because I had him and you, and I was occupied with trying to be you. Being you was kind of an escape from being me. Now, I have to be me, and I don't have him, and I don't have a way to escape from the feeling of loss."

She paused, wondering if she should say it, and then confided, "I hope you don't think I'm crazy—but, I couldn't remember something he said about one of the bookings and I actually picked up the phone to call him and then. . ."

"Oh. No. No. I don't think you're crazy at all. But that's it really. In acting the work gives you freedom to transcend yourself, to leave yourself behind, to be whatever you get lucky enough to be cast in. The work can take you away from yourself. The work can help if you're feeling a bit lost and lonely. Liz Taylor was working on *Cat on a Hot Tin Roof* when her husband, Mike Todd, died. She finished the film. And got nominated.

"You got to inhabit the nurse, Janeen, in Journey and some of the other characters I played during my career. That's the attraction I found in it all these years. Getting to be the nurse, the bar girl, the nun, the Indian, the school teacher. I think you recreated those roles wonderfully well.

"I really feel you should do the remake of Journey. Just the small part of it you played with Prince Richard was masterful—you should really take it on.

"I know you have some doubts, but you should know we all have them, and with time you could get comfortable with taking the risk to do the work. It might be the escape you need."

She listened and said softly, "Sharin, I know you care about me."

She paused. "Let's give it some time. We'll see. Let's just give it some more time."

When the movie opened for its Academy mandatory seven days in Los Angeles it was extremely well received. As good as the movie reviews were, reviews of Jodi's work were even better.

When the movie opened worldwide, with its setting of box office records, Sharin set off on a mission to make sure Jodi won the Oscar for the best actress in a leading role. Even though she had a room full of awards for film work, she felt the Oscar was the only award worth having. Focused on Jodi's winning it, Sharin was relentless.

Other studios launched campaigns for their movies and their stars, but Sharin was on a crusade.

A few days before the nominating ballots were sent out to the Academy members, Sharin called Jodi, who was on a modeling shoot for the opening of a casino-hotel in Las Vegas. She asked if Jodi could spare time to come for a visit in Los Angeles.

Pleased by the invitation, she told Sharin she could be there the next day. She was curious about the out-of-the-blue invitation but she figured maybe Sharin, knowing that she was close by, thought it would be fun to spend a little time together. She was happy Sharin reached out to invite her.

Meeting Jodi at the door herself, Sharin ushered her into the den.

"I'm so glad you could come on such short notice."

Jodi smiled, "No, I'm glad you called, I always like seeing you."

"Well, I have some news —"

Realizing the den was the same room where she told her about Pops' death, she stopped, then groaned, "Oh! This room. This room."

Jodi didn't know what the news was, but she knew it wasn't good.

"Tomorrow we're going to announce that I have pancreatic cancer."

Jodi gasped.

Sharin took her hand and led her to the couch. "I thought since you were nearby, I didn't want to tell you on the phone and I certainly didn't want you to find out in the media. We're too close, now, for that."

Sitting quietly, she let the information sink in.

"Are you in any pain?"

Sharin leaned over and hugged her. "No. Thank you for asking. I haven't told many people but, other than my doctors, you're the only one to ask.

"Most people just want to know how long I have. My doctor said there won't be much pain. But, the answer to your unasked question is—I don't have very long."

"Isn't there anything they can do?"

"Oh. They can keep me comfortable as it gets closer. I can even stay here in my own home, which I want very much. There's nothing to go to a hospital for. Sometimes there's a chance with an operation."

She chuckled, "But, I'm nearing 85 and no surgeon wants to be 'the guy who killed Sharin Mersor.'"

She was glad that Sharin still had her sense of humor.

"Now I know why you blamed 'This room.' I think I could learn to hate this room without too much difficulty. But I'm glad to be here with you. Is there anything I can do?"

"No. The nominating ballots are going out. Since you're now a member, you should vote to nominate yourself. And, any time you're going to be back on this coast, I'd appreciate a visit."

Then she paused, and closed her eyes, "Jodi, I'm sorry, I can imagine what you must have gone through watching your mother — I don't want you to have to deal with—"

Jodi interrupted her, "No. Don't worry. I'll be back in a few weeks and of course I'll be here. But could we maybe move it to the living room?"

They both laughed.

After the public announcement, the press and television shows did interviews with doctors. The speculation was her condition was terminal. She could not have long to live.

In the weeks that followed, the nominating ballots were sent to the Academy members, ballots were returned, and the votes were counted.

Jodi was nominated for Best Performance by an Actress in a Leading Role.

Sharin called to tell her and added, "I know you didn't want to start thinking about the awards show before, but now that you are nominated you better start planning who you are going to wear and who is going to help you get ready. I'll be as much help as I can for as long as I can, but the studio has some old hands with this and they can help you get ready for the red carpet and everything that goes with it."

Three weeks later Jodi was in her apartment in New York, when she got a call from Mattie, Sharin's assistant. Sharin was failing and wanted to see Jodi and she had two favors she wanted to ask.

Jodi was curious about what the favors might be but knew better than to ask for the hint.

Mattie told her that on Sharin's instructions, she had called Edgar to ask him to fly her to the coast as soon as they could make it. Jodi hung up, and the phone rang.

She knew it would be Edgar.

When they arrived at Sharin's home, she was in bed. She looked weak, but, as usual, her hair and makeup were perfect.

After thanking Edgar for bringing Jodi, Sharin asked him for a few minutes alone with her.

"Congratulations again on your nomination."

Jodi smiled, "You already woke me to congratulate me the morning they were announced."

Moving closer to the bed, she took her hand and said, "I'm going to take the risk of making a very poor joke—but are you really dying or just matchmaking?"

Sharin smiled, "Well I am dying, but I'm not in pain, so even if I am doing a little matchmaking, we could both be doing a whole lot worse. But the reason I summoned you," she chuckled at her own phrase, "was because I need you to do two things for me."

"I'm listening."

Taking a sealed envelope from the nightstand, "This is what I would like you to read at my funeral. If you don't mind, open it after I'm gone."

"I hope that won't be for a long while."

"I'm ready now."

Jodi nodded she understood.

"The second favor might take you out of your way a bit."

Smiling, "That's assuming you were planning on attending my funeral anyway."

Jodi laughed, "Don't worry, I wouldn't miss it."

"Good! Then I'll be there, too!" She laughed.

"But the second thing is really strange. Hand me that box on the mantle, please."

Jodi handed her the box.

Sharin explained, "When I got back from the war, and was cast as Janeen in Journey. . . Well, of course you know all that. But what I don't think you know is that I was the one who suggested the scene with closing the dying soldier's eyes, which you played so beautifully. I suggested it because it really happened. I told the writer and director about my experience and the scene was added. Just like it happened, they made the "dying soldier at Anzio" a British colonel.

"And, as he was dying, he asked me to find his brother there to pass on to him their father's watch. It had been given to the colonel as he was the oldest son."

Jodi was curious as Sharin opened the box to show her the watch.

Sharin shook her head, "It was crazy over there. I tried to find the brother, but I was told he was killed in an explosion around the same time the colonel died. Word came back that he had jumped on a grenade or something to save the men around him. There was talk of awarding him the Victoria Cross posthumously.

"When I got home, I found this box that looked like the ones they used to present medals, and kept the watch in it all this time."

Jodi waited.

"Jodi, I just found out that his brother is still alive. He had one of his sons call the studio. The brother was badly mangled in the explosion, but he survived."

She shook her head at the thought of it, "That poor man was hospitalized for over two-and-a-half years after the war as they did operation after operation to piece him back together."

She sighed, "I've seen firsthand what wars can do. He was back in the hospital when Journey played in England and he never saw it. But he saw the remake of that scene in our movie."

Jodi wiped a tear from her eye. She knew what Sharin was going to ask, and was already agreeing to go when Sharin got the words out.

"That's my girl. Did you have any plans to go to England?"

She laughed and dried her eyes, "Funny you should ask. I wrote to Gary and Jimmy about coming to see them around next Thanksgiving. This will give me a good excuse to firm up that plan with them. With the time difference, we don't get to talk much anymore. There's been some noises about a house warming. But, the last thing that I heard about that was they hadn't found a house they both like."

"Good! So, I won't have to feel guilty about taking you too far out of your way. I'll get the details to you. And have my people set up the delivery of the watch for a time that you think you'll be over there.

"Now, please go tell Edgar he can come back now."

Before the voting for the award, Sharin became visibly weaker by the day. But she insisted on giving an interview from her patio.

In the interview she said, "I'm proud to have been an actress and member of the Academy. I'm sure they can recognize what Jodi Worren did on the screen.

"Do I think she deserves the award? I think she did a better job than I did playing the parts I won for. If the Academy doesn't give her the award, I'll have to give her both of mine."

Jodi was touched by Sharin's feelings for her. But she thought that Sharin also saw this award not only as a vindication for having chosen her for the part, but also as a final nod to Sharin herself.

Two weeks before the voting ended, Sharin Mersor died.

All Hollywood mourned. The flags flew at half-staff.

The funeral was held in Beverly Hills a few days before the votes were due.

Jodi thought it natural to go to the huge church with Edgar.

As could be expected, the service was like a Hollywood production. All the speakers, being in the business, were smooth and their remarks well-rehearsed.

The last to speak, Jodi started haltingly. "A while back, Sharin asked to see me. When I arrived, we talked for a few moments but I could see she was very weak. She handed me this envelope and asked me not to open it until after—and asked me to read this today."

She smiled weakly, "Knowing Sharin, we both knew I couldn't say 'No.'"

She paused, "These are Sharin's words:

'Do not grieve.

We all know that the part we play, no matter how glorious, comes to its end.

We should no more grieve the end than we should mourn the beginning—since we know all beginnings lead only to the end.

I have lost so many whose names you know.

I look forward to finding them again.

But, I have long thought of all the boys who begged, "Please nurse, hold my hand," as they lay dying in places like North Africa or Anzio.

It was a profound privilege those men bestowed upon me, then.

It is with a soft and serene sense of peace that I look forward to seeing them again—knowing that they are waiting to hold my hand, now.'"

There was not a dry eye in the church.

On the way back from the funeral, Edgar told Jodi that he had hired Sharin's assistant, Mattie, to work as his social secretary.

"It was something Sharin wanted. When we talked, she told me that Mattie has also been fielding your calls until you choose a new agent. She suggested that I hire Mattie and ask you if you would like her to continue what she's been doing for you too."

Jodi thought about it for a moment and realized it was a generous offer and it would be for the best.

After the funeral, one columnist wrote, "Anyone who bets against Jodi Worren winning the Oscar just doesn't know Hollywood. They don't know the depth of its feelings for tradition in general, and its love for Sharin Mersor in particular.

"Besides, Jodi Worren played the hell out of that part.

"I watched her play the scene in which Sharin accepted her Lifetime Achievement Tony. Then I watched a taped version of the actual event. You could superimpose the two images. It was frightening. Every gesture, every emotion and voice inflection was the same as when Sharin received that well-deserved award so many years ago.

"I couldn't let myself go back and check to see if Miss Worren even blinked when Sharin had blinked because it would've terrified me to find that she did. There's really no question, Jodi Worren should walk away with this award on merit alone."

When Jodi read that, she wondered if Sharin had even orchestrated her own death for maximum leverage.

Slowly Jodi became aware that the time she used to spend on the phone with Pops on an almost daily basis, and then with Sharin after his death, now seemed to be filled with calls from Edgar.

On one of the calls, he asked if he could take her to a dinner promoting a charity that Sharin had cared about and he supported.

She accepted.

Of course, being seen in public together fueled speculation in the media. Later, when he asked if he could accompany her to the Academy Award ceremony, it seemed natural for her to accept.

When award night came, Jodi was relieved that all the preparation for that one night would soon be over. Win or lose, the sun would come up the next day and she would no longer have to worry about all the fashion hoopla and all the preparation for the awards ceremony and the red carpet interviews.

Sitting at her table, she looked around at all the people and all the glittering jewelry. When they introduced the presenters for her category, her mind, again, flashed back to the restaurant when Pops told her about Sharin's interest in her.

During the presenters' banter, she envisioned Pops' wrinkled hands moving above the table like he was massaging a crystal ball and saying "— if God is willing and we stay healthy, we could be sitting here again with an Oscar on the table."

While the presenters were listing the nominees, Jodi—fixated on the phrase, "if God is willing and we stay healthy." She again questioned whether she wanted to win the Oscar.

When she was nominated, she had not felt comfortable enough to vote for herself, since Pops wouldn't be there to enjoy the award with her. She knew he would want her to be happy, and yet she could not think of herself as being happy having this statue without him.

While she was mired in these thoughts, they opened the envelope—and read out her name.

It took a few seconds to sink in.

Edgar had to say, "You better get up there."

She had realized, with the crusade Sharin went on, it had to happen this way—which is why she had prepared a short statement. Her speech was brief. She didn't need anything on paper. It came from her heart.

"I was given the opportunity to play a great lady by that great lady herself. I will always be indebted to Sharin Mersor for her support. I will also always cherish the care and support I received from my Pops Magenwise. While I take this award as your tribute to the work Sharin did and the life Sharin lived, I am so deeply—deeply sorry that my Pops is not here to share this with me. Thank you so very much."

The next morning, Jodi felt both relieved and exhausted. Having received the award, she still wondered if she had truly earned the honor. She was never far from pondering all that had happened to her and was happening to her now. But she wasn't allowed much time to reflect because now there were even more requests for interviews and even more press attention.

She was surprised she hadn't anticipated that actually getting the award would increase, rather than decrease, these demands for her time. But her lack of anticipation was not shared by everybody. She soon found out that her portrayal of Sharin was not the only one that was going to be showing in theaters.

In anticipation of her winning the Oscar, the producers of her first movie had the movie reedited to put back the out-take footage that had been shown to Sharin.

In the re-release, with its big publicity campaign to capitalize on Jodi's acclaim, the movie didn't get any better reviews than it had in its limited first release. Her performance was rated as better than the picture. And then, the questions started as to why her work had been cut out in the first place.

TWENTY-SIX

In the aftermath of winning the award, despite the barrage of offers that Mattie was struggling to field, the only firm commitment Jodi had on the near horizon was to fly to Milan in five weeks for a booking Pops had made. Jodi realized that without work as a structure, things were going to get more chaotic. She was wondering what she would like to do with herself until the Milan booking, when Edgar called.

"I won the auction for the pictures and dinner with you."

"Say that again. You won what?"

"Well, I'm in Japan. But one of Sharin's charities was auctioning off a set of autographed pictures of you and the prize included having you as a dinner partner."

She just let him talk while she remembered that on her second day on the set, when she was more worried about her decision to do the movie than anything else, Sharin had asked her if she would autograph a set of the studio publicity photos so they could be auctioned off at a triennial gala along with the right to have Jodi as a dinner guest. She had agreed and promptly forgot all about it— she routinely signed publicity photos whenever Sharin's assistants asked her, so there was nothing to remind her of this dinner obligation or when it might be happening.

Now, Edgar was on the phone telling her he'd sent one of his people to do the bidding for him, and asking when they could get together. He suggested that it could be at his Malibu house since he was flying to LA. She agreed to dinner in Malibu in two days.

When she hung up, she just shook her head. The invitation gave her something to focus on. She thought she understood his feelings for her, but still she wondered why he went through all the trouble with this auction.

The next day, Mattie called and said that he wanted to do the meal preparation himself and wanted to know if it would be OK if he sent his car to pick her up rather than doing it in person.

Jodi chuckled, "This whole thing has been so strange, seeing Edgar in a chef's apron wouldn't make it any more strange. However he's planned this, it is fine with me."

When the day came—as she was getting ready to be picked up—she had to admit to herself she was looking forward to getting out and was curious about this Malibu house and what he was preparing. Sharin had told her about the remodeling that he had done and how magnificent the house and view were.

She arrived at the house just before sunset. She assumed that if you wanted to impress somebody with a beach-front house, sunset was the time to have them arrive. The side of the house that faced the beach was almost all glass and all four floors focused on the water in such a way that they didn't see the neighboring properties. There was a huge pool and spa between the house and beach and an equally large pool and spa enclosed in glass with a staircase leading down from a second-floor master bedroom. She could see why Sharin had raved about the house. The table set for only two told her they would be eating alone.

He greeted her in the open kitchen. She smiled as he hung the chef's apron, which she almost caught him wearing, on a hook in the kitchen as she entered. He offered a drink, which she politely refused.

He took her hand and led her in front of the pool to a chair on a teak deck that was three small steps up from the sand. They sat and watched the sun go down.

As it disappeared, he sprang up. "Wait here a minute please. I'll call you when things are set."

She sat, and taking a deep breath, let herself sink into the thick, soft cushion on the chair as she looked at the house which seemed all alight.

The lights around the dining area were dimmed and there were lit candles on the table. She thought it could be a scene from a movie.

When they sat at the dinner table, he brought out a roast. After a few bites she complimented him on the meal.

As they were eating, thinking the time was right, she said, "I won't be rude and ask how much winning the auction cost you, but I think we know each other well enough for you to know that if you wanted to invite me for dinner, even if you wanted to do this, you didn't have to go through all that auction process."

He cleared his throat. "The money wasn't important and it was for a good cause. But the truth is I thought about the auction and then sent my man to bid because — well because I knew I didn't want to have the picture in my head of you having dinner with someone else."

Whatever answer she might have expected, she didn't expect that one.

He added, "Once I knew that, I knew I had to stop on the way from the airport and get this."

He reached into his pocket and then slid a box that could only contain a ring across the table

"I've been flying across the Pacific all last night. I think I'm a little too stiff for getting down on one knee, but will this do?"

She opened the box and looked at the beautiful engagement ring. Like the house itself, the ring was very large and very elegant.

She knew if she put it on it meant the she had accepted his proposal.

Instead, she looked him in the eye and said, "It's lovely. But, would you be very hurt if I said I'd like to think about this."

"No. I haven't upset you, have I?"

"No, not at all. It's just so unexpected. I think it's smart to take time to think through big decisions."

"I agree. Don't worry. Take your time."

Trying to lighten the mood he added, "I'm not looking to cast anyone else in the role."

She smiled, closed the box, and left it on the table.

"If you can have your car take me back after dinner I'd appreciate some time alone."

It was not what he was hoping for, but he agreed.

Sitting in the back of the limo on the way back to her hotel room, she felt truly alone. She wished she could pick up the phone and talk to Pops. She would talk to Sharin, even though she was sure what she would say.

The limo turned off the freeway and headed north on the city streets. She watched the few people walking as she reflected on the ring and his sliding-the-ring proposal. She thought that he was nervous when he slid the ring to her. She was aware that many women looking at that house and that ring would jump at the chance to marry one of the richest men in the country.

She assumed he would recognize that too. And yet his nervousness told her he didn't take her acceptance for granted.

She liked that.

When the limo stopped at a light, she watched a couple kissing on a bench at a bus stop. As their affectionate entanglement became more amorous, she found herself thinking about her empty hotel room. Then she thought of how she was going to tell Edgar that she would be honoring the bookings Pops had made for her.

Then she knew—she would only have to make excuses for her prior plans if she was going to say "Yes." She looked at her left hand and imagined the ring. She thought of all the trouble he had gone to—sending someone to the auction, getting the ring, and personally preparing the dinner.

She thought about asking the driver to take her back to the beach house. But she decided not to. She was feeling tired and still wanted to be alone in the comfort of her room.

When she got there, she called Edgar. She was pleased to hear how happy, yet anxious, he sounded when heard her voice. She told him that she accepted. His reaction made her feel she made the right decision.

Afterward, in a quiet moment, when she allowed herself to think about why she said "Yes," she thought of it as kind of a path of least resistance—of going along with something someone else felt strongly about rather than affirmatively wanting it—saying "Yes" because she couldn't think of a reason to say "No."

She wondered, If Pops were alive? She convinced herself that she didn't think of this marriage as fulfilling some last wish of Sharin's. But maybe Sharin was right about being married as a way of getting some stability along with security.

She realized he knew almost nothing about her past. There was not much to her life before the start of her modeling career she felt he should know about or he could relate to. He didn't seem interested in anything but the here-and-now of them as a couple—the public perception of her and that perception reflecting on him. She realized that she didn't know much about him other than he was wealthy and he obviously wanted her.

They decided to keep their engagement a secret until she returned from Milan. Both wanted a small quiet ceremony. There was no family on her side she wanted to invite and he was an only child. He had only an elderly aunt who couldn't travel, and his son announced he wouldn't attend the wedding if his mother wasn't invited. The idea of inviting an ex-wife, with whom relations weren't easy even during the marriage, was a nonstarter as far as Edgar was concerned.

Since the wedding wasn't going to be elaborate, she agreed with his suggestion that they make no public announcement until after they had flown off to Acapulco and gotten married. Even then, they had to deal with paparazzi and a crowd of local people and tourists who somehow had managed to find out about the ceremony.

After the wedding, neither of them was prepared for the pressure that Jodi's increased fame and then marriage put on them as a couple. She now was not only a top model but as an award-winning actress, she was more in demand than ever before. With the articles about her making the transition from supermodel to great actress growing more numerous, the business press also wanted interviews with them as well.

But soon it became obvious to him that even the focus of the business press, whose attention he used to covet, was on Jodi.

All of this had a negative effect on him. He was starting to wonder if being the man who married Jodi Worren was like trading his father's shadow for a new one. He wanted her to cut back on her work and her interviews.

When they had talked about the timing of the wedding, he knew that for at least ten months or so after the wedding, she would still have some modeling and spokesperson commitments. In addition to the work Pops had booked, she let Mattie know that she had certain photographers and designers who she admired and enjoyed working with and she would be happy to work with again. He also was aware she had made a promise to Sharin to deliver a watch to England. Even so, after the wedding, he wanted her to accompany him more for socializing on his frequent business trips and was annoyed when her schedule did not permit it. He started to ask what type of clothing she was modeling and also started to make suggestions about what she should wear when they were out in public and when they entertained his business contacts.

She started to find the questions and suggestions more frequent and his manner more curt. If Jodi, who now had her own sense of fashion, didn't follow his clothing suggestions because she knew that either the color or style of what he wanted was not right for her, he would sulk and not talk to her for a while.

She was starting to feel as though his wanting her to accompany him came more out of a pride of possession than a desire for togetherness. Leaving the apartment one day, as they were heading in different directions—she to a photo shoot in Central Park, not far from their apartment, and he to fly to Boston for a meeting at one of his tech companies—they agreed they had to sit down that night with their calendars and plan when she would go to England to fulfill her promise to Sharin.

Sitting down, looking for uncommitted time, she said, "When I go to England, I want to see Gary and Jimmy. They finally settled on a house outside of London and invited me to visit, and you too, if we're there together." This was the first time he realized that she thought of him going with her on that trip and he was pleased.

As it happened there was a major acquisition he had been working on before the wedding. "I'll see if I can shift the meeting from their office in Paris to the one in London. Or I can just drop you in London, hop over to Paris and be back that night."

He brightened, "We can consider the trip as a belated honeymoon."

She was surprised. She realized without mentioning it that even combined with a business trip, the idea of a honeymoon was more sentimental than she had come to expect. It was almost romantic.

She readily agreed.

Later when she was alone, thinking that he was going to meet Gary and Jimmy, she blushed, remembering what she told them in their first conversations about Edgar. It was the same conversation when they told her they were leaving New York to live in London and were hoping to get enough business to make London their home.

Before the movie finished shooting, Sharin had invited Jodi to attend a charity ball. Edgar, a co-sponsor of the ball, wanted to make sure Jodi knew the invitation was also from him.

Sharin had told him that, after Jodi finished shooting the ballroom scene in the movie, she said, "If this gown was blue instead of this off-color green, I'd be tempted to ask if I could keep it."

Hearing this, and wanting Jodi to attend the event, he rushed to have the gown duplicated in blue and delivered to Jodi with the invitation.

What made Jodi blush now, was having told her friends that after Edgar had gone to all the trouble with the gown, when he escorted her home from the event, he made no move to kiss her.

Jimmy, knowing her ambivalent, sex-coast concept, had laughed.

"This guy sounds like just what you need Girl-friend—a rich older man who is more interested in dress-ing you than undressing you."

Gary had chimed in, "Are we sure this guy isn't one of us?"

TWENTY-SEVEN

They were due to land in London in the early morning. Letting his copilot take over in the middle of the Atlantic, Edgar tried to get some rest before his big meeting.

After dropping Jodi in London, he and some of his staff flew on to Paris.

Knowing Jimmy and Gary were coming to get her around noon to accompany her to deliver the watch, Jodi hoped to take a short nap as soon as she got to the hotel. But she got distracted by the physical layout of the hotel and its furnishings.

She'd been in hotels all over the world but she studied this one, almost like she had never seen or been in a hotel before, because she was aware that the meeting Edgar was heading to in Paris was to buy the company that owned this hotel and several hundred others. He said the deal was for billions of dollars, but since the selling company was drowning in debt he was getting the hotels for a price, in some places, that was cheaper than the vacant land near the hotels.

He'd said, "If all goes as planned, you'll check in as a guest and we'll walk out as owners."

As was typical of these issues, Jodi listened—because she knew this was important to him and she knew he wanted to impress her—but that was the extent of her interest in the details.

Her attempted nap having been unsuccessful, she was ready when Jimmy and Gary came up to the room.

By then she was aware they were going to the home of Sir Thomas Belvedor. He was knighted "for the work he had done to aid widows and orphans, and the shining example he set by his courage and devotion to all of those who had been touched by the cruel horrors of war."

When the studio gave Jodi information for the eldest of his five sons—the one who had made contact when his father saw the movie—she passed it on so Gary could make the meeting arrangements.

As Gary drove and Jimmy navigated, Jodi told them she had gone round and round with herself as to whether she should put the watch and its box in some sort of gift wrapping or leave it just as Sharin had handed it to her. She regretted she didn't know the history of the box. In the end, she decided to let this battered leathery looking box continue to do its job alone.

Turning up the lane to the house, they were surprised to see balloons tied to a fencepost as though they were marking the way to a party. Quickly they came upon the address. There was a gazebo decorated with bunting that looked like Union Jacks and American flags. About two-hundred and fifty people were there with folding chairs arranged in orderly rows on the lawn and more were arriving. They checked the address to make sure they were in the right place. Now, they realized they had underestimated the magnitude of this whole event.

Looking for someone to tell them where to park and what they were supposed to do, they saw a row of chairs lined up in the gazebo and people milling around a frail figure seated in a wheelchair in the center of the row. Jimmy, looking at the mangled old man, with a medal suspended from a full-size crimson ribbon around his neck, inhaled and whispered, "I'll bet that's the guest of honor."

The crowd parted so as not to impede Jodi as she smiled and headed for the man she knew had to be the recipient of the watch. His appearance left no doubt.

To say this man had been blown up beyond repair might have been an accurate description. What repairs had been attempted made it appear as though the doctors had never seen a human before, so they did the best they could to approximate one.

Ascending the few steps, she saw there was a seat for her next to the wheelchair. She stopped and smiled.

There was a hushed, yet audible gasp, as Jodi, without any hesitation, reached out a hand to shake hands. Sir Thomas had long ago taken to keeping the more gnarled parts of his body out of view so as to avoid the look on the faces of those who might see them. He was moved by her gesture. Slowly he managed to get to a stooped but standing position on his prosthetic legs as he reached out what remained of his right hand—which consisted of the stumps of his fingers and most of his thumb.

Taking his hand, she kept her hold as she sat down, while Sir Thomas, with the aid of a couple of his sons, was guided back down into his wheelchair.

Leaning closer to hear him as they talked, she paid no attention to the countless flashes from cameras. She smiled and handed Sir Thomas his family's watch.

He introduced his large family to her.

She thought, What this man must have suffered. Her thoughts turned to Sharin who had not only been a witness to this type of mutilation, but was tasked with easing the pain of those who were suffering and counting on her for care. The words Sharin had asked her to read at her funeral came back to her.

She felt honored Sharin had given her this responsibility. Delivering the watch closed the circle that led from the dead colonel through Sharin to Jodi and finally to this selfless hero.

Getting up to leave, she leaned over and kissed Sir Thomas on the shiny, stretched, scarred graft that passed for a cheek. She simply chose the side closest to her— ignoring the fact this side of his head had neither a jawbone, an eye, nor an ear.

Looking out to the lawn, she noticed there were many more people milling about on the lawn than when she arrived. Jodi sighted Jimmy next to Gary. After nodding to them, they stepped up for a brief introduction before heading back to the car. She noticed several more photographers present. She was more surprised when, as she was getting into the car, some people started chanting, "Jodi! Jodi! Jodi!"

On the drive back, Jodi shook her head, "That was nothing like what I thought when we started the day."

She wondered who called the press, then realized with five grownup sons, Sir Thomas had an army of grandchildren and some great grandchildren; any one of that extended family could have made the call.

Gary said, "Jodi, I felt proud to be there with you. You know one of the qualities I always love about you is your way of treating people like they're on the same level as you. You don't act like you're better than anybody. Or look better than anybody. With you everybody's of equal value."

Jimmy said, "Yeah, what was that Pops used to say? 'You should never look down on someone—"

"'—unless you are reaching down to help them up,'" Jodi and Gary added to complete the sentence.

Jimmy continued "You do that so beautifully well.

"I think it's a gift, it's very special and I love you for it."

She was embarrassed, "I don't see it as a gift. I don't see it as anything special. I saw a man who did an incredibly brave thing. It would have been shameful for me to have seen anything other than that. Sharin told me during the war she didn't date because she saw each man as the mangled corpse he could become. I guess I saw Sir Thomas as the young man who sacrificed his body to save so many.

"In New York I met a man who was run over by a subway train. After I first met him, I came to see him as a man with scars rather than just focus on the scars.

"Remember Wally, the photo editor for Playboy, who married that really heavyset girl, from outside the business. She had this great personality that could light up any room she was in. I really liked her. I was at a party and I overheard some drunken jerk ask Wally how he could marry a girl that looked like that instead of one of the models. Wally very patiently told this fool, 'You marry the inside—you never marry the outside.'"

She continued, "And what is the outside anyway?

"We live in a world of images where beauty and disfigurement are such subjective, relative things."

She turned to Jimmy, "You nearly paint my face to make me look beautiful. We figure the best angles and the right light, but even after Gary takes the picture of the image of me you created, someone else can come along and air brush out my imperfections. I don't think I do anything special."

"Well we think it's special and we love you," Gary flounced in a parody stereotype gay fashion.

"OK you guys thanks. I'm glad you love me—" and trying to imitate Pops, "—but enough already."

The boys just laughed.

As they pulled up to the hotel, a large crowd was forming. They saw Paparazzi everywhere. and wondered what was going on. Maybe Edgar had arrived and word of his big deal was made public. There were two satellite TV vans setting up and then a police truck arrived with barricades. Getting out of the car, Jodi was spotted and the crowd rushed toward them. She'd never experienced anything like this. The surging crowd frightened her. Part of the hotel staff and some policemen escorted them in through the lobby and into the elevator.

Getting to the room, Jodi and Jimmy went to the window and looked down to the front of the hotel. The crowd was getting bigger. It was starting to look like Times Square on New Year's Eve, except now there was a horde of paparazzi and flashes of light everywhere. More police were arriving and some of them were on horseback. They tried to control the crowd. Gary tuned into the TV station that had one of the vans downstairs. They were doing a live broadcast from the front of the hotel as another TV van was arriving. Gary turned up the volume so they all could hear it across the room, and then joined them in looking out the window.

The news report was about Jodi delivering the watch. One of Sir Thomas's sons had many connections to the media. People in England knew about Sir Thomas and his heroic sacrifice. They knew about his struggles to lead a normal life and that, as disfigured as he was, he was able to return home to his wife and twin sons and then managed to have three more children. It seemed all of England knew of him and had revered him for his sacrifice and his many good works on behalf of widows and orphans. They took him to their hearts as a symbol of what it meant to be an Englishman.

News had spread quickly about the mission Jodi had just completed. This beloved old man was shown on the TV starting to weep, "You never get over the feeling of people staring at you. Their revulsion at your disfigurement hammers at your heart. But when this glorious angel took my hand and kissed me, without hesitation or reservation of any kind—bodies did not matter, it was one soul to another soul," he broke down and sobbed, "—it was the first time I have felt truly whole since the explosion."

Some in the mob were chanting "Jodi! Jodi! Jodi! —" Some were paraphrasing the theme song from the movie: instead of singing "Sharin what a life you've lived. Sharin you had so much to give —" they had kept the tune but substituted "Jodi" for "Sharin."

The TV announcer, almost shouting to be heard over the crowd concluded, "She came to honor one of us. These people came here to honor her. This young woman, simply by showing that we are all deserving of care and respect, has generated the kind of reaction that I have not seen since our great rock-star bands," he raised his voice still louder, "—this is truly—Jodimania!"

She was speechless. Not even the fan reaction and the tumultuous click of cameras on the red carpet were like this. Those things could be anticipated. Hiding behind the drapes, she looked out at the chanting crowd. She started to worry that her whole life would change into this kind of spontaneous chaos. And then she thought of Sharin. For a brief moment she allowed herself to wonder if somehow Sharin had a hand in this. She realized how absurd the thought was as soon as it flashed across her mind. And yet, I'm married to Edgar as Sharin wanted, after having won the award she wanted me to win, I'm here on a mission she asked me to undertake, and now this.

Jimmy gave her a playful shove, "Girlfriend, look what you went and did now!" He chuckled, "Wow, J-o-d-i-m-a-n-i-a." Then, looking at her face, he saw she was not amused. She was troubled by what was happening.

Gary watched as Jimmy put his arm around her shoulder to comfort her. Then, studying her himself, he sighed, "I hate to say this, but it sure looks like a quiet visit to our place is out of the question."

Jimmy gasped, "My God, I don't know if Edgar completed his deal to buy this place, but now I wonder if he can get in here with this mob scene."

Gary shook his head, "Even if he gets in, they may have to wait to see if this mob ever leaves before they can get out."

Edgar was on his way to the hotel in a limo along with Timothy Kelly, the retired FBI special agent who Edgar handpicked to be the head of corporate security.

Kelly had been recruited by the FBI after graduating from Fordham Law School. Edgar liked Kelly's looks-like-he-could-handle-anything bearing and, though Edgar could not put his finger on why, he also liked that his identical-twin brother was a priest. Edgar would brag that Kelly was the best man the bureau ever had. He had meticulously tracked down a fugitive who had been on the run for 15 years.

Although there was no set plan, both men knew it would not be long before Kelly was going to retire from his corporate duties and help his younger brother in the Bahamas handle a growing car rental and tour business.

Edgar was elated that he had just completed an acquisition which he thought of as a crowning achievement. Now he was, finally, the owner of the Homeharth Hotel Group which—under several well-known brand names—owned the largest number of hotels throughout the world. Many of the hotels were considered the world's most luxurious. The purchase gave him a vast network of hundreds of properties, which had more than seven hundred thousand rooms. In addition, he now owned Homeharth's management division, which managed hospitality properties for many other hotel owners. This was one of the biggest, if not the biggest, corporate takeover in history.

The two men were alone in the back of the limo and Edgar was saying, "If my dad were alive, I think this deal would get his attention."

Kelly heard the remark, but his own attention was commanded by the growing crowd he saw blocking the street in front of the hotel. He told the driver to pull over and wait.

He approached a police officer and asked, "What's going on?"

"We've blocked off the street because of the crowd. Jodi Worren is in the hotel and all these people showed up because of her."

"Well, how can you help us out here? We really need to get through." Gesturing toward Edgar, "This man in the back is Jodi Worren's husband."

The officer looked in at Edgar who was now sitting up staring at the crowd. "I'm sorry, Mr. Worren, we'll try to get you through this the best we can."

Before Kelly could straighten him out about the name, the officer turned quickly and was rapidly walking toward a mobile command post while talking on his radio.

Edgar slumped back into his seat. It had been a long day. His exhilaration at having made his big deal could no longer sustain him.

When Kelly and the police finally escorted Edgar up to the room, Jodi was still looking at the mob and hoping that, just maybe, some of the people were leaving.

She greeted Edgar with an apologetic shrug, "I have no idea why any of this happened."

Then brightened, "How did your deal go?"

He waved his hand and slumped onto the couch saying that he wasn't in a mood to talk about it.

She made a quick introduction of Jimmy and Gary, but told Edgar they were just waiting for him to arrive so they could say hello and leave.

"We waited until you got here—Jimmy and I didn't want to leave her by herself."

By this time everybody seemed tired—the formalities of greeting and leave taking were almost simultaneous.

Jodi and her friends knew, with the time zone difference, it wouldn't be easy to keep in touch, but they agreed to try.

When Jodi and Edgar were alone, knowing neither of them wanted anything more to do with London, they tried to think of a place they could escape to for the couple of days their schedules permitted them to be together.

TWENTY-EIGHT

After burying Henry next to Bill in the church graveyard overlooking the lake, Harry, Corey, and Dayna had to deal with their loss.

Soon after the funeral, friends stopped coming over with plates of food. Henry's care had taken up a large part of the family's time, energy, and financial resources. With him gone, they had not only lost Henry but their sense of purpose— having lost their roles as his caregivers.

Now, they all had to move back into the areas of their lives that had almost been squeezed shut by the need to take care of him. Dayna could start to focus on school. Harry could pay more attention to the store. Soon, Corey found a part time job with an optometrist.

Slowly the sorrow subsided.

The sense of loss was never far away but it was not ever-present. After a year, Dayna stopped seeing Margaret Solomon. Now, they all had their routines and their distractions. While there was little laughter at this point, they felt there would come a time when they would at least be eligible to laugh.

Harry and Corey didn't consider themselves people to be pitied. So, they spent some effort trying to help people be comfortable around them. However, if the truth were known, they were really not too much into being social to begin with. They had their obligations, but they had always shared the feeling they could get along with just each other's company.

If it hadn't been for work, the activities around Dayna, and the obligation of the fire department, they would have preferred to spend their time as just the three of them.

Gradually, having gone through the ordinary processes of the day-to-day living of their lives— as the emotional distance from the loss grew longer—laughter without regret started to return to the Daweson household.

But there were still times when thoughts of their loss seeped in.

Open school night in the fall was always a nostalgic time for Corey. The Smalsville school had changed very little since she had gone there as a child. Dayna's 9th grade teacher, Mrs. Edwards, had also been Corey's teacher.

Mrs. Edwards told them Dayna was doing well in class, but she was a bit concerned about her social interactions. She wondered if Dayna felt self-conscious about her weight, because she didn't seem to want to run or play much with the other children. She was aware of Henry's death five years earlier. She made some suggestions about getting Dayna involved a bit more socially.

She ended with, "But I have to tell you this," and chuckled, "the other day, on the playground, Dayna was playing alone, bouncing and shooting a basketball. One of the boys came from behind her and slapped it away from her. He got the ball and he was starting to take a shot at the basket and she caught up to him and knocked the ball out of his hands.

"He got angry, mainly embarrassed, that a girl could block his shot. He clinched a fist and started walking toward her. Then his friends jumped between them and stopped him.

"All they had to say to turn the boy around was, 'Hey! You know if you touch her, you're gonna to have to fight Billy Pawl.'"

She laughed, looked at Corey, and continued, "So Dayna has a protector, but I fear not for the same reason you always had the Torey boys a step behind you."

Seeing the quizzical look on Harry's face, she blushed. She owed him an explanation.

"I don't think I'm being improper telling you that—in the past, mind now—all the way through high school, the Torey boys had been so enamored of your missus that Mark broke Tony's arm fighting over her."

Harry smiled at the old story and thanked her for the information.

In the car going home, he laughed, "Tell me about the Torey boys."

She said, "They never had a chance."

"Hey, wait a minute, these are two good looking guys who have a solid family business and this is a pretty small town. In terms of the competition, they had to look pretty good."

"They never had a chance," she repeated more slowly.

He insisted, "What do you mean 'they?'

"They are different people. You didn't like either of them?"

She looked at him and insisted "They never had a chance. I was not going to go through life as Corey Torey!!!"

She nodded her head for emphasis and looked at him to see that he finally understood.

All he could do was laugh and grab her hand.

"So much the better for me."

Arriving home, Harry said, "If it's OK with you I'd like to put up a basketball hoop near the back of the garage."

She said, "That's a fine idea. Maybe the old coach will show Dayna some offensive moves to go with her power defense."

He laughed.

Then pausing, he thought, If Henry hadn't been sick…

Corey, realizing they were thinking the same thoughts, entwined her fingers with his as they both tried to keep from crying.

TWENTY-NINE

One evening, Jodi and Edgar were both returning to New York after not having seen each other for ten days. She had been in the Bahamas on a shoot, happy she could spend nine days with Gary and Jimmy. Edgar was returning from eight days in Japan.

She got to their park-view apartment first. She got a call from Tim Kelly, telling her Edgar's plane had landed and he would be home soon. She thought Kelly was always a bit formal with her. She wondered if he sensed the tensions in the marriage.

When Edgar got home, after what she thought was a rather cool greeting, he plopped himself on the couch and proclaimed himself exhausted. He announced that he had a headache and a really terrible couple of days. He poured himself a double Scotch from the bottle on the end table. He put the glass with the ice against his forehead before downing the drink in one gulp. He poured another, and replaced the cold glass against his forehead.

"Just today, before our flight home, Kelly told me Jason Watler, my college roommate, who I had brought along in this business, has been stealing from me for years. He also got a huge payoff to hide some of the numbers when he was supposedly doing our due diligence on the Homeharth deal."

After another drink he said, "Yesterday, Kelly told me that he had been called by a reporter who said he was not ready to publish yet, he was only hearing whispers, but he was tracking down a lead that Prince Richard's wife made comments blaming you for the breakup of their marriage.

"So," he announced, "I don't want to hear another fucking word about the remake of The Epic fucking Journey with this guy. I don't want you anywhere near him—I forbid you to do it!"

She was startled. "I talked about that movie with Sharin. She told me the part was perfect for me and it would also give a boost to Prince Richard. She hoped I would do it because of her regard for his father. On the other hand, I keep hearing if I don't agree to do the movie it won't get made. Especially, now, with all the publicity about the Colonel's watch.

"Modeling doesn't require big crews, but movies give a very large number of people work. The decision to turn down a project, when a lot of people are depending on me to agree, is harder for me. I don't ever want to be responsible for other people not being able to take care of themselves and feed their families.

"Sure, I have concerns, about Richard's attitude, and my own acting ability, but I'm still not willing to just walk away from the project just yet."

"Listen," he grumbled, "you don't get anywhere in life by worrying about the little people."

He raised his glass in a toast, "Fuck the little people!

"If I have to, I'll buy the fucking studio that has the rights to the movie, I'll just cancel the project, and that will be the end of it."

She was stunned by what was coming out of his mouth. From Pops, she had come to think that if anybody should be called "the little people" it should be those who could help people but refused to try. She decided rather than responding to his bluster, she would wait and see if he was just blowing off steam from a rough day—if maybe it was just the alcohol talking—or if he really thought he could control her and her choice of projects.

She knew there was not a shred of truth to any rumors regarding her and Richard. She noted he didn't bother to ask if there could be any truth to the story. She wondered if all he cared about was the publicity tarnishing his image and being bad for his business.

Without any confirmation that Richard's wife had actually made any statements at all, Edgar said, "That opera-singing bitch thinks that this is the way to get publicity for her husband—to get him more money so her settlement will be bigger, but she's just fucking with my brand."

"Your brand? I don't consider myself to be just another company asset. If all you wanted was a spokesperson for your 'brand,' you could have negotiated that with Pops when he was alive."

He sneered, "I would never have talked to your Jew manager—I have a staff for that."

She just stared. She couldn't believe Edgar, knowing how she felt about Pops, could even think of making a statement like that to her. She was enraged, but she held it in. His prejudice, his alcohol consumption, or a combination of both must have made him lose even the pretense of the civility he had always tried to impress her with.

This was not a lapse she could forget, even if she could somehow forgive it. She was getting ready to remind him—if his college roommate was any example—his "staff" was obviously not as reliable as he had thought. But, as angry as she was, she caught herself. She decided that in his condition there was no point in escalating the argument or even continuing it.

From both Harry and Pops, she had learned the wisdom of knowing what you can control; of picking your fights; of avoiding a stupid tug of war by being smart enough to just open your hands and let go of your end of the rope.

Sadly, she realized that the events of the night were calling into question her decision to marry Edgar, and whether she could she stay married to this man?

Just when she was deciding—you never argue with a drunk, just let him think he won the argument—the phone rang.

It was Tim Kelly. He called to report that Edgar's son was seriously injured in a skiing accident in the mountains of Northern California.

Edgar, visibly shaking as he heard the news, stood up and grumbled, "I'm going to fly out to be with my son. When I get back, we can talk about where you think you fit in this marriage."

In a matter-of-fact tone he said, "We might have to reevaluate where things are going. I'm wondering if we'd be better off if we cut our losses and got a divorce."

Before she could reply, the phone rang again with an update on his son's condition and the hospital he was airlifted to. Kelly said he ordered the jet to be readied. The co-pilot was on the way, but couldn't be at the airport until the morning.

When Edgar said he was going to the airport, Kelly knew it was useless to try to reason with Edgar and tell him he shouldn't try to fly the plane cross-country himself.

As soon as he hung up, Edgar left without saying goodbye or giving her a chance to try to talk him out of flying that night.

Lying in bed, even though she was tired from her trip, she was too upset to sleep. She thought about all he had said and his parting words. She knew, even though it could be considered their first argument, she would have to re-evaluate their relationship. Maybe it was just the stress of the day and the alcohol after all. It seemed a bit hasty on his part. But he never shared much of his feelings with her. Perhaps trouble had been simmering below the surface until the current stresses had brought it to a boil.

Thinking about divorce, she decided to wait and see what the situation looked like when he got back from California. If his son was badly injured and needed help, she might be helpful to them. She could go out to be with them. She wouldn't want to feel she was abandoning Edgar at a time of need. And, a common goal might even make it easier for them to work things out between them. But first, she would have to see if she cared enough to work on this marriage at all. And then, if he cared enough to work on it as well. She knew she didn't have to make any decisions now, there would be time to look at the options when he got back.

Before dawn, unable to sleep all night, as she was still thinking about her wait-and-see conclusion, the phone rang.

It was Kelly.

"I know it's the wee hours of the morning, but I have to see you right away."

When he arrived, twenty minutes later, she could see the news was not good. She thought Edgar had lost his son.

Kelly hesitated, "I'm sorry to have to tell you this. Edgar is dead."

She gasped.

He went on, "His plane crashed into a mountain on the way to California. I'm sorry but I needed to tell you before the press starts calling."

She numbly nodded she understood.

"The local cops and fire guys got up to the scene as quickly as they could but—it was no use."

After a silence, he continued, "His son died a few hours after the medevac helicopter got him to the hospital."

"Oh, how awful!"

She closed her eyes for a second and shook her head slowly.

"Did he know about his son's death before the crash."

He sighed and said softly "Yes Ma'am, I'd just radioed him the news before the crash."

"How horrible for him. To be all alone up there with that news."

He shook his head, "I really feel terrible about this. Now, there's going to be this even bigger investigation. Since he had just learned of the death of his only child, there are going to be questions of possible suicide."

He cautiously asked her, "Did Edgar say anything to you about Jason Watler before he left?"

She nodded, "He told me you said he'd been stealing, and something about due diligence and the Homeharth deal."

Knowing she already knew, he continued, "Well the fact that his college roommate had been embezzling and helped cook the books on this deal. . . Here Edgar's thinking he made this great get-me-out-of-my-dad's-shadow deal and it turns out he got screwed. I mean maybe— well kind of screwed. Yeah, this was a big deal, and really our company is way too big to be hurt too badly about overpaying for the hotels. But, when this all came out, it would have been embarrassing. It's still not a terrible deal, but it's not the home run he was taking credit for.

The whole thing isn't public knowledge, yet. But it will have to come out. And that betrayal might be considered another factor in any of Edgar's decisions."

He grimaced, "Boy, that trip to England—"

She looked at him quizzically.

"He was so proud of that Homeharth deal. He even let on that it was something his father would have been proud of. It was like his 'I'm-as-big-as-my-dad-was' moment."

He shook his head, "In the twelve years I worked for him, I'd never heard him mention his old man once, except when he was hiring me. He saw that I graduated from Fordham Law and he mentioned Fordham was near the boarding school he went to from kindergarten all the way through high school. I was really surprised. I didn't say anything but I thought it was very sad because I knew his parents had a big townhouse a short walk from that school. Why would anyone send a young child to live a few blocks away from home?"

Then he remembered, and grimaced again.

"In the car on the way back, just when Edgar seemed all puffed up, thinking that the Homeharth deal meant he finally made it big on his own, we get stopped at the barricade at the hotel. When I tell the cop we need to get through because Edgar's your husband, the London cop calls him 'Mr. Worren.'"

"Oh, no! Poor Edgar. He never said—"

"—No. He wouldn't.

"He'd just let it eat at him."

She sighed, "He also said something about Prince Richard."

He groaned and exhaled, "When I took this job, he told me anything I heard, he had to hear. Whether it was raw pap or ready for publication—he demanded to know everything I knew. I sure as hell wish I had time to do some checking before I even said anything about that crap. But, if something broke while we were flying home, he would have been blindsided by it as soon as we landed. I am really sorry I had to tell him rank, raw crap like that. And I'm sorry you had to hear it too."

She wasn't going to launch into any defense of herself against baseless hurtful rumors.

She said, "Physically, I don't think he should have been flying. He'd just gotten back, he looked worn out, he said he had a headache and he had a few drinks."

"Yeah, he said he started having the headaches, again, right after we got to Japan. But he said they'd passed before he flew home. A few years ago, he had a series of headaches and went to the Mayo Clinic to be evaluated. He was worried about a brain tumor, but they couldn't find anything, but if they returned. . .

"In Japan, he said these felt like those same kind of headaches."

She asked, "What do you think they're going to find about the possibility of suicide?"

"I don't want to speculate, but, the poor guy—he has to learn of his college roommate, a guy he trusted and brought up the ladder in the business, was ripping him off and then his only child dying in the same damn day? On top of that, this Prince Richard crap. And now you're telling me about these headaches starting up again once he got here—well, knowing him—he was enough of a control freak to . . . Well, let's just say, if he wanted to end it, he was the kind of guy that would want to choose the where, the when and the how. But, until proven otherwise, as far as I'm concerned, it's 'the accident.'"

She nodded.

He shook his head, and said reluctantly, "I know you don't want to hear this now, but you need to know: this whole situation is going to leave you in charge of a huge tangle of an estate—a vast mess of interweaving companies that maybe only he could keep straight. You're most likely the richest woman in the county and right now you have me and about nine-hundred and sixty thousand other employees on your payroll.

"And if Jason Watler was stealing, who knows who else was? Now, I don't want to think Watler could have had anything to do with the plane. . ."

He shook his head, "If the death wasn't a suicide, not only is there a very large life insurance policy, but also if the crash was proved to be due to a malfunction with the plane—and not pilot error—that could add even more treasure to the pile."

Not wanting to speculate any further about all the possibilities, he paused, "If it's OK with you, I can start making arrangements to get his body back here when it's released and while I'm doing that, I can start the process of making some arrangements for the funeral. I'll see if his ex needs anything but I'm sure she is going to take care of things for their son."

Jodi, still numb, slowly nodded her assent.

When he left, she didn't know what to do with herself.

Sitting on the couch, she picked up her feet, wrapped her arms around her legs and rested her head on her knees. She thought about the previous night and about Edgar. She thought about the son—she'd only seen pictures—and the ex-wife, she'd never met who had just lost her only child.

Jodi felt a weary sadness without tears.

Sitting there, her eyes closed and sleep overtook her.

Edgar's funeral was a blur to her. Not knowing many of his business associates, she went through the motions. She felt detached—accepting condolences for a grief she wasn't sure she felt—from people she'd never met, most of whom seemed to be there out of obligation rather than respect for Edgar or concern for her.

The world projected on her the image of the grieving widow just as during the marriage it projected on them the image of a happy couple.

Yet inside, her overarching feeling was one of dread. Yes, the image she conjured of Edgar up in the cockpit, hearing the terrible news about his son, made her sad for him. But, her sadness was mixed with a greater sense of fear for herself. She feared the responsibilities that company ownership and this new wealth would put upon her.

She felt she had allowed herself to drift into this marriage, just as she had been drifting through her life, going from one event to another. She had been glad to let Pops take care of her career and financial matters for her.

Now, in addition to her concern about the people counting on her to make a movie, she worried about the thousands upon thousands of employees and families who depended on the companies for their living. How was she was going to ensure these companies would remain viable? And, with the question about the loyalty of people Edgar had relied on, who could she trust to help?

She had let herself trust Peter and Edgar. But she had misread their feelings and intentions. Now, she feared she could not trust herself to know who to trust.

Sitting through the service she was getting panicked and paralyzed by the thought that she now had truly lost her balance.

As the service ended, she was grieving. Deep down, she was grieving the loss of her self-confidence.

After the funeral, alone in that huge triplex, she didn't know what to do next. She felt like she was totally aimless and drifting. Kelly was going to be consumed by company matters. She felt it would be hard to pull him away from that.

Needing to talk, she felt she had no friend to confide in. That night, as the worry about what was going to come next persisted, it took a long time for her to fall asleep. When she finally did sleep, she had a nightmare.

She could see herself lying on her back, pinned down in the bottom of a huge bucket. The bucket was bobbing and turning slowly in the water. Then, like a casket being lowered into the ground, the bucket, with her trapped on her back inside, was getting lower and lower. The water was creeping higher and higher up the outside of the bucket. Finally, as she was looking up, she could see the water was about to cascade over the rim of the bucket on all sides. The water was going to fill the bucket with her still trapped on her back. Flailing, just as the water began to flood in, she woke up.

Sitting up in bed, trying to figure out where she was, she thought she had just seen her future. She was going to get swallowed up by things she couldn't begin to handle and she didn't know who to trust to help her.

There was Kelly, but she wondered why he had been so quick to point out he was just another of her employees.

Then she took a deep breath and let it out slowly. She tried to calm herself by taking measured breaths. She tried to take her mind off the future by focusing it on the past.

She had known loss all her life. But she could think back to people she had met—people on whom she thought she could rely—people who had helped her just for herself, not because she was beautiful, rich or famous.

She thought her Oscar acceptance speech should have been: "I am here tonight because of two people who are dead and three people I've lost track of."

Now, as soon as she made that speech in her head, she realized what she needed to do to try to regain her balance.

In the morning she called Tim Kelly. "I know this is an imposition, but I need you to find these three people. I'll give you whatever information I can remember that might help you.

"I need you to find Harry Daweson, Jacqui Fykes, and Connie Depanici."

"I'll handle this right away, Miss Worren."

When he hung up, he looked at the list he made during her call and said softly to himself, "Before anything else."

The next day, Kelly called and came to the apartment with his report. "Jacqui Fykes is dead. She died of hepatitis several years ago. Connie's husband, Carmine, survived a car bomb that killed his uncle Leno and two members of his crew who were twins. Then, Connie and Carmine disappeared after being placed in the witness protection program.

"I could call in some favors from old friends, but, if they disappeared from protection, it'll be almost impossible to find them. They might not still be alive."

He brightened, "But, Harry Daweson runs a hardware store in a place called Smalsville."

He shook his head, adding, "It's a place that is actually even smaller than its name implies."

THIRTY

One evening, Corey finished some bill-paying chores, and came to cuddle with Harry on the couch in front of the television. On the screen was an interview with the supermodel, Candy Sherwin. The interviewer was saying, "I understand that you are a friend of Jodi Worren. She's been in the news a lot lately."

Candy smiled, "I was on her first overseas shoot." She laughed as she remembered, "We had finished late the first day and a bunch of us were going to grab a bite and we invited 'the new girl' to go along. We told her when to meet us in the lobby.

"We're all sitting around or draped over chairs in sloppy jeans or torn sweatpants and flip-flops. Well, the elevator door opens and there's Jodi in a dress and high heels—and she takes one look at us and says, 'Oops'—and she lets the elevator door close without getting out.

"In a flash, she's back downstairs as grungy as the rest of us. Well, except for the fact that even without makeup she's…"

She paused to choose her words, "Jodi is like a beautiful, colorful bird that when you look at her, it makes you smile to think God could make a creature like that."

The interviewer said, "I see—"

Candy laughed and then continued, "Let's put it this way, the joke was that the Army wouldn't book Jodi for a recruiting campaign because they were afraid there wouldn't be enough civilians left to run the country!"

The interviewer smiled.

Candy confided, "But you know what? It's OK. Modeling is very competitive but you really don't mind losing a job or a campaign to Jodi. She's really a good person and she works so hard. She's down-to-earth—doesn't put on airs—and she had this really sweet old manager, Pops. He saw her working in a drug store. It was like he found a diamond in a coal bin. When you lose out to her there's no question about whether she did this or that to beat you out of the booking.

"Well, maybe now that she just buried her husband, hopefully the press and the paparazzi will back off for a while and give her some peace."

"I see, well what's up next for you?"

"Well, I'm hoping that Jodi decides to make more movies and do less modeling," she laughed.

Corey looked at Harry, "And why are you watching this stuff?"

He nodded toward Dayna sitting in the back of the room with a bowl of ice cream. "I wasn't really. It was on when I got here. I was just keeping Dayna company and waiting for the basketball game to come on."

Corey said, "OK, so after this is basketball?"

She closed her eyes and snuggled her head on his chest and yawned. "Whatever."

The next day was warmer than usual. Watching the temperature reading alternating with the time on the bank's digital display across the street from the store, Harry wondered if the upcoming summer was going to be really hot. He decided that when he got back from his usual Wednesday lunch, he'd check catalogs and maybe order more fans.

At twelve fifteen, Harry, put the "closed for lunch" sign facing outward on the door and walked across the street to the luncheonette next to the bank.

The place hadn't been redecorated since the late fifties. The wood paneled walls and a black and white checkerboard floor where faded. The white Formica counter had stools.

The group Corey called the "usual suspects" was already in a booth seated on the semicircular faded green Naugahyde on three sides of the faded red Formica table. They seemed to be talking about Harry. Jack Bargers, seated at the back of the booth and facing the door, was the first to see Harry arrive.

"Here's our boy now! How'd you do it, Harry?"

Expecting another one of Jack's jokes Harry played along.

"It was easy."

Then curious, "How'd I do what?"

Willy Cooper, seated on one side of the booth, said, "I knew it, I told you this sombitch would play like he knew nothing about it."

He slapped Harry's hip as Harry pulled a chair from a nearby vacant table and sat down facing Jack.

Frank Peterson, seated across from Willy, said "Well, maybe he doesn't know yet. Jack said he was just told today."

Harry looked at them in turn. He knew if he waited long enough Jack or Willy was bound to tell him what the subject was.

It was Frank who started, "Harry, Jack was just telling us—"

Jack interrupted the banker, "—Boy you really must have stepped in some lucky shit today.

"I was out at the old Cunningham place and that movie star, Jodi Worren, and some out of town architect said she had just bought it and was going to be redoing the whole place.

"They were moving in some furniture as we spoke."

"Jodi Worren? Here? Why?"

"I knew he didn't know," said Frank.

Harry said, "Why should I know?"

Then, realizing most people knew Dayna was a fan, "Dayna didn't say any—"

"You think Dayna's why Jodi said it?" Jack asked him.

"Said what?" Harry asked, wondering when they'd realize he really didn't know what was said.

"Jack said —" Willy started.

"—She said I had to buy everything I used on the house from your store!" Jack finished.

Harry sat back to take in what he'd just heard. He thought about Dayna but couldn't see any connection.

"This woman didn't mention me by name, right? She just said something like, 'I want you to use local people.'"

"No, no. Nice try. She said 'Everything you use on my house has to come from Harry Daweson's store.'"

Now, he knew they were kidding. "C'mon guys. You had your fun. Now, is somebody really taking the Cunningham place? It's been sitting vacant for—"

Willy interrupted, "—Harry, why would a rangy-two-fisted-piece-of-ass like Jodi Worren, be looking —"

"—Oh—My—Fuckin'—Gawd," Jack said through his clenched teeth.

He stared straight ahead, with an awestruck look, and grabbed Willy's arm to try to shut him up.

While Willy was speaking, Jodi had entered the luncheonette and was standing behind Harry.

Frank, hearing Jack's exclamation and looking at his face turned his head to see what Jack was looking at.

Willy, annoyed at being stopped, jerked his arm away from Jack and also looked in the direction of Jack's stare.

"Hello, Coach," Jodi said from behind Harry.

He looked at the faces of his companions. They were frozen in wonder. That look, and the word "coach"— he hadn't been "coach" in a long time—ran though his mind as he turned his head.

First, he saw a woman's feet with bright red nail polish in high heel shoes with almost invisible straps.

Turning further could see her face.

She was smiling, "Hi, Coach, it's me. JJ!"

"JJ? What—" he started.

"—Harry, that's Jodi Worren," whispered Jack, "In case you really didn't know."

Seeing the puzzled look on his face as he started to get up, she grimaced, "I'm so sorry Coach, I really wanted my being in touch to be a pleasant surprise," she said putting a hand on his shoulder. "Not like this. I was going to slip into town and get some of the moving things started before I head to the coast. I wanted to get in touch when I got back later in the week. But, I'm going back to the coast earlier than I thought—and, I was going past here. And, I just thought —"

He shook his head and shrugged, "JJ?— I've seen pictures. My daughter is a big fan—I never—"

"—Well, I go by Jodi now, not Judy, and I'm not the scrawny kid I was when you saw me last," she said, standing there dressed in her high heels, clam digger slacks and sweater.

He recovered enough to say, "Let me introduce you. Well, I guess you already know Jack."

"Yes, at the house this morning he mentioned you all got together here. I'm really sorry about popping in this way."

"—No, no, relax," he went on— "This is Frank Peterson, our local banker. Frank, this is—"

"—Jodi Worren," Frank filled in, standing and extending his hand.

"I'm a big fan. Congratulations on the award."

"Thank you."

"This," Harry continued, "is Willy Cooper he's—"

"Hi! I'm Willy. Can I call you JJ?"

As soon as he said it, he could see the look in her eyes change to ice.

She stared through him and shook her head.

"Only Coach calls me JJ. Why don't you just keep calling me a two-fisted-piece-of-ass?"

Turning to Harry, "Coach, I really have to go, I'm sorry for this intrusion. Can we talk when I get back on Friday?"

"Of course," he smiled, still baffled.

"Can you give me a number where it's best to call you?"

He gave her his home number.

She gave him a quick kiss on the cheek, saying, "It's so good to see you. I'll call when I get back."

She apologized to the others for the interruption, said "Goodbye" and left.

Jack yelled, "Holy Wow!!! This morning it was a loose sweat suit and sneakers! "

"He laughed, "I guess she had to change to go back to the big city."

Then Jack erupted. He screamed, "Two-Fisted-Piece-of-Ass!!!" And messed up Willy's hair with both hands.

"She sure figured Willy out fast!"

"Didn't she do just that!" Frank chimed in.

Harry sat back in his chair and touched his cheek where she kissed him. He had a thousand questions.

How could he have seen all those pictures and not recognize her?

As soon as Jodi walked out, the few other patrons at the counter started talking about what they'd just seen.

MaryEllen, who'd been the waitress for longer than anyone could remember, watched as Jodi got into a car.

Then she shuffled to the table to take the group's orders. Starting with Willy, she couldn't hold it any longer, "You'll have—a Two-Fisted-Piece-of-Ass on toast?" She chuckled.

Everybody laughed.

Jack now was laughing so hard he had tears in his eyes.

MaryEllen, looking at Harry to take his order, asked, "Friend from the past, I gather?"

Taking a deep breath, he let it out slowly, "I haven't seen her since she was maybe fifteen. I was her basketball coach when she was a freshman in high school. I had no idea she was—"

Shaking her head, she attempted to finish Harry's sentence "—was—so—truly—stunning? With a face like that and a body like that? Wow! Ya know, I don't know why I used to think that models had to be flat chested."

She sighed and said to no one in particular, "My goodness. I wonder what it must feel like to be on this Earth and know that—whenever you want to— you can look like that!"

Nodding toward Willy, she repeated Jodi's comment, shaking her hips for emphasis with each word, 'keep calling me a two-fisted-piece-of-ass.'"

She laughed, "Ha!— I'm gonna like her—she's all right!"

The tone of this lunch was now different. He knew that they would have questions about the past, but he knew he wouldn't reveal all he knew about the girl he called JJ.

He sat there thinking, When I walked across the street from the store, I was one Harry to them, and now they're treating me like someone else. He could see it in their body language. As he started to talk, they leaned in to hear him better, as though somehow what he had to say, now, was very important.

But not Frank. He seemed to be spending time going through his own thoughts like he was both mystified and annoyed.

Harry was tempted to ask him, "Why are you so quiet?" just to get the focus off of himself, but didn't want to pry.

Harry had his own questions: why did she want to be in touch with someone from a past most people would want to forget, and how was he going to explain this to Corey? He smiled when he envisioned Dayna's reaction. It would be good to bring some pleasure to his daughter's eyes.

As he walked back to the store, he knew things had changed and there was nothing he could do about it.

It had happened before. If some basketball fanatic found out that he had played college ball with Julius Anderson they would act as though knowing Harry gave them a connection to the perennial MVP even though as a teammate, he was just "Julius" and didn't become the "JayA" everybody wanted to get close to until he worked harder on his game to compete in pro ball.

Opening the store, he checked the time. Corey said she was going shopping with Dayna after school. He figured they'd be getting home around the same time he did. He'd tell them when he got home. He looked through the catalogue to see about ordering fans.

Driving home, the questions persisted. How did JJ become Jodi Worren and what was she doing here? Looking at the fields, and the mountains in the background, he wondered if they were enough to attract a world-famous movie star to live here.

He thought, Einstein said the gravitational pull of stars can bend light. I wonder what her being here will do to Smalsville.

And then there's this thing about buying from my store. When did she find out I live here? That couldn't have anything to do with why she's here—could it?

When he got home, Dayna ran to the door to meet him. "Daddy! Daddy! She's here. She's here. Jodi Worren is here!!!"

He thought for a second, "She's at our house?" he asked in all seriousness.

Dayna seemed annoyed by the question, "Don't be silly Daddy," thinking she was being teased, "Why would Jodi Worren come to our house?"

As Corey came into the hall to greet him, Dayna tattled,

"Mom, Dad's making fun of me! He asked if Jodi Worren was in our house."

She smiled, "Was he very disappointed when you told him 'No?'"

He hugged Dayna, "Sweet girl, I wasn't making fun of you. I never want to hurt your feelings. I need to talk to mom for a second and then we all need to talk."

He gave Corey a kiss and looked to make sure Dayna had gone back to her room.

He felt he better get Corey used to the news before they told Dayna.

Sitting on the couch, telling her what happened at lunch and then about his relationship with JJ, felt strange. It was almost as if he was apologizing for telling her for the first time about another woman from his past, but he never felt that way about JJ. He couldn't get over the bizarre situation.

"All I remembered was she was a scrawny fifteen-year-old girl. Looking back, there was never any hint that would account for her growing up to be —"

"Well, she's not fifteen and certainly not scrawny now. What does she want out here?"

She started to wonder out loud. "If little caterpillar JJ had a crush on you then and now butterfly Jodi—"

Going along with what he thought was a joke, "Well, maybe that's it—she did kiss me on the cheek."

And, remembering what happened he laughed, "That was just after she told Willy Cooper he could continue to call her a two-fisted-piece-of-ass."

"She said *what*?"

He told her how that whole interplay happened.

She shook her head, "This woman must have men coming at her from every possible angle. It must be hard to sort out who wants what." Then, thinking of the absurdity of the situation, she shook her head and smiled,

"But, if she wants you—she can have you. I'm working on dinner."

Grabbing her arm as she was getting up from the couch, he pulled her down into his lap for a hug. "Don't you want to fight for me just a little?"

Looking like she was contemplating, she got up, "Nah."

He followed her into the kitchen to talk with her about how to tell Dayna. After all, they didn't know what was going to happen and didn't want their daughter to get any false hopes about getting to meet her idol. While they were talking in the kitchen, he noticed the light on the wall phone—the home line was in use. Dayna was on the phone; he was sure he knew what her conversation was about.

As soon as he noticed the light was out, Dayna came bursting into the room, "Daddy, you didn't tell me you got kissed by Jodi Worren!"

Harry and Corey exchanged glances.

He shook his head, "Oh, boy!" As he sat down on a chair holding his arms out for Dayna. He wouldn't ask where she heard it because he knew, by now, the only people in the area who had not heard about it were those who were in a coma.

For the second time in about five minutes, he explained that a young girl, who he hadn't seen in well over fifteen years, is now called by a different name and looks so different from when he knew her that he had no idea she was now this famous person.

He realized this was probably not the last time he would give this explanation—and he knew the only one who would ever hear his full recollection of that time in his life would be Corey.

He asked Dayna, "Well, you heard that she kissed me. Very lightly, on the cheek I might add, but did you hear she asked for our phone number?"

"Is she really coming here? Is she really coming here?"

"Whoa! Slow down! She said she wanted to talk and I gave her the number. I don't want you getting your hopes up about anything. All we know right now is she said she'd like to be in touch."

Looking to see if any of his cautionary part of the message was getting through, he resolved that if in any way he could get Dayna to meet her idol, he'd do it.

Corey chimed in, "Actually, I read an interview with her right after the Academy Awards and she said she wouldn't visit any girls whose room was messy or who didn't get their homework done on time."

It took Dayna a second before she realized Corey was kidding.

She groaned, "Maahm!"

Corey was relieved Dayna took it as a joke because, as soon as she said it, she worried Dayna might react badly to any playfulness on a subject she took so much to heart.

Harry fought to keep a straight face.

When Dayna went back to her room, that same feeling that things had changed—that he felt after Jodi left the luncheonette—came upon him again.

He told Corey of his questions on his drive home and Einstein's theory because he realized, for Corey and Dayna, things were changing too.

THIRTY-ONE

Harry was working in the store on Friday when Jodi called the house. Corey was taken aback when she heard a young woman's voice asking for Harry. At first, when Jodi introduced herself, Corey thought it was someone calling about Jodi Worren rather than it actually being Jodi Worren on the phone.

Realizing it was her, Corey said, "Harry told me that he gave you our number. If you want to talk with him, why don't you come for dinner tonight?"

After she accepted, Corey wondered about her invitation. It had slipped out so naturally. While Harry had told her he had given Jodi the number, he hadn't said anything about how and when they were going to get together.

Corey just assumed he'd approve.

She called him at the store.

"I just got off the phone with Jodi Worren. I invited her for dinner."

"For tonight?"

"Yep."

"Well, OK. But the sky looks pretty dark and the radio said we're in for a storm. But let's assume it's on."

"OK. But do you have any idea what this woman eats?"

"Does she need any sort of special diet? I guess I can ask Dayna if she knows whether or not Jodi's a vegetarian.

"Oh, I guess I'll just make my mom's meatloaf and have a lot of vegetables and a big salad."

It was raining hard when Harry arrived and saw Corey and Dayna straightening up the living room.

As soon as he took off his coat, the fire whistle sounded and his pager unit went off to announce a house fire about two miles on the other side of the lake, north of town.

"Gotta go."

"But Daddy! Jodi Worren is coming!

"She'll be here soon, Daddy. Jodi Worren!"

"I know. I'll be back as soon as this fire lets me."

"Harry?" Corey implored as he went out the door, "What will I say to her?"

"I'm sure Dayna will think of something."

Dayna told Corey, "I hope it's a false alarm."

"Me, too, dear, or maybe they'll have it under control quickly. I can't see how anything can burn in all this rain. I'm going to finish making the salad. You can finish straightening up the living room."

Corey went ahead making the salad and thought of things to say to Jodi and tasks to keep Dayna busy while they waited for her to arrive.

Time seemed to go by quickly. The next thing she knew there was a knock on the door and Dayna was flying down the stairs from her room. Corey looked at the kitchen clock and thought—Well, she's right on time.

Putting down the salad bowl and taking off her apron, she started for the door, but Dayna was already there. Corey watched her daughter open the door to find her idol in the doorway.

"Hi!" Jodi said. Then, smiling at Corey, handing her a bunch of flowers continued, "My boots are really muddy, can I just leave them here?"

"That's fine and thank you for these. I'll put these flowers in a vase. Take Miss Worren's raincoat and hang it in the back hall."

Jodi held out her hand to shake with Corey. "You must be Corey.

"And . . .?" Dayna, zipping back from having hung up the raincoat said, "My name is Dayna, Miss Worren."

"Um! Dayna Daweson," she smiled, "I'll bet your dad calls you DD."

Dayna hesitated, "No," she said cautiously not wanting to offend her.

"Well, do you know that your dad called me JJ?"

"Yes. Dad told us about that," she said, mentally comparing Jodi to the room full of pictures she had.

Holding out her hand, Jodi smiled, "Well, how about I'll call you DD and I'd like it if you call me JJ?"

Then, looking at Corey, "Will that be OK?"

Dayna held on to Jodi's hand looking to her mom for the answer.

"Sure," Corey shrugged.

"Whatever you guys want to call yourselves is fine with me."

Dayna was ecstatic, "Mom, can I show JJ my room?"

"Harry's not back yet—he's in the volunteer fire department, and they got a call." She glanced at Dayna still holding Jodi's hand and starting to lead her to the stairs.

"Do you mind?"

"Of course not," Jodi smiled as she tilted her head to let Corey know she was used to the reaction.

"Lead on, DD," Jodi smiled.

Dayna's room was filled with pictures of Jodi from her early modeling days and scrapbooks of other articles and publicity about the movie and the awards. Jodi wanted to seem appreciative of the adulation, but deep down it caused her to worry about someone living vicariously through images of her.

She hoped Dayna had other things in her life that made her happy and fulfilled. When Jodi finished leafing through the last scrapbook, she noticed a black frame standing on the dresser. It looked like a family portrait with another, smaller child in the picture.

Just then the phone rang and Dayna looked at the phone.

Jodi told her, "Go ahead. Go take your call. I'll see you downstairs."

Jodi got to the bottom of the stairs and found Corey in the kitchen.

"It's like a little shrine up there. I don't know that I'll ever get fully comfortable with that. I'm happy that girls like Dayna like me and think they know me—but there are some pictures up there…"

She shook her head, "There's a picture of me on a magazine cover standing next to a palm tree and a ladder. I swear if it didn't have my name on it or if I didn't remember that ladder—I wouldn't know that it was me. I got stuck in the airport for seven hours on the way to that shoot. I flew all night—my eyes were red, I was sick—I had some sort of stomach bug."

She said quietly, "I'm sure I threw up on that tree right after the shutter clicked—but, when they get finished retouching these things . . ."

She sighed, "And then young girls think they are supposed to look like I looked in that picture. I don't look like I looked in that picture!"

Corey grimaced and shook her head slowly, "Hey, it's not just young girls."

Jodi said softly, "I know. I'd like to bring her something of me that's really me— that's not all prettied up."

On the wall near where they were standing was a larger version of the family photo that Jodi noticed in Dayna's room. She pointed to Henry in the picture and asked, "Who's this little one?"

As soon as the question left her lips, the look on Corey's face told her she was about to hear something tragic.

Corey looked up the stairs to see if Dayna was around. Then she started to get teary. Instinctively, Jodi put her arm around her.

Corey told her about Henry and his death six years before.

As she listened, she tried to think back to what she was doing around the time this family was dealing with the death of a child.

She nodded, "So your daughter and I have that in common—we both have lost brothers. Did Coach ever tell you about my brother?"

Corey thought for a moment. "He was the boy that went into the Marines? And then your mom was sick, right?"

Jodi nodded.

Now Corey was thinking of what that must have been like for Jodi.

Corey tried to regain her composure when she heard Dayna coming down the stairs. She turned toward the kitchen, putting her back to the steps to give her time to dry her eyes.

Dayna had a camera in her hand and shyly asked Jodi if her mom could take a picture of them. Seeing the look on Corey's face, she reassured her. "It happens a lot."

Corey said, "By the way, who called?"

"Jenny Masters."

Corey didn't bother asking what this very popular senior, who never once called or had anything to do with Dayna, was calling about.

She just said "Oh. OK."

Corey was taking the picture just as they heard Harry's car in the driveway.

"Hi, Dear," Corey said as he closed the front door.

Jodi, marveling at Corey's composure, walked over to greet Harry. She wasn't going to say anything more about Henry unless someone else did.

Dayna came over to tell him of her new nickname. "I'm gonna call her JJ and she calls me DD."

"Well, that didn't take long. I assume you've seen the room?"

"Yes, it's very nice," Jodi nodded

"What happened at the fire?" Corey asked.

"Not much. It was a chimney fire at the Pawl's place. It's really wet out there so there wasn't much going to happen to the roof and luckily some of the guys live nearby. They used a garden hose and had it pretty much knocked down before we got there with the trucks."

"JJ, Daddy saved Billy Pawl's life," Dayna chimed in.

"Let's sit down before the meal gets cold," Corey said. "We can talk about Billy Pawl while we're eating."

He said, "By the way, it looks like you picked up a nail or something in your right rear tire, it's flat."

"Can we call to get it fixed?"

Corey said, "It's a little late for a local garage to be open. Harry can get you home. It'll give you guys a chance to catch up on old times. Unless you need the car in the morning, we can deal with the tire tomorrow, assuming it stops raining by then."

He agreed, "If the driveway is dry enough tomorrow morning, I'll put the spare on before I go to work and we'll go from there."

Corey went into the kitchen.

Jodi asked if she could help bring things to the table. Corey thanked her and said she and Dayna could handle it. This was a gentle reminder to Dayna who had already seated herself next to the seat reserved for Jodi and was studying her every gesture.

Harry put his hand on Jodi's shoulder and aimed her toward the dining room as Dayna hopped up and retrieved the bowl of salad.

As soon as she reseated herself, Dayna had to tell Jodi about Harry saving Billy Pawl. She frequently looked at him to make sure that she had the details right.

"Daddy had to take a CPR course because he used to coach basket—well, I guess you know all about that, don't you?"

Jodi smiled. "Wasn't that the course you were coming from when. . .?" Referring to the night he found her running away.

"Yep, the very same."

Dayna looked to Corey for an explanation of what they were referring to, but she just shrugged, "I think it was before our time."

Undaunted, Dayna continued, "Well anyway, Daddy knew CPR and he used it on Billy and saved his life."

Jodi said, "On the night he took that course he saved my life too."

There was a long pause and puzzled looks while that information sank in.

Finally, Dayna asked timidly "Did you stop breathing?"

"No." She smiled, "No, I had just stopped thinking. I had some trouble at home with my grandmother, and I made the stupid decision to run away and hitch a ride to New York."

Looking at her, she continued, "Your dad was coming by on his way home from that CPR course, and saw me and demanded I get in his car.

"He took me to see a woman he kinda also rescued and helped turn her life around. She told me what would have happened to me if your dad hadn't come along in time. Later she introduced me to a friend of hers who I could go to in New York."

She sighed, "Now, in a way I'm running away again. I came to Smalsville because I was feeling like my life was spinning out of control. In modeling I always know where the camera is. As your dad, above all people, would know, I wasn't very good at basketball but at least I always knew where the basket was.

"With my current situation I am not sure what the goal is. So, I'm just not sure where I go from here. I was hoping your dad could help resuscitate my thinking and maybe I could gain control again."

Jodi, seeing their stunned looks, smiled at him.

"By the way, I never told you that I knew that the jacket I was wearing—and you said you had found—I knew you had actually gotten it from the thrift store."

Seeing him chuckle, she explained to Dayna and Corey.

"As a kid I was very poor. After my mom died, I had to live with my grandparents who were very poor but very proud. One day, when it was starting to turn really cold, I was at the shopping center and saw a nice warm jacket at the thrift store. But I knew we couldn't afford it.

"A couple of days later, while I was away at a basketball game, your dad brought the same jacket to my house for me. He told my grandparents it had been left in the Lost and Found at school and unclaimed for—I think you told them it was for over a year?"

He just smiled.

"You see your dad knew if he told them he bought it for me, because he knew I needed it, they wouldn't take it—they were too proud to accept charity. So, your dad gave it to them in a way they could accept what I needed."

He shook his head, "I hated having to lie to them, but I knew if I didn't you could freeze to death. But, how did you know it was the same jacket?"

"I recognized the embroidery, like a butterfly, that was used to patch a tear in the sleeve. I noticed it in the thrift store and remembered it when I saw the jacket."

She looked at them. "I kept that jacket for a long time. Even when I went to New York. But by then, I'd filled out a little more and I was making a lot of money modeling, because of my manager, Pops. Then, in talking with him, I realized someone else could use the jacket. When I was getting ready to go to Hollywood, I asked Pops to send it back to the same thrift store and we decided to send a check as a donation. We asked them to use some of the money to lower the price of warm clothing in the winter."

Harry smiled.

During dinner they talked about how Harry and Corey met, and Dayna being born after Corey graduated.

Harry said, "She got a degree in business administration one month and diaper administration the next."

Jodi told them about starting out with Pops, and how there were a lot of people who Pops and his wife had helped get started. Dayna asked Jodi about Sharin and making the movie with her. When Dayna said she had liked the movie. Everyone was surprised when Jodi said she hadn't seen it.

"Sharin used to like to screen her movies to see how she could improve her craft. She told me she watched some of her movies over and over. She had a screening room in her home and she showed me the movies that were the parts of her story I would play. But I was nervous enough while I was making the movie—I don't think I could sit through watching my own performance. I'd only see the flaws. So, I never wanted to see it."

She sighed, "You know, Sharin was old school. She preferred to be called 'an actress' rather than the modern way that some women call themselves 'an actor." But, with what little work I've done, I don't know if either of those labels fits me yet. With Sharin gone, if I want to do anything more in this craft I might have to find a drama coach I trusted or classes."

Dayna protested, "But you won the Academy Award."

Jodi smiled at her, "When you watch the credits at the end of a picture you see hundreds of people made that movie. Someone wrote the script. People found or built the sets. The hairdresser and makeup teams made me look a certain way. The lighting people lit me and the camera people filmed me in the way that the director of photography wanted.

"The director told me, 'The camera is going to be over here. Go over there. Look happy or sad or thoughtful and say these lines.' I did that in my first movie, and I wasn't good enough to be in the final cut of the movie. I did that in Sharin's movie and they gave me an award.

"When I won the award for the Sharin movie, they put me back into the first movie just to make a buck. It isn't like my work suddenly changed—getting better all by itself."

She shrugged, "I don't know. If my work wasn't good the first time. . . It might sound like I am trying to be modest. But, I am just trying to be honest. I didn't have enough of a feel for what I was doing to know if I did anything different in the second movie than what I did in the first.

"It's not like I studied acting and honed my skills. I hear people talking about refining their instrument. I don't know what that would mean in terms of my acting. I don't know what skills to refine.

"It's hard for me to understand. It's like everyone thinks I did this incredible magic trick, but I don't know how I did it, let alone if I can ever do it again."

Seeing they were thinking about what she had just said, she turned to Dayna to ask her about schoolwork.

Later Corey related an amusing incident at the optometrist's office where she had worked.

Jodi liked Corey and how natural she was in her spontaneous invitation to dinner. She knew she was invited as a friend of Harry and not because she was a celebrity.

To her great satisfaction, they all seemed to treat her like just another guest.

She enjoyed watching the playful interactions between her three hosts. Yet, she couldn't forget the loss they had suffered. They were lucky to have each other for strength and comfort in such a tragic time. Watching Dayna, Jodi remembered the loss of her own brother.

After dinner, the three adults knew there was no way Dayna would go up to her room while Jodi was there. Moving to the living room, they all talked for a while before it was time for Harry to take her home.

Corey said, "I've already heard a rumor that you're going to be taking over the old theater in town."

"I didn't even know there was an old theater in town, but I'm open to suggestions."

Getting up, Dayna asked, "Can my dad take another a picture of you and me with my mom this time?"

"Of course."

Dayna ran to get her camera, and then gently pulled Jodi to an area in front of the fireplace. Jodi, placing Dayna in a position she knew would make Dayna look best, put her arm around Dayna's shoulders and Corey's waist. When the flash went off, Harry was amazed by what he saw. It seemed like Jodi knew exactly when the shutter was opening and at that instant was totally still, as if projecting an energy back toward the lens.

Jodi gave Corey and Dayna a hug goodnight and told them she hoped she would see them tomorrow when she came to get her car. Then she and Harry set out for her house.

Getting into his car, he noticed when she sat her short skirt climbed up to where he saw the light brown arrowhead-shaped birthmark on her outer thigh. Remembering it from when she was a kid wearing basketball shorts, he thought, If I had any doubts this woman could be JJ, that would clinch it. He guessed it's the only sign of the scrawny girl that remains on this beautiful woman.

He realized there are some people who—even if you have not been in contact for a long while—when you are reconnected, the content changes but the comfort is constant. Like there hadn't been a separation. His talks with Buddy were like that.

And then he thought, Here I am giving JJ a lift again. For all she had changed, it still felt the same. He felt he hadn't changed that much, although he knew the topics would be far different.

His musing was interrupted when she said, "Coach, your family is lovely."

She lowered her voice, "Just before you came home, Corey was telling me about your son. I am so sorry to hear about that. I can't imagine what that must be like. It's impossible to even imagine how anyone can live through the loss of their child."

He said softly, "Well, in truth, you don't. Or at least not all of you lives through it. There's a part of you that dies and stays forever with that child. But, the part of you that lives builds around that lost part and—with the others in your life—lives on.

"I can still see his brave little face confused by the constant pain. If I tried to think about it calmly and without anything but logic, I would have known that Henry would not live forever—that he—like all of us—was starting to die from the moment he was born. But knowing that on the brain level does not help on the heart level. You can't say, 'OK. If he was born, he was going to die anyway. . .' It just doesn't stop the crying. It just doesn't make it better. It just doesn't."

He paused and took a deep breath, "I couldn't have survived at all if I had to go through it alone.

"Luckily for me and so profoundly unlucky for her, Corey went through it with me. We had a miscarriage before that, so even though Dayna seemed healthy, when Henry was dying there was this fear—a fear that crept into our very existence—about our ability to maintain the life of a child. We questioned if there was something wrong with us, if we passed on something and sooner or later Dayna would..."

He paused again, "And then of course there was Dayna herself and what she was going through. As terrible as the loss of a child is, watching your surviving child deal with the loss is heartbreaking—just heartbreaking.

"But, we had each other. And we had a therapist named Margaret Solomon. We thought we were hiring her to help Dayna and really she helped us all. That woman couldn't have done anything more for us. And the way she's constructed, she couldn't have done anything less. We were truly fortunate to find her.

"Henry is always always close in my mind, but there are two days each year: his birthday and the anniversary of the day he died. . ."

He shook his head, "But you know, there was something weird. The first time we went to see Henry on the anniversary, there were fresh flowers on his grave. We couldn't figure out where they came from.

"Then a couple of days later, one of the guys from the fire department who lives near the cemetery mentioned that he saw the Pawl family at Henry's grave three days before we went. He remembered the date because it happened to be his birthday."

"Three days before?

"Was that the day you saved their son—what's his name?"

"Billy." He said, a bit choked up.

"Yeah. Before hearing that, whenever I thought about saving Billy, it was always a replay of actions—seeing the glove, finding the section of fence, starting CPR. But now I reflect on saving the whole Pawl family from going through the kind of grief that we went through.

"I reflect on keeping them from forced membership in the club no one in their right mind wants to join."

As he thought about the doctor's words,—"that kid stays dead,"—he fought back tears realizing that tears would only hamper his driving.

She remembered the losses in her life.

"Life can be so hard and unfair. But I have to think that my mom—by dying when she did—was spared what happened to my brother."

Thinking about the times that Harry spent with her and her brother as their mother was dying, she said, "I wish I could have been of some help to you, like you were to me when. . ."

"How could you?"

Clearing his throat, "You didn't know. And even if you did know, no one can help. Corey, Dayna and me, we lived it together so we could try to take care of each other. Unless you have lost a child, you can't know. But, in a way you did help—by distracting Dayna."

He explained how Dayna had come across her pictures in a magazine and that he and Corey were pleased to see Dayna focus on something other than illness and hospitals.

She tried to picture a younger Dayna turning the pages of the magazines.

She said softly, "Dayna and I have something in common. We've both lost a brother.

"I hope someday I can find the right moment to talk with her about that."

She paused, "But still, there is something almost obscene when I look back now and realize that while your child was dying, and your family was in so much pain, I was caught up in the stupid superficial world where the major crisis was whether the shoes could be dyed to match the dress in time."

Then she tried to recall, "What was it that you used to tell us about shoes? 'I wept. . .'"

He nodded slowly, pleased she remembered, he continued the quote, ". . . because I had no shoes and then I saw a man who had no feet."

Hearing his voice and his phrases again, she quietly congratulated herself for having known—after her bucket nightmare—that finding him was what she had to do.

Aware that his family's loss had made them stronger, she was comforted by the gracious way that they accepted her intrusion into their lives.

She started to get teary because of the sense of security that being back with him brought her. Realizing this cry had been coming on for a long time now, she poured out her story. She told him about her friendless life in high school after he left, and her three-week period of homelessness when she and her grandparents lived in a church basement because her grandfather drank up the rent money.

He chided himself, "I guess their drinking was worse than I thought."

"Well, in truth, I never said anything about it, and it got much worse after you left. On my birthday they would talk about John, Jr. and what he did when he was that age, and that would always set them off."

She paused, "I guess I didn't talk about it, and couldn't put any of it in writing, because somehow, I thought that that would make it real, and besides when it got so bad and you were already gone there was nothing. . . And I couldn't write that I quit the basketball team—I was afraid I'd be a disappointment to you."

"I wrote but my letter came back as undeliverable. Now I know why."

"My occasional babysitting for Jacqui ended when Naomi finally came home and they all moved to Oakland."

She paused, "I am sorry to tell you, but when I asked this man, Tim Kelly, to look for you—he's the security man for the company— I asked him to look for Jacqui too. He told me she died of hepatitis."

"Oh. That's so sad. She was so young. Did he know when?"

"He didn't say."

She told him that it was through Jacqui that she met Francine who had lived in New York. She told him that her grandparents had died, six months apart, after she moved to New York.

She told him of her life in New York, about Pops, Connie, Peter Warrin and her new name.

Finally, she got herself to stop crying.

It was the first time since confiding in Connie and Pops that she told someone about what Peter had done to her. She could see Harry grit his teeth when she told him about that night. She told him everything including Connie calling Leno and her comment, "Nobody fucks with Gort."

Hearing that, he chuckled and smiled.

She explained that Peter caused her to doubt her sense of self-worth. But, that the life-living-lessons had helped her to move on after that night.

She said, "It was because of your teachings that I was able to keep the name I liked even though I hated how it evolved."

She told him that when she told Pops about the jacket and that she'd lost track of him, Pops said, "Losing track of a mensch like that is such a pity."

She said wistfully, "Pops was such a truly wise, generous and caring man. Among the many things he did for me, he eased my mind making sure I understood whatever might have happened to Peter was not my fault. You and he would have liked each other. He must have known I'd need to find you."

She went on, "After Pops died, I was devastated. I felt lost. By the time Sharin died, I was still so off balance because of losing him, that I allowed myself to stumble into a stupid marriage with Edgar."

"Why stupid?"

"I can't believe I let myself fall into a marriage like that. Looking back, I realize that I had no role model for what a good marriage should be like. My grandparents were both bitter drunks—spiteful, stingy people. I never saw any hint of affection there."

She shook her head, "And, Edgar was so persistent. I hate to say it, but I guess he was a bit of a father figure. I think I must have mistaken his not trying to kiss me initially as a sign of some kind of courtly respect. Which suited me fine, then. But, I should have realized that there was really no love there.

"That marriage was almost like no marriage at all. We made love for the first time on our wedding night. Even then, right after we did it, I thought it had only happened because it seemed to be what we were supposed to do. We were both tired from a long day—it didn't feel romantic at all. And I thought if this is what he wants I'll just go along.

"After that, he didn't display much interest. He worked long hours and we were apart a lot. I was starting to feel that what he really wanted was an ornament, not a wife. We had separate bedrooms. I told myself a joke: our apartment had so many bedrooms that it made no sense to share one. But I was his wife—I should have wanted to make things work out.

"When we tried to have a 'honeymoon' in London, wrapped around a Paris business meeting, we wound up in the middle of this 'Jodimania' and things got worse from there.

"Now, his death leaves me with such a huge financial windfall, and such a convoluted corporate maze, that I feel even more off balance—more isolated from myself. I keep wishing that when Pops wanted to explain the financial stuff to me I would have let him, but I didn't."

She sighed, "Pops talked about a gospel song that said, 'When I look back over my life, and I think things over, I can truly say that I've been blessed—'

"I think that's my life. I think of my career as a blessing. But I don't know if some of the other things that happened were really blessings. So much of what has happened to me was out of my control. I don't feel that I can have any confidence in any problem-solving skills. Everything was so easy. With Peter and then Edgar, almost as soon as I recognized my mistake—the problems were gone. Things were resolved so quickly and with no effort on my part. I get abused by Peter, and the next day he's gone. I realize that my marriage to Edgar has serious troubles, and that night he dies."

She shook her head, "These things just happened."

She sighed, "I know in some ways it's a blessing, but in some ways it's not. I mean I don't know for sure what happened to Peter, but I was relieved that I wasn't going to find him living in my apartment after what he did to me. And I don't want to think of Edgar's death as a blessing, but I was relieved that I avoided the carnage of a Hollywood-headlines divorce. Even if I wasn't looking for anything in a settlement, it would still have been a grotesque, press-feeding frenzy."

She paused, "But these things ending the way they did—well—it's disorienting. It's not like I took some control of my life and climbed out of my mistakes. I know that I've been extremely lucky, maybe even blessed, not to have been more damaged, but I worry—how long can uncontrolled luck last?

"At some point I need to be able to take care of myself. I keep wondering if I'll ever feel like I can make it on my own.

"So, if it's my perception that makes things good or bad, I just don't know—have I been blessed or have I been crippled by the fact that I had no part in dealing with the pitfalls in my life?"

He couldn't answer her. All he could do was listen and try to take it all in.

But, when she told him of Sharin's suggestion about escaping into acting as a way of coping when Pops died, and related her story about Elizabeth Taylor losing Mike Todd and giving an Oscar nominated performance, he shook his head.

He said, "I'm no expert on grief counseling, but that sounds a bit superficial. I think you have to give the grieving process its due. You have to come to terms with the death in order to move on with your own life. You can only escape into a role for so long. When her part in the movie was over, her husband would've still been dead. If she hadn't dealt with her loss by the time the part ended, she would've had to start then.

"Hiding doesn't solve problems it just postpones them."

The rain was still falling when they finished their journey up the long driveway to her house. She invited him in to show him what she planned to change.

"Please, make yourself at home while I get out of these wet things."

He wiped his feet on the mat and hung up his coat. He was surprised at how quickly she had gotten the furniture moved into the house she had just bought. Running his fingers along the surface of a finely inlaid mirror frame, he was looking at a large, but not overly ornate, mahogany desk with a small maple wood inlay of the Scales of Justice that looked out of place in the living room, when she came back.

She was out of her jeans and sweater. She was barefoot and wearing a dark red satin robe that matched the color of her nail polish. She told him most of the furnishings were there already. She just arranged for people to clean up and make it livable so she could stay there. Once they finished the renovation she'd move in some more of her own stuff.

She moved toward the couch and he followed her. He sat down. She sat on the other end and studied him for a moment.

In a low soft voice, her words came out. "As I said at dinner, I see my life as spinning out of control. I need someone in my life who I can trust. Someone to see me for me—not for the image on the covers or the movie posters—that face, that body."

She told him about her bucket dream and then shook her head, "When it was just the 'world class beauty' stuff, it took a while, but I think I was learning how to handle it. I got to where I could almost predict the way men or women were going to react.

"Now, with the award, and Edgar's money on top of all that, I have more people all around me and they all seem to want something. And now I have more things to try to be responsible for than I have ever had to deal with. I don't know what people want, but they all seem to need my attention.

"I don't know who I can trust or, what's worse, I don't know if I can trust myself to know who to trust."

Sighing, looking at him, she smiled, remembering the past.

"You were there for me before any of this. You were there for me, my mom and my brother. You were the only one. You took the time to talk with me when I had nothing. You cared for poor and skinny JJ.

"I need that now. I have some tough decisions to make soon, and I know that I've lost my balance and I need it now more than ever."

The honesty in her voice called him to lean forward to reply.

He closed his eyes and, trying to put past, present, and all that lay in between into place, he waited to find the right words for her.

Finally, he said, "Well, you've come a long way from back then to here. And, it's a long way from our old basketball court to me having a wife and a child, and running a hardware store."

He nodded. "We can work on balance if that's what you need."

She mouthed, "Thank you." The words were silent.

He realized the time. Corey was aware they had some catching up to do and he wouldn't be right home, but he didn't want her to worry about him driving in the storm.

They made plans to talk in the morning about getting her car.

When they parted, Jodi felt tired. She felt that this night she would finally get a good night's sleep.

Corey was already in bed, but she was awake.

He got ready for bed and crawled in beside her. He told her what Jodi told him about the past and why she was there.

He knew Corey would never tell a soul.

"It was interesting what she said about you saving her life."

"I didn't feel that way about it at the time. But when something happens you don't always know how the other person sees it and how it'll play out in the future.

"It certainly wasn't as clear cut as Billy Pawl. But to her…"

She spooned closer into him, pulling his arm around her waist. She told him what Jodi had said about the pictures in Dayna's room.

"It's interesting to me, even with what she says about her balance, she still has that sense of herself—that perspective on what's real and what's not."

She continued, "She's the most seriously gorgeous person I have ever seen. I don't mean just beautiful—even seeing all the pictures of her, I was not prepared for that!

"I can't imagine what it must be like to walk through life looking like that. And you had no clue when she was a kid?"

"Absolutely zero!

"She was just a sad, lanky kid."

"But her hair is the same color, isn't it?"

"Yes"

"And of course, her eyes…"

"Well, I guess I never really noticed her eyes."

"How could you not notice her eyes? They're amazing! You could almost fall into them! I'm not attracted to women, but I do appreciate beauty, and I found myself almost falling into them from across the table."

"Well, she didn't wear makeup when I knew her."

"She doesn't wear much now."

"No. But she didn't wear any then. You heard her. Her grandparents couldn't even afford a warm coat for the kid.

"None of her clothes fit her, but they were always clean. I mean, her grandparents were just scraping by as it was.

"They weren't going to spend money on cosmetics.

"Look, nobody could be more surprised about the way she turned out than me."

"Except maybe her—from what she told you, she's still trying to adjust to it all."

When he told her his feeling about Jodi's energy when he took the picture of the three of them, she agreed.

"I noticed that too when I took one of her and Dayna. It was like she was totally relaxed, yet totally frozen in time for just that moment. Almost like she was controlling the camera from a distance."

They wondered if all models had that quality, or just the good models.

Snuggling even closer, she asked, "Are you tired?"

He grinned in the dark.

He knew what those words meant.

THIRTY-TWO

The next morning was clear. Jodi, already up, was wearing baggy sweats, and lying across her bed reading when she heard two men in the house. She hadn't heard them come in but she could see Jack Bargers' name on the truck outside and she could hear that they were taking measurements.

They were talking as though they thought they were alone. Between one calling out dimensions for the other to record, she heard one of them saying, "Well, I guess Missy is gonna be really pissed."

"Yeah, we hear all that fuss about Missy coming home from Hollywood to be the captain at the game and then Jodi Worren moves into her hometown. What the hell is she doing here anyhow?"

"Making work for us, so don't knock it."

"No. I'm not knocking it, she can bring all her rich friends for all I care. Boss says she had some history with Harry. He knew her as a kid or something."

"Who knows?"

Deciding to make her presence known, Jodi came down the hall and walked toward the embarrassed workers. Seeing her, both workmen jumped. One said, "I'm sorry Miss Worren, we didn't know you were here."

"Yeah, we didn't see any car, so we thought. . ."

"That's OK. No harm done."

Entering the living room, where they were measuring the windows, she asked their names. Jay and Ben.

"My car had a flat and I left it at Harry and Corey's."

She thought for a moment, "Any chance, when you're finished here, you could drop me off there to pick it up, if it's not out of your way?"

They eagerly agreed it would be no problem at all.

While she waited for them to finish measuring for the new windows, she said, "I couldn't help but overhear—if it's not too personal—who's Missy?"

Ben looked at Jay and then shrugged, why not, "Well, every year we have a charity softball game. The faculty and guests against the varsity team.

"It's after their season ends. It's kind of an honor to be the captain of the faculty-and-guests team."

Jay continued, "Missy McQueen grew up here and was, you know, the star of the senior play, the Miss this and Miss that, and then she went off to Hollywood to try to get into the movies. Her mom is on the fundraising committee and kinda wangled the captain's job for Missy this year."

Ben put in, "Yeah, Missy is all stuck up and stuff and she thinks she's the biggest thing this little town has ever seen.

"In school we called her Missy the Queen."

"We were just saying—well, with you here now. . ." Jay's voice trailed off.

Jodi asked, "Do you know any work she's done?"

Looking at each other, they shrugged and shook their heads.

"What kind of charities does the game support?"

Ben said, "Well, last year the money went for a new playground. I'm not sure what they have in mind this year."

"I think I heard a new scoreboard for the gym and if they have anything left over, new jackets for the cheerleaders," said Jay.

"Yeah, Missy was also head cheerleader," Ben added.

Finishing up, they got in their truck to give Jodi a lift to her car.

Pulling up at Harry's house, they noticed several cars in the driveway. Ben said, "There's Missy's mom's car over there."

Seeing her tire was fixed, Jodi thanked the men and said she'd be fine from here. She was just going to tell Corey she was taking the car.

Corey, having seen the truck drive up, was getting to the door when Jodi knocked.

"Hi, Jodi. We were just getting some coffee. Stay for a while and have a cup?"

"I don't want to impose."

"No imposition. This is our Saturday morning committee meeting to get ready for an annual softball game. We have the game to raise some extra money for the school."

She took Jodi into the kitchen and introduced her to Pat McQueen, her sister, Becky James, and Mary Cooper.

Corey gave Jodi a look and said she understood Harry had introduced her to Mary's husband, Willy, at the restaurant.

Remembering her interaction with Willy, Jodi just smiled and only said, "Nice to meet you."

Jodi said, "I don't want to interrupt your meeting."

They insisted she stay.

Corey said, "I better let Dayna know that you're here."

Jodi sat at the kitchen counter while the ladies were at the table talking about publicity, ticket sales, raffle tickets and the refreshment stand.

Dayna came down, sitting with Jodi, she asked her, "Have you ever played softball?"

Jodi noticed the ladies stopped talking and were listening for her answer. "Not since high school gym class—they made us do that, and volleyball."

Dayna told her they had a basketball hoop in the back and asked her to shoot some hoops.

Smiling to Corey that she didn't mind, Jodi said, "Nice meeting you, all," to the committee and went to join Dayna.

When Harry got home for lunch, the ladies were just getting ready to leave. He heard the sounds coming from the back yard.

He asked. "Is Dayna playing basketball?"

"Well, your high school protégé came to pick up her car and, before she knew it, Dayna decided they should shoot some hoops."

Harry took a step toward the back yard, but she grabbed him and said, "Before you go out there, the committee has something to ask you."

Getting to the back yard, he saw Jodi taking a shot. It missed.

He said, "Square your shoulders to the hoop and keep your elbows in."

She turned and smiled, "That's really why I came here. My shot was getting rusty."

Dayna ran over to give him a hug. Jodi went to collect the ball before it rolled down the hill. She walked toward Harry with the ball on her hip and squinting into the sun behind him.

"Thanks for fixing my car—oh, and my shot."

She handed him the ball.

"I've just been deputized to ask you a favor," he stated haltingly, motioning toward the committee women who were looking through the window.

"I don't want you to say anything now, I want you to think about it, and then tell me if it's too much of an imposition."

"Sounds serious."

"Well, depending on your schedule, the committee would like to know if you would consider playing in the softball game."

Dayna became excited, "Oh, please say, yes!"

All Jodi could think of was Missy McQueen.

Putting her hands on Dayna's shoulders she looked her in the eye, then, looking at the faces of the women watching her, said, "Of course I'll think about it."

Lowering her voice told him, "There's something I need to talk to you about first."

She asked Dayna to excuse them so she and her dad could talk privately for a minute. Dayna wasn't happy, but she left them alone.

She told him about the conversation she overheard at her house.

"What do you think I should do?

"I don't want to upstage this girl."

"Well, it was Missy's mother who came up with the idea and Missy's aunt is there and agreed.

"Maybe they both think that more people will come out if you're involved. Missy is still the captain, so it's really up to you."

"OK. I'll have to check my schedule, and I might need to get some things, but it may work out."

They went to catch up with Dayna, who was in the living room with Corey and the other women when they came in.

He said, "JJ needs to check her schedule, but it might work out."

Then added, "Or is it JJ needs to check out Jodi Worren's schedule?"

She smiled, "Well, you know that's a good point. I'd love to be just low-profile JJ here, but that's something I'd like to talk to Corey about."

Saying goodbye to the committee as they left, Harry reminded Dayna to put the basketball back in the garage and went to get some of last night's leftover meatloaf for lunch.

Jodi saw Corey putting the small plates and coffee cups in the dishwasher and went to help.

"I'd like to help out by playing in the game, but also I was hoping to keep my being here somewhat low key."

She looked at Harry and laughed, "Yeah I know, coming up to you in broad daylight in the only eating place in town was not a good start, I was not planning that—but once I knew I'd be passing the place and you'd be there—Anyhow, I guess the question is," looking at Corey, "What kind of publicity do you do for this game? My guess is your friends don't want me to play because they think I'm a whiz bang softball player. So how do I help out and still try to stay somewhat under the radar?"

"Well, so far, the only thing we've ever done is put an ad in the local paper a week before the game, although most people around here know when it's going to be. And then the local radio station will do a public service announcement if you mention their call letters at the end of the spot and thank them for caring."

Jodi thought for a minute. "I guess that would be OK. I assume the people that they would reach are people who probably already know I'm here. If my playing means they're more likely to come, that'd be fine. I just didn't want —"

"Jodimania," Dayna jumped in.

Jodi, looking surprised Dayna knew about that, sighed, "Yeah, that was scary."

"We get BBC news on the public radio station." Corey explained.

Jodi smiled, nodding she understood.

Dayna said, "Maybe we tell the committee that you'll do it if they don't do any more publicity than they've done before, just the stuff that mom said."

Seeing Jodi thinking about that, Corey said, "But, if someone leaks it to the outside press, which you don't want, then you're stuck because, if you don't want to play at that point, the story becomes 'Jodi Worren stands up a local charity.'"

She nodded and smiled at Corey's grasp of the situation.

Dayna looked at Jodi, "Well, now I'm sorry I asked if you played softball in front of the committee people because now someone could say, 'Jodi Worren refuses to help local charity.'"

Jodi, impressed with Dayna's understanding of the situation, put her hand on Dayna's shoulder to let her know it was OK.

They all looked at Harry. "Hey wait a minute. I just came home to have some meatloaf."

Their looks told him he was not going to be able to leave it at that. "OK," he started, "so the way I see it is, you have to weigh the likelihood that people around here learning you're going to play and wanting to come out and see that, against the likelihood that the world finds out you're hiding in Smalsville."

They looked to him for his verdict. "I think your playing in the game helps the game and I think that sooner or later the world finds out you're here anyway. So, I think Dayna's right. you just tell the committee that you're willing to play, but you would prefer not to have more publicity than in the past because you don't think your playing in the game is going to bring paying customers from around the world anyway."

They all laughed.

Jodi said, "OK. Let's try that. I'll check my schedule and make sure I can be here."

He finished his lunch and went back to the store.

Jodi waited until Dayna was out of hearing range.

"Later in the week I'd like to go shopping and buy a few things. I should know by then if I'll also need to get a softball glove and some sneakers for the game. Is there a place to go to do that kind of shopping?"

"There's the mall about 60 miles away where I take Dayna for clothes." Then she remembered and smiled teasingly,

"There's a Winamart there."

She laughed, "Do you get a discount?"

Jodi winced then said, softly, "This isn't settled—and it's unsettling—and more than a little bit embarrassing—please don't mention it to Dayna, I don't want her to feel uncomfortable if we go there, but. . ."

She grimaced, "I think I might own the store, now."

She just shook her head, "One day I can't afford a jacket in a thrift store and now I might own a chain of department stores. And that's based on what?"

Corey, sorry she made the joke, just nodded.

Jodi asked, "But, is there no place closer for you to buy clothes?"

Corey, looking to see Dayna was not back yet, sighed.

"Clothes for me yes—but it's a small local store and sometimes they don't have anything that'll fit Dayna."

Jodi understood, "In fashion modeling the clothes all come in a size six. If you're bigger than a six, it's really tough."

Jodi looked to make sure Dayna was still out before she said, "Can I ask Dayna to be my guide?"

Corey was pleased she asked for permission before inviting Dayna. She knew Dayna would ask if she could accept the invitation, but this way she wouldn't have to disappoint Dayna, if for some reason, she didn't want Dayna to go.

She thanked Jodi for asking and nodded "Yes" when Dayna came back into the room, asking what was going on.

Jodi told Dayna she wanted to do some shopping later in the week and asked if Dayna would show her how to get to the mall. Dayna was delighted. They tried to figure what would be the best day.

Jodi said, "How about Friday?"

Dayna was beaming and then remembered. She frowned.

"Oh, I can't on Friday. I already told Jessie Reed's mom I would come to his birthday party. He's moving away the next day!"

"OK, so let's find another day."

Corey said, "Well, she's having bit of trouble with French. So, you could probably go on Thursday because in her small school she doesn't have French after Wednesday. She should have all her French homework out of the way by Thursday."

"Is there a good place at the mall where we could get something to eat?"

"Sure, Dayna, you guys can go to Marty's Deli."

When Dayna left the room, Corey asked, "Does the change in shopping day really not make any difference?"

"No, it's fine. I know this coming week is all open. And, I know birthday parties are important. Besides, it's good to know that she is secure enough and mature enough to say 'No,' rather than go through all kinds of contortions. It feels more real to hear 'No' once in a while rather than everybody always saying, 'Yes.'"

Corey confided, "I'm pleased she took the risk she might have missed out on being with you. The birthday party is an important commitment. The boy whose party she's going to was one of her only friends at school. He wasn't a popular kid but they hung out together. Then two years ago he had an accident. He was showing off, trying to get attention at a class swimming party, and hit his head in a dive and broke his neck. He was under the water for a while before they could get him out. Now he's in a wheelchair and has some brain damage from the loss of oxygen."

Jodi winced and shook her head.

Corey continued, "His father just split right after the accident. What few friends the boy had, other than Dayna, don't have anything to do with him now.

"The day after the party his mother's taking him to live with her parents so they can help her with him and be closer to a rehab center. Dayna's probably the only child who'll go to his party."

Jodi shook her head, "Oh, how sad for him. But Dayna's caring really impresses me. I wish I had a friend like her when I was her age. She must have had good parents," she grinned, "you must be very proud. Thanks for filling me in about her party."

When Thursday came, Jodi got to the house a little before the bus was to drop Dayna. Jodi, wearing jeans, running shoes, a baggy sweatshirt with her hair tucked into a baseball cap, didn't look at all like a supermodel or movie star. She wasn't in disguise, but she wasn't looking to attract a lot of attention.

Seeing her at the door, Corey realized going to a mall meant something different if you're Jodi Worren.

Jodi brought a present for Dayna.

It was a picture of her and Sharin Mersor.

"It was taken on the set. I'd like her to have this one. It isn't posed or retouched or airbrushed. A lot of things in Hollywood can be so distorted."

She told Corey, "Someone took this photo and made several copies. He told us he wanted us to sign a bunch of them and give them to him for a charity auction. Sharin signed all of them and her people sent them to me so I could sign them.

"Then, her people found out there was no charity—this guy just wanted to sell them and keep the money. I'd already signed a couple that she'd signed and gave those back to her. I still have the rest."

She shook her head, "Sometimes Hollywood's like a minefield.

"I don't know if you read a story saying Sharin and I turned down a $1000 bottle of wine?"

Corey shrugged she hadn't heard anything about it.

"While she and I were having our first lunch meeting, at her favorite restaurant, some man sent over a bottle of wine that cost $1000. And yes, we turned it down."

She looked at her, "I don't think you'd be surprised that, some people try to impress with how much money they have. I think a bottle of wine being worth that amount of money is obscene. Don't you?"

Corey nodded.

Jodi continued, "Neither Sharin nor I wanted to stop our conversation and have a drink with this man. We knew where he was coming from. The fact that his offer was so over the top made it easier to refuse. But if you think about it, we're just sitting there, minding our own business, and this bottle of wine comes into our lives. So, now it's a gossip magazine story. If we accept and let the guy come over to our table it's one story; if we accept and drink it without inviting him to join us, it's a different story—and you see when we refuse it that still gets to be a big story. And it's all because of a move that someone else made—and some waiter peddling the story to a reporter—and then it gets to be all about us."

She sighed, "I know I'm in the image business and the press has its job to do. As Pops used to say, 'When others have nothing, you don't want to be the little girl crying with a loaf of bread under each arm.'

"Most of the stuff that they write about me is good, even though they may get some of the details wrong. But, sometimes I wonder if it has to be so constant and some of it so twisted.

"Pops' brother-in-law, Becher Gold, we call him Goldy, was in very poor health when Pops died. He looked like he was at death's door himself. Goldy made a great effort to get to Pops' funeral. They really loved and respected each other so much. Then later I read in some column that Goldy only came to the funeral because he was savvy enough to know I'd be there and he wanted to get first dibs on representing me.

"That's just so cruel!

"I can only hope he never sees it, although it's hard to imagine he won't. Knowing how he and Pops cared about each other, with Pops gone, Goldy didn't need to court me to get my business. When things got sorted out, if he said his health was up to it, he'd be my natural choice."

She shook her head, "But the papers need to make some things dirty and cheap. I guess it's all about a big scoop to boost circulation. So, it's me and Sharin do 'this,' or poor Goldy is thinking 'that' and saying. . ."

Just then Dayna burst through the door.

Corey said, "Jodi has brought you a present."

Dayna looked at the picture, then held it to her chest and spun around with it and looked at it again.

Jodi told her she wanted her to have a picture of her that was personal and not from a magazine.

She loved how Jodi had signed it, "To Dayna Daweson (DD) from Jodi Worren (JJ), well, we know. . ."

Dayna beamed when she read it and showed it to her mom.

"I guess there's not going to be any confusion about who this was for. Listen, you guys better get going or you'll be driving back in the dark."

Getting into the car, Jodi asked, "Are you going to be looking for a birthday present for your friend's party?"

"No, his mom said they didn't need anything. And my mom said since they're moving the day after tomorrow, getting more stuff would just mean more for his mom to pack."

"I'm glad we could do this today and you'll still be there for your friend."

"So am I. I wish he had more friends then maybe he wouldn't have hurt himself trying to get attention. It was really so sad. He just wanted to be popular and have friends. I think everybody deserves to have friends they can feel good with."

Jodi was impressed by the wisdom and maturity.

"So do I. What about you, DD, do you have many friends?"

"I have a few that I like and I think like me. Now that you're here, some people want to talk to me more, but I think it has more to do with you than it does with me. But I know who talked with me before you came here, and who just wants to talk to me now. I don't want to hurt their feelings, but nobody needs pretend friends."

"Very true, DD. Very true. I didn't have any friends when I was your age."

Having decided she could play in the softball game, Jodi was thinking about be looking for a pair of good sneakers and a softball glove, along with a few other things.

But Dayna, still thinking about her present from Jodi, asked about Sharin.

As they talked about her, Jodi sighed, "Sharin had this idea and now I am being asked to play Janeen Docker in a full remake of *The Epic Journey.* Well, you saw the Life and Times. There's that scene about the making of Journey and a redo of a classic scene from that movie. She talked about remaking the whole movie with Prince Richard playing his father's role. She was impressed by Richard's father and thought it would be a good way to help Prince Richard and it would be good for me too."

"Do you want to do it?"

"I have some major concerns.

"I often go into new things with a fear of failing. Part of me wants the challenge and part of me is afraid of the challenge. With Life and Times, Sharin was there to help me. Obviously, that can't happen now.

"Also, the Life and Times, was unusual because she insisted that it be shot in sequence. Maybe you don't know, but most movies are shot out of order based on things like when certain actors are available or when certain locations are available.

"That seems much harder because one day you could be playing the end of a relationship and then later in the month you're playing the beginning. Maybe she felt that since I didn't have acting experience, shooting in sequence would be kind of like training wheels. Anyway, as people were telling me how well I was doing I couldn't feel it. I heard what they were saying, but it didn't sink in that it could be true. It still hasn't."

"But you were wonderful. And you won the Academy Award."

Jodi grimaced, "Yes. But after you win the Oscar, the only direction is down. I recognize the challenge of trying to pull the rabbit out of the hat again, but I'm really not sure I'm up for that. I'm not even sure I want acting to be a part of my life.

"Also, it's a whole movie and it includes a remake of the scene with the watch. So, there are two things that worry me. People have already seen that scene. Do we have to do it again? And also, when I played the scene while she was there, I knew people would be grading me on how well I did compared to how she did it. Now it's like I'll also be compared with myself as well."

"But has anybody ever just walked in, won the Academy Award and then just quit?"

"That's a good question DD. I have no idea."

She paused, "I never looked at it that way. It doesn't sound so good when you say it that way. But then there's also the thing with Prince Richard. I didn't feel we got along very well on the set. I felt he thought he was movie royalty and I was an outsider. And there are these stupid rumors about me and him."

Jodi looked over at Dayna, "But now I have to deal with that issue in deciding about making another movie with him. On the other hand, when I spoke with the producers about my reluctance to do the movie—I don't feel I can mention the Prince Richard issue with them—they always emphasized the number of people who were counting on me. They said no studio would green-light the movie without me because I played the part so well in Life and Times—and because of the publicity about the watch."

Dayna nodded, "That was that Jodimania thing."

Jodi cringed then sighed, "Yeah, the whole Jodimania thing."

She continued, "They even brought up the idea of wanting to honor Sharin Mersor. Then they said Pops, my manager—who reminds me a lot of your dad by the way—had committed me to do it on the day he died. I know he never would have done that. They're trying to use guilt and to appeal to my feelings about Sharin and Pops. I mean, I get that they really really want me to say 'Yes' to the movie, but I really don't want to play into those tactics. The whole thing is just so unsettling."

Dayna listened and hesitatingly said, "I was unhappy when I heard the story that you broke up Prince Richard's marriage. But then I never saw anything that said any-body ever asked you if it was true."

Dayna, trying to figure out a way of making sense out of rumor rather than it be a total fabrication, said, "I don't remember if there was even a love scene in that mov-ie—because sometimes you read that the couple just got carried away and they weren't really acting."

Jodi laughed, "No, there wasn't. From the script they sent me for Journey there will be a couple of romantic scenes—which for me is part of this whole Prince Rich-ard issue I'm dealing with. But the only scene from Jour-ney that we played together was the one in the field hospi-tal—and in that scene the closest I came to even touching Richard was when I handed him a scalpel."

Jodi liked knowing that Dayna was interested in the truth and wise enough to note that no one bothered to ask her about the rumor.

She said "DD, one of the things that happens when you are well known is that some people want to hook themselves to you or your name.

"I never met Richard's wife, so I'm not sure why she is doing this, or even if it's really her saying any of these things. But either way it's annoying that I even have to consider it all."

"That's sad that people will talk about you without hearing your side."

"The whole thing is sad. But there's nothing I can do about what people choose to say. I know I didn't do any-thing wrong."

"Are you sure that you don't want to do the movie?"

"No. It is a great part and an excellent story. I've been to Paris and I liked it for the short times I was there. But I don't need this movie. If I want to spend time in Paris,

I can just go and spend time in Paris. Right now, I think I might like to spend more time in Smalsville."

Dayna laughed "Smalsville? Well, I like you being here, but, you'll learn."

Arriving at the mall, Dayna was surprised that Jodi took off the sunglasses she used for driving and put them on the dashboard rather than wearing them in the mall.

Jodi saw the quizzical look and smiled, "I don't like the dark sunglasses approach to being in public. I think sunglasses say, 'Look at me, I'm trying to hide.'"

Entering the mall, they saw Missy's mom and aunt who were leaving. Dayna ran up to them and blurted out, "She's gonna play in the game! We're here to buy her a glove."

It took both women a moment to recognize that the person with Dayna was Jodi.

Looking at her, Pat McQueen said, "Is it true? You're really going to help us?"

"Like Dayna said, I'm here to buy a softball glove."

Pat was pleased.

Then taking Jodi aside, "You know I have a daughter who went to Hollywood and she's coming home to be the captain of your team."

"Missy."

"Oh, you've heard of her?"

She brightened.

Jodi figured she better backpedal a little, "Well, I didn't hear of her in Hollywood, but when I was here, people told me she was in Hollywood and asked if I'd met her."

"Well, would it be an imposition to introduce Missy to you?"

"Of course not, no imposition at all. And, if there's anything I know of that might be good for her, I'll let her know."

Seeing how grateful she was, Jodi made a mental note to check to see if there might be some way she could help.

After they left, she asked Dayna about Missy.

"I don't know much about her. She was way ahead of me in school. Mrs. McQueen has some pictures of her that she showed me once."

Dayna's voice told her that something wasn't being said.

"DD is there something else you're not telling me?"

"Well, Mrs. McQueen and Mrs. James are very nice people, but I've heard Missy is kind of stuck up. Really into how good she looks and all. You're so much better looking than she is, and you're not stuck up about it."

Jodi laughed, "Thank you, DD. Thank you very much."

"It's funny that they didn't recognize you."

Jodi just smiled. "Let's go find a softball glove."

The sporting goods store was closed, but the Winamart across the mall was open. As they were walking, Dayna looked at the people they passed to see if any of them noticed Jodi. She was surprised none of the people seemed to recognize her. When Dayna mentioned it, Jodi smiled again

"I like it that way. If I'm out in public dressed up and wearing heels, I have to figure most people think I'm fair game. Usually, if I'm not looking like that, I don't get noticed much.

"Most of the time, when I see a famous person in a casual setting, and if I can't remember their name, I just think they're someone I've met before and I'm not sure where. I imagine it's what happens when some people see me—if they notice me at all.

"There's a story about a famous actress you may have heard of called Marilyn Monroe. She was often called the 'Blond Bombshell' because of her ultra-blond hair and her shape. The story goes that she was walking down a busy street in New York City with a woman friend and wearing a scarf and an ordinary raincoat. They were talking about fame. When the friend said nobody was noticing her, Marilyn said something like, 'Do you want me to be her?' and pulled off the scarf, opened her raincoat, and started to do her hip-swaying walk down the street— and she got mobbed.

"Jodi nodded toward the window of a store with a manikin in the display wearing a skimpy miniskirt and top. "Now, if I was dressed in something like that, with high heels and I did a fashion-show-runway-like walk, the way some people expect to see me, it would probably be different, but not being noticed is really fine with me. I like that this can be just you and me. Just DD and JJ."

Dayna liked that. Then asked, "What was Sharin like?"

Jodi laughed, "Well she didn't have to jump into a Sharin character the way they say Marilyn had to jump into being the Bombshell. Sharin was always Sharin, but she was like a force of nature.

"She had a sense of entitlement. She once told me that before she went off to the war, she thought the world was rigged in her favor, and after she survived the war, she was sure that it was."

Jodi let that sink in, "That doesn't mean that she didn't work hard. She put in a tremendous amount of work on each thing she did. She told me it wasn't always easy for her to disappear into a character. It's just that she knew her hard work would pay off. She knew pushing herself would make her the best. But, when she wasn't submerged in a character on stage or on the screen, she was always her composed, almost regal self. And she didn't need to be anything else to attract attention. The first time I met her, I was sitting and waiting for her in the restaurant, when all of a sudden, I heard people applauding."

Dayna looked surprised.

Jodi laughed, "Yeah, it surprised me too. I looked up and she was walking toward me, smiling, and acknowledging the applause. I stood up to greet her but I was trying to figure out what to do—I was meeting her for lunch, was I supposed to applaud too? She just grabbed my hand and sat me back down. But she wasn't embarrassed by the crowd reaction at all. It was like she was used to it—like she knew she deserved it.

"I'm not sure I'd ever get used to it. I know I'd hate it if every time I went somewhere it turned into what happened in London. But for now, if people in an out-of-the-way place like this think my playing in softball game might get a few more people out to the game, I don't mind trying to do that to help out."

When they found the gloves, Jodi picked out one she liked and said, "You should pick one out too."

"I don't need one. I'm not playing in the game."

"Well, let's get one for you anyway so we can play catch from time to time to help get me in shape for the game."

"OK, but if it's my glove I'll pay for it myself. I have money. Mom gave me some spending money. Here, I'll show you."

She reached into her pocket to take out the money.

Jodi, pleased by Dayna's sense of responsibility, put up her hand—like a crossing guard—to stop her.

"DD, can I win this one, please?

"I know you can pay for it, but I don't want you to spend your money to buy something to help me out."

Dayna nodded, "OK. Thank you."

After paying for the gloves and a couple of balls, they went off to buy sneakers. Jodi asked Dayna if there was anything she'd like to look for while they were at the mall

Dayna said, "No, I don't need anything, thank you."

They walked around looking in some store windows for a while.

After eating, as they were going to the car, they passed a Marine recruiting poster. Jodi stopped to look at it and cleared her throat. "When I first met your dad, it was because of my brother."

Seeing Dayna looked puzzled as to what brought that up, she continued. "My mom was dying slowly and my brother was taking care of us and he was struggling to live his own life. Your dad was his coach. He got my mom some help and spent time with us. My brother, your dad called him 3J, was able to finish school and join the Marines like he always wanted to do."

She paused, "He was killed in a helicopter crash."

"I'm sorry."

"Thank you. Anyhow, the poster reminded me of him.

"And reminded me that we have that in common— we've both lost brothers."

Dayna thought of that as they got into the car.

Starting to drive, Jodi said, "I think you had it worse; at least my brother didn't suffer for a long time, like my mom and your brother did."

Dayna closed her eyes and started to get teary, "When somebody suffers for a long time, you feel so sorry for them that when they die, it's hard not to feel almost good that they wouldn't suffer any more.

"Toward the end, Henry would look at me and I felt so bad for him and I couldn't do anything to help him."

Jodi sighed, "That's the worst, knowing you can't help."

"But this woman mom and dad found for me to talk to, really helped me a lot. She reminded me that I was only a little girl and no one, not even grown up doctors, could help Henry."

Then Dayna said cautiously, "and she told me about dragonflies."

Jodi waited, knowing there was more to come.

Dayna shared the analogy to the life cycle of the dragonflies—not being able to return to the water—just as the therapist told it.

She was finishing when they arrived at her house.

Jodi sighed. She was moved by the dragonfly analogy and comfortingly reminded herself that she, too, was only a little girl when her mom was dying.

She was very impressed with Dayna. She thought, She's clearly Harry's child—and Corey seems quite solid too.

As they made plans to get together to play catch—to break in their new gloves—Jodi realized that a short trip to the mall had ended, but a strong bond between them had begun.

She liked spending time with Dayna.

THIRTY-THREE

From time to time Jodi would go to the house to have a catch with Dayna.

One day, about a week before the game, when she showed up, Corey asked her cautiously, "Have you and Dayna talked at all about her weight?"

Jodi, surprised, assured her, "I would never do that, especially not without talking to you about it first."

"Well, I only asked because I've noticed her eating less and looking at the side of things like the cereal box to check the serving size and number of calories.

"Harry and I have always wanted her to feel good about herself no matter what she weighed, but we know how cruel society can be even with someone just a little bit above the norm."

"We never said a word about…"

Corey made a gesture with her hands toward Jodi's body and verbalized, "Well, you wouldn't really have to say anything."

She smiled, "Anyway, it's fine if she wants to be more aware."

Then she grimaced, "Oh, by the way, Missy came home and told her mom that she'd been in touch with reporters in LA about being the captain of your team and told them when they could watch you playing in the game.

"She said several network celebrity shows want to cover the story."

Jodi shrugged and gave her a weak smile.

Corey said, "Yeah, I know. I'm sorry, but the other big news in town was that Frank Peterson, the local banker, and his family disappeared."

Jodi didn't understand but Corey reminded her, "You met Frank with Harry at the luncheonette.

"They have a little daughter who's two grades behind Dayna."

Jodi was puzzled about the news.

"Well, it seems that Frank Peterson was really a man named Jackson Evant. And he was a fugitive. There's about ten thousand dollars missing from the bank.

"When the Sheriff investigated, he found that Frank, or rather Jackson, was indicted and wanted for arson at a tire store ten years ago, just before the time he moved here. Some sort of radical environmentalist thing."

Corey continued, "Ever since the game started eight years ago. Frank was the announcer. Now, some of the people are thinking that Frank figured with you here, sooner or later there would be a lot of media people around. One of them might recognize him from photos from the past and know who he was. So, he had to take off."

Jodi worried, "Are people going to be blaming me?"

"No. I don't think it's like that at all. There's no blame. But some people are speculating as to why he left when he did. People are aware that things have changed here since you arrived."

Jodi looked at her, "What about you? Have things gotten worse for you?"

"Oh, no!" She said emphatically. "I would never say worse. I do notice that people I was never really friendly with before, you know people I knew by face—and I knew they lived around here—they want to stop and talk now. Often, they ask about you and your plans. I see Dayna gets calls from kids who weren't very friendly before."

Jodi shook her head, sighed, and continued to listen.

"But she's really great about recognizing where these kids are coming from. It's amazing to hear her talking—you know not wanting to offend these would-be friends, but not really wanting to be involved with them."

"She mentioned 'pretend friends' when we were driving to the mall. I knew that she had a good soul. You could just feel it."

Then Corey brightened, "Well, as I said, she seems to be good at dealing with them. And your being here and taking an interest in her has been great for her.

"It's so wonderful to see her happy.

"But I'll tell you what is a bit strange for me. Over the years we've seen the magazines, TV commercials, and then we saw the movie and the awards shows—and now you've been at our house and hang out with Dayna. It's almost like there are two of you."

Jodi smiled, "You know, I also had a similar—like-two-different-people—experience with Sharin. I'd seen her in several movies and interviews before we met and then she was sitting across the table from me. But the strangest time was when she wanted me to see Epic Journey, and some of the other movies that we were doing parts from. She played them for me in the screening room in her home. So, there she was on the screen and sitting next to me on her couch. It does take some getting used to."

Corey said, "But, about you being here… Your being here and playing in the game is going to be great for this place. It's certainly going to mean a lot more money will be raised for the projects that need it. This place could use a good shaking up every so often. So, I'd say your being here is a good thing, all the way around."

Jodi thanked her and said, "Wait a minute, as long as Missy has already outed me, why don't we put it to some advantage? Why don't we say I'll do an exclusive interview with whichever network contributes most to the game?"

"You would do that?"

"I don't see why not? Since my cover is blown any-way, we might as well see if your school charity can cash in."

Then she laughed, "It would be great if we could do it like those interviews with the rebel chiefs."

She smiled. "You know the ones where they pick up the interviewer at his hotel, blindfold him and take him into the mountains somewhere. He gets his big interview, but he doesn't know where he's been."

They were both laughing at the idea when Dayna walked in with her glove to play catch.

Missy McQueen, to everyone's surprise, called for a practice the day before the game. No one had ever heard of a practice before the game. In the past they just showed up and played.

In some years, it was said, there was a tacit agreement that the varsity team was going to win. But Missy wanted a practice, so most of her team managed to show up.

Jodi, wanting to be a good sport, was one of them.

Arriving at the field, she had no trouble deciding which one was Missy. Missy, whose shoulder length hair was a bit too blond, was about 5'5". She wore tight pink jeans and a too-small school sweatshirt showing off breasts that Jodi thought had "work" done on them.

Her jeans were so tight they reminded Jodi of a comment a hair stylist on a photo shoot had made about one of the other models. "Those pants are so tight, you can see that she has a nickel in her back pocket and that the buffalo has a cracked rib."

Jodi introduced herself when Missy hurried over to meet her. Then Jodi met the other members of the faculty-and-guests team. After the introductions and handing out the team shirts they tried to decide who was playing what position.

Jodi said, "I'll play any place where they won't hit the ball."

She wound up in right field. She fielded some fly balls and threw to each base. In batting practice, she managed to hit a couple out of the infield.

When the practice was over, she was complimented on her play by the coach of the varsity track team, Butch Tanner. As Butch was looking to follow up on his opening, Missy cut in between them. Her rear end forcing Butch to take a step backwards, Missy asked to talk to Jodi. She had to look over Missy's shoulder to say goodbye to Butch.

As he walked away, Missy, sang, "You know, he's very married."

"Thanks, but I'm not looking."

"Oh, but I'm sure Butch is. All men are dogs, always sniffing around for their sex needs."

The comment took Jodi by surprise. As they walked together to their cars, she decided not to say anything about Missy having called any reporters.

Instead, she said, "Your mom said you're out in Hollywood. How's it been going?"

"Well, you know, kind of slow. Well, maybe you wouldn't know. You seem to have landed on both feet and climbed straight to the top."

Jodi, readily admitting she had several great breaks, could see Missy wanted to talk shop, but she told Missy she had to get home to make some calls. She would talk to her more after the game tomorrow.

Missy was disappointed.

When she called to find out the latest information on the Paris project, because of the promise she'd made to Missy's mom, she checked to see if there might be anything for Missy.

The next day, Jodi got to the field an hour before the game to do the promised exclusive interview. Dayna rode with her to watch the fifteen-minute talk. By the time they approached the field, the cameras had been set up. Jodi introduced herself to the interviewer and introduced Dayna. Then she took the seat the camera was aimed at. After the focus was checked, and a bit of makeup applied to take some shine off her face, the session started.

She'd already made clear she didn't want to talk about Edgar, the businesses, or the estate. Harry and Corey arrived just as the interviewer started by asking about Smalsville and whether she was planning to give up her 'mansions' on both coasts. She answered that she liked the quiet of the small village and hoped it could stay that way. She noticed Missy arrive and stand near Corey. This time, Missy was wearing the green team shirt which someone, probably her mom had tailored, and the jeans were yellow to go with the shirt and her hair.

Toward the end of the allotted time, the interviewer asked about her relationship with Prince Richard and the status of the Paris movie. She was annoyed by the question but decided to use it. "I have never done anything wrong with Richard. In fact, we've never been alone together.

"I'll be making my decision about the Paris movie soon."

Finally, the reporter asked, "With your career and all your money, why would you risk getting hurt in an athletic event? If you wanted to get money for the school funds, why not just write a check?"

She looked at him as though she was deep in thought, then said, "First of all, no one has asked me to just write a check. My new neighbors asked if I would like to help out by playing in the game. Secondly, I don't think my neighbors are out to hurt me. After all," she smiled, "they're not reporters."

Getting up, she took the microphone off her jersey, turned, and introduced Missy to the interviewer, suggesting he could talk to 'the captain' about the history of the game. Dayna handed Jodi her glove and she went to stretch and warm up for the game.

The game was played in front of the largest crowd ever. As expected, the varsity team won but the score was a respectable seven to five.

She didn't detect any effort by her team to throw the game. She made three plays in right field. All were ground balls past the second baseman. She even managed to get a lead-off base hit—a blooper over the shortstop—but then was stranded on first base.

All in all, she felt the game was fun. Missy came up to her after the game, wanting to talk and saying she was going back to Hollywood the next day.

Jodi was surrounded by people seeking autographs and pictures.

Dayna came up and said she was going home with her parents, so Jodi suggested Missy wait a few minutes and they could talk.

Jodi, seeing Missy was getting more and more impatient while she signed autographs and posed for pictures, looked over to Missy with the silent message, "If you want this job, this is part of the job."

After the last fans left, they were alone. Their cars were the only two left in the lot.

Finally getting her chance to talk, Missy seemed a bit disappointed. Jodi wondered if Missy had greater expectations of what this day would mean. She also wondered to what extent her being there did in fact divert the spotlight from Missy.

Jodi asked, "What's waiting for you in LA?"

Missy answered warily, "Dinner and going to bed with a guy who says he can help me get my SAG card."

Jodi, taken aback by the answer, asked, "Are you sure you want a SAG card now? If you're in the Screen Actors Guild, you can't do nonunion movies."

"I know, but it seems I have been spending most of my time, you know, trying to figure out who it doesn't pay to fuck or suck in that town. Like I said, all men are dogs. I have to give them what they need so I can get what I want."

Jodi looked to see if there was any sign Missy was kidding.

Missy was serious. Then Jodi looked to make sure they were still alone. It sounded like Missy didn't care. Reminding herself she told Missy's mom she would try to help her daughter, Jodi unlocked her car.

She would honor the promise to Pat, even though she didn't think much of Missy.

Getting into her car, she reached into a folder for the Paris movie and took out the card of Frederick Dillhom.

Handing the card to Missy, she said, "There may be a part in this Paris movie I'm being asked to do. I'm told he's the choice for casting director.

If I say 'Yes,' and it gets green-lighted, there'll be some scenes back in the states where they'll need several girls playing student nurses. The job should last three or four days. If lasts at least three days, it can get you that SAG card."

Then added, "You should be aware, I think there may be a shower scene, I don't know."

"Oh, I don't mind a shower scene," Missy said, sticking out her chest, "that's why I got these."

Looking at the card, Missy brightened, "Fred Dillhom! Yeah, I've heard of him," she said, trying to sound more in the know than she really was. Putting her hands on her hips, "You know him, right? Do I have to fuck him?"

She had enough of Missy.

"He goes by Rick, he hates being called Fred. He's happily married, with grown daughters, and he's always a perfect gentleman with me and everyone I know."

She shook her head, "If you approach him like it's a casting couch job, you'll turn him off completely.

"I've really got to go."

Sitting in her car, watching Missy walking across the parking lot to her car, Jodi felt terrible about their interaction. She tried to figure out why Missy had made her react so badly. She perceived her as a sad byproduct of, what Pops called, "our selling of fantasy images business."

She wondered if Missy wasn't just playing a part—if she hadn't cast herself as what some bad B movies made the striving Hollywood starlet look like.

Jodi thought, When I arrived in New York, I had no expectations and no accomplishments to look back on. But, when Missy arrived in Hollywood—with her history of the successes which led to the resentful nickname, "the Queen"—she found all the other small town "Queens" already there.

She felt sad thinking of Missy, and girls like her enduring surgery and worse, in the quest for glamour, fame, and fortune. She wondered if Missy's mom knew that her daughter saw the world in terms of blow jobs and fucking her way to the top. Whatever the top is supposed to be. Was the top a place where the pursuit of glamour, fame, or riches could stop?

A place where no worries existed? Did anyone ever get there?

Jodi rationalized, Maybe she put me off because, while I don't like her methods, at least she seems to have the advantage of knowing what she wants. I don't. I'm still worried about what I want and if I'll know what to do with it. Well, anyway, I told her mom I would try to help. I did what I said. I aimed that interviewer at her. I gave her Rick's card.

But her attempt to make peace with her response to Missy wasn't working. She thought, After all, isn't Missy just seeking the happiness that everybody wants and deserves to have?

She closed her eyes as she remembered Pops saying, "You should never look down on someone unless you are reaching down to help them up." She remembered Connie telling her how she wanted to shield him from his natural instinct to try to rescue Agneta. She could almost hear Pops repeating, "I never want to pass judgment on how people make a life for themselves."

Realizing she had done just that—she didn't like it.

She was ashamed of having done it.

Worse—she feared Pops would have been ashamed of her.

Sighing, she thought, If my work in this "fantasy images business" is even slightly responsible for the dream Missy is trying to realize, then I'm responsible for trying to help Missy realize it—to reach down to help her up.

She called out, "Missy!" And drove over to her. "Look, I gave you Rick's card, but, as I said, I haven't decided on that project yet. Anyway, I've made some contacts in Hollywood, so even if I say 'No,' I can still see if something else might be good for you."

She paused, "I know you're going back tomorrow and I'm hoping to be here a little longer. But, if you want, we can talk more when I'm back in LA."

Jodi thought and then added, "Before I get back—and we have some time to maybe sort through some things— do you have to see that guy you mentioned?"

"I guess I can put that off. It's really me chasing him. I guess I can slow down."

"Good."

Then knowing for Missy's sake she should take the risk.

"OK, now I have to tell you something. Believe me I don't want to judge you or what you've been going through, but I think you need to know—from what I've seen in modeling and the movies—the good agents won't work with girls who are trying to get ahead by giving head.

"The good agents—the kind you need to fight for you to get the best parts—run away from that whole sex-for-work stuff. They're afraid it'll reflect badly on them. It'll hurt their reputations and their other clients.

"They can't survive in the business if people think they're just pimps."

Seeing Missy's downcast reaction she continued. "Look, I know how lucky I've been to get out from under some of the mistakes I've made. Maybe you can be lucky too. We can spend some more time when I get to the coast. OK?"

Missy brightened, thinking of being connected with Jodi in Hollywood, "Sure, I'd like that."

Jodi, feeling redeemed, more true to herself and what she'd learned, said softly, "I'd like it too."

Watching her drive away, Jodi was pleased she'd made peace with her initial reaction.

She thought, Maybe it will all work out for Missy and her mom.

Starting on her way to her Smalsville home, Jodi realized returning to the wider world, and dealing with the issues waiting for her there, could not be put off much longer.

Almost like a prayer she thought—Maybe it will all work out for me too.

THIRTY-FOUR

Harry was at his store. It was near closing time when Buddy Tabor called from Rawlings. They hadn't seen each other since Buddy flew in, after a big win at Madison Square Garden, to attend Henry's funeral.

"Hey man, I saw you and Corey on TV last night."

"What? How is that possible, Buddy?"

"One of the celebrity news shows played an interview with Jodi Worren about a softball game she was about to play in. They showed pictures of the crowd. I recognized you and Corey, but was that Dayna standing with you watching the interview? Man. She's really grown up."

"Well, she's not the only one who grew up."

"How's that?"

"Buddy, it turns out Jodi Worren was a kid that I coached in high school, before I went to work for you.

"She changed her name and grew up so much I didn't recognize her as the same person."

"Wow. So, you and this former kid both wind up in Smalltown. I'll bet she was surprised to run into you.

"If you didn't recognize her, she must have recognized you. After all you haven't changed at all.

"Well, maybe a little slower."

Buddy laughed. "Man. I'll bet Dayna was pleased to see her idol in person. It really must be a small world for this world-class mega-babe—this Oscar-winning-Miss-Solar-System woman—to stumble across you in an outta the way place like Smalltown."

Harry—knowing Buddy's name for the town—was happy to just leave it at that.

He chuckled, "Well, as I so often heard you say, 'Sometimes it just be's that way.'"

Buddy laughed.

Harry asked Buddy about the team for the next season.

They talked about the roster and the upcoming schedule for a while and then both went back to work.

Later, as Harry was closing the store, the fire whistle sounded. There was a grease fire in the kitchen of La Belle Gorda Restaurant, one of the better local restaurants, on the road leading out of town. For the last six years, it's where the fire department's annual dinner dance took place, and was scheduled there again.

At home after the fire, Harry told Corey about the fire and reported his conversation with Buddy. She didn't need to ask if he had said anything about why Jodi came to Smalsville. She knew he wouldn't.

At the monthly fire department meeting later that week, the chief announced La Belle Gorda was closing for two weeks. He asked the members to consider either postponing the dinner dance for two weeks or trying to find some other place.

The vote was overwhelming to postpone.

When Harry told Corey the dinner dance was now two weeks later, she reminded him, that was Dayna's school vacation, and she and Dayna would be in Florida with her sister and mom.

Barbara was not in good health. This might turn out to be the last chance to see her mom.

Harry had to keep the store open so he couldn't go to Florida with them. For something like the dinner, they weren't changing plans.

The next day when Harry came home, Corey greeted him with a big hug. "I've been thinking about this dinner dance. You shouldn't have to go alone. The invitation always says member and 'guest,' not 'date' right?"

She smiled, "So I called Jodi. She checked her calendar. She's flying out to Los Angeles the next day on Sunday but she'd be happy to go with you Saturday night.

"Then I told her that there'll be some single guys at the dance. She laughed and thanked me."

On the Friday night before the dinner, Harry called Jodi to talk about picking her up at her house the next night.

He could tell by her voice something was wrong.

"What's going on?"

"Oh, I've been putting off a lot of stuff while I've been here, and you know I'm flying back on Sunday to have a week of meetings, but I have a bunch of phone conferences tomorrow."

"On a Saturday?"

"Well, I can't put it off."

"Do you want to forget about the dinner?"

"Oh, no. I'm looking forward to it.

"It's just that I have to get through this other stuff in order to get to the fun part of tomorrow."

"Do you want to talk any of that through, now?"

She sighed, "My brother used to quote some cartoon character saying that 'there's no problem so big that you can't run away from it.' But when the problem is inside of you—you just can't run from it."

She took a deep breath, "You know I feel that I have drifted through my life without really taking charge of it.

"As a kid I tried to run once and the cops stopped me at the bus station. I tried to run a second time and you stopped me. For a while, having you and Jacqui, things were better. But now I'm not a kid anymore and the responsibilities are bigger.

"It seems making things better is harder for me to do. I doubt if anyone who has not had the experience of being famous can understand how disorienting it can be. Since I have become Jodi Worren, I seem to have lost myself. When I think I need to start to take more of an active part in my own life, I am not sure who it is that I am—and just what I am supposed to do.

"Pops knew the world so well. As my career got bigger and bigger, I could always count on him to keep the real me from disappearing—he could always keep me grounded. He never told me what to do, but I always knew he was there for me and the way he explained things I could always see the right thing to do.

"I guess I never considered that he wouldn't always be there. You would think with all the deaths in my life I would have expected…"

She sighed, "That first night, when we talked after dinner, I told you that it seemed like everybody wanted a piece of me. Now, it seems that more and more people want a piece, and the pieces they want are bigger, more complicated—have more of an impact on other people."

"Go on. I'm listening."

"I know you are here for me, and since I'm not that kid anymore, like I was that night, I really can't expect you to order me not to go. Now, without Pops, I feel I am going to be lost out there all alone.

"But I can't just ignore it and hide here forever because it's only going to be harder to deal with the more I try to run away from it. My avoiding it this long may have made it worse."

She paused, "Sometimes I feel like my life is a fairy tale that is happening to somebody else. Like there is this hollow Jodi Worren image walking through the world that I'm supposed to catch up with and jump into. I don't dislike her. I'm just not sure how much of her is me.

"The people out there have no idea of who I am and what little I know. All they have are their desires, preconceived notions and expectations. It's almost like most people don't see me at all. My physical image exists, my money exists, my Oscar exists, but I don't.

"I'll never be able to really communicate with people as long as any communication from me is blocked because it doesn't fit through the filter of their ideas about me.

"Pops talked about not being able to live your life from the outside, so you're not always able to see yourself as others see you. But, it's too hard to be constantly trying to figure out how other people perceive my life and be living my life at the same time.

"When you have nothing and you're invisible, you're allowed to have problems and insecurities, but when people think you have everything, then you're not allowed to have problems or doubts or feelings or be scared.

"If I say I want time to think about something, people think I am trying to be coy. People think with all the trappings of what they would consider security, I have no right to feel insecure.

"But I do. I'm just afraid. I'm terrified by this movie thing. I'm afraid of doing it—and I'm afraid I'll always regret it if I don't do it. I'm worried they're going to find out I really can't act. I'm worried that I may discover that I really do want to act—and I'm not any good at it.

"I think that award was for Sharin but, now, it is something I'm supposed to live up to. And no one but you knows what a disaster my marriage to Edgar was. So now I feel like a fraud with the estate thing too. And there's all these responsibilities I have to deal with.

"So, I'm struggling with what to do with the movie business. And, as little as I know about that business—I know nothing about running hotels, factories, mega markets and power plants.

"I'm afraid that if I get it wrong, companies could close, men and women could lose their jobs, and kids won't eat or have warm clothes for winter."

He listened as she continued. "How do I figure out who to trust to deal with all these things or help me deal with them?

"Edgar was a whiz at that stuff and he was getting ripped off by someone he trusted."

She paused, and said more softly, "Pops used to say, 'most people don't do what makes them happy, because they don't know what makes them happy.' I am trying to work on that. I am trying to understand what it is that makes me happy.

But I still don't know if I can trust myself to know what I want. I don't know if I can make myself happy."

She sighed, "I'm sorry for unloading this on you. Does any of that make sense?"

Harry took a breath and let it out slowly. "OK. I think I get it. Pops said people don't live their lives from the outside, so they don't often see themselves as others see them.

"Now, you're telling me that a significant part of that problem is that most people who look at you from the outside don't see you at all. What they see is their expectations of what they think you should be—rather than who you are. Once they have their expectations, they try to get you to behave like they expect—because it validates the expectation, they—not you—created in the first place."

"Yeah. That's it. It makes sense when you put it that way."

"OK, JJ, but aren't these perceptions and expectations that others have just based on their perception of events? You got an award. Most people would see that as good. You choose to see it as a problem because of the perception of what the award meant and how you got it. You have fame and fabulous wealth now. Rather than revel in it, you see it as a problem. You worry about the responsibility and the way the money can distort the way others see you—or the way the fame and wealth keep them from seeing the real you at all."

"That's it"

"But,, you're never going to be able to force a change in the way other people perceive. On some level you have to already know that. You showed the wisdom to realize you could change your perception—you decided you could keep the name you liked although you hated how you got it. Now you need the wisdom to realize that changing other people's perceptions is not within your power. You can put the award on a shelf and just go about your life as if the award has nothing to do with you. You can take the money or give it away if you want to. Some people may notice that you're not meeting their expectations, and they may feel uncomfortable because of it.

Some may reevaluate the way they think of you—and some may not.

"So what?"

"Sounds like we're back to Epictetus."

She said sheepishly, "Pops gave me a book."

He laughed, "Yeah. OK. So, you read the master's work. When I was talking my brand of Epictetus to you kids, let's call it 'Epictetus Lite,' I guess I didn't bother to attribute the quotes to him. But there's a lot of wisdom in what he said.

"Think about it. Is it other people's perceptions you are worried about? Who is so well off that they can give you peace of mind?

"Remember his comments about going to the baths? He said, 'You have to remind yourself that there will be people pushing and splashing. Then you have to remember, while you're going there to be clean—you are going there not only to be clean—but also to keep your inner composure.'"

"I remember that part."

"Well, OK then, let's break the problem into parts. Before you get on the phone tomorrow, try to set limited goals. You know if you want to make this movie, you are going to have to think about what is involved—the people you'll be working with and things like that. You're going to have to focus on how you can do it—and still keep your composure, your balance, your peace of mind. No one can take that away from you unless you let them. Remember his saying: 'No one can hurt you unless you consent'?"

"Yes."

"Did you ever see somebody trying to tease someone who will not let themselves be teased? It looks foolish."

"Give up my end of the rope. Don't consent to be in a tug of war."

"Good! That's it. Try to just gather information. Try to figure out for each of the decisions in these conference calls what the consequences of saying "Yes" or "No" are, and prioritize finding the help you need in making those decisions."

She sighed, "Sounds good. I only hope I can put it to work. Thank you."

"You're welcome, have a good night and good luck on your phone calls tomorrow. I'll pick you up around 7:00."

Getting off the phone, she thought about their conversation. It reminded her of the late night calls she had with Pops. She cried herself to sleep thinking about Pops—wishing she could talk with him again, get his advice, and tell that sweet old man how much he meant to her. And tell him about finding Harry.

Harry said nothing to anyone about who his guest would be at the dinner-dance. Before he went to pick up Jodi, he called Corey in Florida.

She said, "When I asked her about going with you tonight, I told her there would be single guys there—the Torey boys always show up and they're both still single."

"Well, I guess I won't mention they're still single because you broke their hearts. They're your rejects."

She laughed and said, "And, don't introduce her to Billy Brody."

"What?" He thought for a second,

"Yeah. OK, I know—Corey Torey, Jodi Brody. I got it. I got it."

She just laughed.

Jodi had been on the phone all day and just had time to take a shower and get dressed. When she met him at the door, she was just fixing an earring. After opening the door, she turned and headed back down the hall. He was awed by how she looked all dressed up. Stepping into the living room, he noticed a pair of red high heel sandals aimed toward the door. She came out of the hall from her bedroom barefoot holding a red wrap to put over her bare shoulders. Walking up to him, she put her hand on his shoulder to climb into the heels.

Looking at him, she smiled, "How do I look?"

He stared and chuckled. "Do you really expect an answer to that question?

"OK. You look like a movie star."

She laughed.

As he drove, she said, "I'm looking forward to a chance to unwind a bit. Today's phone conferences turned out to be even more draining than I was dreading last night. I've been on the phone all day with people in Los Angeles and New York. It's getting more overwhelming.

"I go to Los Angeles tomorrow. There's going to be a make-or-break meeting on Monday about *The Epic Journey*.

"Then I have some follow-ups depending on which way I go with that. On Tuesday, I have meetings to make decisions dealing with some estate matters. And on Wednesday, there's an all-day meeting regarding the expansion of one of the power plants I'm going to own. Then there's a phone conference at some lawyer's office to get ready for a deposition later in the week for a lawsuit from a man who was stealing from Edgar. And after that some investigators want to continue today's phone conversation in person about the plane crash.

He shook his head as he listened. "Did I hear right? You are getting sued by a man who was stealing?"

"You heard right," she sighed.

"That's the world I'm heading back to. While I'm there—with all of this—I'm going to find time to follow up with Missy.

"But I need to decide if I'm going to agree to do this movie before I talk with her."

Walking from the car to the restaurant, she stopped. She was getting the queasy feeling she often got going to a social event with a large group of strangers.

Asking him to wait for a second, she told him about it and also explained that she'd been so wound up she hadn't eaten all day.

That she would be anxious about a social setting with a crowd of strangers was something he hadn't anticipated. He asked her if she wanted to go home. Hearing his concern, she was comforted knowing he would forgo the dinner and take her home if that is what she wanted him to do. She assured him the queasiness would pass. Just the fact he offered her the option made her feel better. She smiled and straightened her dress and threw back her hair.

"OK. I'm ready. Let's do this."

When they walked into the banquet hall part of the restaurant, the whole crowd went silent. The only sound heard was the sound of Jodi's high heels on the wooden dance floor as Harry, with his hand placed gently in the middle of her back, guided her toward the corner of the bar so he could find the place card to see where they'd be seated.

Since he had not told anyone about bringing Jodi, he was not surprised the card, assigning them to table 3, said "Harry and Corey Daweson."

He got a soft drink for himself. Jodi asked him for a white wine. He was surprised but thought, She's a big girl and knows what she wants. Still, he was puzzled.

Seeing the look on his face, "I know what you're thinking. With her family history?"

She sighed, "But at social events I have a one-wine rule. It allows me to relax and be sociable—be the smiling Jodi Worren people expect."

He handed Jodi her glass, and aimed her toward the two remaining seats at their table, introducing Jodi to the people they passed and then to the couples at their table.

People—even some of the kitchen staff—came to meet her. Some wanted autographs. Others just wanted to talk. Some asked if they could have pictures taken with her. She posed with them and signed autographs.

This was not an unusual experience for her. A couple of the men asked her to dance. As she excused herself and drifted away from the table to accommodate the requests, Harry realized spending the night next to an empty chair was not something he'd thought about when Corey suggested the invitation.

After a few dances, Jodi found herself standing near the bar with the Torey brothers. Tony offered her glass of wine. She hesitated but was comforted by the sight of Harry at their table. She wanted to relax and have a good time—to take her mind off the week ahead.

Being there with Harry, she felt safe. That feeling and because of the effects of the first glass on an empty stomach, she accepted.

Butch Tanner walked in with his wife and gave Jodi a big smile. Mark saw her looking in Butch's direction, "The redhead with him. That's Butch's wife."

Tony said, "In automotive-industry terms we would say, 'She's not original equipment.'"

Mark laughed, "Yeah, his first wife asked too many questions—"

Tony chimed in, "—like why didn't you come home last night, Butch?"

Jodi smiled.

When Mark offered to refill her glass, she was feeling the effect of the wine. She liked the feeling. She had no worry about movies or businesses with nine-hundred and sixty thousand employees.

She accepted.

Everything was going to be fine. She had a warm feeling of calm—euphoria. She felt like she had no cares.

She accepted a mixed drink.

She kidded the Torey brothers, "If I didn't know any better, I'd think you boys are trying to get me drunk."

Tony winked at his brother, "I think she's figured us out."

She laughed.

Then, seeing Harry sitting with his arm draped over her empty seat, thinking how grateful she was to have reconnected with him, she just wanted to fill the seat next to him.

She excused herself and walked back to their table.

She sat down as the meal was being served.

During the meal, the Chief of the department came over. Kneeling next to her chair, he asked if she would present the last award of the evening, the "Fireman of the Year" award.

She looked at Harry. "What do you think? Do you want me to do it? How has it been done in the past? Any special ritual?"

"No. You'll be fine. Usually, the Chief just calls out the name and presents this big plaque to the man. Someone from the local paper takes the picture with the Chief and Fireman holding it up between them, shaking hands and smiling."

The Chief nodded, "That's all there is to it."

She said, "Well I'll be happy to stand behind the plaque as you're handing it like you always do. I don't want to break the symmetry of the shot."

She looked to Harry. "Will that be OK?"

He nodded and the Chief agreed.

After the meal the plaques for the number-of-years of service, and plaques for the number of calls the members had accumulated over the years were handed out.

Then the Chief said, "I suspect a couple of you may have noticed that Winsloh Hardware has made a special contribution to tonight's proceedings. I'd like to ask Miss Jodi Worren to help present the Fireman of the Year Award."

As promised, Jodi stood, walked up to where the Chief was making the announcement and smiled over the top of the plaque as the Chief presented it to this year's winner.

Then the Chief and the Fireman both wanted their own picture with her.

After the pictures, Jodi wondered what award would be good enough to show the fireman who brought her tonight how much he meant to her.

She thought again about their talk last night. She thought about crying herself to sleep. She never wanted to cry herself to sleep again feeling she hadn't fully expressed her appreciation to someone she deeply cared about.

Walking past Butch, to get back to her table, she remembered Missy's warning to her about Butch—Missy saying all men are dogs sniffing around. They all have needs, so she gives them what they need to get what she wants. She didn't like Missy's approach to men.

Jodi thought, Harry's not a dog. What would I want to get from Harry? He's already given so much to show his regard for me—just like he did when he stopped me from running away on that cold night and I was wearing that warm jacket.

She could feel the warmth of that jacket, or maybe it was the wine.

She thought, No, Harry's certainly not a dog. But, he is a man and men do have needs. I know he really cares about me. He cared for me when I had nothing—when I didn't attract attention just by dressing up and walking into a room.

If I'm as desirable as everyone says I am, Harry might desire me but not be able to show it.

Gary used to tell her, "My mother always said: 'If you don't ask, you don't give someone a chance to say 'Yes.'"

But Harry shouldn't have to ask. Corey must know what his needs are—that's why she asked me to come here with him, to take her place tonight. Harry doesn't have to ask. My answer is, "Yes." And maybe saying "Yes," to a man who's a friend I know cares for me, I can have the benefit of that moment of calm and confidence that Sharin talked about.

Back in her seat, she began to questioned her resolve.

Envisioning Sharin hoisting a courage gin-and-tonic, she heard Sharin's voice laughing about friends with benefits and concluding, "It is just sex."

Harry looked at her, silently asking for an explanation, as he watched her fill her water glass from the bottle of wine on their table.

Smiling that she was having a good time, she held up her glass as if to toast him and drank it thinking, This one's for you—and just maybe—me too.

As the drawing for the door prizes was about to start, they got ready to leave. It was obvious Jodi had been a big hit. People tried to get them to stay. She went to the ladies' room while he stayed at the table to give their door prize tickets to their table mates.

He explained, "Jodi has to fly to Los Angeles in the morning, and I want to get home to call Corey in Florida before it gets too late."

Ralph Parker said, "You mean to tell me Corey knows about this?"

Realizing Ralph was kidding, Harry matter-of-factly said, "Sure, Corey suggested it."

June, Ralph's wife, said, "She must have a lot more faith in you than I would in this one," giving Ralph a poke with her elbow.

Jodi returned, they said their "Goodnight," and made their way across the room to the door.

Walking down the gravel path to the car, he noticed she was a little unsteady in her heels. He opened her door and she slid over to open the driver's door. She did not slide back to her side. When he got in, she was facing him, with her arm on the steering wheel. She leaned in and kissed him.

He could taste the alcohol on her mouth. Surprised, he hesitated for a moment with her lips pressed up against his. He thought her kiss to be an inappropriate way of thanking him for an evening away from her worries.

Without saying anything, his shoulder moved her body away.

Jodi, thinking she had made a clumsy miscalculation, trying to kiss him in a parking lot where anyone could have seen them, couldn't make eye contact. Silently she slid back to her side of the car but her hand came to rest on his. She slipped her fingers into his palm and noted he didn't pull away until he started the car.

He drove the short distance to her home in silence.

At the door she fumbled with her keys and dropped them.

When he unlocked the door, she took him by the hand and gently pulled him into the house. She looked back to see his expression. He seemed impassive but she was aware he had not pulled his hand away.

Near the couch, she leaned on him to get out of her heels.

She gave him a long look and said in a kidding, somewhat tipsy, manner, "I think some of the men in that room tonight wanted to go bed with me."

He chuckled, "I see you've developed a good grasp of the obvious."

She gave him a tight hug, pressing her body against his, and whispered cautiously, "But—I know men have needs and you've been without Corey for a while. I know you're going home to an empty house tonight—"

She paused, "—I just want you to know—if it would uh provide—uh, comfort to you—if you want to—you can spend the night here—with me."

He took her arms from around his neck, eased her body away and she folded down onto the couch.

He wondered if he had totally underestimated the motivation behind the kiss in the car.

"What are you trying to do, Jodi? I haven't been with another woman like that since I met Corey."

Looking up from the couch, she said sadly, "Jodi?—not—JJ?"

There was no room for mistaking his reaction. She was afraid she had offended him and had lost him just when she needed him most.

She started to cry.

Seeing her in tears made him sad. He'd just wanted to halt her advance, not hurt her. He sat down next to her and spoke slowly and more softly.

"You've had too much to drink tonight. Let's just leave it at that."

He looked to see if she was listening.

"I'm here. If you came here to find me, you've found me. But, I'm not alone now like I was then. I understood, back then, that the JJ I knew, back then, needed a friend. And I can understand why you need one now.

"I have only a fraction of an idea of what you go through. I've heard you and seen the way people react to you—the requests for pictures, or autographs, your time. I can see how the people here have changed—and how they've changed toward me and my family in the time you've been here.

"I can still be your friend if you want a friend. But me betraying the love and trust of my wife and daughter should not make you trust me any more. If you remember anything about me, you should know I won't hurt the people I really care about.

"If you could get me to change all that—I just wouldn't be the person you needed in the first place. I can care about you, JJ—I do care about you—but it has never been a sexual feeling and I can't be in bed with you now."

He stood up, "Corey and I love each other so much. We've been through so much together. We trust each other.

"She's waiting for my call now. She's never, ever, not once, had any reason to question me. But, if she should need to hear from me that nothing happened between you and me, then I need to be able to tell her what she needs to hear. I never lie to Corey and I will not start now. Do you understand?"

Biting her lower lip, she nodded and whispered, "I know."

Pulling her knees up to her chest, she wrapped her arms around them then realized, "I'm going to be sick."

Excusing herself, she rushed to the bathroom.

He could hear her throwing up.

Walking over to the bathroom door, he knocked softly but they both knew there was nothing he could do.

Coming back in the living room, she shook her head.

Trying to ease back into what she knew would be an awkward conversation, she said, "I'm so glad I'm not one of those girls who need to throw up to keep their weight down."

She sat down, "I finally learned my lesson tonight. It was something I kinda knew."

She paused and reflected, "My brother always referred to our father as an alcoholic or 'that drunk.' He never talked about Mom like that. I never saw her drinking. But, we knew she was dying of liver disease, and I always heard the clinking of bottles when we threw out the trash. Then my grandparents. . ."

She took a deep breath then let it out slowly, "I shouldn't even allow myself a one-wine rule—alcohol makes me act stupid, it looks like if I have more than one glass of wine, I don't know when to stop, and then it makes me sick."

"How many did you have?

"Do you even know?"

"No. I lost count. I think after the second or third I wanted to lose count. And then the last one was to get up the courage to ask you to stay — I was afraid."

"Afraid I'd say "Yes" or afraid I'd say "No?"

She grimaced, "A little bit of both, I think."

"So, what's this all about? Is it just this Hollywood and business situation?"

"That's a big part of it. It's basically all the stuff we talked about before.

"I'm so sorry if I made you uncomfortable. I thought I wanted to show you how much—I thought maybe you needed—I thought maybe if I— Oh, forget what I thought. There's no excuse for it."

He nodded, "OK. So, last night we spoke about what I learned about Epictetus in my college days when I was a Phys. Ed major with a Greek Philosophy minor. Now comes some of my post-college learning."

He sat facing her, "About three years ago, I met a man who was driving cross-country. He stopped in at the store and he saw the fire department placard on my truck outside. We got to talking about fire and ambulance stuff.

"He was a paramedic in a part of New York City that had what he called 'a big knife and gun club.' You can just imagine the bloody stuff he saw.

"He told me about a mandatory stress management program he attended. On the cover of the lecture material was a picture of a legendary yogi standing on a surfboard in some impossible yoga position. The caption was, 'You can't stop the waves!'

"They told him, 'Fear and functioning are not always strangers.' There was a quote in the book that said, 'Leonardo always trembled when he started to work.'

"He realized fear of failure was normal. With what he was rolling into—with life and death on the line—not being worried only meant you didn't understand the situation. He learned, 'The decisions you have to make were hard enough without letting the fear paralyze you. You have to fight through the fear to function. You can't function only when there's no fear. You have to function every time.'

"It put a lot of his life into perspective for him. 'You can't stop the waves' meant the calls for help were going to keep flooding in. The stressful situations were going to keep flying at him. The only thing he could do was to center himself so he could deal with the stress in a way that would allow him to focus—to keep doing his job of taking care of the people who needed him."

He paused, "JJ, you and I know that basketball, or making movies, or other business decisions are not life and death. That doesn't mean your stress and fears can't be real, but you can't let them paralyze you. The idea of being focused or centered is what I was talking to you about when you were a kid. I used the term self-esteem but there are many different ways of saying the same thing. You can call it your focus—finding your center, your inner strength, your composure, your self-worth, or your balance.

"JJ, you know you have a center. You have worth. Now, you need to eliminate whatever is stopping you from finding it again."

He put his hand on her shoulder and looked her in the eye.

He said softly, "When we talked after you had dinner with us, you wondered about your problems being solved for you. Well, it's hard to grow up when you've never had to grow up. But now you have to. You said yourself, people are going to be depending on you. You need to be a person who they can depend on. You need to be there when they need you. In short—you need to grow up and take responsibility for what is—even if you never dreamed it could be."

He asked, "Remember?"

He straightened his shoulders, turned to her and played his old part, except this time much softer since he was not yelling to a gym full of kids.

"It's called —?" he asked, expecting her to fill in the blank as she did when he was her coach.

"Self-esteem," she answered, as though she was that kid again and he had a whistle hung around his neck.

"And can anyone else give it to you?"

"No," she said softly.

Looking at him, she dried her eyes, "Thank you."

She started to ask, "Do you have to tell Corey. . ."

But then decided she didn't need the answer.

Instead, she sheepishly asked, "Can I get a hug and a goodnight kiss for luck if I don't try to seduce you?"

They were both at ease enough to laugh at the irony of her ground rules.

She gave him a long hug and quick kiss on the lips.

After the kiss, holding her at arm's length, he made a show of admiring the woman she had become.

She smiled at his obvious approval.

Shaking his head, as he turned toward the door, "I said I was faithful. I didn't say I was dead. Wow—hell of an offer, JJ. That was one hell of an offer!"

On the way home, he remembered Clarence Gibbons looking at JJ's file and yelling "God. Who the hell would pay to have sex with this?" He had to laugh at the memory.

He thought, Not only was Clarence an unsuitable guidance counselor, but the poor bastard had absolutely no sense of human potential. He wondered if somehow Clarence was aware of who that scrawny young girl grew up to be.

He thought, Not only does little JJ grow up to be Jodi Worren, but she grows up smart enough to know that my Physical Education major had been stealing quotes from my Greek Philosophy minor.

He laughed when he thought, If Clarence were to ask that stupid foul-minded question about paid sex with her now, the answer would probably be maybe—half—the—men—on—the—planet!

Getting home, he realized it was late but when he'd promised Corey he'd call, she said she'd wait up.

He started, "Don't worry, sweet girl, it went fine—we didn't do anything wrong.

"Weebles wobble, but they don't fall down."

"Well, just how far did you wobble?" Corey yawned.

"She seemed to be under a lot of pressure with this movie and estate stuff. And, she let herself have too much to drink.

"She was sick after we got back to her place."

"Poor girl. Is she OK now?"

"Yeah. Anyway, before she threw up, she kissed me in the car, and back at her place she let me know that, considering it was a while since you and I were together, she was available to fill in for you if I needed her to.

"I told her that I wasn't interested in having sex with her.

"I lied!!!"

She laughed, "I hope your turning her down isn't what made her sick. Maybe you were just concerned it would've been the exact opposite of riding a stationary bike."

He laughed, remembering JoBob Trask's lesson on the relationship between anticipation-fantasy and post-participation reality.

"Yeah, that could be it. But, on the other hand," he paused, "she didn't ask me, 'Are you tired?'

"—So, I'm not actually positive she was talking about having sex."

They had never spoken about Corey's habit of using that sex-initiating code phrase.

He listened intently for her reaction, wanting to assure himself his joke didn't offend her.

Corey, recognizing her words, chuckled and felt herself blush.

Hearing her chuckle he exhaled, "She's aware that she was out of line, and she's more than a bit embarrassed by it. There's been some good conversations about what's going on with her. We can talk more about that, if you're interested, when you get home."

After hearing about her day, he wished her a good night's sleep.

"I'll call again tomorrow. I'm looking forward to my girls being home in two days."

THIRTY-FIVE

Jodi, not having slept much, was up early and on her way to Los Angeles. Looking at the clouds below, she fell asleep.

She had a dream.

In the dream, she was barefoot but dressed like she was for the fire department dinner. She was in the clouds, frantically running from a storm until she came to a door.

There were no walls, just the door in its sturdy frame—surrounded by clouds. On the other side of the door was a sheer drop into oblivion.

She was aware that if the door opened and allowed her though, there was nothing on the other side. Holding onto the door handle, she was sheltered and safe.

Awakening, Jodi knew the door was Harry. The supporting frame was his family. She understood the dream's message. Because the door remained firmly closed, she could hold on until she was able to deal with the maelstrom she was fleeing. By holding on, she was able to gain a firm footing. The storm could not harm her.

She was comforted by feeling protected by the whole family. She knew they couldn't regain her balance for her. Only she could do that. But just as the simple act of putting her hand on Harry's shoulder helped her as she climbed into her high heels, she knew if she needed help, this family would provide something solid for her to hold onto so she could steady herself and pull herself back into her own equilibrium.

Thinking of the whole family, she winced. After her offer, he appeared to understand and forgive her, but what about when he told Corey? Knowing she owed Corey an apology, she realized she owed herself one too.

In trying to cope with her fear of being overwhelmed by the decisions she was running from—her fear of inadequacy, her fear of losing control—she had let herself down by drinking.

The wine made her more out of control. She knew whatever her fears might be, she could never allow herself to do that again. She thought, The alcohol solution dissolves nothing but my self-esteem.

I'm better than that. She vowed, I must always do better than that. I will never again let my fear of seeming stupid make me act stupid.

Upon landing, she was greeted by Tim Kelly and taken to the hotel where she would spend the week.

In the morning, he would pick her up and take her on the grueling round of scheduled meetings. But for now, rather than open the Malibu house, she wanted to be at this hotel.

Since the movie, whenever she came to Los Angeles, she was pleased she could reserve the same room Pops had booked for her during the filming.

Entering the room, for a split second she allowed herself to wonder if this was one of the hotels she now owned. No matter. She walked straight to the window.

It always brought a smile to her face when she looked out and saw the "Hollywood" sign in the hills. Unlike the first time she saw it, which seemed so long ago, now—as she looked at the sign—she thought she could see the roof of Sharin's house up in hills not far from the sign.

After settling in, she called room service and she ordered her favorite spaghetti dinner, as she did each time she stayed there. Waiting, reclining on the couch, she closed her eyes and thought about the upcoming meetings. For each meeting she reviewed the limited set of goals she was hoping to achieve.

During the meal, her thoughts drifted to her last phone conversation with Pops. Sitting on the set during the final days of shooting, she re-read the Manual of Epictetus from that first book he had given her.

Later that night, from this room, she talked with him.

"Pops, I was reading the Manual over again—the part that said, 'It shows a lack of education to blame others for one's own misfortunes; to blame oneself shows that one's education has begun; to blame neither oneself nor others shows that one's education is complete.'"

He said, "You may have noticed that part comes from the same section dealing with what your life-lessons coach called 'perceptions' of events."

"Yes, I'm looking at it"

"If we read the two parts of that section together, we can fold Epictetus back on himself, substitute the perception of 'credit' instead of 'blame,' and ask what it shows about our education if we credit others for our own good fortune, take credit ourselves, or credit no one."

He paused, and then said softly, "That is something you need to wrestle with on your own, Jodi. No one sees the world through your eyes. Rich or poor, married or single, from birth to death, your life can only be lived by you. So, in the largest sense, dinner is no credit and there is no blame—there is only you taking responsibility for your own actions, learning from them, and moving on.

"You told me what you went through that night with that man and what it was like when you were a child. No matter what others did in your past, you are no longer in that past, you have to take charge and own your life as it is. And, if not now, when?"

Thinking back, she repeated that last question to herself. If not now, when?

After her meal, feeling the comfort of following her accustomed routine in familiar surroundings, she got up to look at the sign again.

Poised at the middle of the window—watching the sunlight fade—memories flooded in. She pondered how far she had come. She traced her path—from Harry to Jacqui, to Connie, to Pops, then Sharin, and back to Harry and his loving family.

Now, she grasped how that path, and what she learned as she traversed it, coursed toward what lay ahead.

I can't stop the waves.

A sense of resolve came upon her.

While studying that iconic sign—and recalling to mind Pops' reference to Archimedes—Jodi knew she had found her place to stand.

THIRTY-SIX

It was a drizzly Monday, more like fall than May. Corey sat at the table, looking out the window over the pond to the mist on the lake. With Harry at the store and Dayna at school, she was alone in the house. She liked being alone on days like this. She liked the quiet and the calm. But, since the optometrist she had worked for retired five months ago, and she hadn't been able to find works she was feeling guilty about not having an income-producing job.

She still did the books for their store, and had spent the early part of April doing their income taxes.

She was relieved when that tax job was done, but having to come to grips with their finances always made her anxious. So, being home alone on this Monday gave her mixed feelings. She knew as the day went on, she would feel the calm less and the boredom and the guilt more.

Part of her guilt came knowing that if she did have an income there would be no problem finding the money for Dayna to go back to day camp this summer. When she went for the six weeks before the start of eleventh grade, she enjoyed it so much that they thought it would be another good experience for her. But, even with the increase in the business, Henry's hospital bills still weighed heavily on their finances.

Last year Corey's mom had given them some money and they used it to pay for camp, but on the visit to Florida it became obvious Barbara's finances, because of her increased medical needs, were not going to permit a similar gift.

What made Corey feel even guiltier was Dayna saying that she didn't want to go. That only made it worse.

Knowing Dayna had such a great time at camp, they both felt dismayed when they realized Dayna was telling them what she thought they wanted to hear so they wouldn't have to spend the money. They let her know that they appreciated her attempt to spare them the expense, but if they could make it happen, she should get to go.

On the other hand, they still weren't sure they could afford it this year. Now, with the possibility that Jodi might be in Smalsville for the summer, they considered this change in circumstances might add focus to Dayna's previously nebulous comments about not wanting to go away. But neither of them wanted Dayna's plans to depend on the vagaries of Jodi's yet to be settled schedule.

Trying to put these thoughts out of her mind, she sat in her robe at the kitchen table and watched the water dropping off the leaves. She was getting up to pour herself another cup of coffee when the phone rang.

It was Jodi.

She had just gotten back from Los Angeles.

"Oh, hi!" Corey said trying to sound cheery, "Harry's at the store."

"Actually, I was hoping to talk to you if that's OK. Could you find some time for me to come by?"

Puzzled, she said, "Sure, how about now? I'm having some coffee. I'll make some more."

She wanted to ask what it was about but didn't. Knowing Jodi would be there in a short while, she just had enough time to put up the coffee and get into a pair of jeans and a long sleeve tee shirt.

She knew she would have a short time to neaten up before Jodi arrived. She was just getting some papers off the living room table as Jodi knocked on the door.

Going to the door, she realized that in the months since Jodi arrived in their lives, this was the first time she'd been in the house with Jodi without Harry or Dayna arriving. She told herself to be patient.

She'd find out what the visit was about soon enough.

Greeting Jodi, she handed her a cup of coffee as they settled in on the couch.

Jodi knew she would have to start. "I wanted to talk to you without Harry because I owe you an apology and also, I want to ask both of you for a favor. But, I know, even if he likes the idea, if you don't, it won't work."

Corey sat back to let her continue.

Standing up, Jodi walked a few steps wringing her hands, then turned to her. "First, as you already know, when I came here—when I moved into your village, it was because I had the idea that I was spinning out of control. I felt that I needed someone in my life who I could trust."

She sat back down on the couch facing Corey, "Because of everything and everybody coming at me so quickly, I tried to look at my past life and find a time when someone cared just about me—someone who liked me for me not for 'Jodi Worren movie star or wealthy widow.'

"I wanted someone who could see through that. Someone solid to hold onto so it would help me gain control of myself again. And I thought of Harry. I took the chance that because he looked out for me when I had nothing—when I was just JJ—he wouldn't have changed even though I changed so much."

Corey wasn't sure where this was going. But, she was determined to hear her out.

Jodi stood up and started pacing again. "When I got here, both you and Dayna were so very warm and gracious—you both made me feel so comfortable and welcome in your lives."

She looked Corey in the eyes and lowered her voice, "I'm sure Harry has told you about what I did after the dance.

"And I feel deeply, deeply ashamed of making that terrible mistake. I guess at the dinner, I confused Harry being my friend with Harry being a man who might have physical needs—and a man who I wanted to please.

"In the past I've made mistakes pleasing men I shouldn't have trusted. But I knew I could trust Harry, and feeling I owed Harry so much I made a very stupid offer. I still can't believe I made such a stupid mistake. I'll never make it again. I am afraid that in my reaching to hold on to Harry it might have looked like I was trying to pull him away from you."

She paused to look at Corey "I'm sure that's not what I wanted to do. But I understand if you felt that it was. On the plane the next morning I had a dream and realized how important it is to have what your family has—the togetherness, the structural support. I don't know with my family history if I'll ever find it. I've never had a loving supportive family. I had never even seen one. I wish I had, but never did.

"Seeing all of you, I know now how much I would love to have one of my own. And yet I can't think back to what I did that night without realizing what a stupid way I chose to show Harry my appreciation. If I was in my right mind, I would've known that Harry would have thought it more of an insult than an enticement. Especially because of what Jacqui told me happened when she made a mistake like that."

Corey was surprised, "She told you about that?"

"Yes. The night I first met her she said Harry doesn't take advantage. And, on the plane when I was thinking about what a fool I had made of myself, I remembered that—after he left town—she told me what she had done. She said it was a big moment for her because she realized that by not being able to see Harry for who he really was, she was beyond help—she had hit bottom.

"I'm sure deep down I must have known that Harry would refuse my offer—just like he did with her—especially now because he has you.

She looked for a reaction from Corey but Corey just listened.

Jodi continued, "Corey, it's important for me to know I have your understanding and hopefully your forgiveness. When you asked me to go with Harry, I'm sure you didn't think I'd betray you.

"It's important for me to know that I can regain your trust and support. I am truly sorry if I made you feel you cannot trust me to be here. I feel safe here. I feel happy when I'm here. I need to be able to feel that if I spin out of control, there is always a place and people who can help me gain control again. Corey…"

She paused, looking again for a reaction, "I need to know that you understand that I meant no disrespect. And I hope that you can forgive me for causing you any pain."

She sat down on the couch near Corey.

Corey leaned forward.

The imploring look on Jodi's face left her with no doubt about the sincerity of what Jodi has just said.

It made Corey feel sad.

She cleared her throat, "Is that what you want from me? You need me to forgive you for the offer you made to Harry?"

Jodi nodded.

Corey closed her eyes for a second to gather her words.

"He told me when he got home after the dinner. And we've talked a bit since I've been home. I'm sure there was a lot of testosterone in the place that night, and I'm sure you are aware of men wanting you. You knew he and I had been apart. I'm sure because you felt you owed him so much that you wanted to be available to him if he needed it or just wanted it. I get that, I really do.

"Harry and I have been through so much together. He gave up basketball when we needed to be here."

She paused and got melancholy at the memory.

"When we talked about that he said, 'Loving you is what I do best.'"

Corey gathered herself and continued, "Even if anything did happen, on just that one night—if he had given in to temptation—I don't think it would threaten our marriage.

"I don't think either of you want to hurt me. I don't know about most women, but I wouldn't choose to feel my life was destroyed by a single act that really had nothing to do with me.

"I wouldn't choose to give up the life Harry and I have built together—just so I could hate you or him.

"That hate would only make me feel miserable.

"I love Harry so very, very much. And I always want him to be happy.

"If what you offered was what he needed, or if it would have made him happy, I think I would have understood."

Jodi was awestruck as Corey said, "It's the honesty and openness between Harry and me that's most important. I love his honesty. I want him to be able to tell me what makes him happy, so I will always be able to share his joys with him.

"So, even if he had taken you up on your offer—just that once—and he felt good about it, or even if he felt guilty afterward or sad, I would want to know.

"Truth is so much better for our life together than his having to lie about his feelings and feel bad about feeling good."

She put up her hand and cautioned, "Don't get me wrong. I'm not a saint. If either of you had come to me beforehand and asked for permission. . ."

She shook her head at the thought, "But, understanding and forgiveness are much easier to give than permission. I take you at your word that you were not trying to take Harry away from us. I take you at your word, that you just made a mistake and you are aware and sorry for making it."

Jodi nodded.

Corey paused, "As it was, Harry said he thought you had too much to drink. He thought it would not have happened if you had not been drinking. But, even so, as far as he was concerned, he was very flattered by your offer.

"And as far as I'm concerned..." She looked Jodi in the eye and nodded slowly, "I think it comes under the NBA rule: 'No harm—No foul.'"

Obviously relieved, Jodi was grateful for the response. The depth of the feeling Harry and Corey shared was reassuring and inspiring.

She sighed, "Thank you so much for that. It means the world to me.

"Corey, I know that some women might envy me, but in truth I envy you. I wish I had the love you and Harry have. Seeing you two, I think I understand more than ever what true love should mean for me. I realize now that what you two have is what I want from a man. I wish I could find another Harry."

Corey grinned, "On our honeymoon, I talked to Harry about him wanting to find another Julius Anderson. He went into an explanation about why another Julius Anderson probably doesn't exist. I agree that Harry is very special. But I think there are men out there who will love you for who you are, and want to give you the kind of love and pleasure that you deserve—just like I hope there is someone out there for Dayna. My mom used to tell my sister and me, 'There's a cover for every pot.'

"Jodi, just because you've settled for two Mr. Wrongs doesn't mean you can't find Mr. Right."

Jodi smiled at the turn of phrase and was warmed by the idea that she was deserving of love and pleasure. Maybe pleasure in her own right, not just pleasing others.

Jodi's thoughts about being deserving were interrupted when Corey asked hesitatingly, "What else? You did say, 'First.'"

"Well—that was the hard part but only part of it. Yes, I need to ask for a favor." She took a deep breath. "I went back to Los Angeles to try to get some resolution about making this movie. I decided to commit to doing it."

"Well, I remember you said something about a movie you thought you might want to get out of…"

"Right, well that's all changed. I mean I could have gotten out of it. I could have just said 'No.' But, I'm trying to take charge of my life. I can't let fear cheat me out of what could be good for me. I'll never know if I want to pursue acting unless I actually try acting again. I have to take that risk. I mean, in order for me to find out if I can do what I consider good solid work, I have to actually do the work.

"I can deal with my fear of failure. I can even deal with failure itself. And I don't have to let myself be bothered by what somebody says, or rumors of what somebody says or supposedly said, or what's in the press or whatever."

Corey tried to follow along.

Jodi continued, "I felt that I not only had the obligation to myself—to see if I could be comfortable in this craft—but it goes beyond just me. There are many other people affected by this decision. I've been very fortunate and I don't need the money, but each movie project means jobs for lots of people.

"Even more than the jobs, the money they're going to pay me could be put to good use in other ways. So, I decided to change my perception and turn this project into something I wanted to do. Just like playing in a softball game can raise some needed money, I can take whatever money I make from the movie, match it with some of the too much I already have, and start looking for some good causes to spend it on. I'm thinking of starting a charitable foundation."

Nodding approvingly, Corey smiled.

"The next morning, because of the time difference between New York and California, I was able to reach Becher Gold before my first meeting. You remember I told you about him."

"The man you call Goldy?"

She smiled, pleased Corey remembered. "Yes. Goldy. He said he was feeling much better and he was up to representing me. I told him I'd be grateful for whatever time he could give me. He said, 'I'll make the time and whatever arrangement you had with my Pops, just tell me and I will honor that.'

"When I told him my feelings about why I wanted to do the movie, and what I wanted to do with the money, he was delighted. Then, when I told him I wanted to name it the Gold Shield Foundation—Gold Shield was the name Pops used for his modeling agency—I could hear him get emotional.

"He said, 'You remember at the funeral I told you about Tikkun Olam, healing the world? It looks like you are following that precept and I would like, in my own small way, to help you heal the world in any way I can. It will be my honor to help. It will be my privilege to help. Everything WPA does on behalf of your foundation will be free of charge.'

"Corey, after I had made the decision to do the movie, and after speaking with Goldy, it all seemed so right—I couldn't understand why I had trouble making up my mind in the first place.

"But with regard to the actual filming schedule, the plans are scrambled.

"The producers told me that because of some long-term remodeling starting soon, the locations they need to shoot in Paris are only going to be available this summer. They don't want to wait another year or try to find a new location. It's short notice but they want to start shooting in Paris this summer."

Corey shrugged, her body language silently asking, what can be done about that?

Jodi continued, "So, here's the favor—I really enjoy the time I spend with Dayna. And I remember you saying she was having some trouble with French …"

Seeing Corey's obvious failure to make any connection, Jodi hurried, "— since I have to spend the summer in Paris, I was hoping you and Harry would let me ask Dayna to come with me."

Corey sat back. Her eyes started to tear as she envisioned what this invitation would mean to her daughter.

Jodi, not understanding her reaction, and worrying she would say "No," blurted out, "I could get a tutor for her or whatever she needs."

"Oh, no. No, it's a wonderful idea!

"I can't think of anything more delightful for Dayna. But, are you sure there won't be any problem—they'll let you bring her along?"

Jodi, relieved and happy, jumped up and grinned, "Corey, these people want me so badly—especially now after all the free publicity they got from the delivering-the-watch story—I could probably get them to bring this whole village and surrounding towns to Paris if I wanted them to."

Corey, smiling, shook her head and dried her eyes, "Well, I guess I've never had anybody want me that much."

Sitting down and putting her arm around her, Jodi shook her playfully, "I know one man who does." Adding, "And, if it's OK, maybe she and I can visit friends I have near London—if things have calmed down for me over there."

Like co-conspirators they sprang up from the couch when Corey said, "Let's call Harry and check, but I'm sure it will be OK with him."

Standing by the kitchen wall phone together, Corey made the call. Jodi heard her say, "Hi, it's me. JJ is here and she's going to make that movie.

"She's made a very generous and wonderful offer to take Dayna with her to Paris for the summer. And we want to make sure it's OK with you before we say anything."

Jodi, putting her arm around Corey when she heard her call her "JJ," waited while Corey listened to Harry's answer, then hung up the phone, chuckling.

Corey imitated his answer, "He said, 'Paris — really!? That sounds fine to me, but how's she going to convince Dayna?'"

They both laughed.

Then Jodi asked hesitatingly, "Corey, one more favor?"

She paused, "If it's not too much to ask, can you spare some time to talk with me about what you learned when you studied business administration in college? I'd like to know more about business and finance. I missed my chance with Pops. Now, I'm not looking to try to run any businesses or manage any financial matters myself—at least not until I feel confident about what I am doing. For now, I'm going to rely on Goldy and this man, Tim Kelly. Kelly seems solid and Goldy suggested I ask him to sit in on the meetings with me. He's the head of security and knows the ins and outs of the businesses. He and Goldy can see what's what and help me put together a good team. But I'd really like to begin to get my own understanding of that world if I can."

"Well, with these men working with you, it sounds like you're getting a good start. I think the world you're going to be dealing with is a lot more complicated than what I studied, but we can talk about whatever you want.

Sometimes you can't know all the answers, but if you know the right questions and where to try to find the answers. . . Anyway, we can talk and see what we can learn."

"Thank you so much. You know, I watched you handling the details for the softball game. You're very good at that. You're very organized. I'm sure you could help me come up with some ideas for the foundation's money and other things. I think working with you and learning to ask the right questions would be a great place for me to start that part of my education.

"And, if you don't mind—if assisting me starts to feel like a job, we should talk about that.

"Would that be OK?"

"Thank you. Sure. And if it's like a job, we can talk then. In terms of charity, maybe we can start at home.

"With all the money you helped raise with the softball game, the school has what it needs for a while. And they play that game every year.

"But this area used to have a food pantry and it died for lack of support. I was sad when it failed. We could really use a food pantry to help some of the people get by.

"If we could figure out the finances and a central place to put it."

Corey brightened, "Maybe you could buy the old theater after all."

Jodi mused, 'I've seen some places that turn old movie theaters into dinner theaters. If a food pantry shared a building with a restaurant like that. . ."

"Well, the old theater couldn't compete with the multiplex nearby, but something like a dinner theater might work.

"Does Goldy's agency book acts for places like dinner theaters?"

"It might be a little small for some of his bigger names, but I'm sure he'd love to do whatever he can for us. We can always ask. Great thinking."

In talking about the Paris plans, Corey realized she had a lot of work to get Dayna ready and a short time to do it.

Dayna had only one small suitcase, and the handle broke off on the trip back from Florida. She would be home shortly. Corey made a mental list of things Dayna would need and then asked if Jodi could wait for her while she went out to buy some things for the trip.

Epilogue

Getting off the school bus Dayna was happy to see Jodi's car at the house, but noticed her mom's car was not.

Coming in, and putting her books down, she looked around and was puzzled.

"Hi JJ, isn't my mom home?"

"DD your mom went out and she'll be back soon. She asked me to wait for you because I have something to tell you."

"OK." Dayna said, cocking her head to the side.

"I decided to do the Paris movie."

"That's good—I guess."

"I realized I can choose to make the experience into a good thing rather than fear it'll be something bad.

"It'll take up most of the summer," she paused, "and, I'd like it very much if you came to Paris with me."

Dayna was ecstatic, but quickly worried her parents might have some reason for not wanting her to go.

"Oh, I'd love to go, but I have to ask Mom and Dad."

Then impatiently, "When will Mom be back—where did she go?"

Seeing her so happy, Jodi was elated as she told her young friend, "Your mom already talked with your dad—then she went to the mall to buy you a bigger suitcase!"

They both smiled.

www.ingramcontent.com/pod-product-compliance
Lightning Source LLC
Chambersburg PA
CBHW071224300726

48975CB00002B/296